Awakened Deceptions

BeJae Ladd

Ten|16
PRESS

Ten16 Press
www.ten16press.com - Waukesha, WI

Dedication

I would like to dedicate this book to my loving husband, Todd. Thank you for your love and support while I pursued this endeavor. I appreciate your efforts by way of the many meals you prepared and conversations we've had when I wanted to run a chapter by you. Your love and companionship means the world to me. I love you.

And to my Mother, Lula, thank you for believing in me. I miss you everyday.

Acknowledgements

I want to take a few moments to recognize some of the women in my world, without whom this book may not have been written. Karen Copeland, Laura Dauenhauer, Bonnie H, Kathy Ladwig, Marcella Mingey, Maria Rivera, Lisa S, Julia S, and Claire Stangl. Your words of encouragement have been invaluable in this journey.

Thank you to Anne, Peggy and Dominique for your constant support. And of course, thank you Reji Laberje for sharing your pearls of wisdom.

I also want to thank Mary and the ladies of BH, Denise, Dez, Donna, Kathy, Lisa, Maria, Nancy, Shannon, Sherri, and Trish. And my peeps, Kim, Mary Jo and Therese. Your friendship and kind words mean so much to me.

Last but not least, my wonderful editor, Denise Guibord. You are so awesome, and I loved working on this book with you. Your insights and fresh perspectives were so on point, and I am so glad to call you my friend.

In the end, there are many people, family and friends, to thank because you all have influenced my life in such profound ways, but space does not allow me to show gratitude to you properly. Just know that you are always in my heart and I will be forever grateful having you in my life.

1
❧ Gabrielle ☙

New York City – Friday evening, December 19th, 1969

Gabrielle looked out the window at the snow covering the streets in layers of white; glancing at her wristwatch, she saw he was over forty-five minutes late.

"Damn," she muttered, perturbed. "Where the hell is he? He said he'd be here by 5:45." Her brow creased as worry and concern took the place of the irritation she felt only moments ago. *Maybe he's been in an accident due to the snow. No.* She quickly pushed the thought out of her mind. *He's just running late, very late.*

She glanced at the hall mirror as she passed and saw her anxiety evident behind her smoky almond-shaped green eyes. She walked into her small but efficient kitchen and noticed the nervous tension getting to her. At the sink, she turned on the faucet as a wave of dizziness came over her. *That will teach me to go most of the day without eating;* she'd been too nervous to eat, having only had a few nibbles of the supper she'd prepared for him.

She got a glass out of the cabinet and filled it with cold

water and drank the water down in large swallows; it didn't calm her ragged nerves.

The pan was bubbling hot; the mouthwatering aroma of baked sausage, tomato and cheeses filled the air as it escaped from the oven's chamber when she opened it. She set the oven's knob on low as she awaited his arrival. She then stepped through the opened French doors into the living room and stood in front of the fireplace.

The massive fireplace is what had sold her on the old Brownstone. Converted into four separate apartments, each had been period updated to include all the modern conveniences while maintaining its old world feel.

Gabrielle had looked at so many places in New York City and had been just about ready to give up hope of finding the right one. Yet, she refused to do as her parents suggested — -no, more like insisted--she do. They had wanted her to move into one of the costlier Park Avenue addresses. However, Gabrielle did not want her parents in charge of her life decisions any longer; she wanted to do this on her own. Still, her search produced nothing close to what she had been looking for, until she came across this majestic gem.

The sandstone exterior and the structure's front facade drew her in with its embellished bent iron balustrades of the Juliet balconies, flower planters, and high arched windows.

And if the antique tin ceiling in the kitchen or the crown moldings throughout the space weren't enough, when she saw the large fireplace bordered by hand carved wooden columns and a brick opening with a center arch stone, the space spoke to her.

So many architectural wonders enhanced the roomy two-bedroom second floor apartment, like a built-in bookcase in the small sitting area that neatly housed her many books. She loved curling up on the chaise to enjoy her latest read.

Living in Greenwich Village had been a wonderful experience for her and, she liked her new surroundings. It had a completely different vibe than California, and she found the Villagers to be warm, although a little quirky at times, but very friendly. She loved her new space and her neighborhood with its socially and ethnically diverse blend of people. There were little out-of-the-way shops, intimate restaurants, and small theaters with an unlimited pool of talent that could have easily been on any Broadway stage, and everything within walking distance of her building.

Now, as she stood in front of the usually comforting hearth, a foreboding chill raced through her like ice water. And it settled deep within her bones as she tried to find warmth from the fire.

He's just running a little late, she told herself. *Stop your worrying; you're just making yourself sick.*

She walked over to the combination television stereo set and lifted the hinged lid. She turned on the radio just as The Doors' Jim Morrison expressed his words in song to a melodious beat:

You know that it would be untrue
You know that I would be a liar
If I was to say to you, Girl,
We couldn't get much higher
Come on baby, light my fire.

Gabrielle picked up a box of matches from the mantle and went to the large oak trestle dining table. She struck a match and lit the two red taper candles placed into the necks of two empty squat Chianti bottles encased in their own molded straw baskets which displayed dripping remnants of candles past.

She checked her watch for the time once again, which now read 6:36. Deciding a cup of tea might be just what she needed to calm her jittery nerves and settle her stomach, she ran water into a tea kettle, placed it on the burner, and readied her cup with a tea bag.

Returning to the window, she resumed looking out. Outside the snow swirled with large gusts of wind and came down much heavier, accumulating more rapidly as she, much like a sentinel, stood watch.

Her mind drifted back to the auspicious day when she met him, and a reminiscent smile formed on her lips. She pondered a singular thought: who knew her whole world would be so happily turned around and upside-down all by a chance meeting some nine months ago.

4

New York City – Saturday, March 22nd, 1969

That morning, so many months ago, Gabrielle had been working at VonShelles House of Fashion. Her new boss and the head designer, Linda Taylor, had enlisted the aid of Gabrielle and some of the designers to ready the fall design pattern mock-ups for the seamstresses to begin assemblage of the collection's final prototypes on Monday morning.

Gabrielle worked alongside Monty Greer a fellow designer for two weeks, and they had struck up a platonic friendship, at least on Gabrielle's part. Since she'd been working at the fashion house for such a short time, she was eager to prove herself, so coming in to work on a Saturday was fine with her. Besides, she had no one waiting at home for her.

Because she was the newest hire, she readily took direction from the senior designers. But, she loved this part of the process, just feeling the fabric in her hands made her creative artistry flow. After she measured, pinned, and cut the last of the pattern sections of cloth, she helped Monty gather the completed pieces. He then took the cut-outs to Linda Taylor's office for final approval. Meanwhile, Gabrielle and the others cleared the drafting room of debris and packed up their things to leave.

Gabrielle grabbed her jacket and purse and headed to the restroom in the hall. She soon returned to the drafting room only to find it empty. The other designers had left to reclaim what was left of their weekend.

Jacket and purse in hand, she walked down the hall toward Linda's office, whose door was open. Linda leaned over the pieces of material, meticulously checked them, and put them in order. Linda was tall with the salient slenderness of a high fashion model and she looked younger than her thirty-two years. Graced with high cheekbones, large emerald green eyes, and a few freckles on the bridge of her thin upturned nose. Her fiery ginger mane was sheared in a short pixie-cut, reminiscent of Mia Farrow's. She easily carried off the very short hairstyle which served to make her eyes appear even larger.

Gabrielle leaned into the office with a tilt of her head as she softly called out to Linda.

"Knock, knock."

A surprised Linda looked up. "Gabrielle? You're still here? I was expecting Clay--," Linda placed a fabric piece in one of the piles on her large desk. "Never mind, I thought you all left."

Tentatively, Gabrielle entered the office as she spoke. "Looks like I'm the last one." She glanced at the piles of fabric pieces in front of Linda and asked, "Do you need any help? I can stay if you need me."

"No. Thank you for the offer, but there's no need." She said as she shook her head. "I just have to get these in the right order for Monday's rush. Then I'll be leaving right after you." With kind eyes, Linda looked at her. "Thank you for your help today," she inclined her head. "You remind me of a younger version of myself, Gabrielle." Linda continued with a warm smile. "I knew you would be a great addition to our team."

"Thank you, Linda, I'm glad to hear that," Gabrielle beamed brightly. "I'm truly happy to be a part of the team."

"We're grateful to have you, believe me. But for now," Linda gestured her head and eyes toward the door. "I will see you bright and early on Monday morning, okay?"

"Alright, alright," Gabrielle lightly laughed. "I can take a hint. I'll see you on Monday," She pulled on her jacket and secured her purse on her shoulder. "Try to enjoy the remainder of the weekend."

"I will, and you do the same," Linda nodded her head as she spoke through a smile. "Now, get out of here while you still can." She looked at her wristwatch and turned back to her task.

Gabrielle headed for the elevator and pushed the down button; a few moments later the doors opened and much to her surprise there was an occupant.

An equally startled Clayton Butler stood in the elevator. An attractive man in his early-forties, his mostly salt and pepper hair was cut into a short and neatly groomed style parted on the left side. Well over six feet tall, he towered over Gabrielle's five-foot-six frame; his build was lean and almost lanky.

Gabrielle stepped into the elevator and Clayton pushed the button for the lobby as she turned around and faced front with an amused smile; he somehow reminded her of her father.

"Hello," he said. "Miss Lawrence? Isn't it?"

"Hello, Mr. Butler," she turned in his direction. "Yes, it is Lawrence, but you may call me Gabrielle."

He wore an ecru colored button down shirt that was open at the neck and neatly tucked into a pair of dark brown trousers, topped with a brown and tan herringbone blazer. She'd only seen him in his usual dark tailored business suits, and she found it somewhat amusing to see him in his regular clothes. He looked so professorial to her. All that appeared missing, she mused, had been a tobacco-smoking pipe, a bow tie, and suede patches at his elbows.

"Ah, you know who I am." His brown eyes held a bit of surprise.

"I think everyone at VonShelles knows who you are. And thankfully some of my new co-workers have informed me who's who around here." She smiled. "I am, however, impressed you know my name though."

"I usually make it a point to know the names of all of our companies' newest employees," he paused. "It's my small way of being able to personally welcome any new personnel to our little family, so to speak." He smiled. "Therefore, I must say welcome, Miss Lawrence."

"Thank you, Mr. Butler. I think I'm really going to like it here; everyone has been so friendly and welcoming."

"I'm pleased to hear that." He cleared his throat. "Now, you must tell me something, Miss Lawrence," His eyes tapered sternly. "By your presence here today, does it mean

Miss Taylor has you and a crew unnecessarily working on a Saturday?" He half-smiled, not allowing his slanted thinned lips to show any teeth.

Unnecessarily? Gabrielle wasn't sure if Mr. Butler was serious or joking, and she didn't know how to respond. In the end she took him to be serious.

"Actually, Mr. Butler," she addressed him, noting his continued formality with her, "I wouldn't call those here today a *crew*," she pursed her lips, "but even with just a few of us, the work has been completed, and Miss Taylor is finishing some loose ends and will be leaving shortly herself."

Clayton leaned back against the elevator wall and placed his hands on either side of the brass handrail behind him and crossed his long legs at the ankles. He started to say something, but instead he caught Gabrielle's eye and then looked away. Gabrielle stared up at the floor numbers in awkward silence as they seemed to be changing at a snail's pace.

Monty Greer had told her about Clayton Butler recently, but Gabrielle hadn't put it together until now. How he had led the almost hostile way ERB had taken over the fashion house.

Linda Taylor, at the age of twenty-eight years old, had became the Head Designer at VonShelles after the company's founder Erich von Shelley suffered a debilitating stroke that left him completely paralyzed on his right side.

Without the use of his right hand, Erich found himself in the most unfortunate of circumstances for a creative person: a designer unable to put his images onto his sketchpad.

There'd been optimism of him fully recovering but with the passage of time and no progress, hopes of his return soon faded, leaving the future of his successful design house in jeopardy.

His wife Lillian wanted to sell the company outright. But, Erich wouldn't entertain the idea; he'd been grooming Linda to be his Head Design Assistant before he fell ill. He regarded her fondly as a daughter, and Erich delighted in the brilliance she brought with her to his fashion house. Linda had a great sense for fashion and a keen insight for upcoming trends.

She'd been given the opportunity to buy into the business when Erich's health failed to improve. In Erich's eyes if anyone was to succeed him at VonShelles, it had to be Linda, regardless of the fact that she was a woman.

Linda agreed to the buy in, which pretty much wiped out the majority of her savings. However, she liked the division of the company. Erich retained forty percent, his wife Lillian owned twenty percent and Linda acquired ownership of the remaining forty percent. She felt this once-in-a-lifetime opportunity would not only define her career, but also provide security for the rest of her life. In looking over the books she saw VonShelles had always operated in the black, and she had some great ideas she felt would take it to the next level.

With Erich unable to perform any of the daily tasks at the company, it fell to Linda to fill his vacated spot as Head Designer. And much to her chagrin, Chief Operating Officer, the position previously held by the now-disinterested Lillian, also landed in Linda's lap.

Within the evolution of her dual roles, she introduced and launched her own label *Taylor Made* under the VonShelles umbrella and everything took off for her and the company. The new label, coupled with fresh designs, had breathed new life into VonShelles and proved to be a clear moneymaker. Modern women couldn't get enough of Linda's trendy, current, and slightly edgy designs.

That had been four years ago; Linda had since admitted to herself that she struggled to keep it all together. She had been a new business owner, and without the ailing Erich on hand to aid her with the transitions, she found it all difficult.

Lillian offered little to no assistance as she informed Linda that her place was by Erich's side. "I hope you are a strong swimmer, my dear," Lillian had said. "This is a sink or swim kind of undertaking."

To the onlooker the company appeared to have continued success. Linda had even taken quarterly trips to India and China where she special ordered very specific fabrics to aid in her creative visions. The creative end of the business was under control; unfortunately, she found her business acumen left much to be desired. Because in spite of her successful line and other popular designer lines within the company, she found herself grappling to keep the creditors at bay.

Linda hated the thought of defeat after her short tenure of barely four years at the wheel. She swallowed her pride and admitted to Erich and begrudgingly to Lillian that she'd been barely treading water, in fact, was nearly drowning in all the administrative work and desperately needed a lifeline or some sort of help.

Erich called his good friend Elliott Bradford, the owner of ERB National Holdings. Elliott worked with Clayton Butler and swooped up the controlling interest in VonShelles along with all the labels and designers under contract including Taylor Made.

Lillian had gladly relinquished her twenty percent of the company, Erich had preserved thirty-eight percent of the business. Without the necessary funds for legal counsel, Linda represented herself and had only been able to retain a mere thirteen percent of the company with ERB National Holdings acquiring forty-nine percent of the business and thus controlling interest of VonShelles.

That element alone left her feeling ambivalent about her future at VonShelles. While it was true they paid her handsomely for her twenty-seven shares, she still couldn't get over the fact that she had gone back to being just another employee. An employee with stock options, but an employee nonetheless.

In the end, she lost her position as the company's Chief Operating Officer, but rather than lose her altogether, ERB National Holdings retained her as the Head Designer.

She'd become just a figurehead, a fact Clayton Butler made her well aware of. "You can be as creative as you like," he'd told her on multiple occasions, "as long as you mind the budget you've been given. And," he paused, "you can forget about taking any more trips abroad for those overly expensive fabrics."

The deal left a sour taste in Linda's mouth. She didn't mind giving up the COO title and the responsibility that went along with it. She felt she'd given up her dreams of becoming the next Coco Chanel.

One could comprehend the acrimony that Clayton held for her from a business standpoint, what he had perceived as Linda's extravagance had been artistically necessary in her mind. She did what it took to bring her creative vision to life, regardless of the cost for materials or labor, which is what had put her in the financial pitfall.

~ ~ ~

Gabrielle and Clayton reached the lobby and he extended an arm toward the opened doors; she then caught the glint of his gold wedding band on his left hand.

"Please, Miss Lawrence, after you."

She stepped out of the elevator and he started to leave with her, but abruptly stopped and sighed. "I just realized I left my briefcase up in my office." He stepped back inside and pressed the button to his desired floor.

Gabrielle exhaled, glad the little tête-à-tête was over.

2
❧ Gabrielle ❧
New York City – Saturday March 22nd, 1969

Gabrielle turned from the elevator and into the main lobby of the building. She walked past the east side of the building's large but now empty reception desk.

She marveled at the elegant styling of the lobby as she walked through the expansive marbled foyer of The Bradford Building, something she hadn't had a chance to do. On any given day, the lobby buzzed with all sorts of activities and with people coming to and fro. One never really got an actual opportunity to appreciate it as she did now, void of people.

At the building's center stood the enormous freestanding alabaster sculpture. The piece, commissioned by Elliott Robert Bradford himself, erected upon the building's completion in 1941. It beautifully depicted a masculine hand rising from the dirt, littered with fool's gold but within the clutches of the risen hand, a diamond. She felt inspired by the artwork.

Below the sculpture, a bronzed plaque with gold lettering read:

Behold, your diamond in the rough.

Several feet away, behind the sculpture, two sets of exposed staircases on either side rose up to the first ten levels of the building. From her current vantage point they almost appeared to be in a diamond pattern as well, as they soared elegantly upward. The mixture of the glossed varnished oak handrails, decorative wrought iron balusters and stair spindles imbedded in the marble steps, led upwards. The impressive combination of rich materials inspired awe.

Thomas, the door attendant, stood at his post and chuckled to himself as his wrinkled face smiled at her with a twinkle in his blue eyes as he watched her in her wide-eyed astonishment.

"Impressive, isn't it?" His words echoed slightly in the large space.

"Yes, it most certainly is, Thomas, much like the man himself I've been told." She said, "I've heard he was a good man," she paused. "Thomas, did you know Mr. Bradford well?"

The old man stepped out from behind his podium and joined her at the large marble floor medallion embossed with a large gold letter 'B' inlaid at its center.

"Only well enough to say hello and goodbye, although, I'd sometimes have the chance to make small talk with him, because as busy as he was he would always stop and ask, 'How's the family, Thomas?' So he knew me by name," his face beamed with pride. "To know that a man as great and powerful as he was, took the time to remember you and ask about your family, it means a lot to a fella, ya know." He placed his hands on his hips as he continued.

"In all my years working here he'd remember us with nice bonuses on our birthdays and holidays. He placed a lot of value on the people who worked for him and we all miss him. So from what I knew of him, I'd say that yes, Mr. Bradford was a good and generous man." Thomas cleared his throat, looking up at the sculpture.

"Mr. Bradford, designed this building and had it fully occupied when it was completed. All fifty-two floors, filled. And that means both sides of the building, east and west." He gave a nod of his head to put emphasis on his point. "People liked him, ya see? There was something about him that made you just want to be around him." He smiled, practically to himself as if remembering another time.

"You know, Thomas, I believe Mr. Bradford must have also been a forward thinker as well," she remarked. "Because thirty years later, it's still a spectacular building even by today's standards."

"That's because Mr. Bradford had a great mind for detail, Miss Gabi. I can't tell you how many times I heard him say, *'Details, are what stands between a man and his completed goals. A man must mind the details to achieve his objectives.'* It's something I will never forget."

"He must have been a remarkable businessman," she added as she looked around the enormous lobby. "For him to build all of this."

"That he was, Miss Gabi, that he was." Then, almost as

suddenly as it appeared, his smile faded. "His death from that plane crash came so out of the blue. It was awful, just awful. We lost John Butler in that plane crash too," he inclined his head toward her, "you know, one of them small jets."

"John Butler?" She questioned.

"Yes, the father of Clayton Butler. He was on the plane with Mr. Bradford when it went down. It happened just this past January, barely three weeks into the New Year."

Gabrielle now understood Clayton Butler's intensity; *he had recently lost his father*.

Thomas shook his head. "Don't you be believing some of what's been whispered about them though. Some folks just like to gossip, but I can tell you true, they were no cheaters. One of the two girls on that plane with them worked for John Butler. They were both honorable men, and I never knew either of them to do something like that." He paused as he pursed his lips. "It's only been a little over a month or so since the crash. We're still getting used to his Missus running things."

"I haven't met Mrs. Bradford yet, but I have such admiration for any woman who would have the mettle to take on a huge conglomerate such as this." Gabrielle turned toward the doors, speaking over her shoulder as she walked.

Thomas followed and returned to his post near the doors.

"I suppose I'd have to agree with you there, but she doesn't have his heart or his warmth, she's just not that ni..." He quickly clamped his lips shut, as if he'd said too much. "Hey, don't pay no mind to an old fella like me, Miss Gabi." He then remarked with a bit of a lilt in his voice. "Looks like we're out of that cold snap, so enjoy the warmer weather; they say we going to make it to fifty degrees today."

She welcomed the change of subject. "Fifty degrees, you don't say!" She said as she reached the doors.

He nodded as he brought an aged wrinkled hand to the brim of his hat and tipped it to her.

"Take care, Miss Gabi."

She smiled at him as she pushed her way through the heavy glass revolving doors.

Once outside, the warmth from the sun caressed her face and the city sounds surrounded her. Deciding to take a detour, she headed over to Central Park before taking her subway ride home. She wanted to enjoy some of the warmer spring like weather, not exactly fifty degrees, but it felt like a heat wave compared to the coolness at the start of the day.

She bought a hot dog along with a bottle of orange soda from a street vender. With Central Park only a couple short blocks away from The Bradford Building, she headed that way.

After buying a bag of seed for the birds, she worked her way through the crowded street and strolled quickly through the throngs of people already in the park.

With her meal and the bag in hand, she finally sat on her newly found favorite spot, a bench nestled away from the fair-weather crowds at the park. She flung some of the seeds to the ground and ate her hot dog as she watched the birds approach.

Soon, she began contemplating the new life she started for herself; she had been seeking independence and now felt as if she'd found it. Gabrielle had been living in this big wonderful city with all it had to offer for almost two months, and now with her new job, it made her feel as if she really was doing this whole thing all on her own.

Unfortunately, as the dust from her new life's journey had begun to settle, she found living alone wasn't all it had been cracked up to be. Lately, she was overwhelmed with a feeling of loneliness. With none of her family or her old friends here, it engulfed her and dominated her thoughts.

Sure, she had her building's older caretakers, Gustave and Esther Ulrich, but she had hopes of meeting some new people. People closer to her own age, friends with whom she could explore the city with and do some fun things.

Monty Greer asked her out on a date, but she had to think that one through. Primarily, she wasn't sure how wise it would be to date someone from work; while he was attractive, he just wasn't her type. *If we could go out as just friends that might be a possibility. Because right now serious dating or even having a boyfriend is the furthest thing from my mind, given everything that happened back in California with Daniel Walters; that prick tried to force himself on me and had the audacity to try to excuse his actions by calling me a 'dick tease.'*

She smirked to herself. *All he got for his trouble was a knee to the crotch. No, I don't want to even think about the whole dating thing right now.* Beating back some unpleasant memories, she closed her eyes and wondered, *maybe Monty would be a safe bet after all.*

Not quite the fifty degrees Thomas had told her it might be, it felt mild and she enjoyed the warmth from the sun on her cheeks as she tilted her head up and allowed her face to take full advantage of the sun's rays.

The tranquility of the moment suddenly was broken as she heard a fluttering of wings. And seemingly, out of nowhere bounded a humongous beast of a dog who deftly attacked the feeding birds so swiftly she'd barely had a chance to react. As the predator clamped his teeth into one of the birds, she loudly yelled at him and quickly stood, "HEY YOU, STOP IT!"

He stopped and stood motionless with the bird still trapped in his mouth.

"DROP IT, NOW!" She said.

To her disbelief, he dropped the bird onto the ground near the bench at her command as the other birds took to flight and scattered in a rushed frenzy to escape; the dog stood obediently stock-still. He had a collar around his neck with a leash attached that'd been dragged on the ground.

She reached down and took ahold of the leash, pulled the huge dog toward her, and away from the motionless bird. "Hey killer, just where the hell did you come from and what's wrong with you?" She scolded him as his tail wagged at a frantic pace. "BAD DOG! You should know better. Now, SIT!" The dog obeyed.

"You listen well; I'll give you that."

She found his dog tags in the mass of hair around his huge neck and saw his name.

"You seem to have had some sort of training. I suppose you're not all bad, huh, Lobo? But, you SHOULDN'T attack birds." She addressed him sternly. "Now, STAY!"

She kept a hold of the leash as she leaned over to inspect the bird without touching it and could see it was a lost cause. Gabrielle turned back to the villainous dog. A good-looking German Shepherd with a longish snout. His coat looked and felt clean. She crouched down in front of him and scratched him behind the ear. She gently stroked his head and under his chin.

It startled Gabrielle when she heard a man's deep voice call out from behind her.

3
❧ Nick ☙
New York City – Saturday morning - March 22nd, 1969

"Ugh, fuck sake." Nick mumbled, he could still taste last night's liquor in his mouth. He looked over at the unfamiliar clock on the nightstand, it read 6:15 a.m. *Shit, I slept over, and on top of it all, now I'm going to be late.*

He cleared his throat and rubbed his eyes. He glanced over to the other side of the bed. The woman had herself cocooned in the bed sheets and blanket, with only her long brown hair peeking out from under the covers.

Nick sat up and saw the spent condom on the floor. He grinned to himself; *great self-training, even as drunk as I was last night I somehow managed to get the raincoat on.* He got up and headed to the bathroom.

Her bathroom counter contained all the things that promised to make a woman desirable: from lotions to potions and make-up of all sorts. Nick splashed water onto his face.

He stepped into her shower to clean last night's encounter off him, and per his personal hygiene policy he refused to pick up the used soap in the holder. He opted for some of her shampoo to lather his body. He heard her yawn as she came into the bathroom during his final rinse.

"Hi there," she glided the shower door open a bit, "you want company?" She asked.

Even with last night's make-up smudged on her face, she was still a very pretty woman.

"I'm actually done." He turned off the water, "I hope you don't mind that I used your shower, I would have asked but I didn't want to wake you." *More like hoping I could sneak out of here before you woke up,* he thought to himself, *why did I have to take that fucking shower? I should have gotten the hell out of here when I could've.*

In truth, he'd always avoided seeing any woman that he had just fucked the morning after. It was better for them both. He wouldn't have to pretend it could lead to anything, and she wouldn't have to feel used.

"No, I don't mind." She looked disappointed as she handed him a clean towel, she glanced over at the filled bathroom counter and remarked. "I apologize for the mess; I wasn't really expecting a visitor."

Nick quickly dried himself as she watched him in awkward silence.

"Sorry," he said. "I didn't mean to crash here last night. I must have been a little more out of it than I thought."

"Oh, don't get me wrong, I didn't mind, Nick. It was great." She shyly smiled as she eyed his naked body.

"Good to know," he draped the towel around his waist.

"Because, I don't remember much about last night. Like," his eyes blankly met hers, "your name, what is it?" He smiled.

"My name is Mona." She bit her lip seductively.

"Thank you for your hospitality, Mona." Nick walked into her bedroom, found his clothes, and started to get dressed.

"You know something?" She followed him. "You have a great body. I've never seen muscles like yours before, at least, not up close." She opened her robe. "Maybe we could go for round two, to help jog your memory of last night."

"Thanks, but no." He slid his feet into his shoes. "I'm running late as it is, and I have a dog to let out." He didn't want to drag this thing on any longer than necessary, so he headed for the door.

"Will you call me?" Mona asked. "Maybe we can do this again, sometime. Soon?"

"Yeah, sure. We can probably do something some time." *There's no way in hell I'll be seeing you again, Mona. You can bet on that.*

She got a pencil and wrote her name and number down; she placed the paper in his palm as she hugged him. "Call me, Nick."

As Nick left her building he passed a waste paper basket and threw the crumpled piece of paper with Mona's phone number into it.

~~~

After his time at Mona's, he drove home to let Lobo out,

but he only had enough time to let him do his business. He made it to work with only a minute to spare.

Now, it was noon. When he went home to get Lobo, a package waited for him outside his door. He already knew the contents as he could smell the almonds from the fresh *cantuccini* cookies.

He put the package on his dinette table and looked at the small envelope with his name handwritten on it. He just stared at it unopened, but he wondered when his mother dropped them off. *Did she wait for me to leave or did I just miss her?* He didn't have time to think on this right now; he had to give Lobo a long walk and then get ready to meet up with Claudia.

Distractedly he thought about the morning he'd had, the mid-day sun felt warm but the air had a breeziness to it. He especially felt the chill in the shaded areas as he walked Lobo along the busy street. Between the bright sun lit patches on the sidewalk and the cool of the shadows, he felt the sun to be a bit deceiving. Thankfully, he wore his favorite straw ivy cap and a windbreaker.

Nick had learned how headstrong Lobo, a huge German Shepherd, could be. Lobo usually pulled hard on his leash when they were near Central park. Nick took the hint and decided a walk through the park would help burn off some of the dog's pent-up energy.

They started along one of the many paths, and he began to walk at a fast pace just to keep up with the hulking canine. Nick pulled back on the leash, but it had no effect on Lobo as he raced leash length ahead of Nick. *If only Rico had taught you how to walk without pulling an arm off.*

At that very moment a huge gust of wind blew Nick's hat off his head. He instinctually reached up toward his head to grab for his hat and in doing so, he accidently let go of Lobo's leash. Lobo seized the moment's opportunity and took off, speeding away.

Nick chased after his hat in the other direction. He caught up to it, reached down, and retrieved it before it landed in a nearby pond. "Gotcha!" He shouted victoriously as he planted it back on his head with a self-satisfied smile. At that moment, he remembered Lobo, and he couldn't see him anywhere.

"Shit. Wouldn't you know it? Today. He just had to pick today of all days." Nick began running to the path where he lost sight of the dog. "Lobo! Here, Lobo!" He called out, nothing. He ran up this path and that path calling out to the dog. "Lobo. Here, boy. Here!" Still, no sight of Lobo. "Son of a bitch, dammit." He mouthed under his breath.

Nick just saw people milling about, some walking or running along the path, others walking dogs themselves, couples snuggled together, some were lying on blankets, or picnicking with their families. As he passed people on the path he inquired. "Have you seen a dog, a German Shepherd? I've lost him, he's on a leash."

All the people shook their heads in no responses. Nick went back to where he'd lost him and looked all around; he spied an inconspicuous path and ran towards it.

A utopian spot, surrounded by trees and shielded from the wind, but the sunlight flooded the area with warmth. In the distance, he spotted the dog.

Lobo sat on his haunches, and Nick let out a sigh of relief. A woman knelt in front of the dog. She held his leash and pet his head. Her back had been to Nick; he couldn't yet see her face. *Nice ass* he thought to himself.

"Lobo, there you are." Nick called out. "Hey, Miss? I have to thank you for corralling him for me."

She stood up and turned around to face him. "So this killer beast belongs to you?" She appeared to be annoyed.

4
Nick and Gabrielle
New York City – Saturday afternoon - March 22nd, 1969

With the sun in her eyes, she'd been unable to make out his face with only his silhouette visible to her. She turned in the direction of his outline and voice.

"Killer? Beast? You can't possibly mean this dog, he's got to be the gentlest, most loveable dog you'd ever meet." He stated as he continued to move nearer. As he got closer he saw how the sun's rays shimmered through the trees upon her lovely but displeased face.

He lifted his index finger and thumb to his sunglasses and slightly lowered the sunglasses down the bridge of his nose to get a clear un-tinted look. In doing so, he saw her almond shaped eyes. She wore a fitted green cashmere sweater tucked into her hip hugger bell-bottom blue jeans with a large circular silver belt buckle.

The sun's rays strategically spot lit her green and amber eyes and her full lips. Lips, which were pursed together into a firm irate line, yet they somehow managed to look delectable to him all the same. He first regarded her as a potential sexual encounter after assessing her voluptuous body and stunning face, but there had been something more. He felt like his soul had risen from the depths and entwined around his heart.

His reaction to her caught him off guard, and it hit him like a rod of lightning and his mouth went dry; he physically and audibly had to catch his breath.

"Hey, are you alright?" She moved near him, alarm in her voice.

"Me? Yeah, yeah…, me, I- I'm fine. Thanks." He just barely managed to croak out, he'd been strangely jostled by the thunderbolt reaction to her. She was…something more, but something more of what? He'd never stammered in front of a woman before.

He pushed his sunglasses back in place as he quickly tried to gather his composure. "I, I think, I was just so worked up and you know, worried about him. That's all." He paused, not taking his eyes off her. "I think I may have searched the entire park for him." He said.

"Well, Mister," she handed him the leash. "You really need to keep a better eye on your *gentle loveable* animal." Considering his apparent physical plight, her annoyance diminished, just a bit.

"Your dog murdered a poor defenseless pigeon." She pointed to the dead bird near the park bench.

His eyes moved to where her extended finger pointed.

"He did that?" Confounded, he turned back to face her.

"Yes, he did. I witnessed it myself," she continued to look

upset, her eyes fell to the dead bird. "I have been coming here just about every day to feed them and today, well, today this happened." She looked sadly at the bird as she spoke. "You should train him not to go after other living creatures."

"Look, I'm sorry about this whole thing." He said apologetically. "He's never done anything like this before... That, I know of."

She turned back to look at him; his sunglasses shielded his eyes and the straw Ivy cap was pushed down low onto his head covering his forehead.

"That you know of?" She took a few safe steps backward as she suspiciously squinted up at him. "Isn't he your dog?"

"I suppose I have to come clean, no, he's not. I'm caring for him while my... friend... is away."

He sensed her uneasiness as he removed his sunglasses and stuck the arm of the sunglasses onto the vee of his shirt. The gesture made her posture relax as she could now see more of his face and his eyes.

She assessed him as if seeing him for the first time. Gabrielle noticed how attractive the man was.

A radiant white toothed smile adorned his mouth, he was tall, *probably about six foot two or so*, and broad shouldered with a slim tapered waist.

His dark hair hung from under his cap, it fell a few inches past his ears with short neat sideburns. Gabrielle found herself wholly absorbed as she gazed upon his good-looking dark features, and she looked into the bluest eyes she'd ever seen and they captivated her.

She took note of his strong defined jawline, the slight lined dimples in both cheeks when he smiled and the small cleft in his broad chin, she felt the heat rise up to her cheeks as she blushed.

"Let me at least take care of the deceased." He said as he pulled a paper towel out of his right pocket of his jacket and an empty plastic Wonder bread bag out of the other one.

"Would you mind holding on to his leash?" He asked.

His voice pulled her out of her reverie, and she took the leash.

"I see you're a man who comes prepared." She remarked.

He bent and crouched in front of the bench and used the paper towel to pick up the bird and put it in the plastic bag.

"Well, somewhat prepared. Let's just hope Lobo is finished with his business because this is my only plastic bag." He looked up at her with an amiable smile, he stood and reached for the leash. He gently pulled Lobo to him and commanded him to sit, the dog compliantly sat.

He looked at her with a triumphant gleam in his eye and a crooked smile as if to say, 'see, he's not so bad.' Moreover, she'd have to admit that the dog looked as if he'd been trained, well, sort of.

Using his index finger, he pushed up on the brim of his cap, and she then fully appreciated his whole face and saw more of the Mediterranean Sea blue of his eyes as he stood before her with a grin on his handsome face. He reached out his free hand toward her as he spoke.

"Let me formally introduce myself. My name is Nick, Nick Caine with a C and an E." He gestured with the leash. "And the big hooligan next to me is Lobo."

She smiled up at him as she accepted his outstretched hand; She gasped feeling his electrified touch on her skin as he held her hand, which in turn made her feel a series of flutters in the pit of her stomach, and her knees went a slightly weak.

He also felt something he'd never encountered before and noted that his touch seemed to affect her as well. He locked his eyes on hers as his hand held hers securely, but smiled with a perplexed uneasy grin.

To her surprise, her voice became raspy. "Gabi Laurendeau," then her voice faded and her cheeks flushed crimson.

"Come again, I didn't catch that." Nick said.

She attempted to pull herself together as she slid her hand out of his with forced calmness and used the hand to push her hair back behind her right ear. "My name is Gabrielle Lawrence; my friends call me Gabi."

Her mind began doing mental gymnastics, as she marveled at the chain of events that lead to their accidental meeting. Something inside her felt fate had intervened in her life at this moment and sent him to her.

Nick felt heated and removed his jacket, which exposed the true scope of the broadness of his muscular shoulders and arms through his tan colored marble weave pullover.

His biceps formed like mountain peaks. Not that she normally liked that sort of thing, but she found herself drawn to him in some inexplicable way. Without even recognizing it, she snuck more than a few glances at him as he sat on the park bench next to her. She deliberately turned her attention to Lobo and his earlier misdeed as the dog laid on the grass in front of them with Nick holding on to his leash.

"You know, it's kind of sad really," she began, "pigeons tend to mate for life. The bird's poor mate must be going crazy without its companion; don't you think?"

Nick's eyebrows lifted as a grin came to his lips, but he answered her in a seemingly serious tone. "Frankly, I hadn't really thought about it. I'm not an ornithologist and can tell you nothing about the behavior of birds, but I do have a funny feeling that the other bird will be just fine. The flock should see to it." His grin widened as he lightly chuckled.

She cut a sideways glance at him. "You don't have to be a birdwatcher to feel bad for the poor bird, but I have a feeling that you're making fun of me, Nick Caine with a C and an E."

"No, I'm not." His eyes twinkled as the air filled with his lighthearted laughter. "Not really, I just think it's so endearing of you to care about the dead bird and its surviving mate, Gabrielle."

Hearing him say her name felt like a soft caress to her ears, even though she knew he'd been having a good little laugh at her expense. She shifted in her seat.

"You said that you were caring for Lobo for a friend,"

Gabrielle spoke somewhat distractedly. "I suppose that's why you weren't aware of his bloodthirsty palate for birds."

"No, this is news to me." Nick remarked. "I wasn't aware that he had a penchant for the fresh kill, but I have to say, despite this minor newfound character flaw, he's a very good dog. He listens well, and in the time that he's been with me, I've found him to be really smart and a quick learner."

"Well, Nick," she looked down at Lobo, "attacking a feeding bird might be a minor flaw to you, but I can safely bet you that the birds would say it's a major flaw. Maybe while he's in your care, he can learn some much needed social graces."

She crinkled her nose as she glanced in Nick's direction and then down at the dog again. That little gesture she made with her nose intrigued him further.

Lobo's ears perked up as he turned his head toward Gabrielle and looked up at her.

"Do you suppose he knows we are talking about him and his naughty behavior?" She asked curiously.

"I wouldn't be surprised," Nick answered. "I told you he's proven to be very intelligent."

Lobo abruptly stood and shamefacedly moved to her, placed his huge head on her lap, and gave her guilty eyes.

"I believe he thinks you're cross with him. And he's trying to make up with you." Nick remarked with a crooked smile.

"I can see that. Not too subtle, is he?" She placed her hand affectionately on Lobo's head and pet him. "Alright boy, you're forgiven." Her fingers rubbed the spot between the dog's brows as Lobo blissfully closed his eyes and wagged his tail.

"Well now, would you look at that? He is simply in heaven right now because of your magical touch, Gabrielle."

Magical touch – so this man, this Nick Caine, had felt something too, when our hands touched.

Nick asked her to join him for dinner that evening to make up for the ordeal Lobo had put her through with his *bad* conduct; she accepted his invitation and agreed to meet him at the restaurant.

"Until tonight, Gabrielle." Nick's voice seared through her; as they stood together gazing at each other, people passed by them in hurried paces.

"Yes, until tonight." And she broke their visual connection when she crossed the wide busy street as Nick looked after her. Nick and Lobo disappeared from her view as she went down the steps toward the subway trains.

5
❦ Gabrielle ❦

New York City – Saturday afternoon - March 22nd, 1969

Gabrielle found herself lost in thought over this man, this Nick Caine, who had stumbled into her life in a most unusual way, over a dog who had killed a pigeon. But she'd been grateful Lobo had been there, he gave her something to focus on other than Mr. Gorgeous. With his stunning blue eyes, sitting right next to her. And his touch, it had only been a moment, but Gabrielle hadn't ever felt anything such as that before. She had purposely avoided looking at him; but she felt his eyes intently and *unabashedly* assessing her.

Gabrielle absently looked up, and quickly recognized her Bleecker Street stop. She jumped up and made it out just in time as the doors slammed shut behind her. *Snap out of it, Gabi.* She told herself.

She stopped at Wasserman's, a local mom and pop grocery store (minus the mom), the place made her feel at home in a city as large as New York. Once she finished her shopping, Mr. Wasserman handed her a bouquet of fresh flowers.

"You are one of my happiest customers, you always have

such a nice smile." He stated. "Here, you take flowers, Miss Gabi. You take, for you, from me. No charge." He insisted as he pushed the flowers toward her.

With a bright smile she thanked him, sliding the paper wrapped flowers into one of her bags as she paid her bill.

Gabrielle lived a short distance away, but she was thankful when Benjamin, the storeowner's sixteen-year-old son, assisted her by hauling her groceries home in the store's rusted black delivery wagon. The wagon had yellowed newspaper lining it with gate-like wooden sides, and her bags fit perfectly inside the wagon's rectangular body.

A tall gangly lad, Benjamin Wasserman had a pronounced nose. His black horn-rimmed glasses covered his expressive, brown eyes. With a kippah in place at the crown of his head, a mass of loose dark brown curls haloed his face.

They had often talked on their short walks from the grocery store, and Gabrielle knew that Benjamin aspired to be a writer, but he was also a good son. His father expected him to take over the family grocery store, but Benjamin wanted to go to college, and it proved to be a source of anxiety.

Gabrielle didn't want to undermine their relationship, but she tried to give Benjamin encouragement to follow his own path. To maybe look into taking some courses at a nearby college after high school so he could still help out at the store.

As he pulled the wagon toward her apartment, she said quietly, "Have you finished your story about the music conductor yet, Benjy? Remember, I'd love to read it."

Benjamin shyly looked up and seemed to blush a little.

"I guess it's almost done." He eyed the ground. "I'm not sure if it's any good though. Or if I'll even finish it."

"Oh, but you must finish it. It's such a good story."

He hesitated. "My Dad told me that if I don't want to work at the store, I should focus on math and be an accountant, like my cousin Eli. To have something to fall back on."

She saw his look of uncertainty. "I'll share something my father has always said: *'If you insist upon a backup plan, you're just giving yourself an excuse to fail'* only he says it with a French accent." She lightly laughed.

Thanking him for the help, she pulled a dollar bill out of her purse and offered it to him.

He looked sheepishly down at the bill. "I don't know, I don't think I can accept this, Miss Gabi, it's way too much. My dad has me charge twenty-five cents for the local deliveries I do in the neighborhood."

She placed the bill in his hand. "Benjy, to me it's only a dollar. You keep the change for yourself, okay?"

Inside her apartment, she found a vase for the flowers after putting away the last of her groceries. She peeled an orange and plopped one of the large sections into her mouth.

"Mr. Wasserman, you have *the* best fruit." She said out loud as the juice dribbled down her chin.

The phone rang, she wiped her hands, and answered it on the third ring.

"Hello."

"Gabrielle? It's your mother, are you alright? I've been trying to reach you all morning."

"Hello Maman, I'm fine. I had to work at the fashion house today."

"On a Saturday?" Her mother questioned.

"I know, but I'm still trying to prove myself. What's up? Or did you just call to chat?"

"Well, you know how much I love chatting with you, but I have a reason for my call. I've a bit of news," she paused, "and your father is here."

"In California?" There was alarm in her voice. "Is there something the matter?" Gabrielle asked.

"No, dear, everything's fine. Phillipe and Julienne are having their spring breaks from school. Phillipe wanted to go skiing. So we're headed to Aspen for a short vacation."

"Oh, spring break, I forgot about that. I've been too busy getting settled in here."

"No doubt, but, I think you're going to enjoy this new adventure of yours, Gabrielle." She paused. "I wanted you to know where we were in case you tried calling. Plus, your father has a bit of news too."

Gabrielle could hear the smile in her mother's voice and it made her relax.

"I'll let him tell you himself," her mother continued, "he's waiting with baited breath to talk to you, so here he is."

Gabrielle twisted her mouth as she heard the phone being

passed to her father. *Okay, here we go with another lecture.*

"Gabrielle, ma chère fille." His voice was almost lyrical.

'My dear daughter'? So this is how he's going to start his sermon. Nonetheless, she loved hearing his voice.

"Hello, Père. How are you?"

"I am well. It's good to be here with your Mère, but I wanted to tell you that soon I'll be in New York on business, and I would like very much to see you when I'm there."

"Papa," she sighed. "Why do I get the impression you're coming to New York just to check up on me?" Suspicion in her voice.

"That's only because you don't believe me when I say that I trust you to make your own choices. But, Gabrielle, I do."

"Alright," she agreed. "I would love to see you, when will you be here?"

"Not for a while really. I will be there in May, I haven't worked out all the details yet, but I'll be staying at The Waldorf Astoria. I will see you then, we will have dinner."

"Yes, I would love that," she hesitated realizing he wasn't asking. "Papa, if I may ask, what's your business in New York?"

"I'm extending a line from my latest collection into one of the larger department stores there," he paused, "to be, as you say…more main stream. I'm branching out." He chuckled.

"That sounds exciting," she inwardly smiled as she realized how much she missed him. "I can't wait to see you."

Once she finished her conversation with her parents, she went to get ready for her date with Nick Caine.

~~~

After a shower she applied her make-up with care. Not one to wear a lot of make-up, she felt she had the understated look mastered. She went into her bedroom to get dressed and soon had clothes strewn about on her bed.

Her final choice was a sleeveless satin paisley shell with a small cowl collar. She pulled sheer hose onto her shapely legs and secured the elastic over her hips.

Stepping into an aquamarine pleated mini skirt, she tucked the shell in the waistband and then slipped her feet into a pair of black sling-back high heel pumps. She pulled the straps in place as she walked into the hall and dialed the number for a taxi-cab.

She took out her dress watch from the jewelry box, slid it on to her slender wrist and closed the back clasp. A beautiful timepiece made of solid gold and encrusted with diamonds around an exquisite mother-of-pearl face; it had been an expensive gift from her parents when she graduated from design school.

However, she had second thoughts about wearing it and undid the clasp and put it back into the jewelry box. She pulled out her everyday Timex watch and slid the thin elastic metal band over her wrist.

She brushed her hair from root to tip and then flung her hair back as she rose. Her glorious golden brown mane fell loosely and gracefully into place. Gabrielle added a pair of gold hoop earrings to her lobes and some gold bangle bracelets to her wrist. She pulled the mini skirt's matching aquamarine jacket on over her bare arms.

After a final glance at her reflection in the antique Cheval mirror in the corner of her bedroom, she was satisfied.

Not one of my own designs, but it will do nicely.

She looked at the clock on her bedside table and realized there hadn't been time to change purses. She grabbed her daily handbag. *Well, at the very least, it's black and goes with everything.*

Gabrielle raced out of the front door and down the stairs to wait on the stoop for the cab. She ran into Gus Ulrich just outside the building's main door; he had just slid a new label into an identification slot of the mailbox.

Gustave Ulrich was a retired New York City police officer who now worked as the building superintendent, and he had taken it upon himself to look out for Gabrielle as well. He and his wife Esther, both in their late sixties, lived in the first-floor unit of the building as they had for the last fifteen years.

A formidable man, Gus had a huge barrel chest and big sturdy arms; his outward appearance was tough as nails and he seemed rough around the edges. Esther had been his opposite; she'd been soft in speech as well as demeanor. She had a very delicate manner and a softness which had taken its toll on her small slight frame.

Sadly, Esther had miscarried, not one, but all three of her pregnancies early on in their marriage. Coming to terms many years ago that they were destined to be a childless couple, she had in effect became mother to those in the neighborhood who needed one. She and Gus both had informally thought of Gabrielle as one of *their own*, just as Esther had with others on their block. Esther frequently offered motherly, heartfelt and often sage advice (along with a grilled cheese sandwich, a glass of milk and just out-of-the-oven homemade cookies).

Gus shook his head disapprovingly, "Are you trying to catch your death with the cold, Gabi? It's not warm enough outside for what you're wearing."

It was almost like having a substitute for her father right here in New York City; if she didn't know any better, she'd swear her father hired him to keep a watchful eye on her. But it couldn't be the case, because he had lived here long before Gabrielle had bought the building.

She gave him a quelling look, but despite that momentary insolence, she *was* chilled in her lightweight jacket and mini skirt as the warmth of the day had now passed.

Thinking Gus might be right about her outfit, but not wanting to give him any bit of satisfaction, she tried to ignore the cold and his disapproval as she tilted her head in his direction and inquired.

"What are you up to there, Gus?"

"Oh, this?" He pointed to the mail slot. "I meant to tell you. I finally rented the upper unit," He smiled at her as he slipped his screwdriver into a slot on his utility belt. "I think you will approve, rented it to a nice *single* man," His smile crinkled at the corners of his eyes.

"He works nights though. But, I think you should meet him anyway," His smile widened. "I think you'd hit it off."

"Come on now, Gus," She raised an eyebrow. "You know I trust your judgment, but you wouldn't be trying to match me up with our newest tenant now, are you? You know, I can pick out my own dates. As a matter of fact, I'm going out tonight, just waiting for my taxi to get here."

"Taxi?" His mouth kinked judgmentally. "What kind of man is he? That he couldn't come and pick you up himself?"

"Oh, he wanted to, but I chose to meet him. I want to get to know him better before I let him know where I live. A girl can't be too careful, now can she?"

He nodded in agreement. "Good thinking," he said and looked at her with suspicion still in his eyes. "Where is he taking you? Or should I say where are you meeting him?"

This almost feels like an interrogation... Once a cop, forever a cop. "An Italian place on 48th, it's called Mamma Leones. Ever hear of it?" She angled her head.

"Yeah," His mouth formed a reflective grin. "I've been there a time or two, took my Esther and she liked it too. If you like clams, you gotta try their spicy clams- they're out of this world. I think you're in for a treat."

After waiting a few minutes on the stoop with Gus keeping her company, the taxicab arrived just as she was thinking about going back inside to get a warmer jacket, but instead she entered the cab and waved goodbye to Gus.

Her heart raced inside her chest; this is by far the most impulsive thing she'd done since moving to New York City. That is unless, you count riding the subway an impulsive act. *No.* She thought to herself; *a tad bit risky, maybe, but not impulsive.* Sitting in the back seat of the cab, she couldn't help the exhilaration she felt as she made her way to meet the unbelievably Mr. Gorgeous, Nick Caine with a *C and an E.*

6

🍀 Elliott Bradford 🍀

New York City – Wednesday afternoon - January 8th 1969

He had barely recognized her when she stopped him as he got off the elevator.

"Hello, do you have a moment for an old friend?" she said. Her voice, unmistakable. With curiosity, he eyed her as they rode the elevator back up to his office while she fidgeted with the straps on her worn handbag.

The years had not been kind to her, he noted as she somewhat hid behind her shiny, lustrous raven hair.

However, there was no mistaking her beautiful brown eyes that darted timidly away from him.

Once they were in his office she began her tale, telling him she had nowhere else to turn and she hated coming to him with her problem after all the years that had slipped between them. She wrung her hands as she proceeded to beg him to help her. She told him that she *would do anything.* Overcome with emotion, she woefully sobbed as she sank to the floor on her bare knees. He pulled her up from the carpeted floor of his office and took her into his arms.

He held her tightly within his grasp, his mind completely reeling from the enormity of the news she'd just delivered to him in the confines of his superlatively appointed office.

The midday January sun was shining high and bright in the sky. It essentially bathed the busy New York skyline with its glorious golden light.

Vacantly he stared out of the bank of windows in his corner office. The unobstructed view displayed the city as it always had, now somehow it lost its usually palliative effect on him.

He tried to reassure and comfort her; soothingly he stroked her beautiful black hair, it smelled clean and reminded him of fresh flowers. Elliott's eyes soon settled on the mounted replica of his 1940 custom 61 ft. yawl with raised white sails and the name Angel emblazed on its sides.

In that moment, he wasn't sure what he could do to fix it, *her* problem. Yet he vowed to her and to himself that he would damn sure see it resolved, *somehow*.

Firmly she pulled herself out of his arms, he in turn handed her the white Irish linen handkerchief from his breast pocket. She dabbed her tear-stained face and looked up at him, noticing that like a fine wine, he'd aged exceedingly well.

His hair perfectly cut, a shocking white with very little, if any, of his original blonde color. It appeared to her that not a hair on his head was out of place. His eyes, contrasted by the healthy glow of his recently tanned skin, were just as brilliant a blue as the last time she saw them more than two decades ago.

He sat on the edge of his desk; tall, lean and fit, dressed in a tailored navy blue three-piece suit offset by the crisp whiteness of his shirt and the shininess of his black shoes. She'd still been impressed at how shiny his shoes were. So shiny, in fact, she'd told him in years past that she could see her reflection in them.

His presence exuded pure power, a man accustomed to navigating his world with a sure steady hand. She found him to be just as imposing as ever, and her breath had involuntarily caught in her throat.

After she'd composed herself, she pulled her eyes away from him and tried to hand him back his handkerchief, but he gave a dismissive wave of his hand.

"Keep it, and please, don't worry." He rose from the desk's edge. "Everything will be taken care of. This, I promise you."

He stood before her and placed his hands on her shoulders.

"I will make this right, Angel, just have faith in that." Lowering his head, he reaffirmed with a reassuring smile. "Alright?"

"Alright." She sighed with a nod of her head as she fumbled with her purse's latch.

She reached inside the worn handbag, pulled out a large bent manila envelope, and handed it to him with downcast eyes.

"I don't know if you know where he is, but... this really is for both of you."

She decisively tilted her head toward him, her voice

became soft and quavering. "I-I've been kind of saving them, through the years…" Her voice softly trailed off.

He lifted his hand, took the envelope she held out to him, and placed it on the desk behind him.

She glanced at the boat model. "Those were some of my best times." She hesitated. "I-I'm really so…so very sorry about what happened back then and I'm sorrier now for bringing this trouble to your doorstep." Her apologetic gaze lowered even further. "I- I just really want to thank you, for hearing me out and for agreeing to help us."

"Thank me *after*, okay?" He said as he stared intently at her. He put his hand under her chin and lifted her face to his. Then, with his other hand, he moved her cloaking hair out of the way to get a better look at her. He had felt something about her appearance had been off and seeing her face up close confirmed his suspicions.

She quickly turned her face away from him and backed away out of his gentle grasp. Unable to endure his close inspection, her face instantly flooded with color. She quickly raked her hair over her face with trembling fingers to cover what not even her make-up could mask. However, in her heart, she knew hiding it was futile; she saw it in his eyes. He already knew the history of her life, it was so clearly on display. She hung her head and turned to leave, but then she hesitated at the door and looked back at him over her shoulder.

"I need to tell you something else before I go," she cautiously leveled her gaze to his intense blue eyes. "Despite everything that happened in the past, and all of the years," She bit her lip. "I want you to know one more thing; I never stopped loving you, Ell."

His eyes were glazed over, jolted by what he'd just seen and at her words. Grimly he looked at her and managed to say, "Nor I, you." He looked at her; he found that he truly meant it. "I've always loved you, Angel." Then he added. "Even after that night."

"If that's true, everything could have been so different for you and me." Fresh tears welled up in her eyes.

He found himself unusually speechless and at a loss for words as he watched her leave. In his heart, he also knew things would have been very different for them both. *If only you hadn't run away from me all those years ago.*

While his eyes gave off a saddened and desolate mien, he looked at her in her frayed wool coat and worn shoes as she silently left his office.

He dragged himself, on his now seemingly weighted down legs, to his black leather chair and sat behind his sleek mahogany desk. The sadness he had felt rapidly gave way to anger building up inside him.

He grabbed the phone's receiver and dialed a number; someone on the line answered it on the second ring.

"J-John?" He croaked into the receiver.

"Yes, this is John Butler." Wondering how a stranger had gotten his private number, John asked rather brusquely. "Who, may I ask is…" John paused. "Wait a minute, is that you, Elliott?" He asked with uncertainty in his voice.

"Ye-yes," Elliott's voice cracked and resonated with obvious distress. "It's me."

"What in the world? You back from Acapulco, already. I thought you and Margo weren't due back for another week."

"She's still in Acapulco with Penny," he took in a deep breath. "I came back alone. I needed… to take care of some things, here. I wanted to be sure that Erich was sound after the finalization of our deal."

"You don't sound very much like a man who's just come back from a holiday. Forgive me for saying it, but you sound like hell. You did right by Erich; he couldn't have gotten a better deal. So don't trouble yourself. Is there something else, what's happened?" John asked with unease and trepidation in his own voice, he had never known his friend to sound this distraught.

"I think I'm going to need you to cash in on some favors for me, a.s.a.p." Elliott cleared his throat. "I'm on my way to your office; I'll explain it all when I get there. Please, make some time for me this afternoon, my friend." He paused. "This is going to take a while."

He returned the receiver to its waiting cradle and opened the envelope she'd given him. He examined its contents carefully. When he'd finished, he placed the items back into the envelope, excluding two sealed envelopes, which he secured into a locked section of his desk. He closed the clasp with shaky hands and abruptly placed his haggard looking face into the palms of his bare hands.

He then did something he had not done in a long while, not since the death of his first wife Victoria.

Elliott wept.

7
❧ Gabrielle and Nick ❧
New York – Saturday evening - March 22nd 1969

Situated in Manhattan's theater district located on West 48th Street was Mamma Leone's. A favorite spot amongst the locals and celebrities alike, the large building had striped awnings atop its many windows and a curved barrel-shaped canopy over the restaurant's double doors that led out to the street. The entrance was guarded by two stone lions as they majestically sat upon ornate pedestals.

The taxicab stopped in front of the restaurant, and she turned her head to look out.

Waiting outside the restaurant for her, he leaned against the building. His hands were splayed on his hips as his thumbs hooked inside the tops his pants pockets, and he crossed his legs at the ankles. His black slacks clung to his muscular thighs. In a steel gray suede jacket over a black turtleneck sweater, Nick projected subtle confidence.

Sans the ivy cap, she found him to be even better looking than she had remembered from earlier that day. His thick dark hair had been carefully groomed, but for a few errant strands that fell loosely on his forehead.

She saw him tilt his head as he tried to look into the taxicab. Her pulse quickened as she slowly and modestly exited the car exposing the full length of her shapely legs.

He uncrossed his ankles and lifted himself off the wall. He took in a sharp breath upon seeing her.

"Hi, Nick. I hope you haven't been waiting too long."

"Hello, Gabrielle," deliberately and slowly he assessed her from head to toe to head. "Don't worry, watching you emerge from the cab made it all worth it."

The look he gave her made her feel as if her skirt may have been too short, her cheeks warmed as she lowered her gaze; *I'll have to watch that, don't want to prove Daniel Walter's 'dick tease' comment correct.*

"You look amazing." He remarked.

She then looked up at his clean-shaven face. *My God, he truly is handsome. I could get lost in those baby blues.*

"Thank you, you don't look too bad yourself. I'm glad to see you've lost the hat, it's a welcomed sight."

"Are you? Well, thank you, I think." A frown took over his face and he looked her in the eyes. "I wish you would've let me pick you up at your place instead of you having to take a cab alone."

She inhaled and slightly tilted her head back as she looked at him. *Dear Lord, is that Aramis? He smells just as good as he looks.* "Well, Nick Caine with a C and an E, I think I'd like to get to know you better before I have you to my place." She admitted to him and half-jokingly added, "I want to see if you are trustworthy or not. A girl can't be too careful now, can she?"

"Humph," Nick smirked as he opened the restaurant door to allow her to pass. "I think now would be as good a time as any to tell you, I was once a boy scout. Gabrielle, you have nothing to worry about with me. I assure you, I'm very trustworthy."

She arched a discerning eyebrow. "That remains to be seen."

They entered the restaurant; sitting in a high-backed chair in the foyer with all the sovereignty of a Queen was 'Mamma' herself or at least a very close representation to the portrait on the wall.

The décor surprised Gabrielle. An array of paintings covered the walls, plastic grapes hung from the rafters and sculptures resembling classic figures of nymphs, dramatically cast in smooth white plaster holding their heads almost as if they were in agony, greeted her.

Gabrielle watched as Nick and "Mamma" hugged each other warmly and kissed each other's cheeks. Gabrielle felt a tiny bit out of place as she realized Nick has most certainly been a regular here. The staff welcomed him warmly as well, as if he were a long lost relative. They were seated immediately at a table in the back corner of one of the many dining rooms at Nick's request where he assured Gabrielle it would be much quieter.

Silvio the waiter stared at Gabrielle as he spoke Italian to Nick. "Una donna bella."

Nick beamed, nodding in agreement in the direction of Silvio. He began to order wine for them in Italian. As he spoke, his rich voice was deep and captivating; she found herself mesmerized by the very sound. *What is it about a man speaking another language?*

Dragging her eyes from his face, she took the large menu that the waiter had presented to her and began her search through the menu's many offerings.

"I ordered us a bottle of the Barolo Contratto." Nick said.

She looked at the vast menu and saw the wine selections and absently chimed in. "The Barolo is a good choice, but I think that the Chianti would have worked just as well with most of the items on the menu."

"I could change it if you'd like." He said a little amused.

"No, no need. Your choice is fine."

She bit on her lower lip as she now looked at the large menu with clear indecision; he had amusement in his eyes as he quietly chuckled to himself while watching her.

She felt his eyes on her and she looked up at him as a cheerful smile appeared on her lips. "Why are you looking at me like that?" She laughed and pointed a finger to the huge menu. "There's a lot on here." She closed the menu. "Okay, you're the regular here, so what do you suggest, Nick?" She asked.

"I'm ordering the veal parmesan. I also like the lasagna,

and there are the spicy baked clams or maybe you fancy a lobster or a steak. Please, take your time, look over the menu and get whatever you want. But save some room for dessert because the Bugie is sinfully delicious."

With a slight crinkle in her nose, and a tilt of her head she spoke. "That sounds good, I'm always ready for dessert."

"Ah…, you have a sweet tooth, do you?" Nick gave her an easy smile exposing his white teeth. "That's nice to know because dessert is one of my specialties."

"Really?" Her lips curled into a smirk. "So you're a baker?" She appeared unconvinced.

"Is that so hard to believe?" He laughed as he placed his elbow on the table and rested his chin on his raised hand.

"Well, I'm not a baker, not in the true sense. Zabaglione is my favorite Christmas dessert, and I've yet to master it. However, I specialize in a couple of things. I make great *cantuccini* cookies and my cannoli's are mighty tasty. Both are old family recipes, of course."

"Oh, but of course." She grinned. "Truthfully, I'd fancy either, I'll wait with anticipation if you would be so inclined to bake for me some day."

"Nothing would please me more," his tongue slid across his lower lip. "On second thought," he raised a brow. "I can think of some other things that could bring pleasure to both of us."

"Is that so?" She tilted her head.

"Yes, very much so," he paused, and stared almost

intimately at her, "I would also like to bake something for you Gabrielle." He smiled sensually.

He caught her looking distractedly at his mouth; a fresh smile toyed at his lips, and she purposely looked down at her closed menu.

"I think I've made a decision," She placed a hand on top of the closed menu. "I'll order something on your recommendation. It sounds good and this is an Italian restaurant after all. You know what they say, when in Rome… Eat lasagna." She lightly laughed.

~~~

The waiter returned with the bottle of wine and poured some of the liquid into Nick's glass. He tasted the wine and gave his nod of approval; the waiter then poured some in both of their glasses.

Nick ordered their meals as Gabrielle looked around the large dining room, she saw more of the rococo statuaries in their own individual arched alcoves. Gabrielle also noticed other patrons were well dressed and often in large groups; they made the gleeful sounds of people having a good time. More than a few had gargantuan sized pink margaritas in front of them. The atmosphere had a frenetic atmosphere and she could easily see why it'd been one of his favorite places, 'Mamma' and the staff welcomed you and made you feel a part of it all.

He watched her with a smile as she took in the spectacle of the restaurant, but Gabrielle couldn't help but notice how many of the women eyed up Nick, as if he too were an item on Mamma Leones' menu- an item they apparently would love to sample for themselves. And, she noted how he seemed oblivious to the admiring leers and bold stares they sent his way.

"This really seems like a fun place. I can see why you like it here, Nick. Is it always like this? So... Lively?"

"Yes, pretty much. It's usually quieter in this dining room though. There must be a play or a show on slate for tonight. This is the theater crowd and as they say in the theater, timing is everything."

She pushed her hair back behind each of her ears as her eyes lingered on a guitarist playing and singing happy birthday a few tables over. "Well, I have to be honest, I like it here too." She announced as he sighed with relief.

"Good, I was hoping you would." He paused. "I have to tell you this place has a reputation with well-known celebrities. This is where Elizabeth Taylor was not allowed entrance into the dining rooms because she was wearing slacks." He shook his head disbelievingly. "So she and her people had to eat in the lounge instead, if you can imagine that." He chuckled.

"You know, I remember reading something about it." She casually laughed. "Phew, boy am I glad I decided not to wear pants tonight."

He recalled her exit from the cab and thought, *with legs like those, so am I.* "Well thankfully, they don't have those types of clothing restrictions any longer."

Their waiter returned with salads and bread along with large hunks of mozzarella and placed it on the table. The waiter looked at them with a genuine smile and said, "Enjoy it."

As she listened to Nick talk that evening, she learned he was twenty-six years old, lived alone in a one-bedroom apartment on the Upper East Side and he worked for an exclusive private athletic club that catered to some of New York's most elite and very wealthy.

He managed their newly established weightlifting floor, where he was paid just a little too well to want to pursue a job elsewhere. He explained to Gabrielle that his ultimate dream was to one day open his own bodybuilding gym, including a health food store.

He was passionate about his gym philosophy, his eyes lit up and he used his hands to emphasize his points. Upon seeing this she thought to herself, *God, even his hands are beautiful, long fingers with well-groomed fingernails.* Gabrielle felt little tingles and flutters in her stomach.

As she watched him, her mind evaluated him all the while: *this guy is one smooth talker. He is so charismatic, polished, plus he's so easy on the eyes. You had better watch your heart, Gabi girl, because this one could very well take it, and do whatever he wants with it.*

8
 Gabrielle and Nick

New York – Saturday evening - March 22nd 1969

"The combination of the bodybuilding and a health food store would just be so natural."

She listened intently to him.

"It's something I feel is very necessary for optimum health, and they naturally go hand in hand. You get a fit body on the outside with the weights and healthy on the inside with a proper diet, vitamins and nutritional supplements."

"Don't they offer that where you work now?" She pierced a cherry tomato in her salad with her fork.

Nick eyed her as he took a sip of his wine.

"No. They don't, not at present anyway. Because they are new to the bodybuilding thing, it would be a huge undertaking for them to expand any further right now."

"Have you approached them with your ideas? Maybe if you presented them with your concept and ideas, you could set up some sort of a limited partnership. In this one particular area wherein you'd still remain manager, but you would be entitled to a share of the profits of any new memberships that you and your business model generates. Maybe this combination is just what would set them apart from any would-be competitors."

Impressed, he raised an eyebrow toward her; *a beauty with an actual brain, quite a stimulating combination.*

"Would-be-competitors? Gabrielle, I'm afraid that would have to include me." He laughed as he continued. "The bottom line for them is revenue; my current employers would only be interested in this venture if it brought in dollars- immediately. And I know they're not looking for any more partners nor would they be willing to share any of the profits with me regardless of how much effort I put in." He cleared his throat. "That said, when I do open my gym, it will be unique and completely different from what is currently offered anywhere in the city." He took a quick sip of his wine.

Taking a forkful of salad, she observed his animated eyes.

"While I do want my gym to be profitable," he continued, "I'd be more focused on the services and knowledge we'll provide for our members. I want something for the masses, something your average Joe could afford. Health and well-being should not just be reserved for the affluent."

She saw the passion building up inside him as he leaned forward and began talking quickly while his eyes lit up as he poured more wine for them both.

"I think health and well-being should be for everyone too," Gabrielle said, "not just for men, but for women as well. Maybe, it could be your uniqueness, that you include females in your facility."

He looked considerately at his hand as he slid the stem of the glass between his forefinger and thumb. "To be blunt, it takes a lot of hard work and a certain amount of dedication to acquire a well-developed physique. I'm not sure women would be up for that."

"Women are full of surprises, Nick." She arched her brow.

"Maybe, but for now, I think I'll focus on the men. I'll have my work cut out for me because most guys today simply don't have the drive required, either," he paused. "You know, I really should apologize. I have monopolized our whole conversation and have just gone on and on about me and my own pursuits. That's something I don't normally do." He tore off a piece of bread and dipped it in olive oil as he continued. "I usually like to play it a little closer to the vest so to speak, to be a mystery and let a woman wonder about me for a little while before laying it all out there." Suggestively he bit into the bread and with hooded eyes and leaned back in his chair.

"So tell me, Nick," she lowered her gaze demurely as she circled the rim of her glass with her index finger, "have there been many women in your life? Women that you have, in your words, 'laid it all out there' too?"

He chewed the bread and took a slow lazy sip of his wine; at that very moment, the waiter brought their plates as Nick sat up straight with relief.

"I think you're going to love the lasagna here, Gabrielle, it's very good."

Once the waiter was out of earshot, she looked at him expectantly as she prompted him to answer. "Well, Nick?" She asked with a raised brow waiting for his response.

He straightened up in his chair, picked up his fork and knife, and cut into his food. His responded in a casual tone. "I feel as if I've done all the talking, so why don't you tell me a little bit more about you, Gabrielle. How long have you been in been in New York?"

She was aware that he opted not to answer her question; she pursed her lips together as she answered him nonchalantly and a bit succinctly. "I moved here at the end of January so, I've been here just about two months."

"How do you like our fair city?" He asked.

"I like it just fine." She turned away from him.

The silence between them widened as she silently looked in the direction of the accordion player making his way to their table. She smiled up at the gentle round face of the musician while he played a sweet song for them.

Nick reached inside his jacket pocket, pulled out his wallet, and slipped a bill into the accordion player's pocket as he thanked him for playing.

"Grazie." The performer said as he dipped his head in thanks and wandered away to the next table.

Nick had been unable to move his eyes away from her, although she was apparently avoiding looking at him. For fear of messing things up with her entirely, he spoke softly with downcast eyes.

"To answer your previous question," he proceeded thoughtfully and lifted his eyes to her turned away face. "No, I've only shared myself or 'laid it all out there' to a very select few. Really, only once."

She turned back to face him as he continued.

"And, then there is the yes," he looked into her eyes, contemplatively gauging her. "Yes, I have had quite a few women in my life." His eyes lowered as he continued to assess her. "I've known more than my share of lovely ladies," he lifted his brow. "In college 'free love' had been the in thing to do. Everyone did it, and I seem to have carried it over into my adult life; it's not something I'm proud to admit to you." Surprised by his own frankness, his moved eyes away from her as he went on. "You know, as I consider it, I think you would do well for yourself, Gabrielle Lawrence, if you left this table and a scoundrel like me this very instant. I'd hate it, but, I would not fault you in the least."

Her eyes scanned his face, she found his candor to be genuine and felt he looked honestly apologetic about his past dealings with women.

He somberly rested his elbow on the table to the left of his plate and placed his chin securely in the nook between his thumb and forefinger as he curled his long fingers under the side of his jawline.

"And just why is that, Nick?" She asked.

Nick exhaled audibly, as he once again looked into those striking green and amber eyes of hers.

"It's because, truthfully," he paused. "I recognize a rare, sweet innocence about you." He remarked.

"Well, you needn't look so troubled," her hand smoothed her hair back behind her ear, "because maybe I'm not as sweet or as innocent as I appear."

He gave a lopsided grin with a mischievous glint in the sea of blue of his eyes, as he felt hopeful. "Well, *sweet-not-so-innocent* Gabrielle, that's something I highly doubt. But, I do offer you a warning," his eyes meaningfully burned into hers, "if you continue to sit at this table and choose to dine with me knowing I'm a bit of a rogue, then my honesty is simply not enough to save you from the likes of me."

She scanned his face as she lifted her fork and knife, cut into the lasagna, and then locked eyes with him. "And just who says I'm the one in need of saving here, Mr. Caine?"

She moved the fork into her mouth, closed her lips around it and slowly pulled the now cleaned fork out of her mouth while never taking her provocative stare off him.

Nick's eyes were transfixed at her mouth as his breath held in his throat. His tongue darted quickly back and forth over his dry lips as his interest in her further piqued. He pulled his eyes deliberately away from her sensuous lips.

"I have a sinking feeling you may very well be right. Maybe I am the one in need of rescuing here. I'm starting to feel as if you've somehow compelled me to bare everything."

Nick then breathed in deeply, *I have shared with her just a snippet of my past with women and she is still sitting there in front of me.* Exhaling the air from his lungs, he took a momentary pause as an un-expectantly pleased smile came to his lips as he lifted his fork and dug into his dinner again.

"You've had a profound effect on me and in such a short time, and I don't mind telling you that, Gabrielle."

She stopped chewing and cautiously looked at him over her lasagna-loaded fork. "You know, Nick, when I hear you say something like that, I must confess that I'm not sure if you're truly being sincere with me or if you're just feeding me lines from the latest version of the Lothario's handbook."

She lifted the fork into her mouth and watched him as she guardedly chewed; he cocked his head to the side and swallowed before he spoke.

"Gabrielle, while admittedly I'm very experienced sexually, I'm no Lothario. You see, I don't use any so-called lines on women. Maybe I did when in my youth, I would say whatever I felt necessary to gain… access." He assessed her thoughtfully. "However, I have since discovered that women today know full well what they want and are not ashamed to hunt it down and go after it. I find most women are more than willing to initiate an encounter and openly reciprocate sexually."

Nick then looked uncomfortable as he stated plainly, "Gabrielle, I know this may sound arrogant to you, but, you see, women," he cleared his throat. "Well, basically women tend to approach me without much effort on my part." As he averted his gaze downward, ill at ease, he continued. "It's just the way it's always been for me."

She felt it to be a true assessment; there was no conceit attached to his statement, and just from looking around the dining room, some women ogled him despite her presence. Were she not there, many of them would be making their way over to him.

"You can rest assured, I'm not feeding you any lines. I can honestly tell you the truth because I want to start our relationship off right." He remarked.

She picked up her wine glass and swirled the wine inside it before she took a sip. "Relationship?" She questioned as she tried not to let her accelerated pulse rate give her away as she calmly observed him. "Is that what this is, Nick? The start of a relationship."

His look became serious. "That's what it feels like to me," he rested his chin on the knuckle of his raised hand. "So, yes Gabrielle. I believe it is."

She felt uneasy under his gaze and squirmed in her seat; because truth be told, she felt the same way. Telling herself, *this can't be real, it's too soon to feel this way about someone I've just met, isn't it?*

Feeling her senses must be way off, she soon felt the hairs at the nape of her neck rise and bristle uncomfortably. She had learned long ago to listen to her intuition. *Is there something in me setting off an alarm right now? As a warning to avoid this smooth talker, who is undoubtedly trying to disarm my defenses by saying what he thinks I want to hear.*

Then something clicked in her brain, and it irked her. *Whoa, I can't believe it, I almost fell for it hook, line and sinker. This kind of talk is probably the method he uses on women; it's most likely the fastest route to his well-used bed.*

She sat up straight, irritated with herself for the emotions that his words and his sheer presence in front of her had generated inside her, turning her innards into gelatin with his mushy 'relationship' talk.

"Wow! Not feeding me any lines, huh? You know, I think you're as smooth as fresh churned butter. Now will you tell me something, Nick? Is this how all your other interactions with women start out? You invite them to your favorite restaurant; throw in a little dinner and of course, wine. Then miraculously, your promise of" she paused as she made quotation marks in the air with her fingers "of a relationship with you, then you bed them, and when you're done with them, you unceremoniously dismiss them." Her eyes narrowed toward him as she paused. "But, to add insult to injury you've admitted that you don't have the common courtesy to even remember their names," she shook her head, "the poor sad little creatures."

His eyes expanded wide with surprise at her comments; he was offended by her skepticism. "Wow? Wow is right, Gabrielle. I'm going to be brutally honest here, because you have a misconception. One that must be cleared up. I will tell you there is nothing poor or sad about any of the women I've slept with. They have all been women who knew exactly what they wanted and weren't afraid to go after it." He said matter-of-factly.

"If that's the case, then I suppose it proved to be very fortuitous for you, don't you agree?" She pursed her lips.

"Humph," he lifted an eyebrow. "I suppose I did reap the benefits of their forwardness. Nonetheless, as to your other statement, you couldn't be more wrong, I have never brought any other woman-- you are the fir-- you know what? Just forget it, because I don't think you'd believe it anyway."

"Now I suppose you're trying to tell me what?" She scoffed at his statement as she continued, "that I'm the first woman you've brought here to start a *'relationship'* with."

He put his fork down on the side of his plate and looked at her with displeasure; his mouth set austerely as he addressed her. "I wouldn't call what I had with any of the women from my past a 'quote, unquote' *relationship*. As I've said, it was just sex, without the promise of anything more."

He placed his hands on his thighs and braced himself; his jaw tightened. "I am, however, disappointed to hear that you don't believe me when I say that those encounters were of a mutual benefit and no one was hurt by them in any way, because neither feelings nor emotional ties ever entered into the picture, on either side." He lifted his cooled eyes and looked pointedly at her.

"It was almost primal and clearly was about one thing, and that was fucking." He wanted to shock her, and was satisfied when her eyes expanded wide at his choice of words. "Those women weren't shy in that regard, they wanted it, and I gave it to them, but good." He paused to let his words sink in. "And, whether you believe it or not," he continued, "as a matter of fact, you are the first woman I've brought here."

She half rolled her eyes. "This is one of your favorite restaurants and you seem to know all the ins and outs of this place, right down to the little anecdotal stories, yet you tell me you've never brought a date here? You can't really expect me to believe that, now can you?" Not one to be made the fool, she paused with a slant of her head. "Look, I may be new to this city but I can promise you that I didn't just fall off the back of some turnip truck. So, let's just cut the bullshit, okay?"

She saw the insulted expression in his eyes as he answered her tersely. "Cut the bullshit? Yeah, let's do that, shall we? Because you don't know me well enough yet," he tilted his head while he pursed his lips and continued. "But, you will learn pretty quick that I don't appreciate being called a liar."

He scanned the room. "The reason I know the 'ins and outs' of this place is because I worked here for several years while earning my degree." He looked around the room again. "Maybe, it was a mistake meeting you here tonight. Because, clearly, you don't believe anything I've said."

She lifted her eyes heavenward briefly, sighed and then slid her eyes to his unsmiling face. His eyes were upon her as Gabrielle looked questioningly at him. She'd been searching for answers of her own. She just could not wrap her mind around the myriad of emotions enveloping her, with his man across from her.

"If what you've said is true, then tell me, what makes me so different from the rest? What makes me *so* special? You'd ask me here and tell me you want to start a 'relationship'? You only just met me today, for goodness sakes. Tell me honestly that your words are not a ploy just to get into my pants and screw me like you've done the rest." She jutted out her chin defiantly toward him. "Since by your own admission, you are quite the womanizer."

"Gabrielle, I may have used my words to gain my way with some women, but I have not done that tonight. Not with you, I'm not going to apologize or sugar coat the fact that I would like nothing more than to have you naked and in my bed while I have my way with you." His eyes then veered sideways as he found himself preoccupied for a moment with the image of that thought. Then looking a little confounded for a minute, he responded.

"Truthfully, I don't know how to answer your questions. Maybe, it was how we met or maybe the way you looked at that damned park today or the way you look right now. Honestly, I just don't know. But I feel like there is something very real between us. We have a connection; one that I just can't seem to explain to you or to myself for that matter."

Gabrielle looked away from him as she immediately felt contrite for her previous comments, but she had to admit that it did and somewhat still does sound like a few lines of well-honed bullshit to her.

I shouldn't insult him, just because he's getting to me in more ways than one, and in ways I don't fully understand myself either, she faced him again her expression softened.

"Nick, I have to apologize for what I said. In truth, I don't know you well enough to make those kinds of a blanketed assertions about your character or your relations with the women from your past. It was unfair of me to bring it into question, especially after you trusted me enough to tell me about them."

He abruptly looked up at her with sincerity in his eyes while he reached over and took her hand into his. The current shot straight from his hand through her fingers and into the pit of her stomach.

The electrified flutters recommenced, and she unexpectedly gasped. He pressed on with pure resolve in his eyes and voice as he held her hand inside his own.

"Gabrielle, I know what makes you different. Something happened inside me— the moment I laid eyes on you. It happens every time we touch. I feel very literally, drawn to you. You draw me to you like some goddamned magnet."

He looked at her delicate hand inside his masculine palm as his long fingers held her hand in place. He looked up, back into her eyes as he continued earnestly, "This is so irrational and it's coming from out of nowhere, because I've never had these kinds of feelings before. Look, I understand we have just met, but I also sense you are feeling the same pull to me as I am to you. I don't know all that much about how a *real* relationship works, I haven't had any traditional relationships in my adult life."

Gabrielle felt her heart soften almost to the point where it seemed to be melting inside the walls of her chest as she listened to his plea.

"But," he continued, "I need you to know and believe that this *is* the start of something very real for me and I can only hope it is for you too. Because I know from somewhere deep down inside me that we're going to mean a great deal to each other." His eyes bore into hers like penetrating beams of light as he spoke. "I know we were destined to meet at the park today and to be together here in this very place, tonight."

Her cheeks flooded with color as the blood rushed clear through to her ears. Her heart pounded hard in her chest, and she almost felt as if it would burst. She pulled her hand back to break the flow of current between them. His words had indeed struck a familiar chord with her because she was having the same kinds of feelings that he so fervently described. It was all so overwhelming for her.

Attempting to find some composure, she thought to herself, *when all else fails, be the southern belle.* Gabrielle playfully, batted her eyes at him with a broad smile; she dramatically fanned her hand in front of her face and proclaimed in a perfect southern drawl, "Why, Mr. Caine, Sir, I do believe you're making me blush."

Not realizing that he'd been holding his breath so tight in his lungs, Nick exhaled and the relief flooded his face as he relaxed. He was visibly relieved that she had lightened the serious nature of his declarations to her.

9

🙶 Gabrielle and Nick 🙷

Saturday evening - March 22nd 1969

As the night progressed they continued to talk about their likes and dislikes; she found it humorous as he valiantly defended his beloved New York Mets, convinced they were going to turn it around.

She told him about her job and how much she loved it at VonShelles.

"I'm really focused on fashion; I enjoy all of the creative elements involved. From an idea, a conceptual drawing, to picking out fabrics for the final product. The textures, the cut and the styles. I love it."

"As a man, I guess I never thought about fashion beyond going to the store and picking out what I like and what fits."

"Well, we designers make it a little easy for you, by giving you choices."

Nick finished his wine and was about to order more for them until he looked around the quiet dining room. He could see they were the only two people left in the room. "I think they are waiting for us to leave. They have to close this room down and focus on the other dining rooms."

She looked around, surprised by the empty room and the patient face of the wait staff; she swiftly gulped down the remainder of the wine in her glass.

Nick waved the waiter over for the check, and he placed some bills inside, closed it, and gave it to the waiter saying, "Ringraziamenti per tutto. Mantenga prego il cambiamento."

"Grazie, grazie," the waiter nodded with appreciation as he smiled at Nick, and shifted his eyes toward Gabrielle, leaning his head close to Nick's ear, he said, "Si farà dei bei bambini insieme."

Nick gave a light laugh, and patted the waiter on his back as his smiling eyes looked towards Gabrielle.

"È la nostra prima data. Noi non abbiamo nemmeno baciato ancora." Nick remarked to the waiter.

The waiter smiled and nodded in Gabrielle's direction, and she gave him a polite smile in return.

As they left the dining area and approached the foyer and of the restaurant, she looked to him. "May I ask? What did the waiter say to you?"

"You really want to know?" Nick laughed with a grin.

"Yeah, I really want to know." She said with a hint of playfulness in her voice.

Nick's grin still in place. "He told me that we are going to make 'beautiful babies,' but I informed him it's only our first date and I hadn't even kissed you yet."

"Yet?" She folded her arms in front of herself. "What makes

you think I will allow you to kiss me at all?" She smirked.

He pushed the door open and held it open for her.

"I know you will," He winked playfully. "It's inevitable and we both know it. When we do kiss, it will be extraordinary. But I make you this one promise, Gabrielle. I won't kiss you or lay a hand on you in any way, until *you* ask *me* to."

"Well, if you are leaving it up to me," the corners of her mouth rose in a playful smile, "it may take a while."

"Then I guess I'll have to wait, won't I? You will find me to be a very patient man." *A challenge? I'm up for it. We'll see who wears down first.*

Once they were outside of the restaurant and into the chilly night air, she closed her lightweight jacket tightly and held it in place with her fingers. As the cold air overcame her, she absolutely regretted not picking a warmer jacket.

"Thank you for tonight, Nick. I really had a great time, would you mind hailing me a cab, please?"

He looked wounded and frustrated as his brow furrowed.

"Hail you a cab? You don't need a cab, Gabrielle; I can drive you home." He shook his head. "We've spent the better part of the evening getting to know each other. Don't tell me you still don't trust me?"

"No, it's not that I don't trust you. After tonight, I do feel like I can. I just don't want to put you out. I know you live very close by, and to take me home would take you way out of your way." She shivered in her thin jacket.

He ran a frustrated hand through his dark hair.

"Gabrielle, you're not putting me out. I don't mind driving you home. You can trust that I've never taken advantage of a woman before and I have no intentions of starting tonight."

The cold night air made relenting her only real option and she chose not to debate the issue any longer.

"Okay, where is your car?" She asked through chattering teeth.

"You're freezing." He took off his suede jacket. "Here, take my jacket." He covered her shivering shoulders with his jacket. "My car is just up the street."

He held her close under his protective arm while they walked; she was acutely aware of his proximity as she took in the delectable scent of him, mingled with the warmth of his body's heat enveloping her as one arm held her close to him.

As they walked along the sidewalk, the pavement uneven with cracks and exposed holes, she had trouble balancing in her heels and she felt herself about to fall. In order to catch herself, inadvertently she placed her hand on his abdomen to recover her balance. With her hand on his body, her fingers lingered a tad longer than they should have. She could feel his abdominal muscles flex under her fingertips, but something in her made her afraid to look up at his face.

She was grateful when they reached his car; he unlocked the door and opened it for her, she slid inside and pulled his jacket even tighter around her.

Nick walked around to the driver's side, got in, and put the key in the ignition. The engine turned over and purred quietly. As he pulled the car out of its spot, he turned to her. "I have a question, with us being so close to my place. Would you mind if we stop there? I really need to let Lobo out."

"No, I don't mind at all. Poor boy must surely have to go by now."

They soon pulled in front of his apartment building, a gray brick building with a gated side courtyard.

"Would you like to come in? Or wait here in the car."

"I'll wait here, if it's okay," she said.

He was out of the car in an instant and took long strides as he walked toward the building; Nick greeted the doorman who sat behind a desk and soon was out of her sight.

As she waited in the car, she turned on the radio. It was set to a classical station. *Funny,* she thought to herself, *he just doesn't seem like a classical music kind of guy.* After listening to the soothing sounds for a few minutes, she looked toward the building and saw him come through the doors with Lobo on his leash. She watched for a few minutes as Lobo raced around the courtyard. Nick then secured Lobo's leash and he once again disappeared inside the building.

He soon reappeared in the doorway and made his way toward the car. Nick slid into his seat with a smile that soon faded as he looked toward the radio; he tensely half-smiled in her direction and reached over to turn the radio off.

"He's all set and tucked in." He informed her.

Her brow creased with concern. "I felt bad, it's so cold out and I still had your jacket wrapped around me."

His face relaxed as he looked mischievously at her. "Don't worry about it, Gabrielle, I generally run pretty hot."

"Yes, you do." She stammered. "What I mean is…I mean, you…Your hands always, um, seem to always be hot, er… warm." Looking away from him; *what the hell was all of that? Just be quiet, you're making a complete idiot out of yourself.* She felt sure he could see the color spate her cheeks, even in the street lamp lit boundaries of his car.

Amused, he lightly laughed as he pulled the car out of its parked position. "Which way are we going, Gabrielle?"

She gave him her address; they headed to Greenwich Village as Nick expertly navigated his smooth fastback coupe through New York's heavy Saturday nighttime traffic. She observed him out of the corner of her eye while he intently watched the road.

They soon arrived in front of her building, and she began fumbling in her purse for her keys.

"Goodnight, Nick. Thanks for…"

He was already out of the car and opening the door for her. He stood there, offering his hand to assist her.

"Never let it be said that I'm not a gentleman, let me see you safely inside."

Keys in hand she looked up at him as she got out of his car without the aid of his hand. She knew she could not bear to feel his electric touch; her insides were already mush just being this close to him.

"It's okay, I'm home now. I'll be fine." She protested.

He ignored her comment, placed his hand at the small of her back over his jacket, and guided her up the stone steps of the Brownstone. At the building's front door, she handed him her keys not trusting her shaking hands to open the door.

After he opened the door, he gave the keys back to her as she handed him his jacket. Her were eyes downcast, unable to look into his eyes for fear that she would most certainly drown in them.

"Gabrielle, I really enjoyed your company tonight. I would love to see you again."

Slowly she lifted her face to his as she found herself drawn to him, just as he had predicted at the restaurant. She felt a magnetic pull to him. Suddenly, she didn't want this night to end and she heard herself say in a husky voice so unlike her normal voice.

"Would you like to come up for a nightcap?" *Ugh, did I really just say nightcap? I cannot believe how uninspired and clichéd that sounded. It's almost as bad as, come up and let me show you my etchings.* "But," she quickly added, "if you have to go I perfectly understand. It is getting late."

The corner of his mouth raised into a crooked grin as he gazed into her eyes, his voice deep. "No, I don't have to go." With a definite twinkle in his sapphire eyes. "I would love to come up for a *nightcap*."

10
Gabrielle and Nick
Saturday evening - March 22nd 1969

Once inside Nick was impressed, it almost looked like the foyer of a grand home. Complete with Persian rugs and two upholstered side chairs set beneath an open staircase, her building had an air of elegance. He was almost sure the giltwood mirror and side table were authentic.

They climbed the solid walnut staircase with its intricate newel posts and walnut handrails. The steps were adorned with a Persian runner that ran down the center of the whole length of the stairs with golden rods at the crease of each step.

At the front door to her apartment, she looked back at him as she unlocked and opened the door. Reaching her hand inside she turned on the wall switch, flooding the room with soft light.

"I should tell you, I don't have a sofa yet." She said as they entered. "But I'm working on it. I've looked but I just haven't found the right one for the space."

She dropped her keys into her purse, zipped it shut and hung it on one of the hooks of the brass coat tree near the front door. She removed her jacket and placed it on the hook covering her purse. He hung his jacket on the coat tree hook adjacent to hers.

They walked past the small sitting room, where she showed him into the living room. She excused herself and went into the bathroom. She checked her make-up and reapplied her lip-gloss.

When she rejoined him, he was building a fire in the massive fireplace.

"I hope you don't mind, it seemed a little chilly in here, and I know you were cold earlier."

"No, I don't mind at all. I love a good fire."

The living room had two side tables, a coffee table and lamps in place; all that was missing was a couch just as she had said.

"I like your place, Gabrielle. It has so much charm about it." He knelt on one knee in front of the hearth.

"Thank you, I think it's really coming along." Her eyes scanned the room and then settled on him. "So, what do you want, Nick?"

"That's a loaded question, now isn't it?" A smile played on his lips.

"What I meant was, what do you want to drink? I could make coffee or I have red wine, brandy or even some beer, I think."

"I'll have the red wine, but only if it's no trouble."

He moved from the kneeling position and sat on the floor

on top of the large white shag rug with his leg curved under his raised bent knee.

"It's no trouble at all." She walked to the corner of the room and picked up two large zabuton-style pillows and handed them to him.

"You might find these to be a bit more comfortable to sit on. I'm going to change into something a little more suitable for sitting on the floor."

He took the pillows and positioned them on the rug.

In her bedroom, she quickly took off her shoes and stripped down to her underwear and threw her blouse and skirt into a large nearby wicker basket. She stood in front of the antique armoire and pulled out a pair of oversized Le Coq Sportif gray sweat pants from the shelf.

She stepped into the sweat pants and pulled them on up over her hips tying the drawstring tightly around her narrow waist. Then she slipped an oversized sweatshirt over her head, deciding to appear as sexless as possible.

She rolled up the long sleeves and pulled on some thick warm socks and gathered her hair into a ponytail as she soundlessly walked into the kitchen.

What have I gotten myself into here? I hope he doesn't expect anything more than talking.

After opening the bottle of wine, she took down two wine glasses from one of the kitchen cabinet and crossed them at the stems in one hand as she lifted the opened bottle in the other hand.

She returned to the living room, she stopped and stood at the entryway. She saw he'd removed his shoes and was lying on his side atop one of the large pillows. His elbow bent, as his head rested comfortably on the palm of his hand. He stared intently into the fire, the room was dimly lit and the warm glow of the fire illuminated his handsome face.

Watching him, she felt another series of flutters in the pit of her stomach, and they seemed to be triggered by the image he presented before her. Sensing her presence, he looked up at her and their eyes met in the golden luminescence of the room. A crooked smile formed on his lips as she came fully into the warmth of the room; he lifted up to a seated position and reached for the bottle she carried as she sat Indian style on the pillow opposite his.

She placed the empty glasses on the shag rug on the floor in front of her and held them in place as he began to pour the wine into the glasses.

"That's some fire." She commented to him.

"Something I learned from my days as a scout." He replied with a smirk.

"A lesson well learned, as it's quite remarkable."

"Being here with you like this is incredibly nice and much unexpected," Nick's voice, deep yet sensual, felt like a warm embrace and she loved the very sound of it. "I'm glad you asked me up, Gabrielle."

She lifted both glasses up and held one in each hand. "So am I, Nick, I don't know a lot of people here yet, but I'm enjoying getting to know you."

"Same here." He said.

He placed the wine bottle on the table behind him, and when he turned back to face her, she handed him his glass. Their fingers brushed together, and she felt the same electric charge she had felt earlier. She nervously looked away from him and safely into the fire.

Nick, taken by surprise once more, for this was very new territory for him, had never had these kinds of feelings, physically or emotionally, for any woman. He felt this *'relationship'* would need to be cultivated and he had to tread lightly and go at a much slower pace. He most definitely needed to fight the urge within him: *to pull her into my arms and kiss those luscious lips of hers before getting her underneath me and utterly fuck her brains out, but good.* A smile came to his lips at the mere thought of it.

He shook those thoughts out of his head as he heard himself saying, "I like what you're wearing. A bit large for you though, it seems."

She smiled triumphantly as she brought her glass to her lips and sipped her wine. "Well, truthfully they belong to my kid brother and I somewhat appropriated them from him the last time we were both home. He's away at college and I'm here, but I miss him terribly. Wearing these keeps him close somehow."

He took a swallow from his glass as he lifted a bent knee and rested his arm on it as he spoke. "He must be a very large 'kid' brother."

"Oh, he is," she answered him robustly. "He's six two and at nineteen, I believe he's still growing too."

"Hmm, and just where is home Gabrielle?" He leaned back down on his elbow.

"Home is kind of all over. I was actually born in Louisiana when my mother was visiting her family." Her eyes were mirthful. "My early years were spent in Paris, France, up until our mother decided she wanted us to be educated in America, and then we lived by the ocean in California, but we'd spend our summers in Paris. Now, home is here, in New York."

"Paris?" He raised an eyebrow. "I thought I detected an accent of some sort, but I couldn't quite place it."

"You really think I have an accent?" She grimaced. "It must be the result of my varied upbringing."

"It's very slight, but it's really nice, I like it. You know, I've heard a great deal of Paris, but I've never been there. What's it like to actually live there?"

When she spoke, her voice took on an almost ethereal sound. "It's lovely there, and, it's easy to feel as if you've been transported back to an era long gone because Paris is a timeless city. It's very beautiful, the lush countryside, and the city itself." She smiled dreamily. "France's rich history can be seen everywhere with wonderful sights, sounds and smells. And there's La Gallerie LaFayette to appease any shopping need; the space itself is spectacular and a sight to see. For food, Les Deux Magots Saint-Germain des Prés is a favorite of mine. But there many good outdoor cafés, and afterwards a stroll along the Champs-Élysées is so nice as you take it all in."

He smiled as his eyes skimmed the soft angles of her face while her voice became nostalgically reflective with a smile.

"Most importantly, though, are the people themselves; Parisians are wonderful people despite what's been said of them. They're not rude unless provoked to be so," her smile then widened. "The outdoor marketplaces have fresh meats and fruits; And the fashions are so innovative and are bar none, simply the best."

Her eyes brightened even more as she spoke, and he adored the infectious twinkle in them.

"It's actually similar to the Village. And part of the reason I like it here so much."

He watched her keenly, "How did you come to live in France? Were you a student there?"

"Well, yes and no," she paused. "You see, my father is a citizen, he's Parisian and my mother is American. So we lived in France, as well as the States, because each of them held allegiance their own birth country."

"I take it that your parents are divorced."

"Divorced?" Gabrielle's eyes expanded wide at his statement. "Heavens, no. Whatever gave you that idea? My parents are very much married. They both travel to each other's respective countries throughout the year. Unfortunately, my father's work keeps him in France most of the time, but we spend our birthdays and all holidays together and have always spent our summers in Paris as a family."

Thoughtfully, she watched his face as she continued.

"Nick, there's something more I think you should know about my family—and myself for that matter. I am of a mixed background. My mother is Negro, black creole to be exact and my father is a full-blooded Frenchman. So," she paused, "if any part of my heritage bothers you in anyway…"

"Why would you think it would bother me, Gabrielle? It is 1969 after all and while I am aware race relations aren't perfect, I think it's getting better all the time." Nick's expression softened and relaxed as he answered her perceptively. "And to be honest, your racial makeup is, in a word: beautiful. It's given you an exotic flavor that I find alluring."

His smile deepened with unmasked sincerity. "You're a beautiful, intriguing woman, and I want nothing more than to spend more time getting to know you."

"I just felt it important to inform you. In light of the whole 'relationship' thing we were talking about earlier." She lifted her wine glass to her lips and took another sip. "I'm sure it would bother some people, especially here in America, but the French don't give it much thought."

He looked up at her with a playful glint in his eyes. "I suppose I should ask you if it would bother you to learn that my mother is Italian and my father is Irish."

She smiled at his attempt to lighten things up by adding a bit of humor.

"No, it wouldn't bother me in the least." She laughed softly. "You know; I can really see the Italian in you with your dark hair. I suppose I should tell you I like the cultural blend in you too." She looked at him and then her eyes darted away from him. "Now tell me, Italian and Irish- does that mean you were raised Catholic?"

"Yes, I was raised to be a good Catholic boy." Taking a small swallow of his wine, he licked his lips. "I don't know where you stand on religion, so I hope that bit of knowledge doesn't bother you."

"No Nick, quite the contrary." She shook her head, "my father comes from a family of practicing Catholics. While we weren't really raised in any one particular faith, my grand-mère practically lives in the church, and she insists we attend whenever we're there."

"Well, I was raised Catholic, but I'm not really a practicing one, not anymore anyway." He raised an eyebrow. "I went through the motions and took communion, got confirmed, and was even an altar boy; all to appease my devout mother who thought I was destined for purgatory and the final damnation of hell if I didn't. I believe she had hopes it would turn me away from my wild ways."

She smiled as her eyes lifted heavenward and then settled on his face. "A Boy Scout and an altar boy? No wonder I trusted you to invite you into my apartment?"

"Well now, I'm relieved to learn that I was able to quell your feelings of mistrust in me, somehow." He laughed.

"So tell me, did it work? Did you manage to turn away from your *wild ways*' and placate your mother in the process?"

The laughter promptly fled from his lips as he moved his eyes away from hers and thoughtfully gazed into the fire's flickering flames. "Hmm... I sure hope so Gabrielle, not just for my mother's sake but for my own as well. Because truthfully, the life I led in those days, let's just say I'm glad to have left it in the past."

Soberly he went on. "That time of my life...I had to make some tough choices." He took another drink from his glass. "It was hard leaving home and all that I had grown to know. I had to break all contact with my family and the people I cared deeply about, my mother included." His eyes stared unblinkingly into the fire. "You know, I've learned a very hard lesson and it's that you just can't live your life for other people no matter who or what they are to you."

He quickly glanced at her and then focused his eyes on the contents of his glass before he drank down the remainder of the wine in his glass and looked at her a little unsettled.

"Are you telling me you don't have a relationship with your mother?" She queried.

"Let's just say my mother and I live in two vastly separate worlds, and never the twain shall meet. End of story." He ran his hand through his dark hair. "Wow, now that's a pretty heavy subject for a first date, don't you think?" He looked away from her. "Maybe I've had too much wine tonight for my own good, or is it some sort of spell you've placed on me, Gabrielle?"

I just seem to want to share everything with her in any way that

92

I can. If not sexually.

She looked at him and slightly frowned.

"Spell?" She questioned with a tilt of her head. "I can assure you I'm no enchantress, Nick. I'm just a very good listener; however, please forgive me for delving too deeply into an area of your life in which you plainly feel uncomfortable." She paused. "It's all right and most certainly your prerogative, but," she paused. "I think our relationships with our parents can be all telling." She regarded him intently. "It's the primary interaction that molds us into who we are and how we deal with others in the world."

He sat up again and placed his empty glass on the table behind him. "That molding thing may be true for some, but not in my case." His face became somber. "Gabrielle, I'd prefer not to talk about my family, it's a very sensitive subject for me, and I have spent a lot of time refocusing myself and my life. They are not a part of my life, because I'm a self-made man," he said and then added a slanted grin. "What you see, is what you get." He cleared his throat and stood. "May I use your bathroom?"

"Yes, of course," she got up as well. "It's down the hall, the second door on the left."

She went into the kitchen and took out a porcelain platter. She expertly sliced an apple in several thin wedges and placed them on the platter along with one half of boule bread. Taking some cheese from the fridge, she cut several slices off the block and added them to the platter. She also grabbed a cluster of washed grapes and arranged them at the center of the platter.

Nick stood soberly at the bathroom sink and splashed cold water on his face and stared at his reflection in the mirror. *What is wrong with you, man, you nearly told her your whole life story, dredging up the past like that. What are you? Fucking nuts! What is it about her? How does she do it? How does she make you feel like you should tell her everything about yourself? Good grief! If only we could stop all of this talking and get down to fucking. That would put an end to all of this goddamned sharing, but until then, stop it man, get a hold of yourself.* He reached for a towel and dabbed his wet face.

She was placing the platter and a fresh bottle of wine on the shag rug in front of herself when he returned. Taking his place on his pillow, he smiled as he poured more wine into their glasses.

"You must have read my mind," he said as he settled back on his pillow.

She pushed the platter to him.

"Please, help yourself."

He picked up an apple slice and bit into it.

Gabrielle took delight by the manner in which his mouth moved as she blindly picked off some grapes.

She held the grape to her mouth and deliberately bit into it and chewed before she guardedly asked, "Nick, I'm curious about something you said before. About your mother,"

"Gabrielle," he cut her off, "I have an odd question for *you*," he tore off a piece of bread and topped it with a slice of cheese. "Now you can tell me to *mind my own business* if you want to." He pointedly looked up at her as he spoke; his statement was not lost on her.

"You're new to the city and have been only working at your job for a short time," he lifted an eyebrow curiously. "How is it that you're able to afford a large two-bedroom apartment like this in New York City, as well as have it practically furnished already?"

She picked up her glass and nervously took a sip of wine before answering. "Well, Nick, I don't mind the question at all because the answer is simple." She took a breath. "I've found rents to be more reasonable here in the Village. But the big plus is, I personally know the owner of this building," *which is true,* she thought as she continued, "I'm getting a deal on the rent, and the furnishings belong to the building's owner."

"It really is a nice space," his eyes scanned the room, "and you're darn lucky to have a friend who is willing to give you a cut rate on a place like this."

He lifted his wine glass and took deep swallows as he drained it; she took a piece of cheese and nibbled on it.

"How do you like where you live, Nick?"

"My place is nothing special; it's an average small New York apartment." He picked up another apple slice, "I'm actually kind of glad you opted out of coming up to see it. Because it's nothing like what you have here." He waved his hand around the room with a smile.

Sitting so close to the fire, she began to feel the heat, and the only thing she could think to take off were her thick socks, exposing her bare feet with her coral painted toenails.

His eyes fell to her toes like a beam, since it was the only bit of uncovered skin. "It more than serves its purpose though, and like you, I also like my neighborhood." His eyes lingered at her feet as he continued. "It's very close to everything, so close I can usually walk or use my bike to get from my place to where I want to be such as restaurants, stores, and Central Park." His eyes lifted to her face. "Particularly when the weather is good, like today of course. Which leads me to another question that I've got to ask you, do you typically travel by subway?"

"Yes, I do, why is everyone so freaked out by that?" She laughed at the question. "I really like using the subway, it's convenient. Now mind you, I don't use it after dark because I made the mistake once." She slid her eyes away from him as if recalling a particular incident. "Let me tell you, not a very wise thing to do because there can be some questionable looking people approach you while you are waiting for the trains and actually on the trains themselves. So, after dark, I will hail a cab."

"That's good to know," he said as he picked a grape from the bunch and tossed it into his mouth. "As someone just recently informed me, *'a girl can't be too careful.'*" He looked meaningfully at her as he added, "But, in all seriousness, as a native New Yorker I know how true that statement can be. We get some pretty unsavory characters on the trains. Just be cautious, okay?"

"Duly noted, Sir," she brought her hand up in a mock salute as she lightly laughed. "But believe me Nick; I *can* take care of myself." She crossed her arms defiantly at her chest.

"Spoken like a typical woman." His crooked smile appeared unconvinced.

She unfolded her arms and slanted her head toward him. "Spoken like a typical male chauvinist." She pursed her lips.

"Okay sorry, I guess I deserved that." He laughed as he continued. "I suppose that did sound a bit chauvinistic, but I'm not one really. Not in the way that you think."

"I suppose that's your idea of some sort of a breadcrumb, but at least you somewhat admit it," her eyes narrowed a bit.

"Hey, I admit nothing, but tell me why is it if man questions a woman's physical abilities in any way, he gets labeled a chauvinist?"

She raised an irritated brow. "Maybe it's because women are fully capable of doing anything that a man can do and it's simply asinine to think otherwise."

"Whoa there, Nellie, don't get all bent out of shape. I just think there are certain things that men can do and women can't, or at least shouldn't even try to do." He laughed as he picked up another apple slice. He bit into the thin slice giving her a glimpse of his gleaming white teeth along with a jovial grin.

"You know, Nick, it's that kind of Neanderthal thinking that keeps women and men on such an unequal playing field.

Don't tell me you agree with the outdated stances such as '*a woman's place is in the home*' or '*women should be seen and not heard*' or even that '*women should remain barefoot and pregnant*'?"

He gave her a sleepy-eyed lustful grin from his hooded sea blue eyes as they went from her face to her bare toes. "I like the idea of the barefoot part," he looked up to her face, "especially if the feet are as enticing as yours are." His eyes came back up to her face and found she was not amused by his half-hearted attempt to veer off topic, he cleared his throat. "In all seriousness, I feel women are intentionally softer. God made you the weaker sex for a reason, you know."

Gabrielle crossed her legs Indian style and took her feet out of view as she re-crossed her arms at her chest. "Oh really? Now this, I have got to hear. Please tell me, what might *that* reason be, Nick."

The wine had relaxed him, and his eyes dreamily beheld her. "Man, by all intents and purposes, is the hunter, the protector, and the one who does the heavy lifting in the relationship by being the provider, and woman by nature is the nurturer. She balances man by submitting to his authority and tending to his needs- emotionally as well as physically. When he comes home from a hard day of work—of providing—he has desires that need to be taken care of." He lazily smiled with a glint in his eye. "By her being the keeper of the home, she eases his day-to-day burdens. She takes care of him and his needs without question, *whatever* those needs may be." His eyebrow lifted cheekily. "You know it's been said '*behind every great man, is a woman.'"*

"That's an archaic saying in need of some updating; it should be *'beside every great man is a patient woman,'* because she would definitely have to have the patience of a saint to put up with that malarkey." She tightly pressed her lips together.

"Gabrielle, I'm not opposed to allowing a woman to take the lead. I like to see a woman take charge at times."

"Allow? That's what I am talking about Nick, a man should not have the power over a woman and *allow* her to do anything. Women should have the power within themselves to make our own decisions."

He swallowed more wine then slowly licked his lips where a smile formed; he angled his head downward as his eyes glided up at her with a suggestive stare. "You know something, Gabrielle? I like it when you get a little annoyed, your nostrils flair out just a little in such an appealing way." He gave her a wink.

With the downright sexy looks he was giving her, she found it hard to remain angry with him as she tried to stay focused on the point she was trying to make. *He just looks so frigging irresistible, those eyes and those lips are so damned enticing.*

"Don't try to change the subject." She said with a slight smirk; he continued to look up at her lovely face, he could see she was softening.

"Oh, but Gabrielle, I want to change the subject. I don't want you to be cross with me. I think we should agree to shelve the conversation about the differences between the sexes for another time. For when we've both haven't had so much to drink. Agreed?"

Her nose crinkled, as she gladly yielded; she wasn't in the mood to debate anyway. She really just wanted to gaze upon him as she held out her empty glass to him she spoke.

"Alright, Nick Caine, agreed. We will shelve this topic for another time. Because, I can see you are impaired due to drink." She smirked again. "Which leads me to think that I'm able to drink you under the table anyway."

"Is that so, Gabrielle Lawrence?" His lip curled at the corner of his mouth as he gave a crooked smile. "You really think you can out drink me, do you?" His laugh was deep, sensually virile, and filled her warmly.

She beamed at him, leaned forward and clinked her glass to his. "You bet I can," she purred, "because right now, this independent and fully capable woman is quite ready for more and she would like you to pour her more wine, s'il vous plaît."

They finished off both bottles of wine and the platter between them; the fire crackled and gave off a warm soft golden glow as it slowly perished in the dimly lit room. His head rested on his sitting pillow as his quiet breathing became deeper and slower as in slumber.

"Nick?" She said softly with no response. "Nick?"

She let out a soft sigh, *not the traditional first date protocol, but I just don't have the heart to wake him and send him out into the cold of night.*

His face became slack and his body relaxed, so she could get an unsupervised look at him, finding her previous assessment of him still held true. He was unbelievably gorgeous, the crescent scar on his right cheek below his eye seemed to add character to his face. He had thick dark brows with slight arches to them, and long lashes that fanned out at the base of his closed lids.

His Romanesque nose had flawlessly shaped nostrils. In fact, as she gazed upon him she found his entire face appeared to be in absolute symmetry.

Her eyes glided down to his slightly opened lips. She found his mouth faultless and she resisted the temptation to touch his lips or chastely kiss them.

The philtrum above his upper lip had a deep sensual groove, and it made his cupids bow appear to have a perpetual little sexy pucker to them even as he slept. *Those lips look as if they've been designed expressly for the art of kissing* and it made her wonder. *How long can I hold out on kissing them?*

A reasonable amount of a five o'clock shadow also appeared on his face. While customarily considered unsightly, on him, it was positively downright *sexy*. The ideal frame for his face.

He had a few rebellious locks of hair on his forehead, she used a finger to move them back and he stirred a bit. She quickly pulled her hand back away from his face so as not to wake him, and a smile came to her lips.

Aside from his seedy past with women, he seemed to be a decent guy and true to his word- he did keep his hands and *dammit, those lips* to himself. Listening to him talk about his hopes, dreams, and plans for his future, she could not help herself from wanting to be a part of a future that included him.

She smiled as she pulled on her socks, *besides, I do need to educate him concerning some of his antiquated ways of thinking.* Her brow creased and she thought seriously, *I will most definitely have to find out what happened between him and his mother to cause such a rift between them. What was it that he said? 'Two different worlds,' I cannot imagine what could create such a fissure that he no longer even speaks with his own mother.*

A deeper frown formed at her brow, *if he could remove his own mother out of his life for whatever reason, how does that bode for anyone else in his life? Could it be the reason he uses and discards women so easily?*

Only a few glowing embers remained from the fire. She pulled a blanket from the linen closet and placed it on him as he slept on the floor. Picking up the empty wine bottles, she carried them into the kitchen.

Returning to the room she got one last final look at the sleeping Adonis on her living room floor. She smiled and picked up the empty glasses and the platter, then placed it all on the kitchen counter. She made her way down the narrow hallway to the bathroom where she brushed her teeth with weighted lids.

Crossing the hall to her bedroom she closed the heavy door behind her and locked it, just in case she had a sleepwalker on her hands, because a girl can't be too careful. She pushed the pile of clothes from her bed to the floor and slid between the blanket covered sheets. Still wearing her warm socks and oversized sweats, she was sound asleep before long.

11
❧ Elliott and John ❧
New York – Thursday afternoon, January 8th 1969

"Do you believe her?" John Butler asked his friend.

"Hell yes, I believe her." Elliott said. "How could I not? She has no reason to lie, and you've got the proof right there in front of you." Elliott raked his fingers through his thick white hair.

John looked doubtful, but remained silent. *Money can make people do a lot of things, especially lie.*

The distress evident on Elliott's tanned, but now weary looking face. "There's clearly no denying it, John."

"Well, I need to know how do you want to proceed?" John asked as he pushed the bridge of his metal framed browline eyeglasses up in place, the frames matched the silver metallic gray of his hair.

"I want him released, first and foremost," Elliott said decisively.

John wordlessly slid the contents back into the manila envelope Elliott had presented him.

"I know I'm asking a lot and I'm giving you a very short

window in which to operate, but clearly, time is of the essence. I need you to make some phone calls on my behalf and make those charges disappear, today… in some way, somehow. Just work some magic for me as I know only you can."

Elliott sat down in the chair facing John's desk and leaned forward with his elbows placed firmly on his knees as he rested his chin on his raised interlaced fingers his eyes focused at the window.

"No worries, if it's as she said and just a matter of him being at the wrong place at the wrong time and the lack of the proper representation, then we can take care of it. I have several contacts in the attorney general's office who can look into this for me, and I'm sure they can handle this swiftly and with care," John remarked.

Now both men stared out the window at the golden hued sky, and then John looked meaningfully at his friend. "Please, Elliott, consider it done."

Elliott had been quiet for a long moment before he spoke; his voice tinged with uncertainty. "John, you do know I'm very appreciative of everything you do for me, as well as what you are about to do here. I wouldn't trust anyone to handle this for me, except you." Elliott's face remained hesitant as he regarded his friend of more than fifty years. "And it should go without saying that I'm counting on your utmost discretion in your treatment of this whole thing." He sighed heavily as he pressed his lips together.

"Of course." John was taken aback that Elliott would even

suggest he might not treat this matter confidentially; he knew better than anyone how much Elliott Bradford valued his privacy. *This matter was especially sensitive and would require a bit of finesse on my part to keep those close to Elliott, namely Margo, out of the loop.*

"I'll take care of it myself, personally, if it will make you feel more at ease. I want this to be the least of your worries." John then raised an eyebrow, slightly offended. "You know, Elliott, you've been my client for some time now," his eyes lowered, "but more importantly, you've been my friend a lot longer than that. You should know by now that you can always count on me to look out for your best interests and to keep your personal affairs private."

Both men knew the other to be a loyal and trusted friend, and Elliott knew John would do all that had been asked of him in this matter. Yet, he didn't feel the least bit apologetic about making it crystal-clear that he required and expected complete confidentiality.

"I think, I need a good stiff drink," John announced as he abruptly got up out of his swivel chair and strode over to the liquor cabinet. His tall lean frame was juxtaposed by a slight protruding abdomen.

"Care to join me?" He asked lifting the bourbon filled decanter as he looked back at Elliott.

"Yes, I would. Only make mine a double, will you?"

Elliott's eyes were red-rimmed, and he looked as if he'd just been put through a washer's wringer.

As John poured the dark amber liquid into etched Edinburgh Crystal whisky tumblers, making them both doubles, he continued. "You know, Elliott, when I asked you how you wanted to proceed, I was really asking how you wanted to proceed where *your wife* is concerned."

Then suddenly the look that John had missed from his dear friend during their entire conversation made a welcomed appearance as John handed him his drink. The toughness and determination that personified who Elliott Robert Bradford was, had reappeared in his eyes. He took a swallow of the bourbon and looked soberly at John and with a clenched jaw and his mouth set in a tight severe line he spoke.

"I was fool enough to have once loved her. What's more, somewhere inside me, I may still. But for what she's done. This egregious act, it's unforgivable. I don't want to see her or hear another word from that woman again." He took another swallow of his bourbon. "Not ever."

12

🌺 Enrico 🌺

New York – Sunday morning, January 12th 1969

Lathering and washing his long, dark shoulder-length hair and cleaning his full thick beard, he was alone in the open shower room, something that never happened.

He had played a great final game, the water began to ease the tension in his pumped-up muscles, and it felt good on his taut skin. Nevertheless, he had learned to make showering a quick process in here. During his final rinse, he sensed the presence of others and slid his eyes to the left and then the right of him through the steam; *sure enough, it's that asshole Tate Ferguson.* His mind quickly reasoned that his little crew of minions couldn't be too far away.

"Hey Rico, a little birdy tells me you're getting sprung out of here. Did I hear right, ya leaving us?"

"Yeah, Ferguson, you heard right. I get processed out first thing tomorrow morning." Enrico replied as he shut off the water.

"Ya know somethin', Rico? It's a shame we ain't gonna see ya around here no more," he eyed Enrico's wet naked form through the haze, and a leering smile came to his dry cracked lips as he licked them. "Ya really got yourself lookin' really good there, boy, all them muscles. Yeah, ya got a right nice lookin' body; I'm gonna miss seeing it 'round here. I always liked watchin' ya in the yawd."

Ferguson's spoke in harsh strained whispers that echoed within the large area. "Too bad the only time we been together, was yew tellin' me off, 'member?" He chuckled.

"Yeah, I remember. You got in my face and I had to set you straight." Enrico said, he watched him out of the corner of his eye.

"Yeah well, too bad we ain't ever got together in other ways while ya was here. Ya know what I mean? Cuz, that ass ya got there is something special, now ain't it boys?" To which the others laughed and someone from behind him even whistled. "So how's about ya give us a little taste of it before ya go, huh?" Ferguson said as he lewdly licked his lips. "Let's call it a going away party."

Enrico lifted his towel off the hook and dried his face and his hands, but left his body wet as he scanned the shower area. Four of them in all including Ferguson and they were all naked. He quickly determined their number would make it easier. His senses were sharp, prickly in fact, and his brain operated at a calculating and heightened level. However, outwardly he appeared calm and collected.

He flipped his towel out in front of him, and it landed flat on the wet floor of the shower as a constricted smile came to his lips. "You want a taste, huh?" Enrico stepped solidly onto the towel. "Then why don't ya come and get a taste."

Ferguson stepped forward, but Enrico's moves were fast and fluid. Enrico pulled him down, and swiftly had Ferguson's head wedged into a vise grip of his rope like forearm and bulged bicep.

The rage in Enrico's voice was instantaneous; he eyed the other three men. "You fuckin' ass wipes. You gonna come in here and try to rip *me* the fuck off, you picked the wrong one. I ain't nobody's fuckin' bitch, ya dig?" Enrico squeezed harder into the hold on Ferguson's neck, "I never have been and I never will be."

The others started to move in cautiously.

"Don't take another step or I'll snap his motherfuckin' neck, ya dig?" He then directed his voice to Ferguson. "Now you call off your goons before somebody," he tightened his hold further on Ferguson's neck, "namely you, really gets hurt."

Ferguson's freckled face rapidly changed into a deep beet red within Enrico's grip.

Ferguson lifted a hand toward the others to tell them to back off. They tentatively backed away and Enrico loosened his grip around Ferguson's neck and let him go. Ferguson gasped for air, coughing he motioned to the others to go after Enrico.

The largest of the three men charged Enrico, who stood with his feet planted firmly on the towel. Blocking an oncoming punch, Enrico quickly distributed several landing punches in a fury of blinding combinations as he assaulted the man's face, throat, and gut. The man slumped forward as the air whooshed out of him. Enrico grabbed him by the hair and held his head steady. With full force, he brought his knee up hard into the man's face. Bright red blood gushed from his nose and mouth.

Grabbing the man's hand, Enrico pulled back on his index and middle fingers simultaneously and squeezed them together as the man lowered himself down onto his knees in pain. Enrico pulled back hard on the fingers until he heard a definite snap of the joints breaking and the man screamed in agony as he grabbed his floppy fingers.

Enrico moved rapidly to the dry part of the shower. He delivered a barrage of body and face punches to the next man closest to him that sent the man to his knees, but Enrico went down with him as he took ahold of the man's arm and hyper-extended it by placing it over his knee for leverage as he pushed down solidly with the full weight of his body.

The man pleaded for mercy, but Enrico ignored his cries and applied more pressure until it too snapped, and the man howled as he dropped down on the showers floor in pain, all the while Enrico's eyes were fixed on the fourth man.

He recognized the man standing frozen in place, with fear etched on his face. A terrified Sonny Carbone shook his head from side to side.

"Hey, come on, Rico, man. I didn't want no part in this,

I swears. Rico, I swears, on my mother, I didn't." He put his hands up in front of his face defensively. "Please Rico. Don't hurt me…Man, c'mon Rico…PLEASE!"

Enrico stood up and glowered at him, hearing him swear on his mother didn't mean much in here, and it surely didn't make any difference to Enrico, but he decided to let him go so he could get to the ringleader, Ferguson.

"Then get the fuck outta here, ya pussy." Enrico pointed his finger in his face. "I know you're short timing it in here, Sonny, but you better keep your fuckin' trap shut. Don't think for a second I won't find out if you ratted me out, ya dig it?"

Sonny quickly nodded his head, then turned and as he ran out of the shower. Enrico looked back with a slant of his head as he turned his hulking muscular body. Ferguson had backed himself into a corner in the shower, cowering on the floor on his knees. Enrico walked to him as Ferguson began to beg, his voice now high pitched as he spoke.

"Hey Rico, c'mon. Ya don't think this was our idea… Do ya? Somebody's settin' ya up, see? We got sent in here to teach ya a lesson."

"Somebody sent you in here after me? Who was it?" Seeing the reluctance to talk in Ferguson's eyes, Enrico moved closer to him as he pressed. "You tell me, right now!"

"I can't tell ya, he'll make my life miserable as shit in here if I tell ya." Ferguson blinked back; as fearful tears started to run down his freckled face.

In his life, prior to his sentence here, Enrico had been

an associate for the Marchetti family, a well-connected and highly respected gang. They had an affiliation to a major New York crime family. Enrico knew how to make people talk and he had developed an affinity for it.

He placed his hands at Ferguson's throat and lifted him up from the floor of the shower. "You need to be more concerned with the misery I'm about to deal you." He glared hard at Ferguson. "Now, you tell me who sent you and your boys in here and do it now. Because, I ain't got time for no fuckin games."

Enrico bent his head from one side to the other as he cracked the bones in his neck. "We can do this the easy way or it can be hard, either way is fine by me, but you'll be the one who will live to regret it." He hissed while he grabbed Ferguson by his testicles and he began to squeeze, hard.

"Alright! I- I'll tell," Ferguson gasped in pain barely able to catch his breath. "It- I… It, oh God!" Ferguson winced in pain. "Slo- Sloane, he told us to learn ya a lesson."

Sloane? It became as clear as a foggy night to Enrico; Sloane was one of the prison guards. He had told Enrico he could use the showers solo today, telling him, "Seeing as how it's your last day and all, and you've kept your nose clean since you've been in here."

That son of a bitch had it in for me, but why? *I've barely even talked with him. Was he pissed because I'm getting out of this hellhole and he wanted to see me get my comeuppance somehow by way of a prison gang rape?*

"I ought to kill your punk ass," Enrico hissed at the terrified Ferguson, "but that would keep me in this shit hole longer... So count this as your lucky day, ya fuckin' weasel." Enrico gave him a wide yet menacing grin. "I'm just gonna beat the crap out of you."

13
🍀 Gabrielle 🍀

New York – Sunday morning - March 23rd, 1969

The sun bathed her bedroom with streaming rays of light as she leisurely awoke; she stretched her arms above her head with a wide mouth yawn. Then with a start she looked at the clock, it was just after nine. Her bedroom door had remained closed.

Panic gripped her, *what have I done, letting a virtual stranger into my home, gorgeous yes, but still a stranger. Well, somewhat of a stranger. What if he's robbed me? You hear about those things happening in New York all the time. Luckily for me, I didn't wake up dead this morning. Okay, a bit of an oxymoron there, but smooth move Gabi.* She chided herself.

She flung the covers off and scrambled out of the bed dreading what she might find on the other side of the door. From her bedroom closet, she grabbed some old-fashioned protection- a Louisville Slugger baseball bat, a gift from her brother. She could hear him now, *'If I can't be there to protect you, then this will have to do it for me'*, Phillipe said to her. He was her only brother and had always been protective of all his sisters.

She unlocked and slowly opened her bedroom door as she

gripped the bat tightly within her hands. She rushed down the hall and into the living room in her socks. She found no Nick Caine; in fact, the pillows they had sat on were stowed away with the blanket folded neatly on top. The used platter and wine glasses she had left on the counter last night had been washed and dried.

She checked around the apartment, nothing appeared to be missing. Her purse hung on the coat tree under her jacket, just as she had left it, and her wallet was still inside her purse, apparently untouched.

Satisfied she was safe and in no outward mortal danger, she put her bat away in her bedroom closet. She started a pot of coffee and took a shower while it percolated.

Afterwards, she got dressed. Putting on a pair of bell bottom jeans and a white gauzy peasant blouse. She slid her feet into a pair of blue wedge espadrilles and secured a silver chain link belt around her waist.

In the kitchen, she poured herself a cup of coffee and had been so startled by the doorbell buzzer that she spilled a bit of the hot coffee onto her clean countertop. "Damn it!" She grabbed a dishtowel, laid it on top of the spill, and ran to the door and pushed the intercom button.

"Yes, who's there?" She heard the crackling sound come through the wires of the intercom.

"Hello G. L., it's N. C. May I come up?"

Instantly, a smile came to her lips as she recognized his deep voice. She pushed the button allowing him access, and then she opened her apartment door. She watched him as he quietly ascended the staircase.

Gone was his sexy five o'clock shadow she had privately scrutinized last night: now clean shaven and with his damp hair combed straight back with slight curling at the ends. Wearing a beige crew neck aran wool sweater, blue jeans and brown desert boots, he looked like an ad from the pages of *Men in Vogue* magazine.

Wow, how can he look this great in the morning? She thought to herself, *especially after spending the better part of the night asleep on my living room floor.* Yet, there he was, at her door, right in front of her, looking and smelling wonderful.

"Hello, Gabrielle." He happily greeted her.

She smiled up at him. "Hi there, Nick Caine. Come in."

After he entered the apartment, she closed the heavy door behind her and leaned back against it as she evenly stated, "When I didn't find you here this morning, I guess I didn't expect to see you today." Her heart was beating so hard in her chest she felt sure he could see it.

"I should really apologize," he raised a sheepish brow in her direction. "I should have left a note, thanking you for letting me crash at your place last night. I left this morning around seven or so; I had to go home to let Lobo out and feed him his breakfast."

Watching her as she stood there, his own heart raced as he tried to appear calm. "Your floor was comfortable though, I might add." His eyes were glued to her freshly scrubbed face, free of make-up. *She looks even better without all the war paint.*

She blushed under his overt study of her face.

"That's good to hear, but maybe it was because of the pillows and blanket." She eyed the floor. "I wondered about where you were, I suppose I thought... I don't know what I thought, and I guess it doesn't really matter now," her eyes lifted to his, "for, here you are." She looked into his blue eyes and was getting lost in them; she shook her head to clear it as she continued, "By the way, thank you for washing the wine glasses and platter. You really didn't have to."

"No problem," he looked intently at her as he spoke. "It's the least I could do in light of your gracious hospitality. I didn't mind doing it at all."

"So why did you come back this morning?" She asked with a smile.

He pushed his hands in the pockets of his jeans and shrugged his shoulders up towards his ears. "Why did I come back this morning?" His cheeks flushed with a bit of color as he rocked back on his heels. "I wanted to see you again, but I realized you never gave me your phone number, so I wasn't able to call and ask you," he lowered his shoulders. "I'd like to take you to breakfast this morning," he paused, "So, would you, like to go?"

Seeing him blush and appear somewhat unsure of himself, touched her heart as she smiled and shook her head to the negative. "No thank you. I do, however, appreciate the invite though."

This had been a new side to the self-assured man she had dinner with only last night, and she liked it when his eyes broadened in surprise.

"You don't want to go to breakfast? Or is it you just don't want to go with me?" He frowned. "Did I misread something here?"

"No, it's nothing like that, Nick." She turned her head toward the kitchen as she spoke. "I'm making myself breakfast, so how about I make you something here too instead of going out? Would you care to join *me*?"

"You cook?" His eyes sparkled with a smile.

"Yes," she nodded her head. "I'm told I'm an excellent cook. Frankly, not to toot my own horn, but I kind of agree." She said as she tied an apron around her waist. "And, my being a woman has nothing to do with it, if that's what you are thinking, Mr. Neanderthal."

He grinned as he hung his head a little, as he looked up at her with a lift of his eyes and a creased forehead, the expression reminded her of the sexy stare of James Dean.

"I wasn't thinking anything such thing, and I would love to join you for breakfast." He said.

She walked into the kitchen, opened the refrigerator, and asked over her shoulder. "How do you like your eggs?"

Ten minutes later, Gabrielle placed the plate in front of him, his over easy eggs were done just the way he liked them, the buttered toast a beautiful golden brown almost the shade of her silky hair, the bacon crisp, and he thought she made the best cup of coffee.

As she sat across from him, she enjoyed watching him heartily attack his breakfast. Once finished, he announced, "I have to agree with what you've been told. You *are* an excellent cook. This is probably the best breakfast I've had in some time. Where did you learn to master the art of bacon and eggs?"

She sipped the last of her coffee.

"I'm glad you enjoyed it, but believe me, breakfast is not hard to do." She lowered her cup. "Remember, I did spend time in Paris. Which, by the way, is home to some of the best chefs in the world?" She rose and collected their empty plates speaking as she moved them to the counter. "Some of whom didn't mind sharing their talent with an eager-to-learn unofficial culinary student. I was also taught at an early age by a mother who insisted that we all learn to fend for ourselves so as not to be dependent on someone else to feed us when we were hungry."

"You knew chefs who would teach you, unofficially?" He asked.

"Yes-, friends of our family," she kept her back to him as she responded, "and they taught me a thing or two on how to navigate my way around a kitchen."

Squirting some dish soap into the sink and filling it with warm water, she placed the dirty dishes into the sudsy water, scrubbed the plates, and rinsed them.

Nick finished his coffee and joined her at the sink; he

handed her his empty cup and stood close to her as he reached for the towel on the bar over the sink.

"In thanks for feeding me that wonderful breakfast, the least I can do is to help you by drying the dishes."

The proximity of him filled her nostrils delightfully as she inhaled the masculinity of his light spicy woodsy scent.

"Umm, no Nick, you don't have to."

Yet, he picked up one of the rinsed plates and rubbed it dry with the dishtowel.

"You know, if you keep this up, I'll lose all rights to call you a Neanderthal, but truthfully, I can handle this."

"Nonsense, I don't have an aversion to house work. I told you I'm no chauvinist. Well, maybe only in some things." He playfully winked at her, "Besides," he added, "the sooner we get this done, the sooner we can go."

Puzzled she turned to him. "The sooner we can go where?"

He picked up the next dish and dried it. "I'd like you to spend the day with me." He placed the plate on top of the dried one. "Er, that is if you have no other plans. I don't want to be too presumptuous, but I'd like to take you someplace."

She turned back to the sink. "No, I don't have any other plans." Smiling to herself she evenly answered. "I wouldn't mind spending some time with you today."

Once the kitchen was back in order, he asked to use her phone while she went to get ready. In her bathroom, she brushed her teeth and applied some eyeliner and lip-gloss. She heard him on the phone speaking in Italian.

"Ciao Enzo, è Nicolas." He paused. "Sì, sto ancora venire. Essere lì in quindici minuti. Grazie."

14
🌿 Gabrielle and Nick 🌿
New York – Sunday morning - March 23rd, 1969

Gabrielle peered out of the car window as he turned the car toward the Chelsea district, an area she had yet to venture to. Even on Sunday the streets were already filling up with people, and she mused *this is one busy city.*

"We're here." He suddenly announced.

They arrived at a large brick building with a banner over the front. She could not quite make out the name as Nick opened the door and they walked up a flight of wide stairs. The light bulb in the corridor was out, making it dark and a bit ominous.

She felt a little apprehensive as they came upon a wide wooden door; Nick knocked on it. After a few minutes, a short pudgy man in a beat-up tweed flat cap and a worn leather apron opened the door. The men greeted one another with handshakes and they turned to look at her as Nick began the introductions.

"Enzo, this is Gabrielle, the girl I told you about."

His thick mustache covered his upper lip, but she could

tell he was smiling by his eyes.

"Gabrielle, this is my friend Enzo," Nick then added, "he speaks some English, but, it's somewhat limited."

She tentatively stood in the dimly lit hallway as she guardedly spoke to him. "Hello, Enzo, it's nice to meet you." She looked at Nick with bewilderment as she shifted her weight from one foot to the other.

Enzo opened the door wider to let them enter as Nick smiled and stepped aside to allow her passage through the doorway.

Cautiously she peered into the space before entering; her mouth dropped open as she fully entered the room. Nick followed her in as Enzo closed the door behind them.

She smiled as she spied rows and rows of couches and just about every type of chair there was in the enormous space. She heard Nick's soothing voice as he leaned near her ear and said, "I knew you need a couch for your place, and you can get a really good deal here."

Enzo stepped in front of her with a smile below his thick mustache. "You look, you like, you buy, eh?"

She excitedly nodded her head as she started her search. After looking around the space and trying out the various couches for close to an hour, she called Nick over from the counter stool where he sat as he read the Sunday paper.

"I have a question for you." She stated.

He neatly refolded the newspaper, then came and stood in front of her with a smile on his lips.

"I'm a man with a lot of answers, so shoot."

"Why are there no other customers in here?" She asked.

"That's because it's Sunday. This is a workday for Enzo and the guys; the store is normally closed on Sundays. I told him about your couch crisis, so he let us in today as a favor to me. He's a good guy, we go way back."

"Thanks for the consideration, but, honestly I don't think my not having a sofa was much of a *crisis*." She tilted her head toward the couch she was sitting on with a smile. "However, I've narrowed it down to these two; this one is very nice and it's very comfortable, I really like the back pillows. What do you think?" She asked.

He looked over the long bench style burnt orange couch, lifting the pillows to check for softness and then sitting down on the couch. "This is nice." He remarked.

Gabrielle silently smiled as she rose and went a few couches over and sat on a French provincial couch with soft pastel colors on an intricate silk brocade pattern.

He lifted his legs and took a lying down position on the orange couch. "This is very comfortable. I'd wager it might even be a tad more comfortable than your living room floor." He playfully winked at her.

"This is my other choice. It kind of matches the French theme of my place, don't you think?"

He got up and joined her at the other end of the French Provincial couch. "It's nice enough for sitting, I guess, but I don't think it would be so comfortable for reclining on, and it seems a little too formal in my view. Ultimately it's your decision, but I kind of like the other one."

She nodded her head in agreement and went back to sit on the burnt orange couch again.

"The couch you are sitting on would look great in your place, and it's an Adrian Pearsall design." He informed her.

"I don't know who Adrian Pearsall is, but it's really a comfy sofa, and I do like the design. In addition, this one has two matching side chairs; there's only one problem," she twisted her mouth in a grimace. "I hate the color. I know burnt orange is an "in" color right now, but it just seems too garish for my tastes. I like more neutral muted tones."

"Don't worry, that can easily be fixed." He winked at her again; *I am falling in love with his little winks,* she dreamily leaned her head back on the couch's soft back cushion.

He turned his head in the direction of the back of the store and called out.

"Enzo!" Nick hollered. "Ha trovato quello che le piace."

Enzo came out from behind a workbench at the back of the store where he and two other men worked under buzzing fluorescent lights. He zigzagged his way to where they sat.

Gabrielle got up to speak with him. Enzo placed his stubby fingers on his hips; he had a friendly smile under his heavy mustache. "You like? You buy?" He said to her.

"Yes, but I don't like the color." She replied.

"You buy." Enzo repeated with a nod of his head.

Nick rose and spoke to Enzo. "Lei vuole comprarlo. Ma lei

vuole un colore diverso."

"Okay. I change it, I change it." His eyes questioned her. "You like, and you buy, eh?" Enzo said in his broken English.

They walked to the work area at the back of the store and stopped at his bench; it held a large bolts of upholstery fabric and rolls of cording. She picked the colors she liked from his large fabric swatches. With Nick translating for her, she requested a few minor changes to the cushion's design. They went over the price, he guaranteed he would have the couch and chairs completed and delivered to her place in one week, two weeks at the latest.

As they left the building and headed back out into the bright sunlight, she looked up at him and smiled.

"Thank you for bringing me here, Nick, it was very thoughtful of you."

He shrugged his shoulders. "No need for thanks, I'm just happy you found something. Enzo is reasonable, he's fast, and he does really good work; you'll be pleased."

The street was filled with people, mostly families in their Sunday finery. Men and boys were dressed in suits; the women in lovely dresses and some even had on hats, little girls in pretty dresses wore white tights with black patent leather shoes.

"I guess church must be over." She commented with a smile as they began to stroll their way through the crowded sidewalk back to Nick's parked car.

"After all that shopping, tell me you're getting hungry,

because, I sure am." He pondered for a moment then continued. "What do you say to a picnic in the park?" There it was again, his easy smile, radiating from his eyes to his lips.

"I'd say that sounds very nice, but what are we to do for food?" She smiled as well. "Aren't the stores closed today?"

"I know just the place, so leave it all to me." He winked.

~~~

She waited in the car at his request as he went into a small deli close to Central Park and shopped for food for their impromptu Sunday picnic. He'd left the keys in the ignition, she decided to turn on the radio while she waited. She found the station now set to a jazz station, and not classical as it'd been last night; listening, she enjoyed the light smooth sounds. *This music seems more suited to the man, Nick Caine.*

He soon emerged from the deli with two big bags in his arms, and she pulled the keys out of the ignition and met him at the back of the car.

"Please, let me get the trunk for you, your arms are full." She opened the trunk. "That is, if you don't mind assistance from a woman."

With smiling eyes, he placed the bags in the opened trunk. "I'm all for women's rights," he pushed the lid of the truck closed. "I suppose your assisting me means that chivalry can be displayed by either of the sexes."

With a bit of smugness, she grinned at him as they got

back in the car, "Absolutely, now you see how truly useful a woman can be to a man. If given the chance, that is."

He laughed as a mischievous glint appeared in his eyes. "I'll gladly give you the opportunity to show me your usefulness; in fact," his stare turned seductively dark as he gazed at her. "I look forward to it, Gabrielle."

She sucked in her lower lip for a moment at his insinuation as she felt the heat creep up from her neck clear up through to her scalp, but in spite of this, she found she wanted to play along with him a little.

"I thought I displayed it to you this morning by making you a scrumptious breakfast."

He pulled the car out of the parking lot and into traffic as the jazz music played softly in the background on the radio.

"Oh, I won't forget that meal anytime soon, I hope there will come a day when we will eat breakfast together, again soon. I liked waking up in Greenwich."

"Umm..." *More innuendo.* "Waking up in Greenwich and breakfast together again? Sounds like you might have something very specific in mind," her brow arched.

"Who? Me?" His eyes widened playfully and he grinned at her as with feigned innocence. "What makes you think I have an exact occasion in mind?"

"Well, I'm quickly learning, some of your words lay on the innuendos a little thick."

"If I recall correctly, your statement was about a woman's ability to prove how useful she can be to a man, wasn't it? So tell me, Gabrielle, just what usefulness are you inferring to?" Suggestively, his lip curled into a slight smile. Then his eyes were back on the road.

"Yes, I suppose I did, but I wasn't referring to any one particular act. Usefulness or an ability in a woman can take on many forms, can it not? Therefore, it would greatly depend on what you yourself consider a useful ability."

She lobbed the ball back into his court with a smile.

He stopped the car at a red light and glanced over at her, the blue topaz brilliance of his eyes mingled with his sexy crooked smile made her sigh.

"I don't think it would be wise for me to answer that question because I might justly incriminate myself and would be labeled a womanizer or a true Lothario in your eyes," he paused. "Then again, regardless, I'll just say I'm open for anything you might suggest, Gabrielle."

Apprehensive to venture any further down this line of playful banter, she went silent for a moment. She wanted to change the theme of their tête-à-tête, as she now turned her attention away from him and looked out the window.

"You seem to have bought a lot of food for our picnic. There are only the two of us, you know."

As the traffic light changed to red. Nick shook his head and softly chuckled, aware of the swerve in the conversation. "I wasn't sure what you were in the mood for, so I thought I'd give you some options. And this deli will usually give me some bones and day old meat for Lobo."

He proceeded to drive; his eyes now clearly focused on the road. "I was hoping we could pick him up and bring him to the park with us, but only if you don't mind having the murdering fiend with us."

Turning toward him, she smiled with a bit of relief. "I would love to have Lobo with us." Her gaze held at his profile.

"You know, Nick, you don't have to be so formal with me. Seeing how you've already spent the night at my place and all." She laughed, "Please, feel free to call me Gabi."

He smiled, showing white teeth. "Nothing would please me more." He turned his head her way as he lifted his brow. "I would feel privileged to call you Gabi."

The way his deep voice sounded when he said *'Gabi'* sent the now familiar flutter through her.

Outside of his apartment building, she pulled her purse up onto her shoulder as she met him at the trunk of the car and picked up the lighter of the two bags.

"What do you think you're doing?" He said. "I don't need any help; I can carry both bags."

She looked back at him with a tilt of her head.

"I know you can, but I'm helping you," she hugged the bag with both arms and stepped up onto the sidewalk. "I'm a very capable female, I can pull my own weight, Nick."

"Ever the independent woman, eh Gabi?" He laughed as he closed the trunk's lid.

"Something like that, now lead the way, my good man."

Inside his apartment, she glanced around and quickly

determined it was a small space just as he had told her, but it was clean, modernly furnished, and tastefully decorated in masculine tones of browns, reds, and golds.

The honey colored wooden parquet covered the floor; a tiny sitting area had a side table with a lamp upon it next to a sleek camel colored Jorge Zalszupin leather sling chair in front of a painted wrought iron rail; a single step down divided the sitting area from the living room.

"It's not much, but," Nick commented as he led her through the space, "it's what I call home."

"I think it's very nice."

She stepped down the one step that led into the living room where a rich sable colored suede couch sat up against the cream colored painted brick wall. *Wow, what a nice sofa, no doubt some of Enzo's handiwork.* Just beyond the living room was a dinette area with a small square dining table with four side chairs tucked neatly around it. It was situated in front of the only window in the room, although a large one.

She followed him as he stopped and placed his bag on the table; then he removed an obvious barricade meant to keep the dog cordoned off from the rest of the space. Out of the kitchen came Lobo, lowering his front paws as he stretched with a yawn, and then he saw Gabrielle.

He ran past Nick and headed straight for Gabrielle as she placed the bag she was carrying on the table and affectionately greeted Lobo full on as she bent and stooped down in front of the dog. Lobo welcomed her, licking her face and fiercely wagging tail as he sat down in front of her.

"Hey there, Lobo! How ya doing, boy?" She rubbed the top of his head and scratched him behind his ears as he eagerly licked at her neck and chin.

"Look at you. Did you miss me? You are such a good boy, aren't you?" She laughed softly. "I'm sorry you were cooped up all morning while I picked out a sofa." She petted his head some more. "Want to go to the park with us, boy?"

At the word *park* Lobo ran, his nails making scratching noises on the parquet floor as he scampered to where his leash hung on a hook by the door; he barked loudly, and then looked at her expectantly, barking again and again.

"Lobo! Quiet!" Nick scolded him as he emerged from the kitchen; Lobo immediately laid down where he stood and let out a series of whimpers as he waited to go.

Nick turned to Gabrielle. "Sorry, I should have warned you. He goes a little nutty when he hears the 'P' word."

She made a sad face at him. "I'm sorry if I got him in trouble, I didn't know." She looked toward the kitchen and asked. "Do you need any help?"

"If you would like to help with the sandwiches," he grinned at her. "I'd welcome it."

"I'd be delighted." She followed him into the narrow kitchen and tried to mask her delight to be near him in such close quarters.

15

🍀 Enrico 🍀

New York – Sunday afternoon - January 12th, 1969

Before this morning's shower episode, Enrico had tried to lay low the past twelve months while incarcerated; he felt as if he'd done a good job of it. He kept to himself as much as possible and did as the guards told him to do, without his usual belligerent backtalk.

He made time to work out as best as he could in the prison's yard by playing basketball and boxing for cardio. He improvised a prison workout, getting creative by using the bars on his cell for pull-ups, sit-ups, push-ups and he'd even do bed lifts to keep up with his muscular physique. He had found it to be his only form of escape. Without some sort of work out in here, he was convinced he would lose his sanity.

There were a few in here who knew of his affiliation with the Marchetti Family. People were smart and left him alone; however, when he first arrived at the prison twelve months ago, Tate Ferguson had tried to make a move on him and Enrico had to put him in his place. After that he knew the word had gotten out not to aggravate him. His silent bark led to a devastating bite.

Mostly, he had could do as he pleased. Wanting nothing more than to do his time as quietly as possible, he hoped to maybe get out early with good behavior.

What a joke. He hadn't displayed true good behavior since he was a kid. But this stint in prison had changed him. He was determined to show his mother he had it in him to be a good person and alter his life, to be worthy of the love and the devotion she'd shown him all his life and especially since he'd been locked up. She'd written him regularly and even visited him whenever she could. *When that shit father of mine, let her.*

Enrico had been starting to redirect his life, though he had not completely finished with the Marchetti family either. His mother had brought him books on business, which unexpectedly he enjoyed, and more to his surprise, he found he liked learning. It wasn't the chore it had once been in his youth. He had struggled against education in his youth, opting to be too cool for school.

He remembered some of the notes teachers had left on his report cards: *He's a bright boy, if he tried he could do well. He's very capable, if only he would apply himself.*

He now wanted to turn over a new leaf and truly re-assimilate himself. Looking back now, he wished he'd been smarter and turned away from the hood life as Nick had done.

He was sure Nick still had doubts about his rehabilitation; he played back in his head the conversation he had with him that morning.

"Hey Nico, it's me, I don't have much time to talk."

"Okay," Nick paused. "So what's up, Rico? You alright?"

He could definitely sense Nick's eye roll through the phone as he replied.

"Right as rain, so, how was Venice Beach?"

"Let me just say this, brother," Nick replied, "the place truly was a dungeon and the other gym I scouted resembled a pit; I'm confident, we can improve on their model."

"I have no worries; with your smarts and my know how, I know our gym is going to be boss. Hey, one other thing I needed to know before I let you go, did you check? Are you able to take care of Lobo for me? Cause, since Gina and me broke up, she wants him out… Like now."

"Yeah, I cleared it with my building's manager. They only allow small dogs here, so when I told him the dog in question was a German Sheppard, he kind of back peddled a bit, but I told him it would be a temporary arrangement, so he okayed it. How long are we talking?"

"I really don't know, but for sure three months. Four tops. I got word, I'm being processed out of this hole tomorrow; Warden Jenkins is holding a special meeting with my new parole officer, all for yours truly." He gave a slight chuckle into the phone as he sucked in some air. The emotion he felt at hearing Nick's voice surprised him.

Nick became silent for a moment. "Rico, I hope you're taking this thing seriously. Prison is no joke and with you being released sooner than the original sentence; well, let me just say, you just got a gift." He stated.

"I know, Nico, believe me. I am taking it seriously," he paused. "And you don't know the half of it, brother. This place makes Juvi look like a walk in Central. Believe me, I don't need no lectures on that. I'm not sure how this whole release thing got in motion, but I thank God, Jesus, and the Holy Mother it did." Enrico leaned closer to the wall phone and confessed. "I just don't think I could stand it in here another minute," he paused, as his voice cracked a little, but he quickly masked it by clearing his throat as he continued. "The minimum-security facility should be sending someone to pick me up tomorrow, so I got one more night in here."

"I don't want to lecture you, Rico." Nick's voice softened. "I just want you to go straight this time and stay out of trouble." Nick gripped the phone tightly. "What I really want is for you to sever those ties you have with Marchetti and get your life back on track."

"That's what I'm trying to do." Enrico said.

Nick sighed into the phone. "When am I going to see you? Can I come visit you at the new place once you've settled in?"

"No!" He answered emphatically. "The same goes, just like I didn't want you visiting me here." He exhaled. "I don't want you mixed up in any of this shit, so I would rather you didn't. I'd like to hold off seeing you until after I'm done with this whole mess. Okay?"

"Yeah sure, whatever you say." Nick said, knowing by the tone in Enrico's voice that he had to give him the space he'd asked for.

"Hey, I gotta split. Thanks a lot for taking care of Lobo for me; I want you to know I appreciate it."

"No problem, I'll call Gina and make the arrangements to pick him up. Hey, take care of yourself. And watch your back, buddy, okay?"

"No worries there, cause that's what I do best." Enrico said as he hung up the phone.

Nick's words from almost ten years ago filled Enrico's mind, *'Marchetti is lookin out for Marchetti; he left us to rot in here for over a year. He doesn't give a shit about us. Why can't you see that, Rico'?*

Nick had said it to him the day they got out of the Juvenile Detention Center. They had just turned seventeen and had just served eighteen months for the crime of grand theft auto. Unfortunately, Enrico didn't listen.

With their juvenile records sealed, Nick had elected to finish school. He left the old neighborhood and all the illegal wrongdoings behind him. 'Reinventing himself', he had called it, and Nick had even gone so far as to go to an Ivy League college.

Enrico, on the other hand, had just barely graduated from high school. He continued to work for the gang and worked his way up the ranks to become one of Marchetti's best associates. Letting the lure of the money, women, and the power he felt his position had given him, and yet, he liked the job. But as he matured, he came to realize how wrong it was and he needed a change. He now wanted to focus on opening the gym and working with Nick.

Salvatore Marchetti had been something of a father figure for him, since Enrico's own father had been a falling down drunk with abusive tendencies. Just nine years his senior, Salvatore had been Enrico's Caporegime and he'd taught Enrico all he knew about intimidation and leading a group of men to do his bidding. Enrico looked up to him and absorbed all the life experiences Salvatore had to offer. He'd taken Enrico under his wing, and taught him to be tough and a bit heartless when necessary.

Salvatore, the nephew of Vincenzo Marchetti, an infamous kingpin of a major crime family. However, even though Salvatore was his blood, Vincenzo seemed to require more of him, and made him work harder. Salvatore started out as an associate, without his uncle's recommendation. Vincenzo had told him he'd be on his own, *'You gets no handouts, you gots to earn it. The same ways I did'*.

In essence, Salvatore had a lot to prove to the elder Marchetti to earn his uncle's respect and to claim his rightful place within the family. In an attempt to gain his uncle's and the rest of the family's approval, and to get them to take him seriously, he formed a small gang of his own within the family.

Salvatore had evolved from a numbers-running racket and what he called neighborhood security (which only amounted to shaking down some of the local businesses to offer them paid protection), to owning legitimate businesses. However, his vending machines and pay telephone operations were more schemes and fronts: ways to launder money for the crime family.

Yet, he made it crystal-clear to Enrico that since his father wasn't Italian, he'd be limited to associate status.

Enrico's mother was Italian, he loved her and wanted to honor her. He chose to use her maiden name because he wanted nothing from the bastard who was his father. He had also hoped using his mother's Italian name would garner more respect. What he wanted most was to be made. Everyone respected and listened to what made-men said and did.

Marchetti acknowledged his plight, even once telling him. *'You're like one of my own, but the rules are the rules, and they're unbendable. There ain't no way you can ever be a made-man; cause, being half-Italian just ain't enough, especially since that half came from Florence. Hell, you ain't even half Sicilian. You can only go as high as an Associate; if I could change the rules for you, I would, but there ain't no getting around it, Rico. It's just the way it is.'*

Thinking about what had happened today in the prison's showers, he acknowledged that if he had been a made-man, *no one, least of all this fucking nobody Correctional Officer Patrick Sloane would have come after me like that, not for any reason.*

16
 Gabrielle and Nick
New York – Sunday afternoon - March 23rd, 1969

At the park, they ate slowly, sipped wine, played fetch with a very happy Lobo, and they even stopped at the statue of Balto as they left the park and walked Lobo home. With the dog secured in apartment, Nick drove Gabrielle home.

As they stood on the sidewalk outside of her building, she was happily getting lost in his gaze. He slid his hand around her waist and pulled her close to him in an embrace. His mouth came within inches of hers.

She swallowed hard and lifted her face up to his, and closed her eyes awaiting the impending kiss. Instead she felt his lips on her right cheek.

Then suddenly he pulled out of the hold, her eyes flew open just in time to see him backing away from her and tucking his hands safely inside his jeans pockets as he leaned on his car. She longed for his unfulfilled kiss and to be in his embrace.

Speechless and instantly red-faced; she pushed her hair back behind her ears. She glanced up at him and immediately eyed the ground.

"I apologize; I shouldn't have started that," he paused, "I just wanted you in my arms and I did it without thinking. But, I made you a promise, Gabrielle." He looked at her with hooded eyes. "I try to be a man who keeps his word; I told you I wouldn't kiss you, until you asked me to."

She continued to eye the ground. *What is wrong with me? I was about to kiss this man in the middle of the sidewalk, in broad daylight with so many of my neighbors out and about, and on a Sunday no less.*

Embarrassed by her own conduct, out of nowhere she felt the tingle of tears looming at the back of her eyes and a lump forming in her throat. She tried to blink hard and force it all away as she quietly spoke.

"I-I think, I'm the one who should apologize here, Nick," wanting to escape his gaze. "I really just want to go inside now; thank you for a lovey day."

He saw the mistiness in her eyes and he moved in closer to her and pulled her back into his arms.

"Why are you apologizing?" His lips pressed onto her hair as he spoke. "You're upset. You think I don't want to kiss you?" He sighed. "You're wrong there, because, I want nothing more than to feel your lips on mine- I'd like it very much."

She pulled away from him, putting some much-needed distance between them.

"I'm upset with myself because in my current frame of mind, I would have let you; I even wanted you to." She paused as she went on. "That's just not me; I'm not the girl who displays affection in such a public way, especially with some guy I've just met. I apologize if my actions led you think otherwise."

"Some guy? Don't do that, Gabi. Don't minimize our connection by trying to fit us into some senseless time frame set by the prim and proper customs of society; I don't care if we just met. I feel like I've known you my entire life."

He scanned the ground, and looked at her with resolution.

"Forget the stupid promise I made, and the dumb stance I took. I don't want to wait until you ask me to kiss you. I want to do it right now." He started to reach for her. But, she'd found her emotional footing, and she lifted her hand to halt him as a soft breath of air escaped her lips.

"Hey, didn't you hear what I just said? I'm not letting you kiss me out here on the street. Besides, I think your original stance is a good one." A soft smile came to her full lips. "I think I like being in charge, so I guess it's still up to me when or-even if—we venture down that road and partake in a kiss."

At that moment, Gus came out of one of the building's front double doors with a broom in hand. He saw Gabrielle's hand raised to hold the man back. From where he stood, it looked as if she was trying fend off the man's advances.

"You alright down there, Gabi?" Gus asked.

She lowered her hand realizing how it must look to Gus as she smiled and called up to him at the top of the stairs.

"Hello, Gus, yes, I'm quite alright."

His eyes narrowed in Nick's direction. "And who might you be, young man? And just what are you up to?" His voice drenched with suspicion.

She gave Gus a look as if to say 'it's alright and to stop' with his line of questioning as she said, "Gus, this is my new friend, Nick Caine; Nick, this is Gus Ulrich, my building's superintendent."

Nick shot a winning smile up at him. "It's nice to meet you, Mr. Ulrich."

"Likewise, Nick," Gus looked past Nick. "I have to ask, is that your car parked over there?"

"Yes, Sir, it is." He replied glancing back at his car with a smile. "And she's dream to drive."

"Oh she's a beaut alright," Gus remarked, "but wasn't that car parked overnight here last night?" He asked with a raised gray brushy brow, but it seemed more of a statement than a question for he already knew the answer.

"Yes sir, it was." Nick crossed his arms at his chest.

Gus walked firmly down the stone steps and stood right in front of Nick. The superintendent's big-barreled chest as daunting as ever as his aged steel blue eyes narrowed at Nick.

"I wouldn't be doing that too often, if I were you."

"*Really*, is that so? And why is that, *Gus*?" Nick asked with a tilt of his head as he stood his ground.

Wanting to put some space between Gus and Nick because they looked like they were both revving up for a battle, Gabrielle interjected before Gus could answer as she stepped in between the two men. Unflinchingly, she stared up at Gus and with clear irritation as she forced a laugh.

"Gus is a retired policeman who sometimes thinks he's still on the job." She turned toward Nick. "I'm sorry."

"You don't have to apologize for me, Gabi." Gus ruefully twisted his mouth. "Nick is just lucky he didn't get a parking ticket is all I was going to say." He lifted his unruly brows at Nick. "They come through here pretty regular, you know. All the time, marking tires and writing tickets. Just want him to be careful is all."

"Thanks for the information; I'm sure he'll keep it in mind," Gabrielle added, vexation in her voice, "are we keeping you from anything, Gus?"

"I'm just sweeping up the stoop," he looked hard in Nick's direction, and then back to Gabrielle. "I just wanted to issue a little friendly warning to our friend Nick here. Nobody likes getting tickets, now do they?" His mouth thinned into a line.

"I think he got the message. Thank you, Gus." She said with a tense smile.

"I hope that's the case." Gus said as he walked back up the stone steps; he reached the top of the building's front landing and began to slowly sweep as he kept an eagle eye on Nick.

Nick shook his head and raised an eyebrow, he spoke so that only she could hear, "I don't think he likes me very much and from the looks of things, he probably never will."

"What?" She laughed. "Giving up so soon, my good man? Where is Mr. Charisma? You don't think you've got what it takes to charm a cantankerous ex-policeman, huh?"

"No way, cops and me…we don't really see eye to eye. It's like you said, retired or not, he thinks he's still on duty. Besides, I don't think there's anything I could say or do to get on that guy's good side. It's like he thinks he's your father or something."

Nick gave a crooked smile as he looked at her amused face. "And on that note," he sighed. "I think I'd better get going." He gazed into her eyes as added, "I'll leave the timing of our first promised kiss up to you. But, in the meantime," he reached out and took her hand in his, "this will have to do."

He lifted her hand up and never took his eyes off her face as he gently kissed her hand, and he saw her catch her breath.

The sheer voltage from his touch and soft lips on her skin shot through her with its electrified current. Her eyes closed and her mouth opened to the onslaught of the rolling flutters commencing in her belly. She purposely pulled her hand back and out of his grasp.

She instantly looked up at Gus as she remembered his proximity to them. Her eyes went back to an amused Nick who'd now been extracting his keys out of his jeans pocket.

"Now that I have your phone number, is it alright if I call you? Say, tonight? I'd like very much to wish you pleasant dreams before I fall asleep and dream of you."

Still a little shaken from his touch, she silently nodded her head.

Nick's slanted smile showed his amusement, as he looked

up at Gus with a lifted brow and a congenial smile. "It was very nice meeting you, Mr. Ulrich."

She took a mental note at his little stab at trying to charm the old codger; she further noted it had little to no effect on Gus who nodded and said, "You too, Nick. Take it easy."

"I will do just that, sir." He replied. Nick then turned his eyes back to Gabrielle. "I'll talk to you later, stay sweet, Gabi."

She watched after Nick as he drove off, she then sighed with frustration and turned her head toward Gus who'd been briskly sweeping the stoop with his eyes now on his work.

Gabrielle walked up the steps to him.

"What was that all about, Gus? You were quite rude to my friend, and if I'm not mistaken, I do believe you may have overstepped a bit."

"Yeah, I know, I know." Gus sighed as he blew the air out of his lungs. He held the broom with his two huge hands one atop the other as he leaned onto it. "Esther told me not to come out here, but honestly, that guy looks like trouble to me."

"I'm glad to get your opinion, but you'll have to let me be the judge of that. I wish you'd listened to Esther and not come out here when you did."

"I know, it's not my place. And, you have every right to be mad at me. It's just hard for me to turn it off. It's ingrained and still very much a part of who I am." He resolutely sighed, "You know, the whole '*serve and protect*' thing, I guess I just didn't want to see him disrespect you out here with all of the prying eyes of the neighbors."

"He couldn't disrespect me; I wouldn't allow that," she inclined her head. "You've no need to worry, because I have my moral compass intact."

His face contorted. "It isn't your morals that concern me; I'm more worried about his." He sighed, "I've dealt with so many lowlifes that I'm afraid I may have become a little jaded. So, I'm sorry and I do apologize, Gabi."

"I accept your apology." She paused, "I do appreciate your concern, please know that. But Nick is not a lowlife." She took a breath before she continued, "and just for the record—not that I owe anyone an explanation. Nick very innocently fell asleep on my living room floor last night. Nothing happened, as you somewhat inferred by his car being here overnight." Her look became serious. "So you see, things aren't always as they may outwardly appear."

She continued, "I want you to know that you have come to mean a lot to me in my time here. But, I can't have my building's super injecting himself into my personal life like this or behaving in such a fashion."

"You're the boss." He said somberly.

"Yes," she hesitated. "I am. So, I hope I've made myself clear?"

He thinned out his wrinkled lips as he crisply stated with a nod of his head. "Like glass, Miss Laurendeau. Like glass."

17
🌿 Nick 🍀
New York – Saturday morning - April, 12th, 1969

Three weeks flew by, Nick and Gabrielle spent a good portion of that time together. She called him at the athletic club as he worked on Saturday morning.

When he got on the line, she excitedly squealed into the receiver. "Nick! You're not going to believe what was just delivered here at my place."

"Really? Finally," he said in his deep voice and smiling. "How does it look? Do you like it?"

"I love it; Enzo is an absolute master at his craft. I don't know how you knew, but you were right. It's perfect for the space. Come see it for yourself." She took a breath. "Are you almost done for the day?"

"Yeah, I am, as matter of fact," he repositioned the phone between his shoulder and ear. "I'm just finishing things up here, and I could be at your place in about fifteen or twenty minutes. Sound okay?"

"Twenty minutes is just fine," she replied, "I'll see you soon, and I hope you're hungry because I'm just putting the finishing touches on a snack."

"I am. I didn't have time for lunch, but I'm learning your definition of a snack is nothing less than a five-course meal, and I'm thoroughly convinced you're trying to fatten me up. I seem to be the only one taking on the extra pounds from your delicious cooking."

She laughed into the phone; he loved the sound of her laughter, it made him smile and it filled him warmly.

"I'm doing no such thing, I just love to cook, and I'm glad you like to eat," she beamed. "Don't worry, it will be something light, trust me." Giving a playful sinister cackle as she joked. "*Said the spider to the fly...*"

After he hung up the phone, he scanned the empty work out area. Nick walked into the towel room, lifted a stack of clean towels, and placed them onto the shelf in the men's locker room. He heard the door open and close behind him as he arranged the towels when suddenly, he felt a hand reach around and grab at his crotch. A petite hand with cotton-candy pink nail polish could only mean Claudia. She stroked him over his pants, adeptly and knowingly. He felt himself begin to harden beneath her expert fingers; then he heard her voice.

"Where have you been, Nicky?" She purred, "I've missed the hell out of you. I thought you disappeared on me."

Her hand continued to stroke his growing erection as she came around to the front of him and unbuckled his belt and unzipped his pants as she tried looking into his eyes but his eyes were shut tight. Extracting his manhood, his breathing became shallow.

"No, I...I can't, Claudia," he gasped. "I...I'm seeing someone." He managed to utter the words as he tried to catch his breath, but he made no move to stop her as she continued assaulting his body. He groaned as he gave into the feeling.

"Seeing someone? Oh how sweet. Don't tell me you want to be faithful to your someone. Hmmm, from the feel of things, I'd venture to guess that this someone must not be satisfying my boy too well, I can feel how much you want it."

Claudia was a beautiful woman; her long honey blond hair hung loosely around her face. A large pink hair clip held her hair, and revealed her delicate facial features. She had a lean limber body, which he'd felt had been made specifically for sex.

He'd always known her to be a stimulating experience in bed. She'd been open to trying just about anything, no holds barred, and it made being with her even more invigorating.

She went down on her knees and her eyes never left his face. She licked his severely engorged member; and then took the head into her mouth and sucked him while stroking his shaft.

He succumbed to her touch, and he spread his fingers through her hair as he grabbed handfuls of her tresses. He held her head in place as he pumped his hips more forcibly and took her mouth with his rigid member as she sucked him hard and fast.

There was a loud noise outside the door, and they both stilled. He released his hold of head as she removed her hungry mouth and stood.

"I'll meet you in your car," she whispered as she reached into his pants pocket and pulled out his car keys. She kissed his cheek as she murmured in his ear while touching him. "Don't worry. I wouldn't leave you in such a state. We'll finish this, lover." She then slipped out the door.

His eyes filled with hunger, he waited a moment gazing at the ceiling. His cock ached for release as he tucked himself back inside his pants. He stepped out of the men's locker room, peered around, and saw Oscar Jones, the club's janitor pushing a laundry cart as he picked up errant towels.

Nick ran a smoothing hand over the front of his pants and his waning erection. Talk about cutting it close; he shook his head. *What was I fucking thinking? What if Oscar had come in and saw us? This is where I work for fuck sake, and not the place to be caught doing something as inappropriate as having any type of sex. Especially here in the men's locker room.*

Claudia loved the minuscule element of the possibility of discovery, and it was something he himself at one time found enthralling too.

That was before…before *Gabrielle.*

For the past three weeks, Nick hadn't been with any other women, and his body rebelled. He found *cold showers and fisting it* just didn't cut it. It was out of character for him to wait on any woman.

Hell, he hadn't even kissed Gabrielle yet, let alone have sex with her, she'd been a true challenge.

Yet, something in him wanted to prove to Gabrielle that his intentions were honorable and he was worthy, so he wasn't rushing her. He wanted to give her as much time as she needed. But, even to him it was almost absurd, for in his heart of hearts he felt, *she is just too good for the likes of me.*

He knew Gabrielle to be a good girl, despite her words to the contrary; he felt her knowledge was limited at best, and he believed she'd only experienced plain ordinary sex. *Whoever she'd been with, must have been mediocre.* For Nick had been sure she couldn't resist him for long, but Gabrielle had been taking her time, and he'd never known a woman to hold out this long. Which led him to believe that she hadn't gotten it good, yet.

However, I'm more than willing to be the one to take her beyond the ordinary and initiate her into a world of wild, uninhibited, and sometimes kinky sex. My world.

He'd fought those urges within him to crush his mouth onto Gabrielle's. Because, he made a promise to her that he would keep his hands to himself. Looking back now, he berated himself, *how stupid was that? Since, she is nothing like any of the women I've been with before.* He wanted her badly, and not just her lips, but her curvy body as well. This had been new for him; Nick wasn't used to being in a sexless relationship.

Hell, he wasn't used to being in a relationship, period. What he'd been used to, was *fucking* any woman he fancied and at any time.

He secured the gym area and went to the elevator that would take him to the garage and to Claudia waiting in his car.

This little tryst with her was just what his body needed; and it would be just an *encounter*. Much like the ones from his past. He reasoned since he'd been with Claudia multiple times before, this time would be no different. *I'm a man with strong physical needs after all, so dammit, why not?*

As he exited the elevator, he heard the light strains of Beethoven coming from the direction of his car. Claudia had been the closest thing to a relationship he'd ever had, only because they were sexual on a more regular basis and over a longer period, but he had no loyalty to her because he had still slept with other women in addition to her.

And he rationed with himself, if he didn't take Claudia right now, the ache from his blue balls would soon make him implode. Where's the harm in letting this willing woman alleviate that?

He slid into the driver's seat. He had gotten so rigid he couldn't see straight. Claudia's unbuttoned shirt and exposed breasts in the dim light of the parking garage made him harder. He couldn't help himself; he leaned over and tasted her. He thought briefly of Gabrielle, and decided what she doesn't know, won't hurt her.

Nick drove to his apartment and as soon as he closed the door behind them, she undid his belt buckle and the button on his pants before sliding her cool hands under his polo shirt and caressing his hot skin as she helped him out of it. He stepped out of his pants, and Claudia watched as his clothes slid to the floor.

"I never get tired of seeing you naked." She gasped.

"Get out of those clothes Claudia, because you're going to get fucked, but good."

"I'm counting on it." She sharply inhaled following him into his bedroom as she seductively removed her clothing, dropping each item in her wake.

He reached into the top drawer of his bureau, pulled out a condom and ripped it open. He nimbly unrolled the covering over his engorged manhood.

~~~

After taking a shower he called Gabrielle from his kitchen wall phone, his voice just above a whisper. "Hey Gabi, I'm sorry it's taken me so long. I had an unexpected work out with one of our members. So I stopped at my place to take a quick shower and to let Lobo out."

He looked over at the dog on the kitchen floor, Lobo lowered his head to the floor as he disapprovingly eyed Nick.

All of this was been somewhat true, *wasn't it?* He told himself; still he couldn't help the feeling of guilt.

"That's okay, Nick. I understand work comes first, but I can barely contain myself, I can't wait to see you."

He heard the hint of excitement in her voice, and it made him feel more ashamed.

"I mean... I can't wait for you to see how good the sofa looks." She said laughing. Her voice sounded pure and wholesome. Pangs of guilt rose within him knowing that Claudia was still in his bed.

"I'll be there as soon as I can." He whispered.

Nick hung up the phone and heard a laugh behind him.

"Wow, Nicky, it's almost like I'm dating a married man. I kind of like being the other woman for a change." She gaily remarked.

"Only we're not dating, we just fuck. Now get dressed; I don't have time for this crap." He crustily told her.

He felt obligated to drop Claudia at her place, which made him even later getting to Gabrielle's. He nervously ran his fingers through his damp hair as he thought of his beautiful Gabrielle, but was she really his? Would she ever be? He knew in his heart Gabrielle did not deserve someone like him.

Nevertheless, God forgive me, I want her. With all of my being, I want her.

18
Nick and Gabrielle
New York – Saturday afternoon - April, 12th, 1969

Nick stood outside her door after having been buzzed into the building, he took a deep breath and wiped his sweating palms on the sides of his jeans as she opened the door wide.

"Gabi, h- hi," he paused, unable to meet her excited gaze. "I'm sorry that I- I'm so late."

"No worries, you're here now." She smiled as she stepped aside to let him in, her good mood was infectious.

He sniffed the air. "I smell pot roast." He said as he entered her apartment.

"Good nose, it is," she bowed her head with a small curtsy as she closed the door.

"I love pot roast. Now," he awkwardly laughed, "I'm thoroughly convinced you are definitely fattening me up."

"Well, the pot roast isn't ready yet, but I did make you a sandwich. It's on the counter, but first..." She laughed as she took his hand and guided him into the living room where he saw the completed room, the couch filled the empty space along the back wall.

"Wow, Gabi!" He exclaimed. "It looks great, like it was made for your place and the blend of your other items work too. It's a cool funky mix, and I like it." He smiled.

The side tables topped with the Italian Bitossi Rimini blue ceramic lamps complemented as they flanked the contemporary white couch. She had placed the two chairs; upholstered in a medallion Persian blue woven fabric across from the couch in front of the coffee table. The eclectic grouping worked well together.

"It kind of was made for this space, and I had to wait three weeks to get it." She nervously laughed. "You have a great eye for furniture, and I appreciate your sharing it with me, Nick." Her voice had a slight huskiness to it.

"That great eye is something a friend—- I mean an acquaintance- taught me to hone," that friend had been Claudia, he was lost in thought for a second. He soon recovered and turned to her, "I would share anything with you."

His eyes guiltily slid away from her as he walked over and sat on the couch and remarked, "it's really comfortable too."

She joined him, and sat on the cushion next to him. She looked into his eyes and spoke before she lost her nerve.

"I want to thank you for everything you've done. For introducing me to Enzo." She swallowed. "And, thank you for being a perfect gentleman toward me all of the times we've seen each other." She nervously cleared her throat. "So, in honor of me completing my living space, do you think you could give me a- a celebratory kiss?"

He felt himself gulp as he turned his head to face her. Nick stared at her in disbelief; she had caught him completely off guard. Gabrielle's eyes burned with determination into his and he ruefully looked away from her.

Her head tilted to the side as she assessed him, and asked. "Is something wrong, Nick? Don't you want to kiss me?"

Images of Claudia stretched out naked just an hour ago filled his mind, and guilt saturated him.

With hesitation in his eyes he asked. "Are you sure you want me to, Gabi?"

"Yes, I'm sure, I want you to kiss me." The tip of her pink tongue skimmed lightly over her russet lips. "Per our little agreement, I'm doing the asking." She looked up at him with resolve in her amber-green eyes.

He had wanted to kiss her for so long. He pushed the guilt he felt aside, and then without giving her a chance to change her mind he turned his body to her.

His hand began to unexpectedly shake as he tenderly moved his fingertips to the side of her head and into her hair. He slid his hand down and took ahold of her neck with a gentle grasp.

Nick's thumb gently glided along her jawline and stopped as it reached her chin. He tilted her head up toward him, her lips only inches from his.

His jaw opened slightly as he softly pressed his mouth onto hers. He then deliberately glided his lips together and sealed them over her mouth's opening again. He heard her sharply inhale as she closed her eyes and gave in to the sensations of the tender kiss. Nick lifted his other hand and cupped her face; he avoided going all in and only allowed the tip of his tongue to rest momentarily at her parted lips before withdrawing it entirely.

Her hand rose to his hair; her fingers took their due as they slid through his thick locks and she softly tugged at his dark strands. She felt rockets of multiple flutters going off all at once inside her belly as it spread and radiated through her body.

His breath was minty, of freshly brushed teeth, and she found she wanted more of him as her hands reached around and effortlessly glided along the wide expanse of his V-tapered back. Touching him felt so good under her fingers and she pulled him closer to her as they both gently fell back. His body, now half on top of hers. She slid her hands up and down his back as she caressed him.

His breathing had increased and then he abruptly gave her a closed mouth peck on her lips as he lifted himself off of her. He pulled back and sat at the end of the couch, careful not to touch any part of her. His eyes closed tightly. She stared at him with absolute want.

His eyes were still closed as he exhaled, blowing out all the air from his lungs.

Her eyes were drunk with desire, she lifted up onto her elbows as she looked up at him and said breathlessly, "Please. Don't stop Nick, I like it."

He spread his fingers and pushed his hands intentionally along his thighs. "I had to stop, Gabi," he turned his head toward her at a slight angle, "or I'm afraid- I wouldn't be able to, because I liked it too. Maybe I liked it a little too much."

He sighed as he dropped his head back against the couch cushion behind him and looked up at the ceiling as she beheld him with hooded eyes.

"I don't know how far you want to go with this, but if I were to continue kissing you— Gabi, I can't promise…"

She shook her head to clear it of the desire she felt as she got the full meaning of what he was saying. *How far I wanted to go with this?* She wasn't sure; but she was sure that he made her feel things she had never experienced before, and it felt good to have his lips on hers. *Yet, to go further?* She was still leery to delve into that part of a 'relationship' with him, not wanting to end up as just another notch on his bedpost or to become one of the forgotten nameless women of his past.

He had told her he would wait for her as long as it took her to feel comfortable because she was worth the wait.

But am I? Given her inexperience, she now had doubts of her own. She had not shared with him the fact that she was still a virgin for fear that he'd run off in the other direction, given his self-proclaimed knowledge of sex and all it entailed. She wasn't sure he would be interested in taking on a neophyte into the realm of sex, given the experience of the women he had previously been with.

Gabrielle preferred to skirt around the issue of her

experience or lack thereof. She had allowed him to believe she was somewhat experienced. She knew something deep within her wanted to be with him that way. *But the idea of sex, well, frankly,* it frightened her.

Her sister Suzette had shared with her that it was no big deal and that it only hurt the first few times until the body adjusted to being invaded.

Invaded? It reminds me of the Spanish Armada and its failed attempt at an invasion' and the thought of the considerable pain of being 'invaded' down there just didn't sit too well with her.

"I have to apologize, Nick." She remarked and gave another shake of her head as she too sat upright.

"Apologize? You don't need to apologize, Gabi? You didn't do anything wrong."

Nevertheless, hadn't she? A flash of Daniel Walters entered her head as he bellowed scornfully and angrily at her, *'you're nothing but a fucking dick tease, Gabi, and to top it all off, you're probably a lousy lay anyway.'* Quickly, she pushed her hair behind her ears.

"I think I may have led you on, but I don't want you to get the wrong idea or impression here. I'm not ready for us to go any further...at least, not yet."

"Gabi, don't you think I know that by now?" He keenly looked at her. "It's why I stopped myself; you have to know how badly I wanted to go on, to be with you, to have you, all of you," he paused, "but I need you to know, this is not just about me having sex with you." He shook his head. "Sex has been a meaningless act for me to satiate my natural male urges, but, I have lived that life. I want more from you, more from us. The way I feel when I'm with you, I haven't felt this before, not ever. I want to explore it to the fullest. Wherever it may take us. However long it may take us."

Nick lifted an eyebrow as he stated matter-of-factly. "When we have sex," he paused, "it's going to mean something to both of us. It won't be some casual act to satisfy our bodies' desires." Tilting his head away from her as he eyed her with a very uncharacteristic bashful grin. "You are very special to me. I want you to know that."

He took her hand and placed it over his chest. Her fingers felt how fast his heart was beating. "You are the first woman to ever make me feel this."

At hearing his words, she felt her own heart squeeze within the walls of her own chest as it skipped a few beats.

19
❧ Enrico ☙

One of the two transport officers stood near him as Enrico sat just outside the warden's office shackled to the hard wooden bench; Enrico had a slight smile on his face. He listened to them as they spoke and wondered if they knew he could hear every word they said.

His grin widened as he heard the bewilderment in Warden Woodrow Jenkins' voice as he spoke to Enrico's new parole officer Carl Mehring. "How a lowlife like Enrico Bartolini was able to finagle his way into minimum security is beyond me." An agitated Warden Jenkins shuffled the papers authorizing Enrico's release awaiting his signature.

Carl cleared his throat, took off his glasses, and wiped at the lens with a clean white handkerchief. "Well, warden, to be fair, Mr. Bartolini has been an exemplary prisoner while here so the term 'lowlife' seems a bit extreme, don't you think? Besides somebody up there must like him, I guess, because this came from pretty high up. Way beyond my pay grade to know who or to question why."

Warden Jenkins leaned back in his chair, the few strands of hair on his balding head had been slicked down with an oily substance. He interlaced his stubby fingers at his chest just above his protruding potbelly.

"I'm sure you've heard we had a little skirmish in the showers yesterday morning, and I'm pretty sure Bartolini had something to do with it." He pressed his mouth with disdain. "You know, I'm well within my rights to detain and hold him here until after we've completed our investigation on the matter." He narrowed his eyes to make his position clear.

A crooked smile came to Carl's lips; he knew what Warden Jenkins was doing, by digging his heels into the dirt like this. All in effect, to make the point that he was in charge. In the meantime, Enrico would just sit on ice in his prison until the Warden *allowed* him to leave. Carl wanted to wipe the smug look off the Warden's chubby face.

Outside the Warden's office, Enrico's grin faded in a slight panic as he listened attentively.

"That's true, Warden, it's entirely within your rights to do just that. However, as I said, someone wants him out of here, like yesterday. I'm not telling you what to do here," he pushed his wire-rimmed glasses back in place, "but I would think it might bode well for you to sign the damned release papers and be done with him, don't you?"

"Frankly, no. I do not Mr. Mehring." Warden Jenkins's eyes flared at Carl. "Just who is this someone? Why aren't they here talking with me about freeing one of my inmates instead of the likes of you?" His face heated red as his mouth twisted firmly. "I don't appreciate some underling telling me what to do in my prison." He leaned forward as his left hand slammed to the top of the desk. "More to the point, I appreciate it even less when someone decides to pull some invisible strings to release a hardened criminal like Bartolini."

"Yeah, I understand." Carl said as he tried to calm the warden down and make a connection with him on some level. "I don't like the way somebody's pulling the strings here either." He crossed his arms at his chest. "I'm sent here on some fool's errand like I'm some sort of puppet, and hell, even I don't know who *they* are myself."

"I'm glad you see my point, Mr. Mehring," the warden conceded with a nod, "because, whoever they are, they should show some respect for my office and make themselves known to me. Since they are the ones who should be here doing the asking and not you." He slung the unsigned papers on the desk towards Carl.

"As I've said, Warden, I'm not privy as to who they are," he eyed the papers. "But believe me they are not in any position to come a-courting, so to speak." He leaned his elbow onto the chair's armrest. "What I can share with you," he continued as he straightened up in his chair. "I'm told, they are influential and they have it within their power to sway the right people into saying yea or nay to projects," his eyes tapered at the warden, "much like the approval needed for the new guard tower and some of the other improvements you've requested here at this very prison. I've been told all it takes is a phone call."

Carl spoke slowly to make sure his point wasn't misunderstood. He was sure it had hit its mark when Warden Jenkins lifted his brows in acknowledgement. "One other thing I know Warden, this *underling* was told to get this release done." He leaned in closer. "That's why I'm here." The doggedness in Carl's eyes apparent. "To see to it that it gets done." He shifted from his chair and moved closer to the warden as he pressed his index finger on the Warden's desk on top of the release papers to emphasize his point.

"Today!"

~~~

Enrico settled into his new living quarters. The mismatched furniture consisted of a twin bed, dresser, and a desk with a lamp. What mattered most to him was the large curtained window. For the first time today, he sighed with total relief. He felt the nightmare of the last twelve months was finally over.

He opened *his* window; it was freezing outside, but he didn't care. With his eyes closed, he was just glad to feel it and breathe it in. He had yearned for this, the smells of the city. The crisp cold air was the freshness of freedom. The faint stench from the Hudson River wafting his way didn't even bother him. His very spirit had literally been lifted high to the heavens.

This was his new beginning; he never wanted to see the inside of a prison or jail cell again. His resolve had him set to do just about anything to maintain this sweet side of liberty. Smiling to himself, he reached up to close the window and happened to see Carl Mehring standing next to a black town car talking with two well-dressed men.

They didn't look like mobsters to him; *Marchetti didn't keep up with me while I was in the joint, and most likely doesn't even know or care that I'm out. They are too well dressed to be feds.*

The men all looked toward the building, then the taller white haired man started taking long confident strides in the direction of the building's entrance, with the other two men following close behind him.

Enrico soon heard a knock at his door.

"Hey Enrico, you got a minute?" Carl Mehring asked.

"Yeah, sure, Carl," he got a twinge of dread, *have they changed their minds? Are they sending me back?* "What's it about?" He asked cautiously.

"There's someone downstairs who wants to meet you."

He followed Carl down the stairs and into the sparsely furnished day room, it was a shared space for the halfway house residents, only now it was empty except for the two men he had seen talking outside with Carl.

The two men were seated in metal folding chairs at the round table in the center of the room. They both stood to greet him as Enrico neared them; Carl attempted to do the introductions.

"Enrico Bartolini, I'd like you to meet,"

"I'm Elliott and this is John." The tall white haired man stepped up to him as he reached his hand to Enrico. "It's nice to meet you."

Enrico eyed the man with interest as there was something oddly familiar about him, yet he couldn't quite grasp what *it* was because he was sure he had never seen either of the men before.

"Likewise, I guess. So what is this little meet and greet about? You work for Marchetti or something?"

"No, I don't work for anyone, except for myself." Elliott looked confused. "I don't know this Marchetti, but," his eyes tapered intently. "I do know your mother."

"My mother? Wha- what the hell is this?"

"I'm here fulfilling a promise I made to your mother, the result of which is why you are standing in this building right now." Elliott raised an eyebrow.

"You got me out of the joint as a favor to my mother?"

"Yes, I did." Elliott faintly smiled at him. "You see, your mother and I were very close friends some time ago; I felt I owed it to her, and I had it within my power to be of assistance."

Enrico rapidly started to lose his cool. As a bit of anger crept into his voice, he spat out his words. "You owed her a favor, huh? For what? What did she do for *you*, that you were the one who owed her?"

Elliott's eyes narrowed at him, they were both tall as they stood eye to eye with each other. "Now you just wait one minute here, young man," his voice rose with indignation. "I know what you're implying; get your mind out of the gutter. Your mother and I were friends. She helped me through a very difficult time in my life."

Enrico's mouth kinked to one side. "Helped you huh, my Ma ain't got a pot to piss in so, I can only guess as to how she helped you." He shook his head. "I guess my old man was right all these years, after all. She was a *rich man's whore*."

Elliott instantly grabbed the front of Enrico's shirt. "Why you ungrateful," he glowered at him. "I won't have you speaking of Ange... your mother, in that fashion, not in my presence."

Enrico slanted his head toward the hold that Elliott had on him and looked up into Elliott's steely-eyed glare.

As if remembering himself, Elliott abruptly removed his hands from Enrico's shirt and stuck his hands into the pockets of his coat as he resumed talking.

"She's no one's whore; she is a kind, caring, beautiful woman who helped me at a time when I was at my lowest." His eyes held a hint of sadness. "Simply by lending an ear, offering me her friendship, and much needed support after the death of my first wife."

"Well, she ain't so beautiful no more, now is she? He saw to that. Where were you when *she* could've used a friend, huh?"

Elliott eyed the floor. "I didn't know what she was going through; if I had I would have put an end to it."

"Well, I guess it's water under the bridge," Enrico's blue

eyes evaluated him. "I suppose I can't fault you for not knowing." He cleared his throat. "So, Elliott, what you're telling me is all my Ma did for you was listen to you?"

"Angelina was a great friend to me." Elliott's troubled brow furrowed. "She was the only person whom I trusted enough to bare my grief to."

Still a bit unsure, Enrico's mouth curled doubtfully. "And just for that you do me a solid and got me released outa that hole early, huh?"

"Yes," Elliott adjusted the lapels of his cashmere coat, "believe it or not, but, that just about sums it up." Elliott's eyes slid awkwardly toward John Butler who had remained silent as he watched the scene unfold before him. Elliott mutely returned his gaze back to Enrico.

"Look," Enrico said, "it's just that I don't know you, man." His eyes narrowed at Elliott. "But if you and my Ma were just friends, then I guess I got no right not to believe you, so I got no beef with you." He gave him a slanted smile. "Plus, I don't want to seem *ungrateful,* and I do know that if it hadn't been for you stepping up and helping me out, I would still be in there. So on behalf of my mother and me," Enrico then reached out his hand to Elliott. "I appreciate what you did for me, whatever your reasons… so thank you."

Elliott shook his extended hand as Enrico continued. "Cuz, unlike most of the guys in there, I really was innocent, someone set those wheels in motion to put me on ice, but in an effort to change my life, I won't be pursuing it. I'm letting bygones be bygones."

"I think that would be a wise move." A glint formed in Elliott's eye. "And, if you're serious about changing your life and your means of earning a living, I would be happy to offer you a position in my corporation."

Elliott glanced over at John again and then back to Enrico. "Once you've completed the steps you need to do here, of course, and once you've proven to me that you really want to make a legitimate living and make a better life for yourself. That is, if you can clean up your act. Get a haircut and a shave," Elliott smiled. "And if you're not afraid of a little hard work, because with your limited experience, you would be starting at the ground level."

Enrico grinned at him. "I'm not afraid of hard work; who knows, maybe I'll take you up on it if something else that's in the works doesn't pan out for me, but cutting my hair and shaving off my beard—"

"Anything can be negotiated," Elliott interrupted him, "and met with some sort of compromise." He smiled. "Nevertheless, I want to get your contact information, and I will reach out to you when the time is right." He put his hand out to Enrico. "We shall see where you're at, at that time, agreed?"

"Agreed," Enrico lifted a brow, "my handshake is my bond, you have my word on it." He replied, taking Elliott's hand and shaking it, not knowing it would be the last he'd see of Elliott.

20
❧ Enrico and Nick ☙
New York – Monday evening - May 5th, 1969

Nick opened the door to his apartment to find Enrico reclining on his couch, his feet propped up, resting comfortably on the coffee table as Lobo sat obediently near him with his ears alert and perked up.

"Am I your first stop on your first day outta the halfway house? Or did you just come for the dog?" Nick asked grinning as Rico stroked Lobo's ears. "And just how in the hell did you get in here?" Nick said as his set his gym bag down near the door.

"I told your doorman I forgot my key," Enrico smiled as he stood up and gave Lobo a hand signal to stay.

"You're kidding me, that old trick worked, huh?" Nick asked with an amused lifted brow.

"Like a charm." Enrico replied, walking to where Nick stood.

"Don't look so smug, he's new to the building."

They embraced, and Enrico kissed him on the cheek with a sigh of relief. Nick hugged him tighter as Enrico started to pull away. "I never thought I'd be so happy to see your ugly mug again." Nick said in muffled response.

They both bowed their heads onto one another's shoulders cupping the other's head in the palm of their hands as they held on to each other.

"I felt bad for not keeping in touch," Nick continued, "and when I found out you were in prison, I felt like shit for not knowing sooner."

"Yeah, I know. But don't dwell, it's okay," Enrico sniffed back and held Nick at arm's length. "For a while there, I was beginning to think I'd never see you again either."

Nick eyed Enrico, tears stinging the back of his eyes as he blinked hard; he hadn't seen Enrico in many months. "Angelina was on your list of visitors," he stated resentfully, "but not me. Why wouldn't you let me visit you?"

"I just didn't want to pull you down with me, because you got out. And, my promise to you, is that I'm done with Marchetti too." Enrico's stare became intensely serious. "Finito."

"Finito?" Nick asked hopefully.

"Yeah, that's what I said."

"Alright." He paused. "You know, I hated the thought of you in there. I know you can take care of yourself, but I wish I could've been there to help watch your back, like you did for me. Was it terrible?" Nick asked.

"I'll just say this; remember the cesspool the detention center was? Well, this was worse, and I don't ever want to go back." His eyes slid reflectively to the right before they landed back to Nick's face. "But, I'm out now," he quickly grinned, "so everything's copasetic." Enrico said.

"You said you're done with Sal. How did you do it, Rico? Because when I left, I had to bargain for my freedom. What do you have on him?"

"Something you don't need to worry about, but enough about that. It's my homecoming, we have to celebrate." Enrico said as he turned around and headed to the living room to reclaim his spot on the couch. "What do you have to drink around this joint?"

Nick's mouth thinned in a worried line; he went into the kitchen, pulled down a bottle of whiskey, poured some into a glass, and presented it to Enrico.

"Straight, right?" Nick asked.

"You remembered," Enrico grinned as he took the glass from Nick. "I'm ready to work. So let's talk about getting this gym thing off of the ground."

"Wait a minute," Nick looked at him with concern. "You want to talk about the gym?" He sat on the coffee table in front of Enrico. "I need to make sure you're completely done with Sal. I don't want him seeping his way into what we're attempting to do here."

"I told you, I am, now quit worrying. You always did that; drove me crazy, because you worry about every little thing."

"I'm sorry if I can't be the trusting soul you seem to be, but I need to be sure that what you have on him will stick.

Because we both know how ruthless he can be."

"Hey, I'm not concerned about Sal. But, I am concerned about 'The Lady.' Have you seen her?" Enrico asked.

"No," Nick noted the topic change as he looked hard at Enrico, and crossed his arms at his chest, bowed his head, and replied. "I haven't seen her."

Nick's mind went back to a day in January, when he thought he'd seen his mother and he almost ran up to her, but he stood frozen in place at the time as she turned a corner. Or the time he came home to find that she had left a neatly packaged box of *cantuccini* cookies outside his door.

"And, I don't particularly want to." Nick remarked.

"When you gonna let this thing go? She's hurting, Nico. She'd love to see you. With Mother's Day coming up… It'd do you both some good."

"Nah, I told her what would heal our relationship. But she hasn't changed anything. Shamus is still there."

"Forget all that, man. She's your mom."

"You can have a relationship with her if you want, but I'm not." Nick stood up as he continued.

"Case closed. Now let's talk about something else or I'm kicking your butt outta here." Nick warned.

"Alright, because fence mender has never been my thing." Enrico took a sip from his glass. "You got a nice pad here."

"Thanks, speaking of that, where are you staying now that you're out of the halfway house? If you need to, you can crash here for a while."

"I appreciate it, but I got a place, not far from Gina's. My p.o. set it up for me. Once Lobo and me get settled, I plan on getting my girl back." Enrico had a gleam in his blue eyes.

"That's good to hear. Gina's a great girl." Nick replied.

"How about you? You still chasing anything in a skirt?"

"Actually," Nick sheepishly grinned. "I've been seeing this girl since March, and she's making me wait for it. And the funny thing is," his eyes absently slid to the side. "I don't mind too much, because she's that special."

"Wow, you been seeing her since March and you ain't banged her yet? This girl, I gotta see, she must be something else. You're the one-night-stand king: wham, bam, thank you, ma'am."

"Don't get me wrong," Nick remarked. "I'm still having sex. Just not with her..." his eyes twinkled roguishly, "yet."

"You, you're still a sly dog. Me on the other hand, I can't do that, Gina's it for me. Brother, you are playing with fire."

Nick's mouth kinked to the side, *Don't I know it*.

21
🌸 Nick and Gabrielle 🌸
New York – Saturday morning - May, 10th, 1969

Nick had rebuffed Claudia's advances that morning, and in fact, he had avoided being alone with her during the past week. Judging by the icy stares she'd given him when they came into contact at the athletic club when she'd come to swim in the club's pool, it was something she was not too happy about.

But so fucking what, I'm done with her in that way. If Rico can do it for Gina, then I can certainly do right by Gabi. I'm going to be faithful to my Gabi, he loved the sound of *'my Gabi'* and she was his in all the ways that counted except one.

Damn, it's so hard to do the honorable thing, but she felt so right in his arms. He was looking forward to seeing her this Saturday afternoon, and he made special plans to take her out on a rowboat at Loeb's Boathouse.

When Nick arrived at her place, he was earlier than usual; he seemed happier and relaxed, and he smiled when he saw her dressed in red hip huggers, a billowy orange blouse tied at the waist and a floppy red hat.

"This is such a pleasant surprise; I'm glad you didn't have to work late with your client today." She mentioned to him when they were in his car.

"Yeah, me too," he glanced over at her. "I'm actually done working out with that client. I've shown them what they need to know and now it's up to them to apply it." He smiled at her. "And, since I don't have Lobo to go home to anymore, I got here much sooner."

"What?! Why? Did your friend come back to get him?" She asked.

"Yeah, he did."

"Aww... I didn't get a chance to say goodbye. Maybe we could visit him, do you think your friend would mind?" She queried.

"We'll see," he wasn't sure if now was the right time to tell her about Rico *or* their past. But, he thought against it and changed the subject. "I just couldn't wait to see you."

"Same here, I'm happy to see you. I find myself waiting all week for the weekend," she admitted.

They soon arrived at Central Park where they rented a rowboat at the Loeb Boathouse. She brought blankets and pillows so they could get cozy on their ride through the waterways of the park.

As usual, the park was busy with people who had the same idea of boating in the park; the channel was congested with other rowboats and canoes. Nick's powerful arms rowed the boat; as he navigated them away from the crowded waterways.

As he rowed, he slowly watched her and started to say, "The club is having what they call their annual spring fling," he paused as he pushed the oars through the water. "It's their glorified push for new members while appeasing the current members with a huge show of pomp and circumstance. It's a formal affair," he hesitated. "In the past, I've gone stag, but, I'm hoping you wouldn't mind attending it with me this year."

"Wouldn't mind attending with you? Wow! Is that really how you're going to ask me out to such a formal occasion?" She lifted a brow playfully at him.

Always has to be the ball buster, he thought with a grin as he shook his head. "No, you're right Gabi. I can ask you better than that." He loudly cleared his throat. "Ahem," He gave a nod of his head and gallantly extended his hand to hers.

"Gabrielle Lawrence, fair lady, would thoust doeth me the honor of accompanying me to this formal event being hosted by my employers?" Still grinning he asked, "Better?"

She smiled up at him with a little smirk. "Oh, it's ever so much better, Sir Nick. When is this gala to take place, my good man?"

"It's on a Friday night, June sixth, so…" he was slightly apprehensive. "I'm hoping you have enough notice to come up with a gown. The theme this year is black and white."

She lifted an intrigued brow. "A black and white ball?"

"Yes, I think that's what they're calling it. It's where the women wear black and white dresses and the men wear tuxes and give the best penguin impersonations we can." He resumed rowing the boat.

She laughed as she tilted her head at him. "I love parties, especially parties with themes, and I attended a black and white ball once before in France, it was such fun. I didn't know they had them here though, you said it's Friday, June sixth?" She paused. "It sounds like fun... Nick, so yes, I would love to accompany you." And, in her head she calculated that gave her four weeks to design a dress and have it made.

"Thank you, it really pleases me." He smiled to himself, *I can't wait to show you off, my beautiful Gabi.*

The sun was bright and warm, and beads of sweat appeared on his forehead he stopped rowing and pulled a bandana out of his jeans pocket and dabbed his brow. She began snapping with her camera, and she got great snapshots of the Bow Bridge and its mirror image reflected in the water. He steered their boat to the eastern section that was secluded and close to land where the trees dipped their branches into the water. There weren't any other boats about; he dropped anchor in the isolated area and settled back on the pillows and blankets.

Nick watched her as she busily took more pictures of the scenery with her Nikon 35mm camera. Gabrielle briefly turned and smiled sweetly back at him as he took pleasure in watching her.

She has such a beautiful spirit. How did a rogue like me ever get this lucky? She soon turned the lens on him and started clicking away at his handsome preoccupied face. He looked as if he was pondering something important.

Finally ending things with Claudia was the right thing to do. He thought. *It just wasn't fair, not to anyone. Especially Gabi.*

He realized she was snapping his photo, he looked up with a quick smile on his lips as he spoke. "Hey, I thought you were taking pictures of the birds, the trees and stuff."

She continued to click away at him as she lightly giggled, "I think you're the best stuff around," she winked at him.

Her light laughter mingled with the chirping of birds and a few ribbits from a frog in the otherwise quietly stilled air.

"I've never liked having my picture taken." He told her as he reached up and laughingly took the camera out of her hands, and then turned the lens on her as he snapped a few shots. Gabrielle playfully held the sides of her wide brimmed hat, and in another, she puckered her lips as she good-humoredly mugged for the camera.

He placed the camera securely at his side and pulled her down to him. She landed safely on top of him, her amused face right in front of his.

"Why don't you like having your picture taken?" She asked. "You're a great subject because you are indisputably the most beautiful man I've ever seen."

She seized the chance and leaned down to plant a playful kiss on his sexy puckering lips, while he laughed sensually.

"That has to be the first time I've ever been referred to as beautiful, but I think I get to call dibs on that one. I've reserved that description for what you are to me."

Nick became serious as he lifted off her hat and looked raptly into her eyes and pushed some strands of hair away as it fell onto her face. "Gabrielle, you are clearly the most beautiful woman who has ever come into my life and you have completely captured me."

He lifted his mouth and took hers in a passionate kiss; she could feel the pure genuineness within his embrace as he held her tenderly in his arms while his mouth covered hers and his tongue entered her parted lips.

She loved the way she felt when he kissed her, but she had to ask, as she lifted her head to look at him.

"Have I really, Nick? Captured you?"

"How's this for an answer?"

His tongue met hers as they intertwined together in the moist softness of each other's mouths.

She wanted to be nowhere else, only here in his arms. The current his mouth generated through her body was beyond words. Feeling the strength of his hands as he held her in his powerful embrace, his fingers strong, yet gentle as he began to caress her back.

His hands soon went lower until they rested firmly on her buttocks. He began to squeeze and knead at the rounded mounds of flesh of her derrière, the touch of his hands felt wonderful.

She quickly discovered she was powerless to stop him, even if she wanted to, but, she weakly ascertained that she didn't want to. The kisses they'd been sharing in recent weeks had her craving for more of his touch; it'd become overwhelming to her.

She could feel the unmistakable rigid hardness of his manhood pressed up against her yet she lingered there, aware of his sexuality. She started to reach there to feel it with her hands, but she stopped herself. She desperately wanted to touch him, but she wasn't ready for it to go any further. She lifted up off him, but the desire was clear in her eyes.

"Nick I…, I- I just can't." Her eyes were downcast; she was unable to look directly at him for fearing her eyes would give her away as to what her body truly wanted.

"Gabi, this is what happens to me when I'm with you; I can't help what you do to me. You make my cock stand at attention every time I'm with you. I'm a little surprised you haven't noticed."

He sensually pressed his lower lip to the back of his upper teeth as he whispered, "my sexy little vixen, you are my sweet tease." He pulled her back down on the pillows beside him and he held her in place. "You know you drive me absolutely wild, woman." He lightly laughed.

"Nick, I don't mean to tease you, and," she looked earnestly up at him. "I have noticed. But, you need to know I won't be just one of your many," she stopped, unable to say 'women' before continuing. "You mean too much to me, but you also unnerve me a little."

"Gabi, you mean too much to me, too. That is why I've

been taking it slow," he cleared his throat. "I would love to make love to you right this minute, and clearly you've felt it because my body gives me away, but you're too important to me. I will wait as long as you need me to."

"I know your body has needs, so does mine. It's not very ladylike for me to admit it, but I have to be honest with you," she gauged him and looked him in his eyes. "It's your past with women, to be honest, it worries me."

His eyes widened as he asked. "What exactly is it about my past that worries you, Gabrielle?" He was afraid of the answer; maybe she found his past with so many women to be too decadent.

"I-I'm not as experienced as you or the women you've been with." She began. "I can't help but wonder, how could I possibly measure up to any of them?" She paused, turning her head away from him. "My last boyfriend said some very unkind things to me when I," her voice grew quiet. "I don't think I could bare it if you did. What if, after we... what if you find that maybe I'm just not good in bed, and that I am a lousy lay and you waited all this time for nothing."

He released a relieved sigh, placed his hand under her chin, and turned her head back to face him. "Your last boyfriend sounds like an asshole to me." *That's the reason she's been holding back from being with me.* "You think you won't measure up? My Sweetness," using his fingertip, he gently traced the outline of her face, "I'm not worried about it, Gabi, because you'll learn what turns me on, and I, in turn, promise to fulfill your every womanly need and desire."

His hand brushed back more strands of her hair as his eyes caressed the curves of her face.

She gazed up at him with a newfound boldness. "Show me now, Nick. Show me what you like."

"What?" His heart leapt up into his throat. Nick's eyes assessed her with furrowed brows as the back of his fingers gently brushed her silky soft cheek. "Are you serious, Gabi?"

She gulped in some air, but didn't take her eyes off him.

"Very." She replied.

"You really want to know what I like. You want to know what turns me on?"

He paused, undaunted he took her hand into his. "I'd like to feel your hands on me, on my body." Gauging her reaction, he spoke, a gleam in his eye. "I get an inexplicable charge anytime you touch me, and I would love to feel it, here."

He placed her hand on his crotch; though fully clothed, she felt the hardness of his member underneath her palm. She kept her eyes locked with his as she slowly, one-handedly undid his belt and the top button of his jeans. His eyes burned with intensity into hers as she unzipped his jeans one centimeter at a time.

He lifted his pullover enough to expose his flat muscular stomach and encouraged her to help free him of the constriction of his jeans as he assisted her by pushing the jeans down just enough to give her complete access to him.

Wordlessly her hands explored his bared chiseled

abdominals, her fingertips glided down to his member and sent a charge through him that he'd never experienced with any encounter. He stared into her green-amber eyes as her every caress heightened his desire.

"Oh Gabi, that feels so good. Your touch feels so damned good." He closed his eyes to fully experience the feeling, and she stole a quick glance at his erection in her hands. She had a momentary look of both alarm and awe when she saw his nakedness.

Not wanting to disappoint him, she asked. "Does it feel," she paused, "the way you had hoped?"

"Better," he moaned, "your touch...it feels amazing, Sweetness. Absolutely, amazing."

She slid her hand up and down his shaft as she watched him, his eyes closed tightly as he sharply inhaled.

He could not believe they were finally here, at this point, with her giving him a hand job; he was very grateful for the sensations as his cock stood erect, fully engorged inside her soft palm.

"Tell me what you like, what turns you on?" She asked.

"I like everything you're doing, just don't stop. It feels too damned good."

She presumed she must have been doing it right because he groaned in pleasure, his mouth open and eyes tightly shut. "Keep stroking me... just like that. Ahh...Gabi..." he rasped out, and his hands gripped the sides of the boat.

She felt a surge of excitement within herself as she watched his reaction to her touch. A slight smile came to her lips; she felt oddly powerful as she eyed the acceleration of his breathing as his abdominals expanded and collapsed rapidly.

"Sweetness…You're going to make me come undone." His eyes flew open as he locked onto hers and his entire body shuddered as his chest broadened with air and he released.

He was stunned as he silently moved his hand to his jeans pocket, pulled out the bandana, and wiped his abs clean before he dazedly spoke. "My God, Sweetness."

He pulled his jeans up, zipped and buttoned them shut as he relaxed back down onto the pillows. He guided her to him as she rested her head on his chest.

"Was—was it okay?" She asked.

He then gently lifted her hand to his lips and tenderly kissed her fingers as he looked intently in her eyes as he spoke. "I've never been a man who's ever been at a loss for words, but Gabi, you've left me speechless." He paused. "It was good, amazingly good."

"Nick, I'm glad," her words came out slowly, "you liked it." She then turned her head toward him as she gazed up into his eyes. "But, I need you to know… the truth is I don't take sex- or any intimacy- casually."

She felt him squeeze her shoulder, an indication that it wasn't casual for him, as he pulled her closer to him.

"You know," she swallowed as she went on. "I have to share something with you, something that just may explain where I'm coming from. When I was younger, eleven or so, living in California, there'd been a woman who lived near us. An artist— and a free spirit, yet there was a deep sadness behind her eyes as she painted and the sorrow transcended into her work."

Gabrielle spoke softly and Nick listened intently. "I'd walk down to the beach and watch her paint these beautiful ocean scenes, sometimes for hours. Once, I asked her why she was so sad all the time. I was astonished by her answer, and it's something that's stuck with me all these years later. She shared with me she had lost her husband in a car accident. She told me he'd been her only love, her 'heart match,' and she couldn't see giving her heart to another."

Gabrielle's voice had an ethereal quality as she continued. "She said you only get one in a lifetime and if you lose it, as she had, you lose the core of your heart. She told me you can love other people, but your 'heart match' is truly joined to you, connected to you in some divine and intricate way." Her eyes embraced his face. "Nick, I feel as if you're my 'heart match.' You've come to mean so much to me."

He brushed her cheek with the back of his fingers.

"Gabi, I know what it took for you to do that to me. You mean a great deal to me, too. I want to show you how much you mean to me as well." He tightened his embrace around her and held her close.

The birds chirped as their rowboat swayed ever so slightly in its anchored place over the tranquil water's surface.

22
🍀 Gabrielle and Monty 🍀
New York – Monday morning - May, 12th, 1969

Monty Greer had been excitedly talking with the other designers when Gabrielle entered the drafting room. She set up her table to work, and he rushed over to her.

"Gabi, it's happened! My dreams have come true!" He pressed his hands together as his eyes lifted to the heavens.

"What's happened, Monty?" She asked getting caught up in his enthusiasm.

"He's coming, my obsession, Louis Laurendeau himself will be here next week. And you must come to the launch with us, so that we can experience his greatness together."

Her mouth fell open in surprise.

"I won't take no as an answer, you have to come with us." He continued. "Please, Gabi, you must come."

She knew her father had planned his visit for next week, but she had forgotten what a fan of his work Monty was. It was out of the question; she couldn't possibly go to the launch now.

"When is the launch?" She asked.

"Next week Wednesday, we're all going. Even Linda!"

"I'll let you know." She said as he went over to talk with some of the others in the room.

How could I tell Monty that I'll be having dinner with his 'obsession' next Wednesday night.

Wednesday night - May 21st, 1969

"Papa, I'm sorry I couldn't attend the launch of your line. But my co-worker who adores you told me it was absolutely spectacular."

They sat at the back of an obscure restaurant in Greenwich Village; Louis had assured his daughter that he had only wanted to see her and he didn't require a fancy restaurant.

"The launch was fine, too many people though." He smiled at her, his moss infused green eyes toyed with a smile. "You look different, ma chère fille."

She adored it when he called her 'dear daughter', his pet name for her, she grinned her answered to him, as they finished their dessert. "I'm happy, Papa."

"A little independence, it does all this for you?"

"Yes, that, and," she looked up at him bashfully. "I've met someone I really like."

"So, this is the look of love I see on my daughter's face? Who is he? What is his name? What does he do?"

"Slow down, Papa, I think it best if I keep all that information to myself. Because if I don't, I know you will prepare a complete dossier on him, in an effort to control my life again. And, before you ask, he doesn't know who I really am."

After dinner they linked arms and walked to her Brownstone. He liked the apartment and even commented that it was bigger than the place he and her mother had in Louisiana when they were first married.

Her sketch pad was on the table and Louis thumbed through it stopping at her drawing of the evening gown she had designed for the Black and White Ball.

"This is fantastique, Gabrielle!"

"Thanks, Papa." She beamed, "I'm glad you like it."

"I more than like it, I love it. This is why I need you to work for me. I need your vision at the House of Laurendeau."

"I have a job, and it's here. This is where I want to be."

"I cannot believe you don't want to work for me." He said somewhat annoyed. "What you are doing for VonShelles, you can most assuredly do for me- only it will be for your family."

"Papa, I don't want to rehash all of this. Just let it be, and let me enjoy visiting with you." She paused. "I promise you once I've proven myself on my own merits, then and only then will I work for you or even use the Laurendeau name."

23
 Gabrielle and Nick
New York – Friday evening - June 6th, 1969

At the top of a grand flowing staircase; Gabrielle placed her coat check stub into her evening bag. She peered down to the outer lobby of the ballroom from the main atrium of the palatial hotel, her eyes landed on Nick's back as he stood near a sturdy walnut wet bar with clusters of people around it.

A tall attractive man with wild, unruly dark hair and a beautiful blonde-haired woman stood with Nick. The woman stood in the middle of the two men, her hand placed on Nick's forearm as she leaned into him while she talked to both men. Nick appeared to lean away from her as he had turned his back to her.

At that moment, a tall slim brunette walked up to Nick and slid her hand up the nape of his neck as she spread her fire engine red lacquered fingertips through his thick dark hair; with a grin Nick playfully leaned his head back into the palm of her hand. She lowered her hand and rested it on his back and whispered something to him in his ear. Nick turned to her with a devilish white toothed smile, as he shook his head.

The brown-haired woman giggled and shrugged her shoulders looking back at Nick as she walked away. Nick looked at his watch, nonchalantly glanced up, and caught sight of Gabrielle on the stairs.

She smiled down at him, but felt graceless as she slowly began her descent of the carpeted staircase.

His mouth formed a smile at the sight of her; their eyes met, and his companions stopped talking and looked to where Nick's eyes were riveted.

Gabrielle possessed a unique combination of purity and sultriness; her golden-brown hair had been romantically styled in an upsweep as loose curled tendrils framed her flawless face; at her lobes were a pair of black onyx and diamond teardrop earrings that matched the elegant necklace at her throat and the bracelet on her delicate wrist.

The dress she designed hugged her curvy body in a black strapless mermaid style with a sweetheart-topped bodice. Fanning out from below her knees were soft sheer black and white tulle that gave the illusion she was walking on a cloud as it spread out beneath her. Unfortunately, she'd worn heels higher than usual, and coupled with the snugness of the dress, she felt wobbly on the stairs.

Don't fall, don't fall. Just go slow. She told herself.

The man next to Nick let out a low whistle and said, "Oh my Lord, I think I've died and am now in heaven," he swallowed. "Who is that angel? And how can I clip those wings?"

"Sorry, Richard," Nick said with his gaze steadfast upon

Gabrielle's face. "This one is all mine."

"Aren't they all, Caine?" Richard remarked with obvious sarcasm. "But, lucky me, you don't mind sharing."

Nick briefly looked back at Richard but otherwise ignored the comment and moved toward the stairs to Gabrielle. Claudia's hand slid from his arm as he moved away.

Claudia's eyes tapered into tiny slits. She looked at Richard and plastered a cultured smile at her lips. "Looks like someone's found a shiny new toy."

Nick made it to Gabrielle just as she started to fall down the stairs, he caught her as she fell into his arms. He held her in his arms, then helped her to stand upright in front of him.

"Somebody sure knows how to make an entrance." He softly chuckled. "You okay?"

"I'm fine," she blushed, "thank you for being there."

"No place I'd rather be. You look stunning, Gabi."

"You're looking pretty good yourself," she tilted her head toward him. "You are quite fetching in a tux. And, I can see you have the girls all swooning just to be near you."

Nick lifted an eyebrow and looked back toward Claudia who was talking with Richard as she looked at him and Gabrielle.

"Who? Her?" His eyes were back on Gabrielle. "That's just Claudia Avery; she's the wife of one of the Club's partners. She's harmless," his smile broadened, "but tell me, were you jealous?"

"Hardly," she started and then she grinned at him

demurely. "Okay, maybe just a little bit, because she is beautiful, so was the brunette."

"Sweetness, you have nothing to worry about, my eyes are only on you."

"Now that's something I like to hear." She replied and she changed topic and remarked. "It's really crowded in here, isn't it?" She looked away from him as she looked around the space, noting that the chandeliers in the lobby glittered like diamonds above their heads.

"They're only serving cocktails right now, dinner will be in about ten minutes, so everyone will soon be going into the ballroom to be seated."

Nick noticed her necklace and remarked with the slant of his head, "I love your jewels," he then added with concern, "They look expensive, you didn't buy those for tonight did you?"

"N-no," she stammered, caught off guard. "They are b-borrowed."

"Good, I'd hate to think of you spending any of your hard-earned dollars just for tonight. They're sparkly, but I have to tell you, they pale compared to the jewel that you are to me."

"Thank you, Nick." Blushing, she lowered her head.

"You got here just in time, and, Milady," he grinned with a twinkle in his eye. "I still have a particular bone of contention to pick with you." He sighed. "Why didn't you let me pick you up so that we could arrive together?" His eyes stared greedily at her as he leaned in to her ear and whispered. "I want there to be no mistake, I want everyone to know we belong together."

The intimate sound of his voice and words sent a shiver down her spine, she liked the sound of them belonging together.

"I'm sorry, but I just wasn't ready; it took Esther forever to do my hair. Will you forgive me if I promise to leave with you?" She teased, her eyes sparkling.

"I believe it's very possible, but only if you throw in a special *goodnight kiss*."

"I think that can most definitely be arranged," a naughty smile spread at her lips.

A *goodnight kiss* was an inside term for their brand of sex; she had progressed rapidly from *hand-jobs* to oral sex, and she found that she loved watching him come undone. Having that kind of power over him made her drunk, the simple thought of it and him, excited her.

Nick lightly kissed her cheek and whispered into her ear, "I can't wait."

She inhaled his provocative scent, Aramis coupled with his natural essence, *the Nick scent*, she wished at that moment, they weren't on display for all to see, so she could wield her special power over him.

She closed her eyes to the passion building up inside her; this man was hers and she had made up her mind that tonight she would have him fully and in every way possible.

All eyes were on them as they made a strikingly handsome

couple, his dark hair and brows offset by his intense blue eyes. Standing tall in a black tuxedo and black satin cummerbund balanced by his glaring white shirt with ribbed ruffles edged in black at the shirt's front, he looked stylish and debonair. She complemented him well, her tawny golden skin and amber-green eyes that glittered like rare jewels themselves. Her dress clung to her body, accentuating her hourglass figure.

Nick held out his arm to her, and she took it while looking up at him. His pride was undeniable and he felt tiny pangs of constriction around his heart, the ones he got every time he looked at her or if he even thought of her.

They walked her over to the lobby bar where the others stood, and he introduced Gabrielle as his girlfriend to Richard Collier and Claudia Avery.

"It's a pleasure to make your acquaintances," she said to both with a smile.

"So you're the girl who has our Nick all tied up in knots," Claudia smiled brightly, "It's nice to finally meet you, Gabrielle."

"Tied up in knots?" Gabrielle blushed as she returned Claudia's smile. "I wasn't aware that had occurred, but, I suppose now that you mention it." She lifted a brow as she beamed at Claudia. "I guess we are pretty well tethered together."

Nick had a huge grin on his face. "Happily tethered, I might add." Nick said as he turned toward the bar and ordered drinks for them.

Nick handed her a glass of red wine, and then moved and stood at Gabrielle's side and rested his hand at the small of her back just slightly above the generous mounds of her derrière.

"Oh, come now, Nick, you can't invite this enchanting creature here and expect to keep her all to yourself." Richard said taking ahold of Gabrielle's free arm as he led her away by the elbow.

She tilted her head back at Nick and shrugged her shoulders as she walked with Richard into the ballroom where people had started to file in. Nick and Claudia followed close behind them.

Claudia stopped him with a hand on his arm as she leaned into him. "She's a beautiful girl, Nicky; I see why you're so smitten, enjoy your dinner. I've got to locate Harold. Save a dance for me, will you?" A seductive smile lit up her pink lips.

"I'm sorry, Claudia, I'm here with Gabrielle. My dance card for tonight, and honestly every night, is full." He lifted a brow. "But, don't let it prevent you from enjoying your evening."

Nick turned away from her and used long strides to catch up to Gabrielle and Richard just as they were sitting down at one of the round tables. He moved over to them, stood directly behind Gabrielle's chair, and placed both of his hands on her bare shoulders. Nick cupped her bare shoulders and felt her shiver under his palms as he touched her skin, he smiled as he spoke.

"Gabrielle, now you see what happens when a man comes

stag to one of these things? He tries to hone in on someone else's girl." He grinned playfully at Richard. "Very well, tonight you may sit to the left of her, but just know that I'm Mr. Right."

She lightly laughed at Nick's comment as she beheld the elegant ballroom. All the round tables were covered with white linen cloths, along with large black runners placed in the center. The centerpieces had one red rose surrounded by a cluster of white carnations tied with black and white ribbons.

A soft faceted glow emanated from the reflection of candles in crystal holders as they sat atop cut mirror tops on each table. Black fabric draped over the chairs with huge white bows adorning them. Black and white helium filled balloons scattered above the ceiling with silver ties that stretched long in mid-air over the dance floor.

Gabrielle remarked as she looked around the space, "It's really lovely in here; they did a superb job with the room."

"We have but one person to thank for the motif of the ballroom," Richard said with a raised eyebrow. "This whole thing is the brainchild of our one and only Claudia Avery. The woman is a marvel, I tell you. Truly, she's a woman with many hidden talents. Don't you agree, Nick?" He covertly grinned at Nick.

Gabrielle didn't catch the astute wink and smile from Richard to Nick.

Nick nodded his head as he tersely replied, "Yes, I would have to agree, too many to count."

As they ate their dinners she found she liked that two of the most attractive men in room were vying for her attention. If she didn't know any better, she would think that Nick was getting a little jealous over the interactions she and Richard were having. After dinner, the music began, and the band played an instrumental version of Elvis' "Can't Help Falling in Love."

Nick whisked her away to the empty dance floor and held her close. "I can hardly wait for that goodnight kiss you've promised me; I'm getting hard just thinking about your luscious mouth."

"I can see that," she glanced at his crotch. "But you shouldn't say such things, because it makes me want to get on my knees and suck you right here and right now... *Mr. Right.* Gawkers, be damned."

No matter what he said to her, she always seemed to best him in their little game of sexual banter. Gabrielle got to him in ways no other woman had, but somehow when she talked dirty, it amplified his desire for her.

"So how about those Mets?" He said with a grin.

"Yes, Nick, how about those Mets?" Amused, she laughed.

She noticed they were the only couple on the dance floor. She glanced around at the people seated and found that a good many of them were watching them. She further noted, Nick didn't seem to mind that they were being watched.

"To Sir with Love," by Lulu was the next offering from the band, and she smiled at Nick as they danced.

"Nick, just like the song, you've taught me so much."

"You are a wonderful student, but you are teaching me a thing or two as well." He gave her a slanted grin.

They were soon joined by other couples on the floor as they danced to Glenn Miller's "In the Mood" and she giggled to see Nick actually cutting loose and having fun.

"Are you enjoying yourself?" He asked over the loud music.

"I'm having a blast." She tilted her head back. "Wow, Nick, I didn't know it, but you're a pretty good dancer." She smiled approvingly.

"Thank you, but I'm pleased to inform you, I do my best dancing between the sheets."

"You just can't stop, can you?" She arched a playful warning eyebrow, "Are we going to go down that road yet again?" She licked her lips in preparation.

"No, I'm just stating the facts ma'am, just the facts." His eyes crinkled with laughter.

When the song ended, the band started another one, but she was parched. "I need some water, and I have to make some minor repairs." She excused herself and headed to the Ladies room.

Claudia appeared at Nick's elbow. "How about a dance, Nick. Do you have room on your card now?"

"No, Claudia, truthfully, I don't, but maybe," he turned to his left. "Richard, do you think you could take Claudia out on the dance floor? She seems to be in need of a partner."

Richard politely reached for Claudia's hand.

"That's very gentlemanly of you, Richard." She didn't look at Richard as she spoke. "You should give lessons, because some could benefit from them." Claudia leveled her stony gaze at Nick. "I'm sorry, but I've changed my mind; I think I will sit this one out after all. Thank you anyway, Richard." Hostilely she walked away as she headed toward the band.

"Somebody's not too happy with you, my friend." Richard said as he plopped the olive from his martini into his mouth.

"I really couldn't care less. She's someone else's problem to deal with, not mine." Nick replied offhandedly.

"I would have to agree with you there, and I completely understand. If I had the enchanting Gabrielle, I wouldn't care either." He leaned in closer to Nick. "I've got to say, old chum, you are one lucky son of a bitch. To have that beautiful girl look at you the way she looks at you, I'd positively kill for that."

"Believe me, Richard; I know just how lucky I am."

"Not willing to share this one, I take it?" He asked with a sheepish grin.

"Sorry pal. Not in this lifetime, she's all mine."

24
❧ Gabrielle and Claudia ❧

New York – Friday evening - June 6th, 1969

Gabrielle exited from of one of the stalls in the ladies' room as Claudia Avery entered. She gave Claudia a friendly smile as she washed her hands at the sink.

"I love your dress, Mrs. Avery. A Balmain, isn't it?" Claudia wore a very lovely, very expensive Pierre Balmain creation in white.

"Why thank you, it is." Claudia smiled in return with a nod of her head in Gabrielle's direction. "I see you know your designers. And, I must say, your dress is very becoming on you."

"Thank you, it was just finished today. It's why I ran a little late this evening." Gabrielle answered amiably as Claudia turned toward the mirror.

"Hence, the dramatic entrance." Claudia looked loftily at the ceiling then quickly back at Gabrielle. "Finished today? My goodness, did you make it yourself?" She smirked, "My, oh my, Nick has found himself a talented one this time."

This time? "No Mrs. Avery, I didn't make it myself."

Gabrielle said as she now eyed Claudia cautiously sensing this woman did not want to extend a hand in friendship to her. "I designed it and had one of our studio's seamstresses put it all together for me." *Is she being condescending to me?*

Gabrielle dried her hands on one of the towels laid out on the marble countertop; she leaned in closer toward the mirror to put on more of her Clairol Flicker stick lip-gloss. She slid her hands into her elbow length black gloves.

"You're a clothing designer? Now I'm officially hurt," a pout formed on Claudia's frosted pink lips. "Nick never mentioned that fact to me."

"Hurt? Don't be, Mrs. Avery." Gabrielle lifted an eyebrow as she watched Claudia in the mirror. "I can't imagine what I do for a living would never come up as a topic of discussion between you and Nick."

"Oh," Claudia reapplied more of her pink frosted lipstick as she spoke, "you would be surprised at what comes up," she paused and then almost purred, "in our conversations."

She used a fingertip to smooth out the lip color as her eyes narrowed and glided towards Gabrielle's mirrored reflection. "We are really rather close friends, you see."

Gabrielle mutely froze in place as it just hit her, *could Claudia be one of 'those' women in Nick's life?*

"Can you tell me, what exactly *close* means, Claudia?"

Gabrielle's palms started to sweat as she waited for the answer. *Faceless, nameless, women were one thing, but, to be truly engaging in conversation with one of them puts Nick's past into a whole other sphere.* "I feel you're trying to convey something to me here, so please, just get to your point."

"I'm just happy to see Nick has found the girl that has given him cause to," her eyes held a craftiness that Gabrielle found unnerving, "settle down somewhat, or tied down so to speak. I believe the word you used earlier was *tethered.* I just feel you need to be aware of some things," she smiled coyly.

Gabrielle interrupted her. "If you're trying to tell me about his past with women, I'm well aware of it, and frankly I really don't care or trouble myself about who he's been with in the past. You see, it doesn't have any effect on our relationship one iota. And just for the record, I'm not trying to tie Nick down, far from it."

Claudia straightened her back. "Not caring is one thing, but, you must be aware, *our boy* has a voracious appetite in bed. An appetite that hasn't been pacified by just one woman. Since I have firsthand knowledge that you haven't been tending to those needs for him, I feel you need to know."

With Claudia referring to Nick as *'our boy'?* The familiarity within her statement did not lose its meaning on Gabrielle as she shifted her weight from one foot to the other.

Claudia smoothed the front of her elegant one-shouldered beaded gown with a glide of her hand as she continued. "There are plenty of women, just lining up, who would love to see to his sexual needs," she paused with a lifted brow. "Since you find yourself apparently lacking in that particular area."

Gabrielle's eyes narrowed at Claudia's image in the

mirror. "Would that line include the likes of you, Claudia?" She started to fume.

"Heavens no, Gabrielle," Claudia airily laughed. "I never wait in line for anything. Waiting in line for something is for the less fortunate and clearly, my dear, that's not my situation."

"Claudia, your anxiety about Nick's sexual needs are indeed significant, though perhaps they are no longer your concern."

"Perhaps," she turned to face Gabrielle. "But I will say this," she dreamily closed, then opened her knowing eyes. "If you do choose to be with Nick in that way, you simply must have Antonio Vivaldi's 'I Solisti Veneti' as a back drop. Nick is…" She touched her fingers to her frosted lips then extended them in a small flourish with a kiss sound. "Magnifique! Believe me, he does not disappoint. He is an absolute stellar performer in bed. Oh, and regarding being tied down, don't knock it until you've tried it. Just make sure he uses the silk ropes, you'll thank me later."

Gabrielle's face went pallid, *Vivaldi? So, this is the classical music lover. How many times had his damned radio been set to play classical music when I got into his car? Had he been seeing Claudia this entire time? While I was being as intimate as I could be with him, he'd been screwing this callous witch behind my back. Silk ropes? What the hell is that about?'*

As they stood in front of the ladies' room marble sinks, she felt as if the floor beneath her was about to swallow her whole. She silently opened her evening bag and retrieved her coat check stub with shaking fingers. She knew she was playing right into Claudia's hand, but she didn't care. She had to get out of there, out of this place, to get away from Claudia and as far away from Nick as possible.

"What? You're not leaving, are you?" Claudia feigned surprise. "So soon? I'd love to get your number; I'm hoping, that maybe you could design something for me."

"I suppose I could." Mustering up the courage, Gabrielle replied as she gave Claudia an icy stare. "But," she snapped her evening bag shut, "the only thing I would ever design for you is a noose. Fashioned out of those silk ropes, you awful bitch." She turned and pushed her way through the door.

Nick stood just outside the ballroom doors talking with an older man, who appeared to be in his mid to late-seventies when she walked to them. Nick smiled in her direction when she'd reached them.

"Gabrielle, I'd like you to meet one of the athletic club's founding partners."

She could not even bring herself to look at Nick as she robotically smiled at the elder man. The man took her hand, and she heard the good-natured tone in Nick's voice. "Harold Avery, I'd like you to meet my girlfriend, Gabrielle Lawrence. So don't try to push her to purchase a membership." Nick joked.

Harold held her hand in his and kissed her gloved knuckle. "Oh, I wouldn't dream of it." He smiled up at her. "Well now, Caine. You didn't tell me how lovely she was. It's my utmost pleasure to meet you, Miss Lawrence."

Another Avery? *This place seems to be overrun with them.* She quickly recovered as she remarked. "Thank you, Mr. Avery. It's nice to meet you as well. Avery?" She queried. "As in, Claudia Avery?" She held her breath.

"Guilty as charged," His kind weathered face creased with a grin, "Claudia is my wife, but please don't hold it against me." Harold laughed at his own little joke.

Harold Avery is Claudia's husband. He looked old enough to be her father if not her grandfather, she could hear the musical strains of Vivaldi's "I Solisti Veneti" coming from the ballroom.

It all became so surreal to her, *had Claudia planned for that particular piece to be playing right now for my benefit? Of course, she had, a bit of salt for the freshly picked wound.*

She looked at Nick as he tilted his head to her in a perplexed manner; she then moved her dazed face back to Harold. "Mr. Avery, it was very nice meeting you, but, I have to apologize because I was just leaving." She scanned the floor as she spoke. "Nick, could you please get my wrap for me?" She then looked compassionately at Harold Avery, who quietly stood in place as he glanced from Nick and then to Gabrielle as she held out her coat check stub to Nick.

"But Gabi, the night is still young." Nick was puzzled as he took the stub from her trembling fingers. "I thought you wanted to dance some more. Are you sure we have to leave so soon?"

"No Nick, *we* don't have to leave, but *I* do. You can do as you please, because I don't feel very much like dancing or anything else, anymore."

"Gabrielle, are you ill?" Nick moved closer to her.

"No, I'm not ill. I just need to go." Her eyes rose to his and pleaded as her lips trembled. She looked as if she were on the verge of tears. "My wrap, Nick, please."

"Yes, of course. I'll go get it for you." He nodded, turned on his heels, and headed up the stairs to the coat check area.

Harold Avery took ahold of her hand and guided her inside the ballroom. "I know you said you no longer feel like dancing," he smiled with a twinkle in his dulled eyes, "but, you simply must grace me with at least one dance, Miss Lawrence." He smiled at her. "My wife doesn't care very much for dancing with me anymore and I do so miss it. Please, indulge an old man by making me the envy of every man in attendance." He gallantly bent at the waist and kissed her gloved hand again. "So, would you please be my Ginger?"

The music selection changed to *Strangers in The Night.* Coupled with her unexpected feelings of sympathy for the kind elder gentleman, she forced herself to swallow her ire for the time being as the compassion she felt for him overtook her.

"You're quite the charmer, aren't you?" She returned his smile as she commented. "How could I say no to such a genteel invitation. I would be so honored to dance with you, Mr. Avery…, ah, I mean Fred."

25
❧ Nick, Gabrielle and Claudia ❧
New York – Friday evening - June 6th, 1969

Nick headed up to the coat check, but there was no one manning the desk; he went behind the counter and into the coatroom himself, checking her stub's number he reached up to retrieve her wrap. He felt a hand reach around from behind and grab at his crotch.

"Gabi, what th…"

"Oh, come on, Nicky," he heard her voice, but it wasn't Gabrielle's. "You don't think your prissy little girlfriend would ever have the nerve to touch your cock, do you?"

Claudia laughed as he roughly removed her hand from his body and turned around to face her.

"Damn it, Claudia, I don't know what the hell you think you're doing. Gabrielle is downstairs, and I made it clear you and I are finished. I'm not cheating on Gabi."

"Nicky, you yourself have said it time and time again that *blowjobs* aren't cheating. Let's see, how does that catchy little apothegm of yours go exactly? *'eatin' ain't cheatin' and suckin' ain't fuckin.'* Why not let me give you some relief? You know I love pleasuring you. I know you love it too. I miss you, Nicky, it's been way too long."

He pulled Gabrielle's wrap from the hanger.

"Not interested." He stated gruffly as he pushed past her.

Nick soon stood by the opened double doors of the ballroom, there were a spattering of couples on the dance floor. Nick saw Gabrielle as she elegantly danced with Harold Avery. The gentle goodness exuded from her as she looked at Harold. *God, she is lovely.*

Nick glanced about the room and looked upon the faces of some of the other men who were clustered together in small groups; some of them looked at Gabrielle too. They spoke with their companions and looked her way as they stood at the bar smoking cigars and cigarettes while consuming their drinks.

Nick watched Gabrielle, she was graceful as Harold Avery swept her along in the Waltz, but more so, it's the way she beheld him with pure kindness. They were talking as they danced, and Nick could see the warmth of her laugher and Harold's eyes crinkled. Harold seemed to be charmed by her, Nick noted. *Hell, who wouldn't be charmed by her? God, just look at her, she is exquisite.* And though Nick knew Gabrielle to be a keeper, he had come to realize her inner beauty transcended her exterior.

As he watched her, he felt a tight seizing in his chest; his feelings ran deep and he wanted her, to know *her* and all of her intimate places, yet he waited. Honestly, he'd wait for her for as long as she needed him to.

At song's end, Harold took her gloved hand and pressed his lips to her knuckle and Gabrielle slightly bowed her head as she thanked Harold for the dance. She soon reached Nick as he leaned against the doorway holding her wrap. She silently took her wrap from him and threw it over her bare arm as she looked straight ahead and eyed Claudia, who stood at the lobby bar talking with Richard. With an arctic glare fixed on Claudia, she addressed Nick without looking at him, "Thank you for inviting me, Nick; it was a... an eye-opening experience."

Nick's eyes followed her gaze to Claudia's direction and something in his gut suddenly clinched hard like a fist. He knew Claudia had upset her.

Gabrielle headed for the stairs while sliding the wrap over her shoulders and closed the collar's clasp; then she hoisted up her dress as high as she could and hurried up the stairs.

Nick caught Claudia's eye as his mouth pressed into a hard, thin line before he quickly followed Gabrielle up the steps and out the door.

Outside, Gabrielle turned to the hotel's doorman, "Excuse me, I'm in need of a taxi, please." She said as her eyes started to mist with tears.

"Gabi?" Nick said when he reached her, "I can see you're upset," obvious angst in his voice. "Let's talk about it, okay?"

He tried to touch her on her shoulder, but she jerked away from his hand. "The valet will get my car. Please, let me drive you home, Gabrielle." Nick insisted.

"I need a taxi." She repeated to the doorman.

The confused doorman looked at Gabrielle's misty eyes and then back at Nick. Instead of addressing Gabrielle, he spoke to Nick. "Sir?" He asked perplexed.

"She doesn't need a cab." Nick offered. "I'll be driving her home." Nick said as he handed the doorman his valet ticket. "Have the valet bring my car."

Gabrielle was floored; she could not believe the doorman was overlooking her and disregarding her request.

"Look, Ronald," she calmly addressed him by the name she saw on his nameplate. "I'm not sure why you are conferring with him?" Gabrielle looked back at the face of the doorman and evenly stated. "I'm the one who needs a taxi." She pulled a bill out of her evening bag. "Now, will you hail me one or will I have to do it myself?"

Ronald instantly raised his arm toward the taxi stands and whistled. He motioned for a taxicab to pull up to where he pointed. She placed the bill onto Ronald's palm as he rushed to open the door for her.

She let her tears flow as she entered the safe haven of the backseat of the taxicab as it spirited her far away from that place and Nick.

Nick stood beside the doorman as they both watched the taxicab disappear into the night. "I'll be right back," he told Ronald. "Hold my car for me when it gets here."

Nick went back inside, and roughly grabbed Claudia by the arm and pulled her away from the bar. He led her into an alcove away from any curious eyes or ears.

"What's the matter, Nicky? Cinderella leave already?" Claudia smiled up at him. "It's not even close to midnight. With her quick exit one wonders if she had time to have left you with her glass slipper." She giggled.

"What the hell did you do?" He said, placing splayed fingers on his hips. "What did you say to her?" His eyes glared and his breathing came fast.

"You need to calm down, Nicky, because I don't know what you're talking about; I had nothing to do with your 'little' girlfriend running off like that."

"I don't believe you. You had a hand in this, of that I'm sure. Gabi was fine and having a good time."

"Maybe she just realized what she's up against, and she knows she's just not the girl for you. I mean, come on." Claudia mockingly pouted her lips as she disdainfully sniffed the air. "She even has the nauseating scent of innocence; it seems to ooze from her, through every pore." She narrowed her eyes. "There is no way in hell she could ever satisfy a man like you. Nick, you yourself have to know it. I know she's a pretty girl, but pretty girls are a dime a dozen around here."

Frustration taking hold, he raised his hands and interlaced his fingers and placed them on top of his head. "You told her about us, didn't you? I know you did; this is all because of you." He lowered his hands and crossed his arms at his chest, but he knew he wasn't blameless in any of this either.

"So what if I did, I did you a favor. Because she'll never sleep with you; she's too virtuous for it."

"You're a fucking cunt, Claudia." He spat his words.

"I'll be your *fucking* cunt any day of the week, Nicky." She lowered her voice seductively. "Because unlike the little babe in the woods you have there, I'm more than willing to be your sex puppet. You can do anything you damn well please with me and you know it."

"It's not about sex!" he snapped. "She means...," he breathed in deep. "This has gone way beyond anything involving sex. Can't you see?"

"Good grief, Nicky." Her brow arched as she pressed her lips together. "Don't tell me you've gone and fallen in love with that... 'little' girl." Her mouth twisted with disgust. "Don't you know love is just not in the cards for a man like you?" She put her hands on her hips. "You would have to wine and dine her, shower her with flowers and words of undying love and devotion in order to have her. She would expect you to *'make love'* to her, not fuck her. We both know fucking is all it's about for you, that's all it's ever been about; licentious *'fucking sex'* is you at your best."

The riposte of her words made him flinch.

"You're not the boyfriend type," she continued, "you don't know how to be a boyfriend. You are the sort of man who has one purpose and one purpose only, to please women—many women—sexually. You have a gift, my darling, and it would be sinful to waste it on one woman and clearly this 'little' girl wouldn't know how to appreciate the talents you are in possession of."

Suddenly, he dropped his hands to his sides as they clinched into tight fists and his eyes filled with distress and alarm. "Just shut the hell up, Claudia." *Could she be right? Maybe I'm not the boyfriend type. But for Gabi, I'll give it my best effort, that is if she'll let me; I've got to fix this.*

"Claudia, you know I've always counted you as a friend, we've shared a lot, and I'm not just talking about sex." His eyes narrowed at her. "But if you've blown things for me with Gabrielle," he pointed an angry finger in her face. "You need to know I will never forgive you for it. Do you understand me? Not ever."

Nick turned and walked away, and she threw invisible daggers to the back of his head with her frosted pink mouth set in a firm straight line.

26

🥀 Gabrielle and Nick 🥀

New York – Friday evening - June 6th, 1969

Gabrielle had a good bottle of champagne in a bucket of ice in front of her. Little did she know that she'd be holding the filled fluted glass of the golden bubbly liquid alone. She sat on her couch and sadly listened to one of her favorite albums, *Tom Jones: The Golden Hits*, just as 'I'll Never Fall in Love Again' played. Still fully dressed in her ball gown, she'd kicked off her heels and thrown her wrap over a chair.

This night did not turn out at all the way I thought it would; if it had, Nick would be here with me right now in the midst of making love to me for the first time as I had planned.

A few weeks ago, she had shared with her sister, Suzette, the feelings she'd been having for Nick. Suzette encouraged her to be practical and get on some sort of birth control. Gabrielle had typically found Suzette's advice to be sensible and sound, so she listened, and she'd been on the pill for a month.

Suzette told her she should be okay to have sex without the fear of pregnancy by now. "What's holding you back? If you have feelings for him and don't want to wait for marriage, then why not?" Suzette also shared with her, "First-time sex is a way to fully experience that special oneness with someone you care about."

However, Gabrielle knew she couldn't be the free spirit in regards to sex like Suzette was; but she had confided that she thought Nick had been the one. Now as it turned out, she had been miserably mistaken. Her thoughts were interrupted as she heard the loud buzz of the intercom; in stocking feet she went to the door, her dress dragging on the floor behind her.

Knowing it had to be him, she spoke into the intercom. "Go away, Nick."

"Gabi, we need to talk." He said through the speaker. "You have to give me a chance to explain."

"I can't talk about it now. I'll call you tomorrow, we'll discuss it then."

"The hell we will! I'm going to stay right here until you open this door," he stated. "We need to talk this thing through and right now!" His tone became softer. "Gabi, come on. Just open the door so we can discuss this."

"I don't want to talk. I can't… not right now. Please, I need you to go away."

"How can I fix this, if you won't talk with me?" He asked solemnly.

"There's nothing for you to fix. I don't want to talk to you or even see you right now. Just stop all of this… and leave me alone." She paused, and then threatened, "Don't make me call Gus."

"Gabrielle, you can call whomever you damn well please, but I'm not going anywhere until you hear me out... I'll wake up this entire goddamned building if I have to."

Something in his voice had articulated to her that he would most assuredly do it, and she sighed heavily.

He heard the buzz at the door to allow him access, and he quickly ran up the stairs to her front door.

She opened the door, but stood in the doorway blocking the doorframe. "I don't want to talk with you, Nick. And I won't have you disturbing my neighbors with any of your bullshit, so please, try to at least act like a gentleman and go away!"

He swiftly placed his hands on both sides of her waist and without warning, he easily lifted her up off the floor where she stood.

"Goddammit Nick! You brute! You put me down, this frigging instant!"

Nick ignored her reprimanding cries as he carried her effortlessly though the doorway and into the apartment under her kicking protests as he closed the door with a back kick of his foot.

"Well, you're going to talk with me," he said gruffly and then smiled just a little, "like it or not." He walked with her in his lifted hands and then plopped her down onto the couch in the living room.

"You know what, Nick? You're an ass." She hissed at him as she glared up at him, the sheer and tulle fabrics of her dress looked like a tangled mess around her legs.

"So, I'm an ass," he threw his hands in the air. "Believe me, I've been called worse."

"Oh, I can believe it, and I'll bet you anything, whatever you were called was probably well deserved." She straightened up and lifted herself up off the couch. "How dare you force your way in here like this?"

"We need to clear the air. Gabi, and to do it, we have to talk. I need to know exactly what happened."

"What happened?" She scowled. "Your 'girlfriend' Claudia Avery is what happened; she met up with me in the ladies' room."

She placed her hands defiantly on her hips, her eyes narrowed as she fixed them directly on his deep blue irises, Nick's jaw visibly clinched hard with tension as he lowered his eyes and focused on the floor.

"Claudia is not my girlfriend," he immediately looked her square in the face. "You are, and I want to keep it that way."

"Well," her head slanted, "you have a funny way of showing me when you invite me to a function where a woman you are currently screwing is in attendance, along with her long-suffering husband."

He felt the air get thick, and the heat crept up his neck and flushed his face. He untied his bowtie, but left it hang loose around his neck as he unbuttoned the top button of his shirt.

"I'm not screwing her," he looked away, "not any longer. And for the record, I haven't for a while."

"Not for a while, huh? Oh, well, I guess that makes it all alright then." She replied, her voice snarled with sarcasm. "I'm surprised you're not patting yourself on the back for that one, Nick." Continuing, she shook her head in disgust. "I can't believe you think it's okay to have slept with her at all. How you could even talk with poor Harold, let alone work for him," the repulsion on her face clear and sure, "knowing you've had sex with his wife behind his back is entirely beyond me."

"Wait a minute," he shook his head. "Longsuffering? Behind his back?" He gave a hollow laugh as he rolled his eyes upward, and took a deep breath. "Harold knows all about it; as a matter of fact, he encourages it. And what's more he likes to watch."

Gabrielle's jaw dropped wide open, struck mute by this new disclosure. "Likes to watch?" She questioned him to be sure, of what she had just heard. "Watch you having sex with his wife?"

Nick mutely nodded his head, but looked away, unable to keep eye contact with her.

Her mouth formed an incredulous 'O' as she shook her head in disbelief.

"Just what kind of people are you?"

"Immoral ones, I suppose," he looked remorseful. "But, Gabi, I've told you I stopped seeing her in that way. It's not what I want. You are all I need; I only want you."

"Ni-Nick, in light of this new revelation... I'm sorry to say it, but I don't even know who you are. I don't know if I can turn a blind eye to this or to your past... I thought I could, but now I'm not so sure, especially when it's been thrown so deliberately and so blatantly in my face." Pain filled her face as she frowned. "Just, how many Claudias are out there?"

"Gabi, she's been the only woman I'd developed the closest thing to any type of relationship with." His tormented eyes gazed at her. "We were friends before we ever..." He shifted his weight from one foot to the other as he raked his fingers through his hair. "Before we ever slept together." He cleared his throat; it suddenly felt scratchy as if he'd swallowed a sheet of sandpaper. "Gabi, I know I have no right to ask, but," he heavily sighed. "Can you find it within your heart to forgive me for putting you in the position where you had to be subjected to the Avery's without warning or the benefit of the knowledge of our sordid history?"

"If you are looking for some sort of absolution here, Nick," she solemnly shook her head, "that is something not within my power. You'll have to see a Priest for that, because to me, this whole situation goes way beyond immoral."

"No, Gabi, you *are* the only one who has that kind of power over me because yours is the only forgiveness I need or want." His brow furrowed. "I don't need to have to confess anything to a priest and be told to say a bunch of Hail Mary's or Our Fathers to clear a troubled conscience; I knew what I was doing. I also knew on some level it was unquestionably decadent behavior," he exhaled. "But I seized an opportunity to sleep with a willing woman." His sapphire eyes turned dark. "With no strings attached, like most any young red blooded male would."

He watched her with intensity as she stood, dazed.

"I just hope I haven't lost you, or what we have, over this. Something I did in my past," he extended his hands to her with his palms up as he said with his guilt-riddled voice. "Because believe me, she and any other woman I have been with is my past. Gabrielle, you are my future."

She continued to look troubled; tears pooled in her eyes and threatened to fall, sadness filled her throat in a huge lump as her voice cracked.

"I tho…thought we were headed in that direction, towards a future together." Her disheartened eyes half closed as she looked down and then back up to his downcast eyes. "You said you hadn't been with her in a while. Can you tell me what 'a while' is? When was the last time you slept with Claudia or any other woman for that matter?"

He lowered his eyes even further knowing he had to be honest and come clean to her if he had any hope of receiving her forgiveness. "Ahh…," he paused, "I finally ended things with her about a month ago."

She silently let his response sink in.

"A month ago? Nick, that's barely a week before that Saturday, when we were in the rowboat, the first time that I… I touched you…" Crestfallen, she lifted her face towards the ceiling. "This is just too much for me to take in." She wiped away at the tear as it fell. "I don't know if I can move past this, Nick."

With the realization that he'd most definitely been sleeping with Claudia while he'd been seeing her, Gabrielle now understood Claudia's meaning from their conversation in the bathroom: "That's how she knew we hadn't slept together, isn't it? You had to have told her, to keep your relationship alive. So she could take care of your carnal needs, because as Claudia informed me, I'm sorely lacking in that area." Her head throbbed and somehow the room seemed to be spinning.

"Hold on a minute here," he shook his head. "I've never told Claudia anything about what we've done or haven't done; it's none of her business."

"If you never told her, then how did she know, Nick? How did she know to insinuate I was unwilling or incapable of satisfying you if she had no idea?"

He thought back to Claudia's comments that first time in the locker room after he had started seeing Gabrielle. "Gabi, when you and I started seeing each other, I had stopped seeing her. I did, but unfortunately, it was short lived. She caught me off guard one Saturday and my body responded to her touch. I-it needed, release. So, my guess is she only assumed that…"

"That your needs weren't being met." She finished his sentence for him as she moved to the couch and sat down, not trusting her legs to hold her any further.

He knelt on one knee before her and looked up into her stunned tortured eyes. "I'm so sorry, Gabi. Please, forgive me, for my body's weakness and my stupid mistake of misleading you about what I had with Claudia."

"You keep asking me for forgiveness; I don't know who you think I am, but I'm not some holy person you can ask such things. I'm just a woman who has foolishly fallen for a man who has such little regard for me. So little, in fact, he could carry on an affair with another woman with nary a thought for me or my feelings."

"Gabi, I do care about your feelings, can't you see that?" With anguished eyes, he beheld her. "That's why I'm here, and it's why I broke it off with her." He felt his chest tighten and squeeze with the hearing of her declaration she had fallen for him, because he knew he felt the same way about her, but telling her right now would just have a hollow ring to it.

"You know what I think? I think you broke it off with her when I started satisfying a little bit of your sexual needs by stroking you and then ultimately giving you blow jobs and not a second before." She turned away from him, and for the first time, regret entered her heart.

"No! I had decided long before that, I felt guilty seeing her. Guilt is something I've never felt before where any woman was concerned. I realized I couldn't continue seeing her when I knew I had definite feelings for you. The only things about our relationship I've shared with her is, honestly, my feelings run deep for you and I'm way past the desire for just sex."

He sighed as he rested his head in her lap, closed his eyes, and slid his hand along her bare forearm. She inhaled at his touch and closed her eyes as she listened to him.

"I felt like I was deceiving you, and I couldn't do it to you any longer. I didn't deserve you then or even now, Gabi, because you *are* too good for me."

She fought the impulse to run her fingers in his hair as his head lay upon her lap; she lifted her arm out of his reach and crossed her arms tightly at her chest.

"Maybe it's not that I'm *too good* for you, Nick, maybe it's just you're *too bad* for me."

He turned his head to face her and opened his eyes to gaze upon her face. "I pray that's not the case Gabi. I'd like to think I have some redemptive qualities within me. Qualities I thought were long since dead inside me. Having you in my life, I have felt them reborn. What I feel for you is real, Gabi, and it makes me want to be a better man. I want to show you I can be the man you deserve. The man I know I can be, for you and for us. You are the best thing that has ever come into my life."

She was quiet for a moment. "I think you, or the man I thought you were, does have redemption within him," she lifted her eyes to the ceiling, "but honestly, right now, I'm having a hard time seeing him." Her chin quivered.

He lifted up from the floor and sat next to her on the couch as he took her hand into his own. "Look into my eyes, Gabi; you know I'm being completely honest with you. My soul is bared for you, right here, right now."

She solemnly considered his eyes.

"Look, Sweetness," he looked down at their hands. "I know I fucked up, royally." He blinked hard. "But we have something here, can't you feel it? Because I do. We're meant to be together. I don't want Claudia or any other woman. I only want you, my sweet Gabrielle." He moved in closer to her and landed a light kiss on her cheek. "You're all I ever think about." He lightly kissed her other cheek. "Day or night, with or without sex." His lips landed on her forehead as he pulled her into his arms. "You consume me, Gabrielle, wholly and completely."

"Nick...I really do feel you're being genuine in what you say, but I also feel..." She pulled back out of his embrace as she paused. "No, I more than feel it, I know you're like fire for me. I know I should take off running in the opposite direction for fear of being burned by you," her voice became hauntingly soft as she lifted her face and looked into his eyes. "But, I find myself feeling so much like Icarus right now. I'm being compelled by some force greater than myself or my own natural instincts to fly even closer to you and your burning all-consuming flame." She took in a sharp breath. "Because Heaven help me, I want you too."

Another tear fell down her cheek; he leaned in and tenderly slid his fingers under her chin holding her face to his as he kissed her tear away. The taste of her salty tear on his lips prompted him to speak.

"I will never make you cry again, I promise. It rips me up inside to see you cry or to see you upset." He took her into his arms in an embrace that encircled her, never wanting to let her go. Nick pulled back just enough to gain access to her waiting mouth as he took her lips, gently at first, then with an urgency as he felt her hand reach into his hair.

Her spread fingers lithely caressed his scalp as she grabbed at his thick strands; her touch anywhere turned him on as evidenced by the bulge forming at his crotch.

His mouth took hers in a kiss that left her breathless. He felt her pushing at the lapels of his tuxedo jacket to take it off. He quickly helped to remove his jacket and threw it to the floor behind him as he looked back at her and could see the desire alive in her eyes.

"I want you," her voice smooth as silk, but laced with heady desire, as if it had been plunged into vat of nothing but pure arousal. "I want all of you, Nick."

"Gabi, this is about you, Sweetness, I want to make you feel good. I want to take care of you, take care of your needs."

"Tell me what you want me to do."

"Get undressed," he stated, his voice powerful. "I'll do the rest."

27

🌸 Gabrielle and Nick 🌸

New York – Friday evening - June 6th, 1969

Gabrielle stood in front of him; she reached to the side of her dress and unzipped it and watched him with heated eyes. His eyes followed her fingers as she slid the dress off her body and kicked it away. His eyes feasted upon her as she stood before him in a black strapless corseted bra and lace panties peeking out under the matching black garter.

He inhaled at the sight of her; from his seated position on the couch as he felt the continued rapid growth between his legs, but he reminded himself. *This is not about you, it's about her, making her feel good.* He found it difficult to not just throw her down on the couch and plunge himself inside her.

"Gabi, you are even more beautiful than I ever imagined," he swallowed. "You're exquisite." He began to take control, but not wanting to alarm her, he decided to pace himself as he reached for her hand and told her hoarsely. "I want you to enjoy what I'm about to do to you. Because, Sweetness, I'm going to make you feel things you've never felt before." His blue eyes darkened as they scorched intentionally into to hers.

Taking his outstretched hand, she swallowed. She felt a throbbing between her own thighs and the weight of the ache had been driving her insane as she wanted him to finally take the ache away.

He guided her closer to him, and she now stood directly in front of him as he looked up at her face and let his eyes scan her body. His cool fingers slid smoothly from her hips to the metal closures of each of the stays as he undid them; freeing the tops of her nylons. He secured the silky material within his fingers as he glided the nylons down. His hands akin to a flame skimmed down her legs to her feet and she lifted each foot out of the sheer material. His hands cupped and squeezed her buttocks as he inhaled, and then gently tugged at the elastic of her panties while caressing her body as he lowered the flimsy fabric to the floor; he looked up to her face, stood up, and kissed her parted lips. Their tongues ardently met and merged. She felt weakened from the passion and clung to him.

"Will you lay down for me, Gabi?" He hotly said in her ear.

She lowered herself to the couch and wordlessly looked up at him.

Nick removed the cummerbund and his shirt, exposing his powerfully built torso, his dark chest hair glistened in the dim candlelight against his olive toned skin. The sight of him made her bite her lip, her eyes glided over him as she watched him disrobe. He proceeded to remove his shoes and socks, but kept his pants on.

Nick removed the back cushions from the couch and threw them to the floor; his legs bestrode her, his face over hers as he began kissing her. His lips covered hers as his torrid moist tongue slipped in and out of her mouth. He moved to her neck and gently nibbled the tender flesh. His every touch awoke yearnings deeper than she'd ever thought possible.

He brought his mouth to her ear where he whispered, "You are all I ever want Gabi, only you." His hot breath sent pulses into her ear and scorched her.

He moved his mouth to her ample breasts as they spilled precariously out of her corset exposing a meager sliver of her areolas, and he began to lick at her nipples until they were both completely out of the cups. She moaned under him as her fingers found his hair and tugged as she held him selfishly in place requiring him to nibble and flick at her nipples. His mouth on one of her breasts as his nimble fingers grazed and rubbed her other nipple until it puckered and ached for attention.

She felt as if she would go insane from all the newfound sensations her body welcomed; she felt as if she'd opened up like a spring flower as it kissed the morning sun.

Nick placed his mouth on the other breast giving it equal time; her body wriggled beneath him as he heard moan after moan of pleasure escape her throat. Placing both of his hands on her fleshy peaks, he pushed them together as he consumed both of her breasts expertly sucking one and then the other.

Skillfully he kneaded them with ravenous fingers; he unhooked her corset like an expert and started to move his mouth down her body, his tongue lapped at her smooth flat belly. He landed his open mouth to her inner thigh. His teeth began lightly nibbling at the delicate skin as her body shivered in delight. He moved his hands underneath her bottom, caressing and clutching at her buttocks as his tongue slid to the inner part of her thigh.

His head inching ever so close to her opening and she soon felt his tongue flicker over her clitoris as he inserted his adept tongue in and out of her opening while squeezing her buttocks. The erotic sensations fired through her whole quivering body and she gasped, as he began sending her ever closer to the brink. Her body arched as she moaned and sighed into the splendidness of the feeling.

"You come so good, Sweetness," he sighed "and you taste so sweet." She heard Nick's voice in the distance as the waves of released pressure began to run through her, rushing like rapids within her body. Her breath hitched in her throat as she moaned again without even realizing it.

"You are so wet," he sighed longingly. "If I were to take you right now, my cock could slide so easily inside that sweet box of yours."

"Ar- aren't you going to?" She breathlessly gulped.

His eyes shut tightly against his own want of her as he blew out his frustrated air.

"Ohh baby...My Sweetness," he groaned. "I didn't know we would be doing this." He paused. "I, I don't have a condom to protect you, you know, from pregnancy and I-"

"I'm on the- the pill, Nick." She revealed to him between ragged breaths.

His mind whirled for a moment as an eager optimistic smile played at the corners of his mouth; nevertheless, he kept himself in check.

"Are you sure?" His eyes, hooded from his own built up craving. "You know this will change everything between us," he paused. "By doing this, you are agreeing to be mine and only mine for all time. You sure it's what you want, Gabi?"

"I haven't been more sure of anything in my life." Her chest rose and fell with each breath. "I don't want anyone else, I only want you, I want this, with you because..." she blurted out. "I love you, Nick."

Hearing her words, his heart leapt; he caressed her thigh and placed tender kisses along the soft inner flesh.

"God Gabi, you mean so much to me." He buried his tongue into her as he licked and suckled at her sex while his fingers gently massaged at her desire swollen folds as she moaned through the shockwaves her body produced within her orgasms.

"You are everything to me, my sweet Gabi."

She could barely hear him as the blood whooshed in her ears. She squeezed her eyes shut as she felt the last of the shockwaves and opened her sated eyes to look at him.

Wordlessly he pushed himself up off the couch; standing up he unzipped his pants, pushed them down along with his boxers and stepped out of them.

This had been her first time seeing him completely naked; his body was indeed magnificent, a true work of art molded within human flesh. She caressed his firm chiseled muscles and rock hardness of his carved backside with her eyes, the view of his body had her in awe.

He threw his pants on top of his jacket and once again he was over her, finding her mouth, and lowering his hot moist tongue in a kiss to her mouth.

His hands soon found their target between her legs, and he felt for the slickness there and began to massage her as she squirmed under his masterful fingers. As his fingers entered her his manipulations made her gasp and hoarsely she called out his name; not being able to hold off any longer.

It was all the invitation he needed as he took ahold of himself and began to slide his inflamed tip up and down along her moistness and he began his entry into her tender folds. He heard her gasp again and again as he inched his way into her.

"Ohh...Such a tight, tight box," he held himself in check. "You feel incredible, Gabi."

Accustomed to always using a condom when having sex, Nick discovered having his bare cock sliding inside her coupled with her tightness gave him unbelievable sensations, and he found it difficult to harness them.

"You...feel so good." He gulped, "you make me want to explode." His eyes were tightly closed as he slid in and out of her. "I don't know if I'm able to hold back... I'm trying not to come."

He soon gained control, slowly at first, but as soon as he felt her starting to accommodate his size, he started to speed up his thrusts into a steady rhythm. He began to drive harder and deeper inside of her, and he felt her quivering, tightening even further around him.

He wanted to see her, needed to see her eyes, to see the pleasure on her face. To make certain she'd been enjoying it as much as he'd been, because he wanted this to be about pleasing her.

Nick opened his eyes to look at her, but what he saw wasn't a look of pleasure on her face; her brows were pinched together, and she winced as if in pain. Tears slid from the corners of her eyes and streamed down her temples.

"Gabi," he froze, "are you alright?" The alarm and concern in his voice obvious. "Sweetness, am I hurting you?"

"It's..." she took in a few jagged breaths. "I'm fine. I'll be okay...," she took another ragged breath. "I- I knew the first time would hurt, but... I'm all right."

He was stunned. "What do you mean... the first time?" His eyes pierced through to hers in the softly lit room. "The first time...with me right?" He asked.

"No. M-mine." Her voice faltered, she took in another lungful of air. "It's... my first time, Nick."

He felt how tight she was- the tightest he'd ever had- but he chalked it up to her youth and limited experience. His eyes glazed over while he got the full realization of what she had just said; instantly he pulled himself out of her and lifted off her. His mind in a whirl as he sat back on the bare back frame of the couch, near her feet.

I knew she'd been a good girl, but a virgin? That explained it. Why she made me wait to have her, she wanted to make sure I was the one to give herself to. She truly is an innocent just as Claudia said. How could I have not known? She watched him and lifted into a sitting position and slid to the other side of the couch and pulled her legs underneath her.

"Wa-was I that bad, Nick?" She felt prickles of imminent tears in her eyes, her worst fear realized. "Am I, a lousy lay?"

"A lousy...?" He eyed the ceiling with a dazed questioning look on his face. "Why didn't you tell me you were a virgin?" He asked hoarsely.

She was quiet for a moment before she answered him.

"You've been with so many experienced women," she paused. "Women who know what to do." She cleared her throat. "I just didn't think— I knew my lack of experience might make me bad in bed. And judging by your reaction, I can only guess, I was right."

"Right? No, you couldn't be more wrong, good God, Gabi. I could have made this so special for you?" Remorse cast a shadow on his face. "I wouldn't have taken you on this goddamned couch for one thing. I would have made it better for you and not plunged myself into you as I did. If I had known, it wouldn't have hurt so much."

"I'm sorry I didn't tell you, Nick, but, I'm okay."

He moved to face her, reaching up he cupped her face

lovingly in his hands and kissed her lightly on the lips.

"Gabrielle, you mean the world to me, don't you know that? I never want to hurt you. If I had known the precious gift you were giving me..." he gently kissed her again. "Let me start this whole thing over, I want to make love to you, the way I should have done in the first place." He pressed his forehead against hers. "Will you let me- let me make it special for you, somehow?"

She nodded.

He rose from the couch, took her hand, and lifted her effortlessly into his arms; she wrapped her arms around his neck and laid her head on his shoulder as he walked, cradling her in his powerful arms over the threshold of her bedroom.

Nick gently placed her on the side of the bed in the softly lit room. He leaned in and tenderly kissed her and then took her hand and brought her up to him and removed her garter belt; his sigh came out almost a growl as he ran tamed hands over her body.

Her skin sprang to life under his touch; she felt her body's want reemerging despite the soreness she felt. She turned and pulled the bedspread back on the bed exposing the crisp clean white sheets, she turned back to him.

His hands were in her hair removing the pins, as they held her hair loosely in place; she shook her head to let her hair cascade about her shoulders. She stood before him in nothing except the black onyx and diamond jewelry adorning her lobes, neck and wrist, they sparkled and shimmered in the softly lit bedroom.

Seeing her naked with her tousled hair, in wonder he spoke. "Gabi, you are, without a doubt," he swallowed hard, "the most beautiful woman I have ever seen."

He kissed her selflessly, cupping her face gently in his hands as his hands began to slide down to her neck and then her shoulders as he pulled her close to him in a loving embrace, wrapping her up in his arms, his mouth on her neck.

"Sweetness, you feel so good in my arms. I never want to let you go." He felt the squeeze in his chest around his heart again. Then slowly and lovingly, he made love to her. Nick revered and cherished every inch of her body with kisses and sweet caresses; his firm hands and fingers acting as conduits of pure pleasure and they brought her body to soul-aching heights of ecstasy.

When he entered her this time, he took care as he inched his huge member into her womanly folds watching her face the whole time to be certain he wasn't hurting her as he stared raptly in her eyes.

"Gabi, you mean the world to me. You have to know, you're my everything." His mouth covered hers; his kiss soft and slow.

She arched her body to take him more fully; ignoring any pain she felt because the enjoyable sensitivity of having his mouth on her as she felt him inside her filling up her womanhood outweighed any discomfort.

She clung to him, pressing her fingers on to his hot taut skin.

Feeling the ripples of his solid muscles beneath her fingertips, her senses deepened as she drunkenly inhaled him in. Her head pressed back into the pillow while he kissed her neck. He let his tongue get a taste of the delicate flesh covering her throat, she moaned under the subtle soft nips from his teeth.

With practiced fingers he kneaded her clitoris and felt the walls of her womanhood tighten further still around his rigid member in a true vice grip, and as she came, he slid slowly but gently in and out of her.

His testicles were wound so tight; he had been ready to explode ever since he had entered the rose petal softness of her sex the first time. The pulsations he experienced were like none he had ever felt before; he yielded to the pressure built up inside him, he quickly discovered his physical and emotional sides colliding, intersecting together, and leading him to an unbelievable and nearly ethereal release inside of her.

He ejaculated with such force; he could not control his own moans and cries of pleasure. Her name on his lips. "Gabi, my Sweetness" he uttered in gasping breaths. "My sweet, Gabi."

His skin glistened with sheens of sweat. Her hands were upon him as she soothingly stroked the firmness of his moist muscular back, he heard her words, they touched him deeply in his heart.

"I love you Nick." She gasped. "I'll love you forever."

He collapsed on top of her and felt her heartbeat beneath his chest; he was drowning in the overwhelming feelings surging within him.

His arms were on either side of her. "You are my entire world, Gabi." His mouth covered hers with a kiss; sated, he reluctantly pulled himself out of her. His damp back landed on the cool crisp sheets.

"Sweetness, you have nothing to worry about because," he paused breathing heavily, "you are incredible. Amazing. I only hope, I made it alright for you."

"It was good for me, too." She quietly responded.

"Liar," he grinned at her, "but, Sweetness, I promise it does get better. Please, trust me."

"Nick, rest assured, I did like it," she asserted. "The way you touched me and the things you did to me with your tongue..." she blushed. "It was indescribable."

"Gabi, I'm glad you enjoyed it. I wanted to make this all about you, but I have a feeling, I may have let my own selfish need to satisfy little 'Marco' get in the way a little bit." He pinched his fingers close together to indicate an insignificant amount.

"You've given it a name?" She asked with a soft laugh.

"I think all men name their Johnsons, it's a little friend that never leaves you. I don't think calling him 'it' would be appropriate." He smirked.

She yawned as she snuggled up to him resting her head on his shoulder, and she sleepily looked up to his face.

"Believe me, Nick, there is nothing little about you or Marco." She yawned again. "You are both larger than life itself, but I'm sure I will get used to it, now won't I?"

He pulled her closer to him. "Absolutely." He happily kissed her and glanced at the bedside clock.

"It's getting late." He brushed back some wayward strands of her hair from her face. "Do you want me to go? As we both know, Gus gets up awful early."

She opened her eyes just a crack and looked up at him with a smile. "No way, I want you to stay; I want to wake up in your arms, Nick. Don't you worry about Gus or anyone else, because, I couldn't care less?"

He tilted his head to hers. "Good. I was hoping you'd say something like that, because I'd like to stay." He gave her another peck on the lips. "Now, you close your eyes," he ordered. "I'll be here when you wake up."

She closed her eyes with a satisfied grin on her lips and she burrowed closer to him, with his arm around her.

He watched her as she slept; he knew he loved her. Yet, he'd been too afraid to say it aloud to her. For fear if she knew the hold she truly had on him, she could break him.

He didn't like the knowledge of her, or anyone, having any kind of power over him, but, she did indeed have it. Tonight proved it to him in spades. Just her saying she questioned having him in her life, it wounded him somewhere deep inside.

Knowing he'd almost lost her for good- it felt like he was falling into the abyss, an enormous chasm with no feasible way out. *Damn you Claudia*, he thought, with a spark of anger.

Because of you and our shared past, I almost lost the one who holds my heart securely yet so innocently within her grasp, my beautiful Gabrielle. He pressed his lips to her hair as he vowed. *I won't ever let anything put a wedge between us again. Not ever.*

28

🌿 Gabrielle and Nick 🌿

New York – Friday morning - June 20th, 1969

She loved birthdays, especially her own and today was June 20th, her birthday. Gabrielle was working at her drafting table at VonShelles when she got a call from Regina, the fashion house receptionist. Gabrielle smiled to herself because Regina had informed her of a delivery waiting for her at the main floor reception.

In the elevator, she pushed the button for the lobby; *What did Maman and Papa buy me for my birthday that they couldn't send to the brownstone? It must be something very expensive and super extravagant if I have to sign for it personally.* She shook her head. *Not very low profile, Papa.* Last year's gift had been enough to buy a small Island, but, she had settled on buying the Brownstone instead. Still, she couldn't help but get a tad excited.

The doors opened and she exited the elevator; her gaze glided to the reception desk and immediately she saw a huge bouquet of red roses spattered with baby's breath throughout.

"Oh wow, are these for me, Carol?" She asked, awed by

the beauty of the perfect red roses. "They're beautiful."

"Somebody must really love you." Carol smiled at her.

Gabrielle turned the large vase of the flowers around and peered through the lovely stems.

"There doesn't seem to be a card." She frowned toward Carol. "How can you be sure that they're for me?"

"Oh, they're for you alright, all twenty-four of them."

"Did you say twenty-four?" Gabrielle's lip curled into a smile.

"Yes, I did. Twenty-four roses, I counted them."

Gabrielle's eyes twinkled as she thought *they must be for me.* "Okay Carol, where do I sign?" She asked with a grin.

"There's the delivery man over there," Carol smiled, her eyes moved toward the lobby chairs. "I think you need to see him about a signature."

Gabrielle turned around to see Nick sitting in one of the white leather lobby chairs watching her with amusement as he rose from his seat. She felt her heart skip a beat as she rushed over to him and abruptly threw her arms around him in an embrace and squeezed him tight. She let go as she looked around red-faced at the busy lobby. She placed cool fingers to her warmed cheek and looked up into his smiling blue eyes.

"They are positively gorgeous. Thank you, Nick, but you really didn't have to go to all of this trouble."

"Trouble? It was no trouble, and it's the least I could do to help my girl celebrate her twenty-fourth birthday." He lifted an eyebrow. "You didn't think that I'd forgotten, did you?"

"No, I just didn't expect this," she sheepishly grinned.

Nick took her hand into his. "What kind of boyfriend would I be if I didn't get flowers for you?"

She immediately felt that now familiar lurch in her heart, filling her with emotion, along with the voltage surge all the way through her fingers clear to her pelvic region. She crossed one leg in front of the other as she squeezed them tightly together. She was sure Carol, who had not taken her eyes off them, could see the desire starting to build up inside her.

"You are a wonderful boyfriend, because I love them."

He looked adoringly at her.

Gabrielle found her eyes betrayed her as she looked at him with a mixture of absolute love and carnal craving for his rock-hard body.

"I'm happy you like them, but believe me, I don't want to stop at just flowers. I would like to take you to lunch, are you free?" His eyes burned with an ache of his own to possess her. "To let me, *take* you."

His words sent a shiver down her spine.

She gave a throaty laugh. "I'll make myself free; let me go upstairs to get my purse and tell Linda."

He leaned in close to her ear then whispered. "Do you think you can make a pit stop into the ladies' room and remove your constricting panties?"

"Are you kidding me?" She gave a small laugh.

"Do I look like I'm kidding?" His hooded eyes sensually

accessed her. "I'm very serious. I like the thought of having complete access to you."

Her heart was beating a mile a minute. "Give me a few minutes, I'll be right back."

~~~

After finishing her favorite deli sandwich in her chosen delicatessen with Nick seated across from her, she smiled.

"How's your birthday going so far?" He asked with a sparkle in his eye and a grin on his seriously handsome face.

"So far it's been great, all because of you, Nick."

He took the last bite of his sandwich and finished off with a large drink of his water as he smiled at her.

"However, I feel positively brazen without my undies on. Why did you request for me to go panty free anyway?"

"I like the notion that I could place my hands under this table and reach between your legs and strike gold."

"Gold? Hmm… If you keep talking like that, I'd say it would be more like a river waiting for you to ride like the Rapids."

She seductively licked her lips as she smiled at him and reached over with her napkin to wipe a bit of mustard from the corner of his mouth. "I only wish I could lick it off." Her voice became sultry.

"It's your birthday, so I'd be careful for what you wish for today if I were you, Gabrielle." His deep blue eyes were suddenly aroused as he watched her. "Because I can most assuredly make it happen. Come to think of it, I know what I'd like to lick."

Then without giving her a chance to respond, he pushed to his feet, took her hand, and gently pulled her through the busy delicatessen toward the restrooms. Looking around to make sure the coast was clear, he pulled her into the Men's room, guided her into one of the stalls, and locked the door behind them. Her laugh was naughty as he pressed her up against the door and crushed his mouth on hers and kissed her deeply, his tongue proficiently took her mouth.

"I've been waiting to do that all damn day." Nick breathed near her ear. "God, Gabi. The thought of your sweet spot being so unfettered, you drive me crazy."

"Do I?" Her breath caught in her throat. "You do the same to me, Nick."

"Thinking about you without any panties on has my cock on edge. I want you, Sweetness. Right now."

He slid his hand up her skirt and his fingers met their mark. "Oh, fuck yes, that's what I like to feel. My sexy woman, wet and wanting."

He undid his belt buckle and slid his pants down as he sat on the toilet seat. He pulled her to him and she widened her stance over him before sitting on his knees. He told her to put her legs on his shoulders, he placed his hands under her buttocks and lifted her up to his waiting mouth as his tongue filled her as she quaked under the sensations. She crossed her legs at the ankles as her legs rested on his back. Delighted sighs of ecstasy escaped her as she reached out with her hands to the stall walls for balance.

Nick worked her into a frenzied state, he was doing some amazing things to her as his astute tongue lapped and stroked her sex. She couldn't hold back as waves overtook her to the welcomed heights of euphoria. She moaned blissful cries and felt her legs go a little limp and she found it hard to hold onto the walls within the sensations of the orgasm.

"This is the best part of my lunch, but now," he growled, his voice deep. "I need to be inside you, Sweetness, where I belong."

Nick began to lower her onto his erect member; she let down her legs and straddled him. Taking charge, she began riding *him*. Nick was usually in control, and she had no problem with it, but at this moment, she felt eager to take over. She placed her hands on his shoulders and looked him in the eyes. She kissed his mouth slowly as she inched herself down onto Nick's hard cock as she raised her body at a pace of her own. His cock filled her up in ways that made her body quiver, and she sped up until she felt herself come again.

"Fuck sake... You're already so tight... But when you come, Sweetness, you're... going to... make me detonate."

"That's the idea... because," she gasped out her words. "It's my birthday... I want to... to make... you come with me."

"Keep doing what you're doing," he panted back at her. "You will most definitely get your wish."

29
❧ Gabrielle and Nick ❧
New York – Friday afternoon - June 20th, 1969

Back in the empty elevator of The Bradford Building; Nick pulled Gabrielle into his arms and kissed her mouth and began lifting her skirt. He gazed at her through half-closed lids.

"I can't get enough of you, Gabi."

He pressed himself onto her, and she could feel the definite rigidity of him against her and desire began to rise within her too, her body just seemed to have a mind of its own when it came to Nick and she wanted him, until she heard the ding of for her floor. She purposely pulled away from him and smoothed her skirt back in place as the doors opened.

"I find you to be absolute trouble, my good man."

"As are you, Sweetness." He blew the air from his lungs. "Just give me a minute, will ya?"

She smiled to herself; men just are not able to hide their desire as well as we can. "Are you having hard times there, Nick?" She playfully batted her eyes at him, and held the elevator door open. "And to think, it all started with a simple kiss."

"That's where you're wrong, Gabi." A small grin appeared on his sexy puckered lips. "There's nothing simple about kissing you, vixen." Trying to compose himself, his eyes scanned heavenward as he repeated under his breath. "Baseball... Baseball..." He then suddenly announced. "I think I'm now ready to meet the illustrious Linda Taylor."

Gabrielle introduced Nick to Regina, the VonShelles receptionist, and as they passed her desk, Regina fanned herself with her hand and mouthed, 'He's gorgeous' to Gabrielle.

Gabrielle gave him the dime store tour of the fashion house, showing him the drafting room where she worked and one of the four showrooms housed on their floor with their finished Autumn and winter collections on display.

Nick commented with a befuddled shake of his head. "Summer has just started and you've already finished winter clothes? Now, that's just plain crazy to me."

"Well, in fashion you have to stay ahead of the seasons. The winter lines were done for Fashion week back in March, and what you see here is what the buyers selected and now they have to be ready for mass production."

"If you design something so far in advance, how can you know if people will like it?" His brow lifted inquisitively."

"That's my job," she raised an eyebrow up at him. "To create something that will set a trend and thereby convince the public that they like it, want it and just simply have to have it."

They soon stood outside of Linda's office. Gabrielle and Linda had grown close in the past few months and would go out for drinks and occasionally dinner after work some evenings.

Gabrielle poked her head in the office, she found Linda on the phone, but she motioned for them to come in as she finished her call and hung up the phone.

They walked fully into Linda's large office, which had been tastefully decorated with a Scandinavian modern flair. Linda stood and stepped out from behind her desk and stretched out her hand to him. "You must be Nick; it's really nice to meet you. Gabi has told me so much about you, I feel as if I already know you."

"It's nice to meet you too, Linda." He accepted her hand. "I hope Gabrielle shared only good things." He said with his winning smile.

"There are only good things to tell," Gabrielle beamed beside him. "So you've no need for concern."

After a bit of small talk, he gave his regrets and informed them that he had to go and return to work himself.

"I'll walk you out." Gabrielle told him. "I need to pick up my roses from the main lobby anyway."

He smiled in Linda's direction. "It was good meeting you, Linda."

"Same here, Nick." She replied. "Maybe we can all have dinner sometime."

"I'd like that," he nodded. "I'm really sorry I have to rush off like this, but duty calls."

"Oh please, don't apologize for being a dedicated working man. Work only serves to build character." She glanced at Gabrielle then back at Nick. "Just do something nice for our Gabi, since it's her birthday."

Nick's smile slanted. "Trust me, Linda; I intend to make this a special day for her." His eyes regarded Gabrielle tenderly as he subtly slid his hand up along her spine.

Linda smiled favorably, taking note of the looks they were exchanging with each other as they left her office.

~~~

There were other people in the elevator as they rode down; Nick held her hand in his and spoke quietly in her ear.

"I'm planning dinner at my place tonight; I'll pick you up here at five."

"Nick, you've done so much already. You don't have to-"

"I do have to." He cut her off. "Besides, I should make good on my word to Linda and make this day extra special for you," he winked at her. "Tonight, I will do just that."

As they were exiting the elevator, Gabrielle bumped into Margaret Bradford who was with her assistant, Penelope Peters, as they entered the elevator to take them up to their offices on the fifty-second floor.

Margaret's fine features made her an attractive woman, but these contrasted with the slight edge of her steely personality.

With her gray pale blue eyes expertly lined with a semi thick brown liner at the upper and lower rims of her eyes, she left the corners open to make her eyes appear larger. Her blond hair was cut in a stylish bob, shorter in the back with chic long angled sides and bangs across her forehead.

Gabrielle had only briefly met Margaret Bradford once before, and because of this, she felt reluctant to do an introduction, but she also felt she should at the very least say something.

"Excuse me and good afternoon, Mrs. Bradford." Gabrielle said to her, but noticed that Margaret's eyes were transfixed on Nick's face with a look of surprise as her head and shoulders gave way to a slight tremor.

Gabrielle ignored Margaret's reaction at seeing Nick.

Margaret quickly poised herself as her eyes slid with recognition to Gabrielle. "How very good it is to see you again, Miss Lawrence."

Gabrielle was astounded; *whoa, she remembers my name?*

"And just who do we have here?" Margaret's voice was even and cultured, but her eyes were back on Nick. "I've not seen you here before, young man. Are you employed in the building? A new designer at VonShelles, maybe?"

"No ma'am, he's not a new employee," Gabrielle spoke up. "Forgive my lack of manners. Mrs. Margaret Bradford, I give you Mr. Nick Caine," she then added with a smile. "That's Caine, with a C and an E."

"It's a pleasure to meet you, Mrs. Bradford." Nick cordially smiled in her direction.

"The pleasure," her eyes narrowed at him as she now thoroughly disregarded Gabrielle's presence. "I can assure you, is all mine, Mr. Caine."

Nick was used to dealing with women, and he knew a come-on when it presented itself. Time was, he would have jumped at the chance to have an attractive woman such as Mrs. Bradford as his latest conquest. That was his life before Gabrielle had seized his heart; he responded to her with a closed-mouth smile and a slight nod of his head in her direction.

He turned his full attention to Gabrielle. "Gabi, I really do have to get going. Remember, I'll be here at five on the dot to pick you up." He swiftly took her into his arms and kissed her on the lips in full view of Margaret and Penelope.

Gabrielle felt the color heatedly rise to her cheeks as he released his hold.

Nick gave a formal nod of his head, "Mrs. Bradford." He said in her direction as he whisked past her, using long deliberate strides to the revolving doors.

30
❧ Margaret ❧
New York – Friday afternoon - June 20th, 1969

At thirty-six years of age Margaret Bradford had been much younger than her late husband, and their age gap spanned some twenty-nine years.

Her path to being one of the city's most wealthy women started unremarkably as the daughter of an un-wed teenage mother who had been disowned by her family; then after her mother's untimely death when Margaret had turned sixteen years old, she had connected with an uncle she never knew she had. Her uncle paid for her secretary school, but upon graduation he informed her she now had the tools to make her own way in the world.

She started with ERB National Holdings as a typist in the steno pool, and soon worked her way up to be Elliott Bradford's executive secretary when his secretary quit the job to get married. Margaret quickly set her sights on the widowed business tycoon, and they were married within six months.

Her station in life had vastly improved the day she married

Elliott Bradford. They had fourteen years of what she would call wedded bliss; she did what was expected. She joined the usual ladies' clubs, she shopped, lunched with all the high-brow wives of her husband's business associates, and she ran the household all while presenting herself as an eye-catching symbol for Elliott's arm.

It had been five months since Elliott's death, and with him leaving no apparent heir, Margaret was the sole beneficiary of his vast fortune, which included his business holdings. But the *pièce de résistance was The Bradford Building*. When it was said and done, she had become one of the wealthiest women in America.

After a short mourning period, she relished taking control of Elliott's multi-million-dollar corporation and showing the *boys* on the board she could manage the company as well as, if not better, then Elliott had. Knowing she would have to pass muster with them had been the least of her worries, for she had learned from the best. Her husband was the most astute business man she'd known. Under his tutelage, she acquired the kind of knowledge one could only obtain by watching and shadowing a master.

After Elliott's ill-fated death, she drew a hard line in the sand and eliminated the men she knew wouldn't follow her lead; in doing so, she earned the respect of the ones who remained. Having been taught to be a shrewd executive, she wasn't afraid to get her hands a little dirty when need be. As Elliott had drilled into her head; *'Sometimes the only way you'll find your diamond in the rough, is once you have sifted thoroughly through the muck.'*

She sat behind her desk in her huge corner office, which had only months ago belonged to Elliott, she swiveled from side to side in her white leather chair behind her sleek glass desk (she'd put Elliott's mahogany desk in storage along with some of his other things some time ago when she redid the offices to suit her own modern tastes).

"Of all the dumb luck, can you believe it, Penny?" She said almost giddy as her eyes filled with mirth.

Her personal secretary, Penelope Peters, took a seat in front of Margaret's desk. Her long platinum blond hair pulled back into a bun at the nape of her neck and accentuated her pretty face. Her makeup was understated, but she'd placed emphasis on her large brown doe-like eyes they were thickly lined in black.

"Are you sure it's him? I mean the photo you have is so old." Penelope fidgeted with the hem of her skirt.

"Oh, it's him alright, those eyes are unmistakable. I can't believe he just waltzed right in here, into my building of all places."

"Or rather just waltzed right out of." Penelope remarked as her eyes lowered to the floor aloofly.

Margaret disregarded Penelope's indifference as she smugly went on. "I've been searching for him for how many months? Thanks should go to our designer Gabrielle Lawrence; otherwise, I'd still be trying to track him down."

She lightly laughed. "Caine with a C and an E, indeed."

Her eyes gleamed happily. "Now all I have to do is to keep a close eye on him." She slanted her head. "Actually, on second thought, I would like Riordan to do a thorough check on our boy." Resting her elbows on her desk, she tented her fingers together and tapped her raised fingertips to her lips. "Let's see what he's been up to all these years, and I want to know when he changed the spelling of his name."

Penelope's eyes continued to focus on the floor. "I'll take care of it, Margo, the securing of Mr. Riordan."

It was then Margaret acknowledged Penelope's forlorn expression. "Penny, I haven't forgotten about what you asked me over lunch. The subject is not dead yet. But, this Nick Caine revelation means I've got to get a handle on things first. Acceptable?"

"Not dead yet? That statement alone, leads me to believe it soon will be. I don't think you're even going to give it your full consideration."

"I said I would think about it; Penny, give me some credit, won't you? I am known in this town. Anyone who's someone, knows of me. I have slowly brought these fools around to see that I am their equal, enough so they would even want to do business with me. They are beginning to see me as more than just a woman or more than Elliott Bradford's rich little widow."

She looked thoughtfully at Penelope. "If I do this and am recognized, do you know what it would mean for me? I'd be a laughing stock, who would dare work with me then? I would be ruined." She resolutely shook her blonde hair. "This could very well be courting disaster for me, don't you see that?"

"Margo, baby...," Penelope, pleaded her case. "I just want to do something normal and go out to a club for drinks and a little bit of dancing with my girlfriend. The place I'm talking about is discreet and it's out of the way. It's somewhere down in the Village. I know the clientele is not the crowd you're used to, but," she scooted on to the edge of her chair. "But we can have a great time while being ourselves. There's no judgment there, because it's one of the few places around for people like us."

Margaret didn't like the sound of *'people like us.'* She certainly did not like the idea of being around a group of what she deemed substandard people. *The idea of pretending to fit in with them is just about as appealing to me as sticking needles into my eyes.*

Nevertheless, Penelope had demonstrated her loyalty repeatedly. Margaret found because of her loyalty, she would do just about anything for Penelope.

"I've said I'm thinking about it, Penny, alright?"

"That's all I ask, is for you to consider it." A glimmer of hope sparked in Penelope's eyes.

"I'll let you know and soon. In the meantime," Margaret lifted an eyebrow. "How about you go and lock the door and get naked for me? You know how I like to have you after lunch."

The corners of Penelope's mouth curled up in a ready smile as she immediately rose and walked to the office's door.

"Your wish is my command." Penelope stated while locking the door. She turned back to face Margaret, their eyes caught each other's and she slowly walked back to Margaret. Penelope began unbuttoning her silk blouse.

31

❧ Gabrielle and Nick ❧
New York – Friday evening - June 20th, 1969

Nick arrived right on time as she stood outside The Bradford Building hugging her birthday flowers in her arms. She could smell the wonderful aroma of dinner as she entered his car; he had stopped at Mamma Leones prior to picking her up.

"You went to Mamma's?" She asked.

"Yep, I said we would have dinner at my place, not that I would make it." He smiled as he headed for his apartment, "I want you to enjoy your meal and not suffer through my cooking."

She stepped out of her shoes as she entered his foyer, she placed the flowers on his coffee table, "I'm glad I decided to bring them home, they're so beautiful. Now we can both enjoy them. With this heat, they probably would have died over the weekend."

She looked around the room. "You know something? It feels so odd, not having Lobo here." She commented to him as he unpacked their dinner.

"You must miss him too." She remarked, "Did you ever ask your friend if we can visit him?"

'My friend,' how can I tell her Rico's more than a friend? Nick's brow furrowed as he moved and stood next to the table. "No, I haven't. I've been way too busy."

He quietly went to work filling their plates. "Dinner's on, so let's eat." He held out her chair for her.

After their meal, he presented her with a platter of home-made *cantuccini* cookies. "I promised you these a while back." He shyly grinned at her. "Sweets for my Sweetness."

"Oh Nick," she exclaimed after trying one. "These are heavenly. You *are* a great baker."

"Not really, but I wanted to make them for you."

She noticed how unusually quiet he'd been during dinner and dessert, but she filled the silence with talk about work. Afterwards she helped as he cleared the table and they went into the kitchen to clean up; she washed and he dried.

They retreated to the living room where he turned on the stereo to a nice jazz station. He joined her on the soft leather couch and sat next to her. Facing her, he anxiously yet tenderly cupped her face in his hands, tenderly kissed her lips, and held her quietly in an embrace.

Still noting his quietness, she finally flat out asked him. "What's going on? You're being way too quiet, what's put you in this brooding mood, is something wrong?"

"No, nothing's wrong," he paused. "I don't even know where to start with this." He sighed. "It's just-," he hesitated.

"I want *you*, Gabi. So much and it petrifies me sometimes." With his impenetrable gaze, he looked into her eyes. "I have never wanted or needed anyone in my life before, especially not the way I do you."

"You want me? You've no need for concern, because you have me. I'm yours Nick, I'm all in."

"There's something I want to give you." He said abruptly.

He wiped his damp hands along his thighs, and reached behind one of the sofa's pillows and pulled out a small teal blue box with a satiny white ribbon neatly tied in a bow. His smile was almost shy as he nervously grinned at her.

"It's a birthday present."

"Wh…what is it Nick?" She stared at the box in wide-eyed wonder, as her finger slid across the embossed silver lettering.

"Just a little something to help you remember how much you mean to me, but I guess you won't know what it is until you open it." His smile broadened.

Carefully, she untied the ribbon, then lifted the lid off the box and pulled out a white velvet jewel box. She opened it to reveal a gold necklace with two interlocked hearts, and a floating shimmering stone at its center.

"It's a moonstone, I'm told it's the preferred stone for the month of June."

"Oh Nick, it's beautiful." She freed the intricate gold chain from the jewel box and held it out to him. "Please, will you put it on me?"

She turned her back to him and lifted her hair to allow him

access to her neck. After he clasped the necklace in place, he began kissing the back of her neck.

"Never take it off, as long as you wear it, you'll know what we mean to each other." He said nuzzling her ear.

"I'll wear it, always. I promise." She came to realize his mood had been his nervousness at giving her a gift of such significance. *A big step for him.*

She gasped as he undid the back buttons of her top and slid his fingers smoothly over her bared skin as he undid her bra. She turned around to face him; allowing her seductive eyes to take him in. She felt her breasts slide out of the bra cups as he gave a low sexy growl.

"You are so breathtaking, don't move. Just, give me a minute." He pushed himself to his feet and left the room.

After a few minutes, he called out to her.

"Gabi, can you come in here?"

She entered the bathroom to find him in his boxers; standing near the tub filling with bubbles. Lit candles were placed at each of the tub's corners.

"What's all this?" she asked with a smile.

"For your special day, I wanted to indulge you a little, so I drew you a bubble bath." He pinched his eyebrows together with a matter-of-fact grin. "I'm going to need you to disrobe and let me get down to some serious pampering."

"You really are all I could have ever hoped for. You're wonderful."

She removed her clothes as he watched her with lusty

appreciation. The heat in his eyes grew as she stood before him wearing only a smile and the necklace he had just placed around her slender neck.

"You like?" She asked as she flung her hair over her bared shoulder.

"I more than like. You could come over here and feel how much I like, but it wouldn't be fair, it's not my birthday. You're the one who's getting taken care of here."

He reached for her, placing his hand at the side of her neck as he slid his splayed fingers through her hair. Nick's hands continued to her waist as he lifted her high enough until she was just above him and she gazed down at him.

Her hands went around his neck as she lowered her head and sealed her mouth to his with a kiss, her tongue melded with his. Without breaking their connective kiss, he lowered her into the bubble bath. The tepid water felt refreshing and served to cool her hot skin, she removed her hands from around his neck as she adjusted herself in the bubble-filled tub. Nick lowered to his knees outside the tub and reached for a washcloth.

"This is blissful." She said happily and rested in the tub.

~~~

The morning after her birthday, Gabrielle made coffee in his small kitchen. She wore one of Nick's t-shirts and stood barefoot as she peered into his nearly empty refrigerator and twisted her mouth.

Wow, he really is a typical bachelor. There is nothing to eat here, except last night's leftover lasagna, cold cereal or fruit. At least the cantuccini cookies were homemade.

She prepared their bowls and coffee cups and placed them on the small dinette table, he stepped up behind her and nuzzled her neck.

"Hey there, Sweetness, I reached for you," his hands slid around her tiny waist, "but you were gone. What are you doing? You're supposed to be in my bed, naked with me."

"I would be there still, but my tummy growled at me."

He gave her a soft nip with his teeth on the tender flesh of her neck; she smiled as he gave a soft low growl, "Now I'm growling at you."

"Hmm…that feels good, my budding Count Vlad." She turned around. "But, this," she kissed his mouth. "Feels even better."

He teased in his best Dracula voice, "I vant to kiss your neck."

She laughed as she wrapped her arms around his tapered waist, "Kiss away then." She stretched her neck and raised her chin to look into his eyes as she embraced him. "I just love being in your arms like this, I feel so treasured."

"You are treasured. Gabi, my wish is to put you on the pedestal you deserve, to show you how precious you are to me."

Nick held her in his arms and kissed the side of her head;

he smiled when his eyes caught sight of the filled cereal bowls on the table.

"Aww, would you look at that, you made breakfast."

"Well, sort of, I could have made you a better breakfast, but your provisions are sorely lacking."

She let go of him as she turned around to go get the milk out of the fridge.

"You need to go to the grocery store, my good man. You can't live on protein powder, a little fruit and coffee alone, you know."

"I usually grab something on my way to work," he smiled, a slow sexy smile at her, "or, I just eat at your place." He cocked his head and became serious. "Since I don't have Lobo here anymore, I just don't do as much shopping anymore."

"Oh Nick, you miss him, don't you? I know I sure do."

Not wanting to let on how much he actually missed that dog, he stated briskly. "It was time; he'd been a major pain in the ass anyway." Nick paused, "I had to work around his schedule, had to be here to feed him, let him out, brush him, and bathe him. He really was a lot of work."

"I'm sure you don't miss the work, but I still miss him though." Her eyes perked up. "Hey, maybe we could go visit him today, maybe your friend would let us take him out for old times' sake. I loved taking him for walks in the park with you; he really is a great dog and he did get over the bird attacking thing."

"Speaking of attack," Nick said, wanting to change the

subject. "I know what I'd like to attack right now." He eyed her up and down. "You look great in that tee shirt of mine, but after you've had your breakfast, I want to see how good you look out of it."

She boldly reached over at him then pulled at the waistband of his boxer's and let go of it with a snug snap. "Likewise, my good man, likewise." Her eyes twinkled, "I want you to know how much I enjoyed my birthday, you made it special. You are most certainly the best boyfriend this girl could've ever asked for."

"I'm not done yet. I have one more surprise for you."

"Nick, you've done more than enough. I mean, with the flowers, last night's dinner, the splendid bubble bath and my necklace," her hand went to the gold chain around her neck. "Which, I love, by the way." She smiled brazenly. "Not to mention the great lovemaking last night. What more could I ask for?"

"My aim is to please, Sweetness." His look became thoughtful. "I'm glad you liked the things I did Gabi, this whole *being a boyfriend* thing is new for me. But as I said last night, you have captured my heart, and I think it only fitting that you should wear a symbol of it. I wanted you to know, you've found your *heart match.*"

It's the closest he had come to saying he loved her. She'd been waiting to hear those words. She had wanted him to say them on his own accord without any prodding from her.

"Oh Nick, it means so much to me. You have to know I

feel the same way." She then playfully grinned at him. "Okay, now," she excitedly asked, "what's my other surprise?"

"I know how much you like the folk musician Richie Havens. Well, a buddy of mine is holding two passes to an outdoor music festival where Richie is slated to play. If you're interested."

"You bet I'm interested, when is it?" She then scrunched her nose. "And what does one wear to an outdoor music festival?"

He laughed. "It's not until August, so you've got plenty of time to figure that one out."

32
❧ Margaret and Penelope ❦
New York – Saturday morning - June 28th, 1969

At one in the morning, Margaret could still feel the club's loud music vibrations in her chest. The drinks were weak, and the smell of cheap perfume mingled with the stench of cigarette smoke filled the air. Nevertheless, overall she had to admit they were having a great time.

The walls of the club were painted black, taking the room into near darkness. The first of the two dance floors had so many people on it and made movement nearly impossible. Just beyond the length of the long bar in the packed club had been a second dance floor. With closed eyes, Margaret allowed herself to sway back and forth to the music.

She opened her eyes and looked over at an entwined couple dancing next to them. She marveled to herself, the drag queen was beautiful; his looks could rival that of any woman's.

Margaret herself chose to go barefaced, she wore no make-up for fear of being recognized. Her hair was slicked back and tucked behind her ears. Wearing black slacks, she had chosen a white sleeveless silk shell that glowed to an almost neon blue under the clubs' pulsing black lights. The lights set their faces in almost eerie shades; illuminating them, as well as the whites of their eyes and teeth.

Penelope happily put her arms around Margaret's neck, and kissed her full on the mouth and much to her delight, no one seemed to notice or care. Margaret could feel herself start to relax and flow with the crowd.

As she musingly thought to herself, *Penny had been right, it had been fun and so freeing to be able to loosen up and be ourselves out in public--with people, 'just like us.'*

After dancing, they headed over to the crowded bar and pressed themselves to the counter where they ordered more drinks.

"Are you having a good time?" She shouted to Penelope over the noise with a grin plastered on her own face.

"I am," Penelope happily yelled back as she took Margaret's hand and kissed the inside of her palm.

"I love you, Margo, thank you for tonight. It means so much that you'd come here with me."

"I love you too, Penny. More than you know." She smiled back. Penelope had seen Margaret at her worst, yet still showed true loyalty to her.

"After all I've done, you're still here with me."

"Forever, Lover, forever."

They finished their drinks, and she soon discovered that Penelope appeared to be feeling no pain and, in fact, she'd become more than a little tipsy. Margaret had little tolerance for drunkenness and thought people shouldn't drink if they couldn't handle their liquor.

Penelope frowned as she saw Margaret look irritably at her watch. It was 1:10 a.m., and Penelope kissed her and put up her finger up in the air for one more dance.

They were on the edge of the crowded back dance floor as she held her close. They wrapped themselves in each other's arms. Margaret did feel good holding the girl she loved in the embrace, in public, without any judging eyes to mar or criticize the love they had for one another.

Suddenly she felt a big hefty hand on her shoulder as someone pulled her back into reality. She focused her eyes to see her driver Curtis Graves. It'd been loud in the clubs, but even louder on the dance floor; she could not hear what he was saying. Nonetheless, she did not misread the look of alarm in his eyes. He urgently motioned for her to follow him.

She took ahold of Penelope's hand and pulled her along. She followed through the hole Curtis created with his large body through the throngs of people; there had to be over two hundred people in the hot cramped night club. She wasn't sure how it happened, but Penelope's hand pulled away from hers and they were separated. Soon outside the club, Curtis quickly led Margaret down the street to the parked car.

Safely inside the car, Margaret looked out the back window of the car; her eyes locked onto the club's entrance to see if she could spot Penelope, but she couldn't see her. Margaret did see several police officers congregating outside at the Club's entrance.

Almost immediately, a patrol wagon pulled up in front of the building. The officers converged onto the building and pushed their way through the main double doors of the club. With a shudder her eyes widened, it was a raid. Thanks to her driver, Margaret just narrowly escaped the bedlam, but Penelope was still inside.

The scene behind her became utter chaos; crowds were quickly forming outside on the street in front of the club. The fifteen minutes they waited inside the car seemed like an eternity. The police eventually led out a string of patrons they placed into the waiting wagon. They soon got into a tussle with a very butch blonde lesbian who'd been handcuffed, but somehow she'd been struck over the head with a baton during the fracas. She wildly looked at the crowd and shouted at them.

"Why don't you guys do something?"

It was all the prompting the crowd needed. Some people began angrily yelling at the police. The officers started to let some more of the people inside the club go, and that's when Margaret spotted her.

Penelope had her hands cuffed behind her, and she had been crying as evidenced by the streams of black mascara dripping from her eyes and running down her rouged cheeks. She looked frightened. Her blouse gaped open, her breasts exposed. The police officer inappropriately grabbed at her breasts as he removed her handcuffs; the scene incited some in the crowd even further.

"Curtis, help her!" Margaret wailed from the back seat of the car. "Go get her, please!"

"Yes, ma'am." He jumped out of the car and removed his jacket, as he worked his way through the crowd and ran to Penelope's side. Placing his jacket around her and shielding her, he swiftly walked her to where the car was parked and helped her inside the back seat with Margaret.

People in the crowd were still shouting, and someone started throwing coins at the police, then some threw bottles. The horde of people swelled to dangerous numbers, too dangerous for the police officers present as they were in no position to manage the angry mob.

"Get us out of here!" Margaret bellowed. "NOW!"

Curtis slowly maneuvered the car through the crowd on Christopher Street as the protesters yelled at the police. He curved the car toward West Fourth Street to get out of the Village, and he headed up town toward the haven of Park Avenue.

33
❧ Margaret ❦
New York – Wednesday morning - July 2nd, 1969

In the days following their night out, Margaret had scanned every newspaper she could get her hands on. She read all the reports she could find on the raid at the Stonewall Inn. Only the newspapers were calling it a full-fledged riot. One paper even captioned the melee:

HOMO NEST RAIDED QUEEN BEES ARE STINGING MAD

In all she'd read, there was no mention of Penelope. Still, Margaret did not sleep well that night or the entire weekend for that matter. The mere thought that she had come so close to being exposed, completely shattered her. Her nerves were on edge to the point that she had become physically ill.

On her first day back to work since the incident (having stayed home in hopes that everything from the horrible night had died down), she found herself in the private bathroom of her office as she succumbed to the nausea. She threw up her meager breakfast, and when she tried to flush the toilet, it didn't work.

Well, that has to be the cherry on top of an already crappy day. Back to work at her, desk pen in hand, she heard a knock on the door, and Penelope entered the office without waiting for Margaret to respond and closed the door behind her.

"I didn't see you come in, Margo." Penelope's weary eyes fearfully scanned Margaret's face.

Margaret looked up at her from behind a pile of papers on her desk. "I know," she tilted her head. "I came in early."

Penelope looked as if sleep had been eluding her too. "Margo, please don't be angry with me." She nervously bit her lip. "You must know--I'm sorry about what happened last Friday night."

"I'm not angry with you, Penny. I just have a lot of work to do, as you can see." Margaret pointed to the pile in front of her.

"If you're not angry with me, then why haven't you returned any of my calls?" She sucked in her breath. "Margo, I waited for you to call me all weekend and these past two days."

"Have you seen the newspapers, Penny?!" Margaret snapped as she put her pen down. "If you had, then surely you can understand why I've been incommunicado these past few days. I hope you appreciate that I was this close," she pinched her fingers together, "to being caught up in that whole terrible mess." She grew more agitated. "I have worked too goddamned hard and have done too much to get to where I am today. It would have been catastrophic for me and my standing, not only in this corporation, but in this town as well."

"I know, Margo, but please don't shut me out."

"I'm not purposely shutting you out, Penny; I just needed some time to process this whole thing." Her mouth hardened as she went on. "My entire life could have ended in one night. So forgive me if I'm a little shell-shocked, won't you?" Her eyes narrowed. "You do realize that fact, don't you? It has been a lot for me to take in. Nevertheless, I will say this, I hope you enjoyed your little night out amongst 'people like us' because it shall never happen again, at the very least, not with me." Margaret raised an agitated brow.

"I know." Penelope's dejected eyes slid away from Margaret. "It was foolish of me to think that we could be like everyone else." Her hand flew to her mouth. "I've never been so humiliated in my entire life." Her voice quivered.

Margaret felt a brief stab of guilt; she had only been thinking of herself and the repercussions of what might have happened to her that night. When in reality, Penelope had been the one who endured something awful. "I'm sorry we didn't talk about it that night, before Curtis dropped you off at your apartment." Her voice had softened a little bit. "Tell me, dearest, what happened to you inside the club, when we got separated."

Penelope sat down in one of the chairs in front of Margaret's desk and sighed. Her platinum blond hair flew wispily around her troubled face.

"I remember, I was a little tipsy, not drunk." She emphasized while looking into Margaret's eyes, "We were dancing, just like any other couple, and I felt so good, you know? Then we suddenly started to rush through the place. I bumped into people, trying to keep up with you, but someone pulled me by my other hand, then I stumbled and fell onto the floor. The man held me tightly by the wrist, and he pulled me up from the floor. When I got up I had lost sight of you. He said to me, 'what's the rush?'," tears began to well up in her eyes, "from there on, it all happened so fast. I learned later the man who had me by my wrist was a policeman, only he was dressed in normal clothes. They turned on those harsh white lights and made us all line up; then one of the male officers grabbed me- between my legs and felt me…" she sniffed back, "he said, 'I just want to make sure you're not hiding a dick down there.' Then they made us go into the restroom with a female officer to further prove that, we, the few of us there, were in fact women." Tears pooled in her eyes. "They handcuffed me, and the female officer ripped open my b-blouse to check. They had us stand in line again while they checked our IDs." She hugged herself as tears fell from her eyes. "They took me outside, then another officer grabbed me and felt my breasts as he un-cuffed me and said I was free to go. The next thing I knew, Curtis rescued me…thank God."

Margaret handed her a Kleenex from the box on her desk. "I don't know what to say, other than I'm sorry that you had to undergo such brutality at the hands of those who have sworn to uphold the law and protect us."

Margaret realized Penelope's detention by the police just further confirmed that she had just narrowly missed an exposure of her own. Thank God for Curtis, indeed. She made a mental note to increase his pay.

"I'm sorry I put us--you--in that position, Margo," Penelope blew her nose. "I should have known better."

"I could have said no, told you that it was too risky, but I agreed to it. Let's not dwell on it any further. We shall not speak of it again. It's done and over with." Margaret wanted to change the subject as she scanned her desk. "Has there been any news from Riordan? I'm still waiting for his report."

"No, I haven't heard anything yet." She cleared her throat. "Since we're closed on Friday, I told him we needed to hear from no later than Thursday."

"Good, he has until tomorrow to connect with me then. It will be interesting to see what he has learned; keep me informed." She picked up her pen. "That will be all, Penny. As you can see, I have a mountain of paperwork to get through."

"Yes, Margo." Realizing it was back to business as usual, she rose to leave. "I just have one question. Do you still want me to go on holiday with you?"

Margaret became thoughtful for a moment. "Yes Penny, I do, I think we need some time alone in a safe place to reconnect. Time away and a change of venue will be welcomed." She smiled warmly up at her.

Penelope felt as if a load had been lifted off her as she

smiled back at Margaret. "I think we need some time too, I can't wait."

As Penelope reached the door, Margaret remembered something. "Oh, Penny, by the way, I almost forgot, place a call to maintenance and have someone take look at my toilet; it appears to be out of order."

"Alright, I'll take care of it."

A few minutes later Penelope buzzed on her intercom. Margo, I have Patrick Sloane on the line and he insists that you will take his call."

Margaret paused for a moment. "I will take his call, Penny. But put it to my private line."

The line rang. "Hello, Patrick. It's been awhile. What do you have for me?"

A man's voice replied. "I'm sorry about not getting back to you before now, but, I got a line on where he is now."

"You disappoint me, Patrick; you still haven't told me how Bartolini got out of prison unscathed in the first place?"

~~~

Before long, the building's maintenance man was in Margaret's private bathroom working noisily on her toilet.

After about a half hour of the loud clanging, Margaret opened the door and yelled over the noise.

"How much longer is this going to take?"

"I'm sorry about the noise, Mrs. Bradford, it's these old

pipes. They were custom made over thirty years ago, so I'm just trying to get these new ones to fit."

"Carry on then." She said as she backed out of the room.

Margaret felt the urge to go. Not wanting to get caught using the employee's restroom much like the angst that a teacher would have felt to use the students' bathroom, she discretely walked down the hall into one of the women's restrooms and was glad to find it unoccupied.

She went into the last stall, and just as she'd finished up, she heard a couple women come in to use the restroom. She sat frozen as they used the facilities and when they were at the sinks, one of them started talking as she lit a cigarette.

"Hey, you used to live in Greenwich Village, didn't you?"

"Yeah, I did."

"Well, you were gone the last few days, did you hear about what happened there last Friday night? There was a raid on one of the gay bars that turned into a full-fledged riot." She said.

"Oh my gosh, that's awful. Was anybody hurt?"

"I don't know, but the homos were fit to be tied, they were throwing all kinds of things at the police. I heard it was a bad scene. I also heard the police do these raids all the time, but this one went bad real fast."

"They do? What do you think happened? I mean, if they do these raids all the time, what made this one different?"

"I don't really know, but maybe the gays got tired of being pushed around by the police and decided to fight back.

Someone told me there was an unidentified blonde dyke who started it all when the police were roughing her up. She yelled at the crowd, 'do something' then the crowd started throwing stuff at the police."

"That's incredible and horrible at the same time."

"Any bets as to who the blonde could have been?" She snorted and laughed. "My money is on Margo or Penelope, because I don't care what anybody says, I think those two are together. If you know what I mean." She laughed again. "I would bet Margo is the guy, she's power hungry just like a man. And let's not forget that Margo's been out sick the last two days, wink, wink."

"You may very well be right," her friend lightly laughed. "But you had better not let her hear you say that or hear you call her Margo, because you'll be out of here on your ass."

Margaret was seething in the stall. If I could recognize their voices, they would *both* be out on their 'asses.'

The second female continued. "Besides, that's not fair, I've been out of the office for the last two days myself because my mom was sick and needed me. Either way, I don't think Margaret Bradford would be caught dead in place like that."

"That might be true, but maybe, just maybe, it's why Elliott cheated on her; he needed some love from a real woman instead of the ice queen."

"Oh, come on now," The second woman said. "Those girls were nothing but common trollops and hardly the class act that Margaret is. She may be a lot of things, but Margaret

Bradford is one beautiful and elegant lady."

"I know that, silly. You don't think I was serious about anything I said, do you?" She ran water on her cigarette and threw it in the trash and washed her hands.

"With the way you were talking, you could have easily fooled me."

"Nah, I was just kidding around." She said as they exited the restroom.

Margaret sat in shock; her blood had rushed to her face. *People actually speculated about me and Penny.*

She poked her head out of the door to be sure the coast was clear and headed straight for her office. Penelope was there at her desk outside Margaret's office; she looked up and smiled, but Margaret wordlessly walked past her as she went into her office and closed the door.

Penelope entered shortly after and spoke over the clanking noise. "I have good news for you," Penelope said, starting to look more like her put-together self. "Mr. Riordan called. He has your report ready and would like to see you today, if you have the time."

"That is good news. I'll make the time, check my schedule. Call him back and set it up." She paused as her eyes slid away from Penelope's face and down to the papers in front of her. "Penny, I'm sorry to have to tell you this, but I've decided to go on holiday without you."

"What? Why, Margo?" The shock in her voice was plain.

"I'm thinking of making it a work function in place of the

actual holiday, and I'll be inviting some of the board members to join me instead."

Penelope's smile flattened as she silently stared at Margaret before she asked. "If it's a work function, shouldn't I be there? I am your personal secretary, after all."

"Let me think about it and I'll get back to you on the whole thing, but right now, set things up with Riordan. I'd like to see him in the conference room so I won't have to put up with this blasted noise, and make it sooner rather than later."

34

❧ Gabrielle and Nick ❧

New York – Friday afternoon, August 15th, 1969

Richie Havens had become a new favorite artist of Gabrielle's since moving to Greenwich Village. She and Nick had been driving for over two hours when they came upon the venue for the concert– a farmer's field in a very rural setting. Nick parked his car along the side of the road, as did so many others. They walked the long distance as Gabrielle looked around with wide-eyed wonder at the field turned into a standing, sitting, or lying-room only outdoor concert.

As she eyed the scene, she couldn't believe the enormous crowd and the way some of the concertgoers were dressed. She asked a girl with long messy hair dressed in a three-tiered floral skirt and tank top to take a picture of her and Nick in front of the massive mob. Gabrielle began photographing the crowd of people. Some of the men wore tie dyed t-shirts, fringed suede vests, or they were shirtless all together. Long hair, afros, headbands and love beads were everywhere. For Gabrielle she saw inspiration and envisioned ways to translate some of the funky styles into mainstream fashion.

With a mixture of ethnicities, it proved to be a true melting pot and they struck her as being a fun-loving group as a good many of them flashed the two-fingered 'V' sign for peace as she snapped their images. In her neighborhood, there were a few street musicians who could have been called hippies, but seeing so many mellowed out people on a scale such as this, it stirred her creatively.

Quite a few of the concert goers had set up tents, while others were lying down or sitting on blankets bobbing their heads to the very loud music. A pungent scent filled the warm atmosphere with an earthy aroma that floated all around them; Nick scowled and informed her the area stunk of marijuana. "Try not to inhale that shit," he frowned tilting his head back at her, "it will stunt your growth."

"Well," she shook her head, "that's going to be hard to do because the smell seems to be everywhere."

He turned around and cupped her face in his hands. "My sweet Gabi, I just continue to corrupt you, don't I? Now I'm exposing you to a drug riddled music festival." A grin spread on his lips as he kissed her forehead. "I suppose the contact high from a little weed won't kill us, now will it? And who knows, you might even like it." He laughed.

"Nope," she beamed. "I don't think weed is for me; I'd much prefer a glass of wine."

She slid her arms around his waist and allowed the *love everyone* vibe guide her along with its relaxed wave. "I hope you know that I think your other forms of corruption, up to this point, have been very gratifying experiences for me," she said.

"Good to know." He replied loudly over the music with a smile.

She followed Nick as he sliced their way through the jubilant yet mellow crowd of people; Richie Havens was already on the huge stage performing.

They both had special passes around their necks that got them closer to the stage, and soon they stood in front of the wooden fenced area along with other people who were taking photos of Richie Havens and his bandmates. Just beyond them was the stage. Nick stood behind Gabrielle with his arms around her as she leaned back onto him allowing him to cocoon her within his arms. They let Richie lyrically move them with his soulful offering of "I Can't Make It Anymore," and the music had them swaying back and forth. Richie's enthralling raspy, yet smooth voice held the crowd as his vocal cords caressed each word as he moved everyone with his frenetic guitar playing.

On the stage in the background a tall skinny man in dust-covered jeans and a black t-shirt moved band equipment around until he spied Nick in the crowd. With a look of recognition and relief, he exited the stage. As the tall man moved toward them, Nick explained that he was his friend Jerry Millner, and he had gotten them their plum tickets and passes.

Jerry approached and shook Nick's hand. "Hey Nick, I'm

glad you made it." He spoke over the loud music.

After Nick did the introductions, Jerry frowned at Nick. "I could really use your help, buddy."

"Oh, so that's why you offered me the tickets, want me to work for them, huh?" Nick laughed.

"Hey, you're the biggest guy I know." Jerry grinned as he looked over at Gabrielle. "Do you mind if I borrow him for a few? I need him to lend me his muscles."

"No, I don't mind." She replied over the noise.

"Are you sure?" Nick said to her with concern. "I don't want to leave you alone."

"I'm not alone, look at all these people, I will be okay. Go on and help Jerry, I'll be fine right here."

"Alright, I won't be gone long, Sweetness." He replied.

Jerry and Nick walked around to the side stairs of the stage leaving Gabrielle in front of the fence. She soon saw Nick in the background as he helped Jerry move some large heavy sound equipment around on the stage.

She stood there bobbing her head to the energetic offering of "Handsome Johnny" and a couple of other songs. Gabrielle enjoyed Richie's music as he went into a spirited version of "Freedom" that soon morphed into "Motherless Child."

A shirtless man with his t-shirt hanging from his back pocket passed by her, but he stopped directly in front of her, and with wild eyes, he looked at her with a half-baked leer. "Hey there, little mama, you look like a freaking beautiful flower just ripe for picking! You want a hit?" he fanned a lit marijuana cigarette under her nose.

She shook her head at him. "No, thanks." She looked to the stage trying to avoid eye contact with the man in front of her.

"You don't know what you're missing, little mama. Ya sure?" He waved it under her nose again.

"I said no, and I'm not your little mama. Now buzz off and leave me alone." Her eyes glared at the man and then went back to Richie on the stage.

"Buzz off? I'm already buzzed, you can be too, little mama. I got to tell you it feels so fucking good."

"No thank you, I don't need your weed to feel good."

"I got more than weed though," he nodded his head at her. "We can go on a real trip. I think that you're gonna love it." He extinguished the marijuana cigarette by pinching it with his fingers and stuck it into his pants pocket. "Come on, you're coming with me. I can show you how to really party." He grabbed her by her right arm and started to pull her along with him.

Caught off guard, she tried to jerk free from his hold. However, high or not, he had been stronger than she thought. And he was, in fact, pulling her behind him. She needed to get a foothold so she could free herself.

As they got closer to the fence opening, she looked up and made eye contact with Nick, who was still on the stage helping move the large amplifiers. She still struggled to free herself from the man's grip.

She just lifted two of his fingers from her arm and dug her

heels into the grass beneath her feet, stopping the forward motion. She was about to knee him in the crotch as soon as he turned around. Before she could do it, Nick instantly appeared.

"Take your filthy hands off her before I break you in half, you son of a bitch!" Nick snarled as he squeezed the man's wrist tightly and broke the hold the man had on Gabrielle's arm.

She tried to protest. "It's okay, Nick, you don't have to-"

Ignoring her objections Nick pushed the man back towards the wooden fence.

"What the fuck? Don't push me, man!" The man regained his balance and looked hard at Nick.

"Just wait, I'll do more than push you. You fucking idiot!"

The man threw a punch that Nick blocked before striking back, hitting the man in the face and knocking him against the fence. Blood sprang from the man's nose.

Gabrielle could not believe the scene in front of her; stunned, she rubbed at her now freed arm.

The man scowled at Nick. "Who the hell are you, man?" Raising his fingers to his nose, the blood smeared across his face as he crudely wiped at it. "I'll kick your ass, man." He made a fist that he threw in Nick's direction.

Nick was done talking, he grabbed the man forcefully by the throat.

"LET HIM GO, NICK!" Gabrielle shouted pulling on his arm.

He released his hold as the man coughed and clutched his throat, reddened from Nick's grasp. "Don't ever grab a woman that way again!" Nick warned him. "Especially when she's my woman!"

"Hey, I'm s-sorry, man. I thought she wanted to party. I didn't know she had an old man. I thought she was alone. Free for the taking."

"Well, you thought wrong because she does have an *old man* and he happens to be me. Now, get out of my sight before I change my mind and finish what I started."

"Okay man, you don't have go all Sonny Liston on me. I'm going, okay?" The man scurried away holding his nose.

"Hello, Mr. Neanderthal!" She angrily glared up at Nick. "What in the hell was that all about?"

"You've got to be kidding me! Unbelievable!" He balked at her. "He had his hands on you, and I'm the one you're pissed at. What did you think I was supposed to do, Gabi?" He glared back at her.

"Nothing! I didn't need you to do a thing, because I had it all under control!" She shot back at him.

"Like hell you did. If I hadn't stepped in, he would have taken you to God knows where- and given you whatever he was on." His jaw clinched hard.

"I didn't need you to go ballistic on some drugged-out jerk; I was freeing myself from his grip." She countered.

"You know, maybe he already slipped you something. Because for you to be cross with me right now is insane.

Did the smell from the weed make you high or something? Because right now, Gabrielle, you're talking fucking crazy!"

"Go to hell, Nick!" She glowered at him.

"I feel like I'm in the fucking Twilight Zone, because you are being beyond ridiculous."

She spun around and walked speedily away from him as Richie Havens finished his set with the last few bars of "Freedom." Nick followed her in silence as they worked their way through the hordes of people. As the darkness of the sky slowly crept upon them, they finally reached his car; both angry at the other for different reasons.

So much for a fun outdoor concert. He turned on the radio and they drove the two hours back to the city without talking. Her head turned away from him, she sulked as she looked out into the darkness of the car window.

~~~

They arrived outside her apartment and Nick parked the car.

"Do you want me to come up?" He asked her.

"You've got to be kidding me. No." She replied as she opened the door to get out.

"Gabi, wait," he stopped her as he spoke in a rueful tone. "I don't really know what I did for you to be cross with me. However, I'm sorry for what I said. You're not crazy, insane or ridiculous."

She sat motionless; her back stiffened as she listened.

"Still, you need to know something," he sighed heavily as he spoke, "when I saw that guy with his hands on you like that, it made me angry. It made my blood boil." He wrapped his hands tightly around the steering wheel and pressed his forehead against the top of the wheel, as if steeling himself to go on. "I wanted to do more than just punch him in the face. If you hadn't stopped me, I'm pretty sure I would have."

"That's why I'm angry, Nick." She turned to face him closing the car door, the streetlight giving her a dimly lit view of his inclined head.

"You came charging in like the friggin Calvary. You always want to protect me. But, you need to know something about me: I can take care of myself. I don't need a protector."

"Hmm…" He lifted his head. "That's good to know, that you're prepared to stand up for yourself, that you don't back down. It's one of the things I admire about you." He sighed. "What you need to know is," he stared straight ahead. "I knew someone who couldn't do that for herself, and she became his weekly punching bag, suffering abuse at the hands of her own husband."

She remained silent and watched him in the darkness. He continued, "Nevertheless, she refused to leave him because of her faith. The church wouldn't support her in leaving him. Even though it was a well-known fact that she was an abused woman. The church did nothing to help her out of that ghastly marriage. In essence they told her to suffer in silence." His jaw clenched visibly. "I wasn't able to protect her then, and later, when I could, she wouldn't let me help her, like it was her penitence or something. I had to walk away from that situation and from her because if I didn't, I think I would have killed him. I haven't seen her since."

"My God, Nick, your mother? I'm so sorry, I had no idea."

"I don't like talking about it, or about her, because I've always felt helpless where she's concerned. Gabi, I know you think I'm some chauvinistic asshole with a large sense of my own machismo, but I'm quite the opposite. I think women have a voice and men ought to contribute to their ability in exercising it."

Unable to look at her, his eyes focused on his hands that still gripped the steering wheel. "From what I saw growing up and from what I experienced myself," his finger went to the crescent scar below his eye. "Those awful scenes have stuck with me. If a man is harming a woman, I will not hesitate to step in and stop that threat. That's something you need to know about me."

"That's the problem, Nick; I just don't know who you are. We've been dating for months, and this is the first time you have shared a glimpse with me about your formative years."

"You know more about me than most. I just don't like talking about that time in my life."

"I know. Anytime I've tried to learn a bit about you, who you were as a youngster, you just clam up or change the subject all together."

"I've done many things I'm not proud of, and I've associated with quite a few bad people in the process. I escaped that life, Gabi. I don't want to dredge any of it up to pollute the place I'm at right now. What would be the point? It's over and I've moved on away from it."

She watched him in the darkness and could sense the pain he was trying to squelch down inside himself as he leaned his head back against the headrest of his seat.

"Gabi, I need you to trust me on this and not push the issue. No good can come of it."

She reached over, placed her hand on top of his and gave his hand a soothing rub. "I do trust you, I just wish you trusted me enough to let me in. But, I won't press you about it, because it's your story to tell. You can tell me in your own time, when you're ready."

35
❧ Nick ❧

New York – Tuesday afternoon - September 16th, 1969

When he rounded the corner of the reception desk at the health club, Nick saw Margaret Bradford. He wasn't all that surprised to see that she had sought him out; he knew she had sparked some sort of interest in him when Gabrielle introduced them at The Bradford Building a few weeks back.

She appeared softer and more vulnerable than the last time he'd seen her; she stood in front of the bronzed plaque listing the names of the club's benefactors. He silently assessed her, an attractive woman smartly dressed in a tailored cream colored pantsuit with a pale blue scarf softly knotted at her neck that seemed to equal the color of her large gray-blue eyes. Her blond hair looked different, but still expertly coiffed in stylish layers. He watched as her fingers smoothly slid across one name on the list.

Nick rested his hands on his hips. "Ahem," he cleared his throat. "Mrs. Bradford? You wanted to see me."

Startled, Margaret slightly jumped and turned to face him.

"Mr. Caine, I was just," she looked back at the names on

the wall. "Did you know my late husband had been a member here?" She turned around to fully face him and smiled warmly.

"Yes ma'am, I am aware of that fact." He replied.

"Ma'am?" She lightly laughed. "I'm not sure when I became a ma'am, but in any case, I really do prefer Margo." She eyed him curiously. "I have to ask, were you ever privileged enough to have met my Elliott by any chance?" She spoke, her voice even and controlled.

"I did speak with Mr. Bradford on occasion when he'd come here; I think the last I talked with him here was a few days before his death. We had a brief conversation. He seemed to be a decent man, very likeable."

"Hmmm, yes, he was." She softly replied, lowering her eyes.

"I'm sorry for your loss, but I'm sure that's not the reason you're here." He asked guardedly, "How can I help you?"

"Help me?" She laughed gently and tilted her head to him. "On the contrary, it is actually I who intends to help you."

"I don't catch your drift here. I don't recall ever asking for your help with anything, Mrs. Bradford."

"That didn't come out the way I intended it- what I really should have said is that we can be of service to each other."

"How's that?" He shrugged his shoulders. "I still don't follow; I haven't a clue as to what you're talking about." However, he felt he had an idea, *all the talk of her dead husband, she's probably looking to get laid.*

"Oh, you will, but I must confess. I'm not in the habit

of discussing any type of business in this manner, Nick." Margaret pursed her lips with smiling eyes. "I think we should converse about this, say, over lunch, today."

"Business?" His eyes squinted. "Please, tell me, just what kind of business you're talking about, Mrs. Bradfor..., Margo?"

"Maybe I didn't make myself clear," she said, "or perhaps you didn't hear me. I said, we should discuss this over lunch."

"I hear you loud and clear, but you're not saying much."

"I will have plenty to say. Join me at the 21 Club at noon today. Trust me, your entire future may very well depend upon it." Then without a word she turned around and walked through the main doors of the health club without looking back."

Nick stared after her as she entered the back seat of a black chauffeur-driven limousine.

~~~

Nick arrived at 21 Club and informed the maître d that he had a meeting with Margaret Bradford. The maître d looked disapprovingly at Nick's collared polo shirt as he disappeared into the small room behind him and re-emerged with a jacket and tie in his hands.

"Sir, would you mind buttoning up?" He handed Nick the clip-on tie and a large sports jacket. "It's our policy."

Nick sighed; the large jacket fit snugly as he pulled it on

over his muscular biceps and clipped the tie in place at his polo shirt's opening.

"Follow me, Sir." The maître d said with superiority as he led Nick to Margaret's table.

Nick stood edgily behind the chair facing Margaret. "Alright, I'm here. So let's talk."

"Please, sit down." She stated tersely with a stiff smile as she looked around the room; people were beginning to stare.

He rolled his eyes, sighed, and sat down in the chair.

"I took the liberty and ordered for both of us. I hope that's okay." She smiled cordially.

"That's fine by me," he shook his head impatiently. "I really don't care one way or the other. Unless you get to the point pretty damned quick as to why you needed to see me *so urgently*, I'll be leaving anyway."

"I suppose I can dispense with any of the usual pleasantries and get right to it then." Her stare determined. "I'd like to offer you a business deal."

"A business deal?" Nick's handsome face held a bit of doubt as he suspiciously watched her. "I'm listening."

"You may or may not be aware of this, but ever since the death of my husband," she paused and straightened up her back. "Elliott Bradford was the glue that held this company together," she swallowed, "with his passing, much of his responsibilities have fallen to me." Her eyes shrewdly measured him.

"I'm still confused, what does all of that have to do with

me?" He questioned.

"I'm getting to that; I've discovered that since I have ultimate control of ERB National Holdings, it just doesn't sit well with some. And many business men, if you can call then that," she paused, "for truthfully, I use the term loosely." Her mouth twisted irritably. "These men have chosen not to renew their leases with us and have vacated some prime space in The Bradford Building, solely because a woman is at the helm." She took a sip of her water before going on.

"I now find that I have excess space in my building. Therefore, I need new tenants, and it's been recently brought to my attention that you are planning to launch a health club in the not-too-distant future." Her eyes tapered. "I'd like to have your business; I'm hoping you would consider placing your club in The Bradford Building."

Nick shook his head as he lightly chuckled. "Thank you for the offer, but I'm in no financial shape to be able to afford neither the renovations nor the rents that you would charge at The Bradford Building." His lips held his smile.

"I'm aware of your financials, Nick. Don't make the mistake that some men do, believing that just because I am a woman, that I would overlook that very important fact. I don't enter into any venture, business or otherwise, without knowing precisely what or whom I'm dealing with."

"You know about my finances?" His mouth coiled as his jaw tightly clinched. "How's that possible?"

"My husband left me well off. I am, in fact, a very wealthy

woman, and it's afforded me a certain amount of influence in this town. Given that element alone, I make it my business to know all there is to know about my future business associates," lifting her hands, she interlaced her fingers and continued, "which includes the recently released, Enrico Bartolini."

Nick's eyes widened at her disclosure, as he defensively stated, "I don't understand; you know all of this, yet, you still want to do some sort of business with us. Why?"

"To help, Nick, I'm aware that you've gone to some banking institutions for traditional loans to get this thing off the ground, and I'm also aware that you've been turned down flat. I'm sure Mr. Bartolini's record hasn't helped you in that regard."

His eyes squinted suspiciously at her. "And you have no problem with Enrico's record? I still ask the question, why is that, Margo?"

Confidently she smiled. "I want to be very clear; it's you I want. I'm banking on you, because on paper, your credentials are impeccable. You were amongst the top of your class at Columbia Business School, and your current employers speak very highly of you." She paused, gaging him as she took another sip of water. "Let's just face this head on, Mr. Bartolini is your unfortunate baggage. I know that to have you, I must accept him."

"That's not completely accurate." Nick readjusted himself in his chair. "To be fair, Enrico is not 'unfortunate baggage,' he's my family. All he needs is a fresh start. And he does have some good business ideas as well." Nick's eyes were downcast as he said the words, finding it hard to defend Enrico due to his own misgivings where Enrico was concerned.

"Be that as it may, Nick, you can be his champion all you like. I'm willing to overlook his past brushes with the law because of you. It's you who will take this business where it needs to go, I'm assured of that."

"Thank you for the vote of confidence, but our plans are only in their infancy. We are in no way, shape, or form in the position to be considered a business yet."

It was her turn to dryly laugh as she looked pointedly at him. "Please don't underestimate the power of money; anything you can dream is accomplishable. I'm prepared to be a silent partner in your club, and only after it's up and running and making a decent profit, of course, would you be expected to reimburse me on my investment."

With a slight tilt of his head, he asked, "What are your conditions, Margo? I've been in the business world long enough to know that there are always conditions."

"I have placed no conditions or stipulations on this project, other than expecting your highest degree of discretion, of course."

He looked bewildered for a moment as his eyes settled on her face. "Why me, Margo?"

"It's simple really; I like your ideas, and I think having a health club in our building will be an added bonus for our current tenants. I want to extend the services you plan to offer as a benefit to them; also I need the public to see there is absolute confidence in the current management of The Bradford Building, as well as in ERB National Holdings."

Inwardly, she smiled, as she could see the wheels of possibility swirling around in his head like the innards of a clock as she spoke. "The only way to achieve this feat is with new business and that's where you come in. On the surface it will appear to be new commerce for ERB, but no one will be aware that it's actually me who is assisting this venture by financially backing your athletic club."

Intrigued, he allowed himself to give her a slight smile as his eyes twinkled. *She wants me because she thinks that I'm hungry enough to let her orchestrate everything behind the scenes, and I am, aren't I?*

"We do have capital in our stronghold, miniscule by your standards, I'm sure. But we were letting our money grow while the gym plans were being fully developed." He stated.

"Growing at the current rate of interest, you would be very old men by the time you would accumulate what I'm offering, but mind you, I do understand Nick. I trust you will discuss this little undertaking of ours with no one except Mr. Bartolini and obtain his silence as well?" Her eyes then appeared steely cold.

"Keep in mind that your discretion would also have to extend to one Gabrielle Lawrence."

She silently watched his expression change as his bewildered eyes met hers. She let that little tidbit sink in as she finished her sentence, "And, unfortunately, I must also inform you that my offer does come with a deadline." She paused. "I'm allowing you until the end of business day tomorrow to give me your answer."

Nick conceded with a nod of his head. "You will have an answer by tomorrow. And you have my word; I will be discrete and speak only with Mr. Bartolini about this opportunity." Truth be told he could answer her now; they would be fools to pass on this offer.

His glass had condensation droplets on it that slid to his fingers as he lifted it for the first time for a sip. *It will be hard not to share any of this with Gabrielle, but if Margo is on the up and up, and I have a feeling she is, all of Rico's and my dreams just might be coming to fruition.*

"Ahh, our meals have arrived." She smiled at the waiter who had just brought them the house specials she had ordered for each of them. "No more talk of business; let's eat, shall we?"

Nick could scarcely eat the food placed in front of him with his mind doing cartwheels. He politely nodded and smiled, but he wasn't even really listening to her anymore. Barely able to contain himself, he couldn't wait to tell Enrico about their stroke of good fortune.

36
🌸 Nick and Margaret 🌸
New York – Monday evening - October 20th, 1969

After getting all the legal documents signed, notarized, and squared away, he noted that Margaret just seemed pleased to have them sign on the dotted line and to break ground on their project, albeit very quietly per Margaret's provisos. Only a handful of people knew of the construction of the impending health club.

Club, Nick hated the word, to him it meant a place for the wealthy and certainly not the clientele he wanted to attract. He wanted a place for die-hard lifters who took the principles of body building seriously. So, to him this wasn't a club, this was a GYM, his gym, yet he knew he had to play along with Margaret. Margaret bankrolled a significant amount of funds for the build; however, he intended to pay her back every red cent of her investment.

By the end of October, Nick spent his days distractedly working at his job at the athletic club, but by night, he could be found at The Bradford Building in the roughed-out space, working in secrecy with Enrico and Samuel Burton, the architect who Margaret had hired to make their vision come to life. Those blueprints displayed their hopes and dreams as they lay spread out on Sam's worktable.

Enrico spent all his time on the second floor with Sam, helping with the planning, measuring, and even with some of the construction once it began. To see Enrico so happy and cheerful made it all seem worth it. Nick hadn't seen him like this since they were kids, before they both got mixed up with Marchetti.

He did, however, have mixed feelings about not sharing any of it with Gabrielle, but secrecy had been Margaret's only stipulation or she could pull the plug on the entire project. He had too much riding on this to let that happen, because not only did his future depend on the outcome of everything, but Enrico's did as well.

This had been the fresh start Enrico needed to turn his life around, and Nick was acutely aware of how much he owed it to Enrico to give him that chance. Gabrielle would just have to understand the position he had to take by keeping her in the dark about the whole thing.

Gabrielle barely noticed his absence most evenings because her schedule at the fashion house also kept her busier than usual, but despite this, he hadn't missed calling her every night to wish her pleasant dreams as well as spending time with her on their shortened weekends.

Everything began to fall into place; he had but one worry: money. Their capital (his and Enrico's pooled assets) was quickly being depleted. Considering this, Nick realized that Margaret had invested the lion's share for the modifications needed. However, he kept a running tally as to what they truly owed Margaret so they could pay her back.

Enrico had told him not to worry because he had some hidden assets that would more than cover what they owed. Nick hoped this was true; he further hoped those 'hidden assets' were not in any way tied to their old business associates, namely one Salvatore Marchetti. He most certainly did not want this project poisoned by their nefarious past business associate.

Nick would much prefer to owe money to Margaret Bradford and pay her back when they could, allowing her to be the silent partner she had proposed to be until they could buy her out of the partnership, which had been one of *his* stipulations.

He walked around the space situated on the second floor of the west end of the building and approvingly exhaled. The raw area was enormous. The carpenters had already roughed out some of the areas, and Nick found that Samuel Burton had a way of listening to him and capturing everything on Nick's wish list, only he made it look better in his renderings than Nick had imagined.

Nick's office was to be large with its own private bathroom complete with a walk-in shower; fittingly Enrico's office would mirror Nick's just on the other side of the reception counter.

"It all looks great, Sam." Nick's deep voice echoed in the

vacuous space.

"I'm glad you approve, Mr. Caine. Now if you could just look over here, at this section," Samuel walked him through an area that had been cordoned off by sheets of opaque plastic. Beyond there were eight wide steps, once they were at the top Samuel pointed to a long area that had large pipes snaking beneath what appeared to be a built-up hole in the floor.

"The high ceiling in here will really make this work out well, it's where the lap pool is going to be situated, the area has been steel reinforced and the plumbers installed the piping along with the drainage pipes. The masonry workers are due tomorrow to tile up the sides of the walls, and-"

Nick frowned. "I thought we scrapped the plans for a pool to cut down on some of the expenses, Sam."

"It's my present to you," Margaret said from the bottom of the steps, she walked up the stairs and stood behind Nick. She slid her hand up his arm as she moved close to him. "I wanted to thank you in some small way."

"Margo, installing that pool is not a small way," he paused. "We really need to talk." He turned his head toward the architect. "Sam, could you give us a moment?"

"Yes, of course, I'll catch up with the foreman. I have some things I need to run by him anyway."

Once Sam was out of hearing range, Nick turned to face her. "Look, Margo, I know you are more than aware of our finances, so you know we're rapidly approaching our maximum. We're in no position to be able to afford-"

"Relax, my dear boy." She cut him off. "As I said, the pool is my gift to you for working with me on this project and adhering to my requests, so just be gracious and accept it." She leaned closer to him. "Trust me. There are no strings attached to it, alright?"

In his dealings with her she has been on the up and up, but something inside his gut had told him that those words *'no strings attached'* just might come back to haunt him.

37
❦ Gabrielle ❦

Linda loved this time of year at the fashion house; even with the pressure from all the tasks that needed to be completed, she somehow felt less stressed than usual. She was happy that things were humming along in its own chaotic loveliness. Everyone had been pulling his or her own weight, and they were producing some amazing designs. Her current designers impressed Linda, and she appreciated how invested they were in VonShelles.

Monty, a true star in the traditional sense, his style of design tended to lean toward the classics, focusing on women's shapes and feminine silhouettes. His creations were similar to Oscar de la Renta or his personal favorite Parisian designer, Louis B Laurendeau.

Monty patterned his design style after Laurendeau, he had been impressed with the French designer's ability to drape the female form with miles of fabric while making her look sleek and sexy. Laurendeau had successfully evolved his LBL brand from his haute couture collections to popular ready-to-wear options that were now available in stores and accessible to the fashion conscious American woman.

Then there's Gabrielle, she proved to be Linda's modern girl, her prodigy. She had an avant-garde approach to design that Linda felt gave her the ability to create spectacular images. Some of which, Linda felt, had an edginess that rivaled her own past Taylor Made collections. Gabrielle used colors and textures to advance her renderings into unique yet marketable offerings.

Linda had ordered take out for her team and was just about ready to go pick it up when she got a call from Clayton Butler who wanted her to come up to his office. A smile played at her lips as she thought of him, and she pulled her compact out of her purse to refresh her lipstick and face powder. She fluffed her hair with her fingers as she saw Gabrielle walk by.

"Gabi, can you come in here for a minute?"

Gabrielle stood at Linda's door and leaned in. "Sure, what do you need?"

"I was going out to grab some dinner for everyone, but I just got called to attend an impromptu meeting with Clayton Butler on the fortieth floor." She scrunched her nose. "I hate to ask but, would you mind terribly, going to pick it up for me?"

"No, I don't mind. I could actually use the distraction."

"That's great! You're a lifesaver" She smiled as she put the bills into Gabrielle's hand. "Here's the money and the order number."

They both headed for the elevators and each entered their own elevator; Linda went up as Gabrielle took the down car.

As Gabrielle exited the elevator, she unnervingly observed the deserted reception desk, even Thomas had left for the day. Only wall sconces lit the darkened lobby; however, the light coming through the front windows of the building illumined the area.

She then saw two figures near the stairs at the center of the building, and she'd been taken aback to see that one of the figures was Nick talking with a man she'd never seen before, and it looked as if they were about to take the stairs as she called out to him in surprise.

"Nick? What on earth are you doing here?"

Startled, Nick turned to face her and his face went white. "Hey Gabi," he said as he quickly recovered. "Just the person I'm looking for."

"That's odd that you would look for me over there, since I work on this side of the building."

"I know... I was helping this fellow with directions." He tilted his head toward Samuel Burton.

"Thank you for your help," Samuel said, nodding his head to Nick, "I think I can find it from here." He remarked as he headed up the stairs.

"I'm glad I caught you," Nick walked to her. "I knew you'd be working late again, I hoped I could take you out to dinner?"

She smiled; seeing him made her realize how much she

missed him, and she wished she could do more than just a dinner with him. Her body, as tired as she was, longed for him and his touch as she audibly groaned.

"I can't leave for dinner, but if you like, you can join me as I run an errand for Linda to pick up dinner for the crew."

"I'd be happy to." He tilted his head and kissed her. "I've missed you so much, Gabi. Saturday nights and Sunday mornings just aren't enough." He wrapped her in his arms and held her close.

"I've missed you too, I'm sorry." Her brow furrowed, "I've been so busy with work, and I know I've been a bit neglectful. Everything's so hectic at the fashion house. Right now, all I've been doing is eating and sleeping fashion." She shared a hopeful smile. "Our deadlines for press week will be met soon, then things will ease up, and we can get back on track."

He walked the short distance to the deli with her and found himself itching to tell her why he'd really been at The Bradford Building, but he refrained. Once she had purchased the food, he helped her carry it all back to the hungry designers on the twenty-second floor; she walked him back to the elevator.

"Thank you for being so understanding about my work. This really is important to me; we'll be together this weekend. I promise." Her hand touched the necklace he'd given her.

He kissed her. "I know how important your work is to you, and I also know that if the shoe was on the other foot, and it was me who had work obligations, you'd understand as well."

"You're right, I would." She gave him a peck on the lips. "We're trying to tie things up here tonight so we won't have to come in tomorrow. I should be done around nine-thirty or ten. Can I call you later?"

"You absolutely can."

He went back down to the second floor and worked with Enrico, Samuel, and the carpenters for a few hours. But, after seeing her, the thought of Gabrielle being only twenty floors away made it hard for him to concentrate.

"Hey, Nico, I can see that your head's somewhere else." Enrico said. "Why don't you get outta here, go be with your girl. Sam and me, we got things under control here."

"Are you sure, Rico?" Nick gave a crooked smile. "I don't want to leave you guys with all of the work,"

"Everything here is copacetic, brother. Now go."

Nick went downstairs to wait in the lobby for Gabrielle, the illuminated alabaster sculpture caught his eye. For the first time he saw the words written beneath it in bronze:

Behold, your diamond in the rough.

Those few words struck a chord in Nick as it seemed to speak to something within, something he couldn't understand. *Maybe, it's because I've been working in the roughed-out area and once finished, the gym will be my diamond...*

Well after 10 p.m. she and some of the other designers exited the elevator. It stunned her to see him sitting in one of the lobby chairs, his legs stretched out in front of him as his feet rested on one of the glass tables.

"Hey lady, you need a ride?" He smiled up at her. "Your chariot awaits."

Monty Greer smiled at Gabrielle. "I guess you don't need a ride from me tonight after all. Enjoy your weekend, I'll see you Monday." He said as he joined the others as they walked toward the doors.

She smiled at Nick. "You waited to drive me home?" Her heart melted.

"Well, not the whole time. But yeah, I guess I kind of did." He stood up. "So, shall we go?"

As exhausted as she'd been, she found a new burst of energy flowing from within. "I'm more than ready because tonight and the next two days you have me all to yourself."

"Hmm… The thought of having you for the next two days is tantalizing. Are you sure you're up for it?"

"Oh, I'm up for it. Lead the way, my good man."

38
❦ Nick and Enrico ❧
New York – Sunday evening - October 26th, 1969

Nick returned home that Sunday evening to a ringing phone and he quickly picked up the receiver.

"Nico, I need you…at Gina's…hurry." Enrico pled, his voice garbled. Nick heard wheezing and knew he had to get there, and fast.

Ten minutes later Nick slammed on the brakes as he pulled up in front of Gina's apartment building. She must have been watching for him because she met him at the door.

"Nick! Thank you for getting here." Her skin was pale, and her large brown eyes were filled with distress, as her long dark hair up in a messy bun. There'd been drying blood on the front of her blouse and jeans. The hallway and her door had blood smeared in a haphazard attempt to clean it up.

"It's bad…" her eyes gave way to the fearful tears about to brim over. "They beat the crap out of him."

"WHAT! Someone beat up Rico?" His eyes expanded wide in disbelief. "You've got to be fucking kidding me!"

"Not someone. More like some ones, you know Rico. He's

317

the toughest guy around; he's always been able to take care of himself." Her brow furrowed with worry as she wiped at her tears. "There had to be more than one guy to do this to him."

"Where is he?" Nick asked.

"He's inside," her breath hitched in her throat, "see if you can get him to go to the hospital. I cleaned him up the best I could, but there was just so much blood." She sniffed back using her knuckle to wipe her nose. "Be warned, he's talking out of his head." She said as she quickly led him through the door to the apartment.

Nick's heart sank, and a knot formed in his stomach. A shirtless Enrico, laid out on Gina's couch, his face hardly recognizable. It was a swollen mess, at his throat blood oozed through the crude bandage that Gina had put upon it; a stream of blood seemed to be coming out of his ear.

Visible bruises already formed on his ribcage, and it also looked as if his hand had been broken. Nick could see the definite outline of a shoe heel imprinted upon it.

"Who in the hell did this to you, Rico?" Suddenly, his voice filled with rage. "I'll kill the sons of bitches!"

"Mar... chetti's... goons." He wheezed. "Ki..., killed... Lo bo."

"Lobo's dead? For fuck sake!"

"I wa...want t-to do good... Make Nicolo... p-proud." He wheezed. "Keep... your hands... off, don't you hit... her."

"What? What are you talking about, Rico?"

"Remember... Sal's caddie? Want... one jus'... like... it."

Enrico wasn't making any sense. Nick looked in Gina's direction with concern. "You need to call for an ambulance!"

"No...No...amb...lance." Enrico objected. "Won't...let you hurt him...he's my bl...blood. One m-more job-Sal...No amb...lance."

Gina did not move a muscle; she remained frozen in place and looked helpless.

"For fuck sake, Rico, you need to get to the hospital, and I don't want to hurt you further trying to haul you in my car." He sharply looked over at her again. "Gina, call that goddamned ambulance, NOW!"

~~~

After Enrico and Gina were loaded into the ambulance and on route to the hospital, Nick followed the trail of blood that led to Gina's apartment from a nearby alleyway. Enrico had been staying at an apartment near Gina's, Nick recalled what Enrico had said to him a while back: *I'm going to do all I can to win Gina back. I will be as annoying as hell, but I'm gonna get my girl back.'*

Huge dumpsters loomed in the alley, overflowing trash cans lined up against the buildings. Smears of blood on a building's wall confirmed it to be the site of the attack. Nick realized it had been a perfect spot for an ambush, there were many places to lie in wait for the unsuspecting Enrico. Some cans had been knocked over, their contents spilled out onto the ground along with two bloodied cast-off two-by-fours atop the trash heap.

His brow furrowed as he caught sight of the stilled bloody body of Lobo. The dog had been shot, a piece of blue fabric caught in his teeth. Nick fell to his knees, his face twisted painfully as his hand reached out and smoothed some of Lobo's blood caked fur. Tears stung his eyes as a guttural yell filled his throat and he croaked out.

"Why'd you do this Sal! Why?"

~~~

Nick sat in one of the many olive green Naugahyde and metal chairs in the waiting area of the emergency room as he waited for word on Enrico's condition in the busy waiting room. Gina by his side, still wearing her shirt and jeans caked with Enrico's dried blood. A dazed expression plastered on Gina's ivory face, and she stared blankly ahead under the fluorescent lights.

Nick ran a tense hand through his thick dark hair. "How in the hell did this happen?"

"I don't know, Nick." Gina wearily shook her head. "All's I know is that there was this knock at my door, see?" Her Bronx accent eternally present. "I open it and I sees Rico bleeding, all ova in the hallway. I got him inside and tried to bandage the cut on his neck. He had me call you; I put the phone to his ear. You know the rest."

She looked purposely at Nick. "We broke up, ya know? He calls me, a few months back, tells me he's going legit. I tell him: 'don't tell me Rico, you gotta show me.' I told him not to come around me if he was still running with those thugs." Her voice became thick and garbled, she swallowed.

"I want a better life, ya know? Kinda like what you did, to get away from all of that mess." She tried to hold back tears, but she couldn't and started to cry. "I really love him, but I can't be a part of that... that kinda life, worrying about him. Wondering if he killed somebody, then get sent back to prison. Or if he's been hurt, like now or worse yet, that he's dead."

Overcome with emotion, Gina sobbed; Nick put his arm around her and held her in a comforting embrace. All the while he realized he felt the same way Gina did. He had told Enrico as much, and he had distanced himself from him. He had kept him at arm's length by not including him in his life. He hadn't even told Gabrielle about him.

At first, Nick had doubted Enrico's claims of rehabilitation since his release from prison; he thought Enrico would resume his life with the organization. When the gym project with Margaret came about, he saw the hard work and efforts that Enrico put into designing the space, he even helped in the constructing of the club by wearing a construction hat and getting his hands dirty.

In his heart Nick knew he owed it to Enrico to show a bit of faith in him. After seeing Enrico's battered and severely beaten body, he now fearfully wondered, *what if he dies and I lose that chance.*

Well past midnight a doctor came into the room with a grave expression and looked around the room at some of the other people before settling his gaze upon Nick and Gina. "You're Mr. Bartolini's family, I presume?" He stated.

Fear gripped Nick's chest like the jaws of a vise as he gulped some air into his constricted lungs and stood. "Yes, doctor," he looked over at Gina. "We're his family."

"I'm Dr. Logan and I'm caring for Mr. Bartolini. I should begin by telling you he's a very lucky man. His injuries were extensive. Apart from the obvious external things you see, such as the deep laceration to his throat; we have sutured the area and have dressed his wounds. He has some internal lung bruising along with three broken ribs from blunt force trauma; we've bandaged his ribs to aid in the healing process." Doctor Logan hesitated, "Also, after performing some x-rays, we discovered he has a fracture to his skull."

Nick took ahold of Gina's cold trembling hand as the doctor continued.

"Which has resulted in a concussion. And there's a fracture to a bone in his left hand. Thankfully, it was a clean break. Given time he should be fine."

"Doctor Logan," Nick's brow creased with worry, "is he really going to be alright? He wasn't making much sense."

"If that's the case, it was due to the concussion. However, I expect him to make a full recovery; the facial swelling should go down in time; what he needs right now is rest and time to heal. You can see him if you like, but just know that he's pretty out of it from the pain medication and the concussion. He won't be making much sense right now either."

Moments later Nick stood over Enrico's abused but bandaged body, and he felt tingles behind his lids as he looked down at him. "Rico, brother, I love you. You have to get better so that we can take care of those sons of bitches who did this to you."

Gina looked up at Nick with tears streaming down her porcelain cheeks as she winced at his words.

"What are you talking about, Nick?" She swallowed in some air through her sobs. "You have to let this go, you heard him, it was Marchetti's men who did this to him. Don't you go and do something stupid, leave this alone." With wide fearful eyes, Gina implored. "Do you want to end up in the hospital bed next to him? You should be telling him *not* to retaliate. Just let it go, please." She wiped at her tears with the back of her hand. "You were always the levelheaded one; don't tell me that now I gotta try to talk some sense into you too."

He placed his arm around her quaking shoulders. "No Gina, you don't. I promise I won't do anything stupid." He pulled her more fully into his arms as she sobbed. "Because I know you're right. I just got caught up in the moment; it hurts the hell out of me to see him this like this." He released his hold on her, his pained expression locked onto Enrico as he continued. "I'm sorry, it's just my anger talking, I didn't mean to add to your worry."

Even as he said the words to her, he inwardly seethed as he vowed to find those responsible for putting Enrico in that bed. He'd make them pay, and payback would extend to Salvatore Marchetti himself if need be.

39
🕸 Nick and Gabrielle 🕸
New York – Friday afternoon - October 31st, 1969

Nick caught his breath. "I've been trying to reach you for hours; the receptionist said you left the fashion house a while ago." The distress in his voice evident.

"I just got back from my doctor's office." She gave a labored sigh, "he squeezed me in, I was his last appointment and it took longer than I thought."

"Doctor's office?" He questioned with alarm. "What's wrong?" Nick had spent the better part of the last week making sure that Enrico was all right, and he had talked to Gabrielle every day. So he knew she was safe. Now a fearful thought flashed in his mind. *If Sal has done anything to harm Gabi in any way, he's a dead man no questions asked.*

"Nothing," she sniffed back. "Or at least, nothing serious, thank goodness. I just have a case of the flu. I'm sorry I didn't call you." She paused. "Actually, I feel absolutely awful."

Nick took in a breath and spoke. "No worries, Sweetness, I'll be right over."

"No Nick, I don't really feel up to having company over.

Plus, I don't want to expose you to this."

"I'm not company." He said matter-of-factly.

She weakly grimaced. "Are you sure you want to chance it though?"

"I never get sick, so I'll take my chances. You go straight to bed and rest up. I'll be there soon to take care of you."

Nick stopped at a pharmacy and a local delicatessen before heading to Gabrielle's brownstone. He let himself in with the key she'd given him some time ago.

He placed everything in the kitchen, got out the tea kettle and filled it with water, and put it on the burner. Pulling a serving tray out of the sideboard, he positioned a soup bowl on it and filled it half way with the hot chicken broth from the deli, adding some saltines to the tray just as she weakly walked down the hall toward him.

"Nick, you're here. You truly don't have to be; I don't want you to catch this." All color appeared drained from her face as she stood shivering in her chenille robe. "I will be fine. So you can go, really."

"Hey, no arguing! Now back to bed with you." He sternly stated. "Gabi, like it or not, I'm taking care of you."

Not having the energy to protest any longer, she meekly surrendered. She nodded with a slight frail smile, turned around, and headed back in the direction of her bedroom.

The tea kettle soon whistled its readiness; Nick poured the hot water into a teacup and placed it on the tray along with a glass of white soda. He expertly balanced the filled tray as he managed to navigate his way over to the bed where she'd taken a seated position and pulled the covers over her legs.

"Nice balancing act," she weakly remarked. "I'm impressed. Your days at Mamma's have really paid off."

"Yes, I guess something good came out of my time there, if nothing else, your approval makes it all seem worth it."

"Even though," her brow furrowed. "I wish you hadn't bothered, Nick. You've gone to so much trouble, and I'm not able to keep anything down."

He filled a spoon with the thick pink liquid. "This is to help your tummy feel better, and here are a couple of aspirin to help with any other aches you might have."

Realizing that arguing wasn't an option, she took the aspirin with water first, and then she let the Pepto-Bismol slide down, coating her throat.

He lifted a spoon. "Chicken broth," he said as he moved the spoon to her mouth, "this will make you feel better, take it in small spoonfuls." He ordered.

She dutifully sipped the soup until it was gone. She even nibbled on a saltine and took small sips of the chamomile tea.

"Hmm… It's good, nice and hot. It feels good because I am literally chilled to the bone."

"You're cold? I'll run a hot bath for you."

~~~

He stayed with her the entire weekend caring for her,

feeding her and waiting on her. He truly had been the best medicine she could have asked for.

Sunday morning, she awoke feeling better and back to her old self. Nick slept on her bed, sprawled out on his stomach in only his pajama bottoms. She quietly slipped out of the bed.

Famished, she went into the kitchen and started a pot of coffee as she prepared two bowls of oatmeal sprinkled with cinnamon and brown sugar. She even added cubed apples on top of the cinnamon and brown sugar the way her mother used to make it. She poured two glasses of orange juice, filled two cups with coffee and placed them on the tray.

She walked toward the bedroom and saw Nick as he came out of the bathroom. His dark hair sexily disheveled and with more than a five o'clock shadow on his face, he sleepily blinked.

"What gives? I'm supposed to be taking care of you, not the other way around, remember?" He rubbed at his eyes with a yawn.

"Well, this," she gestured with a lift of the filled tray, "is just my way of showing you my appreciation for all your care and concern. Now," she ordered, "back to bed with you, my good man."

"Someone's pretty spunky this morning, aren't you?" He smiled. "Glad to have you back, Sweetness."

"Thank you for taking such good care of me, I've never been the best patient when I'm sick. So in spite of my objections, it really meant a lot to me."

"Well, I'm glad you feel that way, because I ran into Gus last night when I went out for our dinner. I told him you were under the weather and that I was staying in your guest bedroom. Not sure he bought it though."

"Don't worry about it, I'll deal with Gus. I'm just so happy you were here." She reached out her hand to his face and her fingers met his three-day growth.

"Sorry," he said apologetically pinching his brows together in a sensual scowl. "Forgot my razor, so I haven't been able to shave."

"Hmm, I think I like it," she informed him as she stroked his hairy jawline. "It's really kind of sexy on you. I think I'm finding it to be a real turn on." She looked lustily up at him. "After you've been fed, I'm going to jump into the shower and then I'd like to show you my appreciation, appropriately."

"I'll let you shower, but only if I can join you."

"That sounds downright scandalous. What would the neighbors say?"

40

❧ Nick and Salvatore ❧
New York – Sunday, November 23rd, 1969

Salvatore Marchetti was a good-looking man with brown deep-set bedroom eyes, a narrow aquiline nose and an olive skin tone that complemented his wavy black hair parted on the side. He had a thick but neatly trimmed mustache above his full lips. Salvatore sat in his wooden swivel chair with its riveted black leather padded seat and slatted back. The king of his world, and he loved the view from his top perch.

He was counting cash from last night's receipts, a task he preferred to do himself because as his Uncle had instilled in him: *'Never let someone else handle your money, do it yourself, so's you don't get ripped off'*.

His desk had been situated in the back of his office in his newly acquired nightclub; Sal had *convinced* the previous owner to retire, took it over, and renamed it Club Ten-O-Nine. The door to his office stood open; he could hear one of his men raise his voice.

"What tha fuck!"

Anthony 'Big Tony' Rizzo who was sitting at one of the

tables just outside Salvatore's office, abruptly stood; in doing so he knocked over his chair with a loud thud from the table where he played cards with four other men.

In his office, Salvatore quickly slid the cash he'd been counting into the middle drawer of his desk and locked it. He instantly opened the top right drawer, pulled out a handgun, chambered a round, rose from his chair, and went to his office door.

"Where the hell did you come from?" Big Tony said with astonishment in his voice.

"I'm here to see Sal, so get him for me or get out of my way and I'll find him myself." Nick's voice calmly said.

A heavy set man with dyed black hair slicked back that accentuated his hound dog baggy eyes, he said, "You know I can't let ya do that, Nick," Big Tony looked back at the office and saw Salvatore standing in the doorway.

Salvatore gave a nod of his head to Big Tony, as he tucked his handgun at the small of his back, securely in his waistband. He walked toward the doorway.

"The boss says okay, but I gotta pat you down first."

Nick's eyes locked on Salvatore's as he lifted his arms to allow Big Tony to frisk him.

"He's clean, boss." Big Tony stated with labored breaths.

Nick walked over to Salvatore. "Hey, Sal."

"Nicolo, I was wondering when I'd see you shine around here."

"I'd ask how you're doing," Nick said as he entered the

small but purposeful office. "But, from the looks of this place, you're doing well for yourself. This is a long way from running numbers and pay phones."

"I can't complain, life's been good to me. So how about you? How ya been, Nicolo? I haven't seen you in a bit, looks like life's been treating you pretty good too."

"Like you, I can't complain much," Nick shrugged his shoulders, "who'd listen anyway, am I right?"

"I suppose so," Salvatore went behind his desk, sat down in his swivel chair, and placed his hands on the padded armrests, "so what can I do for you? I'm sure you didn't stop by here just to catch on old times now, did you?"

The room reeked of stale cigar smoke mingled with Sal's signature Old Spice, that as usual, he seemed to have doused himself in.

Salvatore grabbed a bottle of bourbon from the bottom drawer of his desk and poured some of the tawny liquid into a glass waiting on his desk.

"Can I offer you a drink, Nicolo?"

"No thanks, I don't want a drink. I like having a clear head, especially when I'm talking with you."

"Suit yourself, but I tend think clearer once I've had a drink." He took a swallow from his glass. "Ahh, now that hits the spot." He smiled at Nick. "Nice weather we been having for November, don't ya cha think?"

Nick's eyes narrowed as his jaw clinched hard. Salvatore was going to make him bring up the subject himself.

"Yeah, the weather's fine. But, I didn't come here to talk about the weather, I came here to talk about Enrico."

"I had a feeling that's why you were here, but Nicolo, that wasn't supposed to happen. I did hear he's going to be okay though. That right?"

Enrico had been healing up since his beating four weeks ago, the facial swelling all but gone and his hair had started to grow out from where they shaved it. Nick had decided to wait until Enrico was out of the woods and well on the mend before having this sit down with Sal, without Enrico's knowledge.

"If your definition of okay," he continued, "is a cracked skull and broken ribs, a busted up face and hand, then I guess he's doing great."

"Look, I know what you're getting at, I told you I didn't order it."

"You're the new Underboss, Sal, no one would act alone and do what they did to Enrico without your say so."

"I guess I got me a loose cannon on my hands," a wry smile slid to Salvatore's lips, "the helps not what it used to be, but he's being dealt with."

"So you're telling me that you didn't order your men to beat the crap out of Enrico and kill his dog?"

With a glum expression, Sal shook his head. "You know that's too bad, I always liked that dog."

"Glad to know you feel bad about the dog," Nick smirked. "I guess Enrico's injuries mean nothing to you."

"Well, Rico's still breathing, the dog ain't."

Nick was having a hard time keeping himself in check as he sat before the seemingly nonchalant Salvatore.

"You know something; I would really like to meet your loose cannon. He has to have some cannonball-sized stones to go out on his own like that. I'd like to have an old-fashioned talk with him, to see for myself."

"Whoa, when did you get so tough, Nicolo?" Salvatore leaned back in his chair. "You were always the brains not the brawn. That was always Rico's department, so, you put on a few pounds and now want to go all G.I. Joe, huh? Not your usual smarts."

"I guess things change over time in the grand scheme of things." His eyes went dim as he pressed on with resolve. "Can I talk to the guy, Sal?"

"I guess it's true what they say, having all those muscles does seem to make a guy dumber. I already told you he's being dealt with," Salvatore's face became hard as he sat straight up. "Don't come in here trying to tell me how to run my people, Nicolo."

Salvatore lifted his glass and took a large gulp as Nick shifted in his chair.

"Just for the record, I did send them to talk with Rico. But only because he owes me money."

"Enrico owes you money? How's that? Because the way Rico tells it, it's you who owes him." Nick's eyes tensed. Enrico had told Nick in the hospital that Salvatore had his cash and he went to get it.

"I did owe him money; I'd been holding it for him while he was in the joint. But, when he came to collect, he found out that there was this little filly in the third that had six to one odds You know how much Rico likes the ponies. I'd swear it's like his kryptonite or something. Anyway, he lost that bet, and now he owes me twenty-five thou."

Nick eyebrows raised, "Twenty-five thousand dollars!" Floored, he could not believe it.

Enrico lost everything on a friggin horse? Typical for him to neglect to tell me about that fact, but still, he didn't deserve to be beaten within an inch of his life over a fucking debt.

"When was this horse race?" Nick asked.

"A few weeks back, he bet his whole roll." Salvatore said.

Nick eyed a photo on Salvatore's desk; it was a rare photograph of Salvatore and Vincenzo, along with much younger and skinnier versions of Enrico and Nick in front of Salvatore's brand new red Cadillac.

"Are you running things differently now, Sal? Time was you would give more than a few weeks before you released the hounds over a debt that size." Nick cocked his head with an edge. "I guess the fact that Rico's worked for you all these years just doesn't count for much now, does it."

Salvatore's eyes went even harder as he took stock of Nick.

"I treated him good when he worked for me, and don't forget that I let you walk away. I never bothered you about the money you got from my uncle. And, I let you have the life you wanted. Didn't I?"

"*Let me walk away*? Don't make me laugh." Nick shook his head with a slanted smile. "I can see it still sticks in your craw that Vincenzo pulled some strings to get me in at Columbia and paid for my schooling and that he never wanted anything in return."

With a clinch of Salvatore's jaw, Nick knew he'd hit a nerve, as he went on, "And I think we both know the reason you didn't bother me, and it didn't have anything to do with you letting me walk away. Keep that part straight, all right? Because what I had on you then, I still have on you. And don't you forget that you still had Enrico under your thumb, so really you got the best of both worlds, didn't you?" He raised an eyebrow. "You got my silence and you got to keep your best associate."

"I don't give a shit what my senile old uncle did for you. But, our little arrangement was just between us. That's how you set it up back then, remember." Salvatore replied.

"I do remember; I'd been pissed that Enrico didn't want to leave with me back then. But with that said, you know Enrico, Angelina, *and* Gina are my family, and I want no harm to come to any of them or anyone I care about."

"Nicolo, our deal was said and done; you can't come in here and try to change it now after all these years. We shook on it, that's our honor code, and you know it."

Nick did know it; a handshake was the bond that meant everything in this world. No one would dare break his word on a handshake. Without the seemingly *simple* gesture of a handshake, the honor among thieves, there would be complete anarchy.

Only he regretted it now that he didn't include his loved ones under his get-out-of-the-mob-free card. He looked over at the photo again; things were different when Uncle Vincenzo was still in power. But, Vincenzo had lost his place at the table all because a hit man's bullet left him infirmed.

Salvatore now looked over at the photo too, and soon his eyes were back on Nick. "He quit on me," Salvatore spat out angrily, "told me he wasn't going to be working for me no more, so I guess now he gets treated like anybody else who owes me money."

Nick's jaw clinched, but then Salvatore's eyes relaxed.

"If you want to clear his debt for him, you're more than welcome to. Just pay me the money owed, and I will forget about you, Rico, and *your entire family*, cause without me getting my dough, they're all fare game."

He glanced over at the photo again and then back at Nick. "Do you want to take over his debt?"

"Yes, I'll do it. What other choice do I have?"

"When it comes to our familia, sometimes the choice is made for you." Salvatore smiled. "You got my word they will all be safe, and just for old times' sake." He extended his hand. "On that, Nicolo, I offer you my hand."

Nick took Sal's hand and shook it. *Where in the hell am I going to come up with that kind of money?*

"How long are you giving me?" He asked Salvatore.

"Hey, we are still paisans, aren't we? I know that it's a lot of money. With tomorrow being Thanksgiving, I'm feeling generous. So for you, my brother, I will give you give you a few weeks-that puts us right around Christmas for you to get me my money." He smiled. "We'll call it my Christmas present to you and Rico."

Some Christmas present, only Sal will be getting the friggin twenty-five-thousand-dollar gift.

41
Nick and Gabrielle
Thursday – Thanksgiving Day, November 27th, 1969

The delicious aromas coming from Gabrielle's apartment wafted through the whole building as Gus and Esther came through the door. Esther held her famous pumpkin and pecan pies, one in each hand.

"Oh Esther," Gabrielle declared, "they look wonderful."

"Thank you, I only hope they taste wonderful as well, I fear they weren't my best batches."

"Looks great to me," Linda Taylor said as she came through the door as well. "I can't wait to dig in." She had piggy backed in on Gus's and Esther's entrances as she carried a jelled cranberry mold.

"Linda, the cranberries look good too. I can't wait to get this feast started." Gabrielle stated with a grin as she took Linda's coat and hung it on the coat tree. Their friendship had emerged into a sister-like bond.

Linda looked around and spied Gabrielle's large trestle table festively set for eight with a pumpkin and gourds in various shapes, colors and sizes along with candles.

Mr. Wasserman and Benji were already sitting in the living room. Nick crouched in front of the fireplace, working on building a fire as he added the kindling under the red oak logs placed on the cast iron grate.

"Need a hand with that fire, Nick?" Gus asked.

"No, but thanks for the offer," Nick replied as he lit the kindling, and the fire came to life. "I think I've got it under control." He stood up and surveyed his work.

"Nick's got the whole building-a-fire thing mastered." Gabrielle said. "Besides Gus, you're always working around here, and today, I want you to just relax for a change. What can I get you to drink?"

"Well, if you want me to relax. I guess a beer would be nice if you have it." Gus replied. "And, if you wouldn't mind turning on the Lions-Vikings game." He chuckled.

"One beer, coming up." She said to Gus.

"I'm rooting for the Lions. Who do you like in today's game, Nick?" Gus asked.

Gabrielle smiled; Gus truly seemed to be trying to find some common ground with Nick.

"The Lions don't have a chance against the Vikings; this is the Vikings' game to win." Nick replied.

The doorbell rang and Gabrielle buzzed Richard Collier into the building and met him at her door.

"Gabrielle, it's really good to see you again. Thank you for having me." Richard's eyes devoured her.

His leer made her a feel a little uncomfortable as she

politely replied. "Welcome to my humble home, Richard."

"I'm sorry I'm a little late, I had a devil of a time finding a wine that goes with turkey." He held two bottles of wine out to her. "So I brought red and white."

"A gewürztraminer and pinot noir. I think both will go well with dinner. Thank you. Please, come in."

She showed Richard into the living room where the other men congregated, and he stood next to Nick after the introductions.

"I think you're wrong, Nick, the Lions are good." Gus had countered.

"Oh I don't know, Mr. Ulrich, I think I have to agree with Nick, the Vikings are going to win in this match up." Benji chimed in, happy to be included in the adult male discussion instead of being treated like a kid.

"You are wrong, my son," Mr. Wasserman said, "the Lions are going to reign superior, and they'll claim the victory today."

Richard leaned into Nick and whispered, "I didn't figure you to be the Norman Rockwell type, Caine. I mean look at this group. They're all so folksy. Let's see, we have the couple from American Gothic over there, I'm not sure where they've hidden their pitchfork though. Geppetto and his wooden boy and that redhead Linda, hmmm… with more hair, she's a perfect version of the foxy X-Men's Scarlet Witch."

"And just which character are you, Richard? Maybe you're the big bad wolf? Don't think that I didn't see how you were eyeing up Gabrielle. You need to remember she's mine, as I've told you before, mine alone. So back off."

"Simmer down, old chap. I know it must be love or else you wouldn't subject yourself to this little homey scene. Besides, red over there looks very promising."

"Which team are you rooting for in today's football game, Mr. Collier?" Benji asked.

"Today's game?" Richard jovially remarked. "The Lions, of course."

Ignoring the men in their sports talk, Gabrielle turned to Esther. "What about for you, Esther, what can I get you?"

"Gabi, you don't have to wait on me. Let me help you in the kitchen so that the men can watch their football."

Not the time to get into a women's liberation discussion with old-fashioned Esther, the women went into the kitchen.

"I notice you have me sitting across from that Richard guy," Linda remarked to Gabrielle eyeing the leaf shaped place cards on the table, "please don't tell me you're trying to set us up or something."

"No, I'm not trying to set you up with him. However, if I were," she smiled coyly, "he's good-looking, don't you agree? Tell me, what do you think of him? Could you be interested?"

"He's very good-looking, but no. I'm just not interested."

"Linda, he could be someone to do things with, like share a meal, a play, or whatever. It could be good for you."

"Gabi, I'm fine. I like my life the way it is, and I prefer to be alone; I'm on a quest of self-discovery. And, to learn all about one's self, I'm afraid one must do it solo."

"Well, I wasn't setting you up anyway. Nick invited him." She frowned. "Nick said Richard doesn't have any family close by and would be all alone for the holiday. How could I say no?"

~~~

In the end, the Vikings won the game with a final score of twenty-seven to nothing. After the game with the guests seated around the dining table in their assigned seats, Gabrielle presented them with the beautifully browned bird as she placed the turkey on the table.

Nick stood and began carving the turkey as Gabrielle went and sat at the other end of the table and beamed at the scene in her home. Surrounded by people she cared about, her hand went to her touchstone, the heart necklace around her neck. She felt she had plenty to be thankful for.

"That is a lovely bird," Mr. Wasserman proudly said. "And, I know for a fact that it's kosher because Miss Gabi bought it from my store."

"A kosher bird? It might look good, but I'll bet that it's going to be way too salty." Richard exclaimed with wide eyes.

"How rude of you!" Linda said as she gave Richard a hard glare. "You haven't even tasted it yet; maybe the polite thing to do would be for you to keep your comments to yourself like a true gentleman."

"I'm sorry, but I've had kosher turkey before, it left me so thirsty I was drinking water for a week." He smiled at Linda with a flirtatious wink. "Besides, who said I was a gentleman?"

"An assumption on my part," Linda wryly replied.

"I soaked it twice in clear clean water, Richard, so you shouldn't worry." Gabrielle interjected before Richard could respond. "So let's dig in."

~~~

After dinner the men went into the living room while the women cleared the table and began the clean-up in the kitchen.

Richard pulled Nick aside. "I can take only so much of this domestic scene, Nick. Can we get down to the real reason you invited me here?"

"I guess you know me better than I thought. You're right, I need to ask a favor. A loan, as much as you can spare."

"Wow, I wasn't expecting that. Christmas is right around the corner, and I'm flying home to Montana to see my folks, so my funds will be tight."

"I understand, thanks anyway."

"Now wait a minute, Nick, I said my funds will be tight, not that I couldn't help you. I could spare say, three thousand dollars. Would that help?"

"That does help, thank you. I appreciate it." Nick gave him a grateful nod of his head. "I'll pay you back, with interest."

"I'm not worried about it. Besides, what are friends for?" Richard's eye then wandered over to Gabrielle as she wiped down the table, her backside to them. Richard eyed her with a slant of his head. "You sure I couldn't get you to change your mind about Gabrielle? She's a lot of woman, maybe too much for just one man, don't you think?"

"Hell no, I don't think. I would never share her with you or make her part of anything like that. If that's why you're loaning me the money, then forget it. I'll figure something else out."

"I'm joshing," Richard grinned. "I know she's gotten under your skin. Never thought I would see the day when a woman could tame the roving eye of the infamous Nick Caine."

"Shut up, Dick." Nick scowled at him.

"Have you told her how you feel about her yet?"

Nick was silent.

"I'll take that as a no. She's beautiful, charming, she cooks-that turkey dinner was amazing! And, she loves you--and for the life of me, I don't know why. But, I suppose not telling her is a bit of hubris on your part." Richard thoughtfully said. "But if I were you, I wouldn't let pride prevent me from telling her everyday how I felt about her."

"I plan on doing just that, Richard. I bought her a special Christmas present for her finger."

"Blessed Mary! You're going to propose?"

"Keep your voice down, will you." A smile on his lips.

"I will miss our little jaunts with the ladies," he paused,

thoughtfully stroked his chin. "I've missed them since you met Gabrielle."

"Well, I haven't. She's all I need or could ever want." Nick's smile deepened.

"I'm happy for you. I've said it before, but you are one lucky son of a bitch."

"I do feel lucky."

"And hey, no worries where the money is concerned, the banks are closed until Monday. I'll get the funds to you as soon as possible."

"Thanks," his lips curled in a smile, "now stop ogling my future bride."

They both laughed as they joined the other men.

42
Nick

With time running out on his deadline with Salvatore; Nick called in every debt that was owed to him. With what he had in his own emergency fund and what he had borrowed from Richard, he still needed fifteen thousand dollars.

She has money and lots of it, she spends at least twenty grand on her yearly wardrobe alone, and I will pay her back as soon as I can. Nick stood outside the door to her penthouse apartment, and while he'd been grateful she took his call, he now felt sick to his stomach as he knocked on the door.

Wearing her customary pink, she resembled something right out of a Frederick's of Hollywood catalog. She wore a short satiny robe tied at the waist along with a pair of spiky black heels.

"Nicky, I'm so glad that you called. I feel as if I haven't seen you in such a long time."

"I know, Claudia, my fault, and I apologize for that."

"You're look good though." She said as she closed the door behind him.

A Bach tune played ever so subtly in the background.

"You too, you look as beautiful as ever."

"What brings you into my neck of the woods, Nicky?"

"I need your help." He avoided looking at anything but her face.

"You said that on the phone. What can I help you with, darling? You know whatever it is, you can count on me." She smiled lustfully at him. "You have but to ask."

"I need a loan," he took in a deep breath, "and it's sizable."

"A loan, as in money?" She asked with a tilted head.

"Yes, as in money."

"How much do you need, Nicky?"

"I need," he paused. "I need fifteen thousand dollars."

"Hmmm, fifteen thousand? That is sizable," she smiled. "But it shouldn't be a problem, when do you need it?"

"As soon as possible." He sighed, the relief flooded his face as he replied.

"Would a personal check be okay? I could get it for you right away, today even."

"Thank you, Claudia, a check would be great. Just make it out to cash." He smiled. "You are a complete lifesaver. I want you to know this means a great deal to me. I won't forget this, and I'll pay you back every cent, with interest."

"That's fine, Nicky, I'm not worried; I know you're good for it. And I'm not hurting," she then came close to him and brashly put her hand on his crotch, "for money at least." A kittenish smile came to her frosted pink lips. "I think we ought to solidify our little deal, don't you?"

"Claudia, I…" He knew what she wanted. "We're friends, aren't we? Can't you just, do this for me without…"

"Look, Nicky, you were the one who came to me. And you know how this town works. I scratch your itch, you scratch mine and so forth."

"It's just that, I'm with Gabrielle and I…"

"I don't care if you're still with her or not," she said with agitation at his reluctance to play with her. "I just need you to get hard for me and right now, *friend*."

She untied her robe, it fell open exposing her lacy pink bra and matching garter belt. Sheer black hose embraced her shapely legs. There was a time, just seeing her like this would have incited an eager response from him, but not now.

"I have some new little accessories for us to try." She hummed as she pulled pink fur lined handcuffs from her robe pocket and lifted them up for him to see. She ran her other hand over his crotch again only to find him still soft.

"I haven't been with anyone except Gabi since… I can't do this, not to her. She trusts me and I… I'm in love with her."

"Are you serious? Trust? Love? Don't make me laugh. So what, you're in love with her, big deal! I don't give a shit. That doesn't change our deal, so you had better figure out just what you *can* do, Nicky. Especially if you expect me to hand that kind of money over to you, because I'm giving you fifteen thousand reasons to get hard for me."

He felt he had run out of options, as he closed his troubled eyes. He knew what he was about to do was so wrong, but in order to get the money to clear up the debt and keep those he loved safe from Marchetti's crushing arm, the choice was clear; he knew he had to fuck her.

He thought of the only thing that could put him in that state: Gabrielle, her skin, her hair and her beautiful face. But, he heard Claudia.

"That's it, now you're getting nice and hard."

He grabbed her by the arm and roughly pushed her towards her bedroom.

"There's my tiger," she purred, "you know I like it a little rough."

"Do you have a condom? I didn't bring one."

"I've got everything we need, Nicky."

On autopilot, and just going through the motions, he pictured Gabrielle in his mind as he played Claudia's game.

~~~

Afterwards, he felt sullied and went into her bathroom to shower, he just needed to get clean. In an effort to wash away the act of being with Claudia, he wanted to erase the fact that he had just done the *unthinkable*.

He'd cheated on Gabrielle and he felt horrible.

In his rational mind, he knew it had been the only way to pay off the debt. That debt had loomed heavily over his head like a guillotine's blade for the past three weeks, because not only was Enrico's ass on the line, his was too. Regretfully, he felt that the price tag to clear up this whole mess may have been too high a price to pay.

After he dried off with one of her fluffy pink towels and dressed once again, he saw her in the doorway wearing her robe and a satisfied grin.

"You were great, as always. I left something on my nightstand for you." She said walking out to the living room.

Good, at least this part of the nightmare is over. I'll pay Marchetti the money and make this up to Gabrielle, somehow.

He'd just finished putting his shoes on as he walked to her nightstand where he found the envelope. He opened it and counted the bills inside. His jaw clenched hard as he went to the living room and found her reclined on her cream-colored sofa resting her head on a silk embroidered pillow.

"What the hell is this, Claudia?" He shook his head at her. "Two hundred dollars?"

"Oh, that. I wasn't sure how much stud services were going for these days. But Nicky, no worries you earned every penny."

"Stud services! You fucking cunt! You're toying with me? You're playing more of your fucking games."

"With the way you treated me at the Black and White ball, Nicky, you're lucky I gave you anything at all."

"You're lucky you're not a man or I'd throw your ass right through that wall." His heart sunk with the realization as he grasped her intentions. "You're not giving me the money, are you?"

"I fully intend on giving you what you asked for. However, for the rest of the money, fourteen thousand eight hundred dollars to be exact, you will need to come back when Harold is here. I'm sure he'd like to see what he's paying for." Her eyes became gleeful. "Let's make next time a really good show. Can you bring Richard again?"

"Whatever *this* was, I thought friendship was at the core. But it's over now, I won't darken your door again, *we're* done." He took the money-filled envelope, crumpled it in his hand, and threw the wad of cash at her, as he walked out.

He felt defeated and back at square one, only now to add insult to injury he had betrayed Gabrielle on the grandest of scales for absolutely nothing.

With his time limit quickly approaching, he began to get panicky. Minutes later, he found himself in the lobby of The Bradford Building taking the east elevator up to the fifty-second floor.

43
🍀 Clayton and Margaret 🍀
New York – Thursday afternoon - December 18th, 1969

"Margo, we need to have a conversation," Clayton Butler said as he entered her office. He looked grave as he uncomfortably approached Margaret's desk, his eyes averted hers, "it's of a delicate nature."

"Don't be so ominous, Clay." She placed her pen down on her desk as she watched his uneasy stance. "Spit it out."

"Well, first and foremost; I want you to know I'm not in the habit of listening to gossip. However, when that kind of talk leads to disparaging remarks about this company in any way, I feel it's my duty to address it." His eyes locked to hers as his brow shot up austerely.

"What kind of gossip do you mean? What could hurt ERB so much that it would have you so vexed?"

"I'll speak plainly. There's talk, it's been said that you and Penny are," he crossed his arms at his chest, "together."

Her face went as white as the sheet of paper she'd been writing on. "But, what do you believe Clay?"

"Come on Margo, I've known you for over 15 years. I'm

no fool, and what you do in the privacy of your own bedroom is of no consequence to me...unless that behavior threatens what Elliott has built here. I will not let your little dalliance jeopardize his legacy."

She interlocked her fingers and pressed her lips to her raised hands. "Where did you hear this *gossip*."

"A very reliable source. But it really doesn't matter, Margo, because if I'm hearing it, then our stockholders, board members, and tenants might be hearing it as well."

"Would it matter to them to know that you yourself are having an affair?" She shot back at him. "If not them, then perhaps Patricia would like to know."

"You've got to be joking. You're trying to threaten me? I'm probably the only ally you have here, but if you think that I'm afraid of exposure," his eyes narrowed as he challenged her, "guess again."

"No! Clay, I'm sorry." The fear in her eyes apparent. "I shouldn't have said anything. Please, forgive me?"

"I don't care how you do it, but you get a handle on this. Elliott was like a second father to me, and I will preserve the reputation of his corporation with my dying breath." He'd become furious and didn't care that she looked like a mouse caught in a maze. "The only reason you're in that chair is because I helped get you there, because you were Elliott's wife. I would have no problem having you removed as CEO, and believe me, I can get the votes. Then you can go back to living your life of shopping and sleeping with whomever you choose." His voice rose with ire.

"Clay, I know you're angry about what I said; please know that I would never say anything to Patricia or to anyone. I'm really sorry." Her eyes darted back and forth in fear as she went on. "I appreciate everything you've done for me, and I thank you for giving me a heads up. I will fix this."

"I warn you," his lips pursed. "If you don't get this taken care of, I think you ought to gracefully resign from your post as CEO of ERB, before I have you removed." He walked out of her office.

In a panic filled moment, *I have to let Penny go,* she put her face in her hands and sobbed. A few minutes later she went to her bathroom and washed her face. She returned to her desk, and buzzed for Penelope, *might as well get it over with,* but Penelope's voice came over the intercom and held a bit of surprise.

"Margo, you have a visitor. It's Nick Caine."

44

❧ Gabrielle ❧

New York City – Friday evening - December 19th, 1969

The tea kettle screamed, announcing its readiness and roused her out of her musings; she poured the hot water into her waiting cup and blew at the hot liquid before she sipped.

She needed to get her mind off Nick and the snowstorm outside, and soon her thoughts were full of the unsettling day she had at work. There'd been so much hustle and bustle in the city today, more than usual. People rushed by with filled shopping bags of either gifts or groceries. The predicted snowfall had people preparing for a weekend in or an exodus out of the city.

In this morning's meeting, Linda was all business as she delegated the tasks for completion by day's end. Before she dismissed them to their assignments, Linda fretfully informed them that the board members for ERB were coming down to their floor sometime that afternoon. The news had the team worked up and it appeared as though they were feeding off of Linda's anxiety at the ERB board's impending visit.

Unflustered, Gabrielle took the news in stride. She went

into the drafting room and began a sketch on her pad; her fingers deftly moved her sharpened pencil, and her drawing began taking shape. She drew a single off-the-shoulder bra top knotted on the left shoulder and a form fitted bikini bottom single knotted at the right hip.

With her pencils, she colored the drawing with soft delicate strokes- securing fabric swatches to her sketch, she then tore the drawing from the thick pad of paper and laid it aside as she started a new sketch.

Linda walked by, eyed Gabrielle's concept, and picked up the completed sketch. "Great, Gabi. Give me more like this."

Continuing her observation walk about the room, Linda stopped at other designers' tables and offered valued input by way of praise, as well as critiques. Linda tried to present a normal air about herself, yet Gabrielle saw through the facade. She knew Linda's unease stemmed from the 'take over' by ERB. Elliott Bradford, who had garnered the deal, had been killed in a tragic plane crash almost twelve months ago. Gabrielle wondered how things would have gone with the fair-minded Elliott in the lead. Dealing with Margaret had often been distressing experiences for Linda.

Margaret had been what Linda liked to call a *sometimes person*, in that *sometimes* she could be cordial and *sometimes* she could be a real bitch. Linda had shared her misgivings about Margaret with Gabrielle one evening when they had gone out for impromptu drinks.

Gabrielle continued sketching with a discerning eye, and

after about her eighth conceptual drawing, she heard Linda's nervous voice in the foyer. "Margo, I didn't expect your visit so soon, but yes, of course, you and the other board members are more than welcome to see our young designers at work." Said Linda as she ushered Margaret Bradford into the drafting room.

Dressed in an expensive designer navy skirt suit with a cream-colored blouse and cultured pearls at her throat, her very look and demeanor conveyed money and authority. She carried herself in a regal manner, as if she were royalty.

Four well-dressed men in dark suits and wide ties followed closely behind Margaret Bradford. Penelope Peters, with her platinum tresses pulled into a bun, and impeccably dressed in a slender black pantsuit shadowed behind them, with a clipboard and pen in her hands.

Gabrielle recognized one of the men as Clayton Butler, the CFO for ERB National Holdings; he casually eyed the anxious Linda as she spoke.

"All of our designers have been assigned different aspects of our upcoming summer and even our fall lines." Linda stated.

Clayton nonchalantly looked around the room as Margaret made eye contact with Gabrielle. Even though her table sat furthest from the door, Margaret had been in the lead as they all headed right to Gabrielle's table. Margaret's eyes squinted as if she were eyeing up an opponent.

Linda caught up to her and beamed, "Margaret Bradford,

this is Gabrielle Lawrence."

Gabrielle's mouth formed a polished smile at her, even though Margaret regarded her in a dissecting manner. Nevertheless, Gabrielle extended an outstretched hand to Margaret, who ignored it as she picked up Gabrielle's completed sketches. She barely looked at them as she kept her adversarial gaze on Gabrielle.

"I know exactly who Miss Lawrence is. We've met before, haven't we?" Margaret practically sneered at her.

"Yes, Mrs. Bradford, we've met before, but, only in passing." Gabrielle responded somewhat carefully as she tried to gage the woman's mood.

Taking note of the antagonistic tone in Margaret's voice, Linda remarked, "Gabrielle has been assigned to swimwear for our summer 1970 line. She is one of our most promising young designers." She added informatively.

"If this is what you call 'promising', Miss Taylor, then frankly, I must question *your* judgment." Margaret narrowed her eyes into slits and then turned her head to challenge Linda full on. "Although, your decision making hasn't been your long suit now, has it?"

"Margo!" Clayton Butler tried to interject.

"Clayton, please." She glanced back at him and then back to Gabrielle. "I'm merely stating a fact, and in regards to this woman's so-called talent. Frankly I just don't see it. This is not at all what I would call 'promising.' It's amateurish at best, and it's just not good enough for this great fashion house.

Erich would be aghast were he to see this."

The room became stark still as she tossed the sketches back towards the drafting table, and a couple of them slid off the table and fell to the floor. Margaret did not miss a beat as she watched Gabrielle, whose smile had faded.

"Now, my advice to you, Miss Lawrence, it is Miss, isn't it?" She beheld Gabrielle with a mock questioning look. "My expert advice as one who can and does buy clothing from all corners of the globe, and as CEO of this company, Miss Lawrence, is for you to get back to the proverbial old drawing board." Her head lifted haughtily. "You see, raw talent for design has to be in your blood, in your genes, so to speak. In viewing your sketches, it is now apparent to me that you've got a lot to learn, my dear. You can either get serious and learn it, or might I suggest, you can get married and let a man take care of you."

Margaret snapped her head with superiority and adroitly moved to one of the other designer's table as both Linda and Gabrielle's eyes displayed shock.

Linda mouthed to Gabrielle, *'what the hell?'* Gabrielle was dumbfounded, but Linda quickly caught up to Margaret as she marveled over the drawings of Monty Greer whose drafting table was two tables away from Gabrielle's.

"Now this is what I call talent…" Margaret said loudly so that all in the room could hear.

Clayton Butler lagged behind at Gabrielle's table as the others followed Margaret over to Monty's table. Clayton gave

Gabrielle an apologetic look, his short salt and pepper hair shimmered under the bright lights of the drafting room. He bent down and picked up her cast-offed sketches from the floor and handed them back to the shaken Gabrielle.

"I'm very sorry, Miss Lawrence." He murmured, so that only Gabrielle could hear. "She can be a bit insensitive at times, but please, don't take it personally. It's just her nature."

Don't take it personally? How could I not? A bit shaken, she mutely nodded and gave him a crumbling smile.

"Tha…Thank you, Mr. Butler I appreciate your kind words."

He graced her with a compassionate smile. "You're welcome, Miss Lawrence." He gently patted the top of her hand and returned to the group of board members.

She turned to her drawing board and tried to commence another concept. But with shaky fingers and hand, she hadn't been able to translate anything to the paper. She now felt the anger rise within her, *why had that woman sought me out?* Margaret had indeed singled her out, despite what Clayton Butler had said. *That woman had been deliberately harsh to me.*

Gabrielle had never imagined she would ever be on the receiving end of Margaret Bradford's dreadful tongue. *In your blood? I've got that one covered. But, for all she knows, I'm just an ordinary designer just like the rest of the group.*

Gabrielle tried to keep her ire from frothing over. She spied some of the other designer's tentative smiles. Margaret Bradford glanced back at her with a satisfied victorious air.

The group had finished its tour in the drafting room and had left the area, but Gabrielle could hear their muffled voices as they headed into one of the fashion house's showrooms where some of the completed spring line was on display.

Monty Greer walked over to Gabrielle. "Don't listen to her, Gabi; you are a wonderful designer." Then he said while looking around at the others in the room, "I wish I had just one ounce of the talent you have."

She smiled kindly at his gentle round face. "Thank you, Monty. I appreciate it."

As soon as Margaret and her group were gone, Linda appeared in the doorway of the drafting room. "Everyone, I have an announcement to make. Due to the impending weather, we will be closing the fashion house early today. I know most of you have plans for the holiday, so finish up your projects and get a jump start on your two-week hiatus."

The group cheered and clapped their hands.

"You all have until one o'clock to complete what you're working on, so that gives you about forty-five minutes to clear up and get out of here."

"Gabi," she turned her head toward Gabrielle. "I need to see you in my office."

The other designers watched Gabrielle as she put her pencil down and went toward the door; Linda waved her hand in the air. "The rest of you can get back to work."

Linda walked to the back of her office where her credenza housed some of the best scotch whiskey in the city. She took out two tumblers and with her back to Gabrielle and asked, "Rocks?"

"Yes, please." Gabrielle responded with a sigh.

Handing one of the glasses to Gabrielle, she walked behind her sleek mahogany desk, which had been clear of the traditional desk accessories, all except for her telephone and an elegant Tiffany Damascene harp desk lamp.

With her drink in hand Gabrielle swirled the glass with the caramel colored liqueur as the almond-marzipan aroma drifted upwards to her nose as she took a drink. She had to admit, it truly *was* good scotch. She allowed it to glide smoothly down, heating the back of her throat.

"First and foremost, I have to ask. Are you okay?" Linda asked with true concern.

"Yeah, a little bruised I think, but I'm fine." She nodded.

Linda scooted her chair further under the desk and asked her directly. "Now, I need to know. What in the world did you do to that viper to piss her off?" She asked in a somewhat amused yet serious tone. "And pissed off, she was, believe me."

"I honestly have no idea. I've only talked with her twice in my whole ten months here." She lifted her right hand and pushed her hair behind her ear and stared at Linda.

"You know," Gabrielle looked blankly at Linda. "Someone told me that I shouldn't take her words personally and that it's just her nature." She paused. "But, how else can I take what she inferred about my work?"

Gabrielle felt something grip in the pit of her stomach as she mentally pondered. *With her comment about designing being in your genes, has Margaret Bradford discovered my secret?* Gabrielle reasoned with herself that it couldn't be the case because Margaret would have said something to her before now if she had found out, *wouldn't she?*

"It sure seemed personal to me." Linda remarked, lifted her glass to her lips, and took another drink.

"So, I wasn't imagining it? She singled me out specifically." Gabrielle lifted a brow.

Linda set her glass in front of her, placed her elbows on the top of her desk, and interlaced her fingers as she rested her chin on her finger bridge. She spoke knowingly, "Oh, my dear friend, not only weren't you imagining her attack on you, she even had a few jabs for me. That bitch went after both of us. My only question is why?"

"I thought I'd been the target and you just got caught in the crossfire. You mean to say, you think she intentionally went after you too?" Gabrielle asked.

"Absolutely." Linda affirmatively nodded her head.

"I now see what you meant when you said she could be a bitch. She's so calculating."

"Precisely my point," Linda said slowly, "in past dealings with her I know that she's only a bitch if she has an axe to grind. When I get back after our break, I'll make it my business to find out what this was all about." Linda lowered her gaze with a raised eyebrow as she silently wondered, *has Margo found out about my secret.*

"There was some reason she felt the need to berate us in front of everyone." Linda's eyes tapered. "There's not a doubt in my mind that she wanted to put both of us on notice, and the public lashing she just gave us in front of the board members and *our team* was just the icing on the cake. She wanted to discredit us both, all in one fell swoop. That little display was to make us look incompetent and worst yet, my friend, that *'sometimes'* bitch thoroughly enjoyed every single moment."

45

❧ Gabrielle ☙

New York City – Friday evening - December 19th, 1969

Holding her hot cup of tea, Gabrielle stood at the window and resumed looking out for Nick; she had so much to tell him. She anxiously wondered *How will he take the news? Will he be angry or hurt that I didn't share this with him sooner?*

Seeing his Mustang GT fastback coupe slowly trekking its way through the snow as he parked in front of her building, she let out a sigh of relief.

She watched him tightened the fine wool scarf around his neck to protect himself against the cold; she'd gotten it for him because his old one had been worn through. Nick crossed over the un-shoveled walk and reached the drifts of the ankle-deep snow-covered steps; he swore at the snow that had entered his boot as he then entered the warmth of the brownstone.

He took the inside stairs two at a time and soon stood outside the door, which she opened before he could use his key. Gabrielle greeted him as he dropped his keys into his coat pocket as his eyes drank her in. Wearing little make-up, her almond shaped eyes had only a thin line of black eyeliner while her full lips were tinted with her russet gloss as she smiled at him.

Her hair hung loosely at her shoulders but away from her face and was held back by a wide multi-colored headband. She wore the dress she'd worn to work that day, a long sleeved deep mustard colored mini dress trimmed in two inches of beige fabric at the hem; she wasn't wearing any hose on her shapely legs, but she had on cream colored pumps.

Her beauty never ceased to take his breath away. Nick took her hand, and the electricity between them created undeniable sparks as he pulled her in close to him and placed his hands around her tiny waist.

"Hey there, gorgeous." He said quietly.

"Hey there yourself, handsome. I was getting worried. You're so late."

"I know, I'm sorry- I had a few things to take care of and the snow was very slow going, but I'm here now and I couldn't wait to see you to do this." His mouth covered hers, and his minty tongue keenly sought out hers.

Together their tongues mingled in a slow circular greeting; then without taking his mouth away from hers, he backed her into the apartment and used his foot to close the door behind him.

He whispered in her ear. "You are so precious to me, Gabi. Don't ever forget that." He began to nuzzle her neck as he pulled her tightly to him and held her.

She felt him hardening against her; she softly moaned

and slid her hands inside his coat as she began to caress his muscular back before she slid her hands down and took ahold of his backside, squeezing his chiseled buttocks with her hands.

He reached behind and easily took one of her hands and pulled it toward his front and placed it on his hardened member. "Feel me here, Gabi," his voice needful, "feel how much I want you. Always, remember that. I want you and only you."

She kissed him and lightly nibbled his lower lip as she felt herself wanting him too. Her knees becoming weak from her body's want. Despite the need building up inside her, she pulled out of the embrace and cleared her head with a shake.

"Oh Nick, I want you too." She replied breathlessly. "But we have all night, there's no need to rush." She inhaled. "Let's slow things down a bit."

Tonight was too important, she had significant matters to discuss with him, knowing all too well the path that his kisses led them to. Gabrielle needed to keep her wits in check, "I made some of your favorites," she gestured to the nicely set table with a wave of her hand. "I even included a tablecloth to give it a real Italian feel. But, we do have to eat before it becomes inedible."

Nick looked over at the table and then back at her; his mouth formed a slight smile as he expelled the air out of his lungs in an effort to repress his need of her.

"Okay, Sweetness. Have it your way."

His hands were damp as he planted a kiss in her palm as he reluctantly let go of her hand. "You've gone to all of the trouble to make dinner," he nervously laughed. "The least I can do is eat the wonderful meal you've prepared." He removed his scarf and coat then hung them on the coat tree.

"It smells great, and the tablecloth and candles are nice touches."

She inhaled, "Thank you." She loved his scent, as it gently lingered in the air.

He took off his damp boots and placed them on the boot tray. "Aside from the strolling accordion player and the huge pink margaritas, I'd almost swear I was at Mamma Leones, but it's nicer here and thankfully quieter."

"Well, I don't have an accordion player or the margaritas, but I do have the stereo on and a wonderful bottle of Cabernet Sauvignon on the counter just waiting for you to open it."

He playfully tilted his head in her direction. "Putting me to work, are you?"

"I think we need something to keep your hands busy while I finish up things in the kitchen."

"Well, I suppose I could help you with that. Seeing as how you've done so much already." He lifted an eyebrow to her with a crooked smile.

"My aim is to please," she curtsied. "And, for your tasting pleasure I've made zabaglione for dessert."

"You did?" He sounded pleasantly surprised. "I haven't had that in quite a while, not since my--my mother made it."

His voice became quiet. "How did you know to make it for me?"

"I remember you telling me once that it was one of your favorite Christmas desserts," she winced, "I hope I did it justice because it was my first time making it."

"I have no worries." He became quiet for a moment. "Thank you, Gabi." He paused. "You seem to always go the extra mile to make me feel-" Nick stopped and then awkwardly cleared his throat before his voice became light again. "A woman who cooks, tidies up, and takes such good care of me. Hmm, how could I dare ask for more?"

The banter between them became light, he liked when they would verbally jaunt back and forth, it made it all seem so normal, and he needed normal, tonight more so than ever.

"Well, I'm not sure what more you would ask of me." She answered him teasingly.

"Shall I make you a list?" He asked playfully.

"I can only imagine what would appear on such a list." She sultrily bit her lip.

"Let's see, number one, you are very easy on the eyes. Number two, you're confident and I like that. Number three, sexiness, you could corner the market on that. Number four, you keep everything ship shape around here and you even pitch in at my place, shall I go on?"

"You are familiar with the adage, *'the way to a man's heart is through his stomach'* are you not? I believe I have that one covered too, don't you think?" She countered with a smile.

"Yes, I totally agree," he then became somewhat serious, "because you are the only woman who has my heart. I need you to know that, and always remember that, Sweetness."

Her brow lifted quizzically at him. "I know, Nick."

A log loudly slipped off the grate in the fireplace. He went to the living room, shifted the fallen crackling burning piece of wood back in place with the poker, and added another log to the fire. He quietly stared into the flames as a shadow of melancholy crept into his now darkened blue eyes.

After stoking the fire and listening to the console playing a soft tune, he silently moved into the kitchen to the sink where he washed his hands and opened the bottle of wine on the kitchen counter.

"I can't wait for you to meet my family," she was saying as she busied herself in the kitchen.

He quietly walked to the table and poured the deep red liquid into the two glasses on the table. She spoke as Nick continued his task, but he had a troubled brow.

"I know you're going to hit it off with Phil, he is such a great guy. He likes sports like you, so you have that in common." Gabrielle continued talking as she carried a small basket with sliced garlic bread.

He tensely took a long drink from his glass.

"My sisters, are just going to love you, so will Maman."

Noting that he hadn't responded to any of her comments, she looked at his face and saw the concern upon it. Nick's ordinarily sparkling eyes had taken on a new darkness, and he seemed so deep in his own thoughts that he appeared to be a million miles away. He wore the blue turtleneck she had bought for his birthday two months ago, and she admired how good he looked in the color, but then she noticed his jaw clench with tension.

"Nick, you alright?" She softly asked as she reached out and stroked the top of his hand. "Why do you look so glum?"

He looked a little unsettled when he glanced at her, she had pulled his thoughts back into the present.

"I'm sorry, Gabi. I just have a lot going on right now."

"I can see that, and I have a few things going on as well. Things...we need to discuss, so let's have dinner and talk." She paused. "You're hungry, aren't you?"

He looked up at her fretful face with a ghost of a smile on his lips and placed the wine bottle on the table.

"Truthfully," Nick said as he picked up his wine glass and drained all the liquid; he licked his lips and closed the space between them, pulling her into his arms.

"The only thing that I'm hungry for, Sweetness, is you."

He kissed her slowly and deeply with such intensity that it startled her. He tasted of the wine, and she momentarily gave in to the passion and kissed him back. Her hands reached up and ran her fingers through his thick dark locks.

He easily scooped her up in his muscular arms, and she began kissing his neck. He smelled so good, wearing his usual Aramis. She loved the woody spicy scent mingled with his Nick scent; it was so heady to her. He carried her through the hall and into the dimly lit bedroom.

"What about dinner?" She murmured cuddling his ear.

"Dinner's gonna have to wait," he said as he gently laid her on the queen-sized bed. "Me, on the other hand," he reached down to remove his socks and threw them onto the floor. "I can't wait; I have to have you, now."

Gabrielle lifted up onto her elbows and watched him with a salacious smile. "Then we won't wait." She said, no longer wanting to push her body's need for him aside any longer either.

He watched her with a hooded carnal glint in his eye as he pulled his turtleneck sweater over his head and revealed his muscular frame. His fine dark chest hair trailed down his well-developed abdominals. "I have been thinking about you and this all day long." He threw his sweater on a nearby chair.

She moved to the edge of the bed in front of him and pulled him by his belt buckle placing him between her spread legs. She undid his buckle and exposed the top button on his jeans; with swift fingers she unbuttoned it. She quickly unzipped the zipper, and pushed his jeans and boxers to the floor around his ankles before he stepped out of them.

She took his cock into her hands and slowly stroked it paying special attention to the head of him. He was so hard and she loved the feel of that hardness in her hands.

"You like this, don't you?" She asked him huskily.

"Yes," he said hoarsely. "I love it when you touch me."

"I can tell; Marco gives you away." Gabrielle said as

she continued to stroke him; his breathing increased as he moaned, standing completely naked in front of her. "I love looking at your body; you are like a work of art that has come to life just for me." Her voice had a sultriness as she stroked him and touched his abdominals with her other hand.

"I love your eyes on me because, tonight this is all for you." He looked directly at her. "As much as I enjoy this, you touching me. Right now, Sweetness, I need to be one with you. Inside you." His fingers met at the nape of her neck and unzipped her dress. "Get this thing off." He commanded throatily. "I want you stark-naked. I know that I could make love to you, but tonight," he paused cocking his head to one side. "I want to fuck you, but good."

She licked her lips and stood, her dress fell and pooled at her feet. She removed her bra, and stood before him only wearing her white lace bikini panties and cream colored pumps.

"I've been imagining how good you'd look for me tonight." He said with an intake of air at the sight of her. "But, in the flesh, you have surpassed anything my imagination could ever come up with."

She smiled and raised her hand to remove her headband, she tossed it on the dresser; her fingers raked through her hair as she shook her head to let the loose curls cascade around her bare shoulders.

He took a breast in his hands and bent his head to kiss her erect nipple as he used his agile fingers to softly squeeze and caress her other nipple. She moaned letting her head fall back as she succumbed to the feelings that had started to ignite within her. He moved his mouth to her other breast, and her body shuddered as she sighed with want; she felt the deep throbbing between her legs.

Nick lifted his head and ran his tongue up along the vee of her collarbone and up her neck. He kissed her neck, and his lips moved up to her chin and upward still until he located her mouth where his tongue met hers. They fused together in a hot fervent kiss; she pulled back and inserted her thumbs in the thin waistband of her panties and slid them down her hips, past her thighs and down to her feet. She stepped out of her panties and started to remove her heels until Nick stopped her.

"No, leave your shoes on. You look so damned good." He gazed at her slowly from head to toe as his eyes beheld the vision of her naked body before him.

She knew he liked looking at her body, so she let him have a good long look as she walked around to the other side of the bed and pulled the bed covers back. She then started to lie down on the bed, but he stopped her.

"Wait a minute, Gabi, I just want to look at you." His eyes drank in her image as if trying to commit every inch of her body to his memory. "You look amazing," he swallowed. "Now, will you lay down for me, Sweetness."

She adjusted herself onto the bed. He joined her in the bed, as he lifted her legs and held an ankle in each hand. Kissing her ankles, he found her gardenia scent intoxicating.

He ran his hands up and down her legs. "God," he marveled, "your skin is like satin." He slid his lips, tongue and teeth along her shapely leg. His hand continued its descent down her inner thigh until he was caressing her sex, his nimble fingers made her moan with desire.

Her back arched up as she gasped at the pleasure. "Nick… That feels so…oh, so good."

"Sweetness, you're so soft and wet for me, just the way I want you." He continued his manipulations of her most intimate parts. He took the head of his cock and slid it up and down the slickness of her opening. She moaned and moved her hips up to get more of him as he pulled himself out of her reach and he then brought himself back to slide along her opening. He did this slow excruciating dance of pleasure over and over again.

Gabrielle quivered from an intense yearning. "Nick, please," she said breathlessly. "I want you." She inhaled through her shuddering body. "Don't tease me." She pleaded with a shameless whimper. "Give me all of you."

He slowly entered her and rhythmically pumped himself inside her until he felt her tighten around him calling out his name in her orgasmic cry. He squeezed his eyes shut and paused as he held back. He pulled her shoes off and tossed them to the floor. With her legs on his shoulders he lifted her hips up to him as he plunged deeper into her.

"You feel amazing. I love it when you come, you get even

tighter." He thrusted himself deeper inside of her as he rolled his hips. "This is where I want to be, inside you, forever."

Their connection had taken on an almost primal tone as she dug her fingers at his sides and moaned with quickened breaths. She gave way to the sensations and the emotions, and she felt a tear slide down from the corner of her eye and glide to her ear. *Everything is going to be fine, it just has to be.*

Their eyes locked; he'd always loved to see her face when she orgasmed. She could see the yearning in his eyes, but it seemed to be mingled with something else. She lowered her legs and wrapped them around his body as his thrusts became slower, more measured.

She couldn't place the expression in his eyes as he watched her, but it held some degree of sadness or acceptance. Not sure what the intensity of his eyes meant as she tightly pressed her fingertips onto his moist muscular back and pulled him closer to her. The orgasmic crescendo rose inside her, they climaxed together in a swelling of rushing waves through their intertwined bodies.

He stayed in position just watching her beautiful face unwaveringly, then he slipped out of her and lay next to her on the bed. The music from the radio, wafted into the stilled room as Frankie Valli crooned a familiar tune:

Pardon the way that I stare.
There's nothing else to compare.
The sight of you leaves me weak.

There are no words left to speak.
But if you feel like I feel.
Please let me know that it's real.
You're just too good to be true.
Can't take my eyes off you.
I love you baby, and if it's quite all right,
I need you baby to warm the lonely night.
I love you baby.

46
🍀 Gabrielle and Nick 🍀
New York City – Friday evening - December 19th, 1969

Gabrielle basked in the afterglow and snuggled even closer to him with her head on his chest. Nick had been quiet and deep in thought as he distractedly smoothed Gabrielle's hair with his hand.

"That was wonderful," she purred with a smile as she ran the tips of her fingers through his chest hair, "I think I like it when we *fuck*. How was it for you?" She asked coyly.

Nick took his fingers and placed them under her chin to lift her face to his and kissed her lips tenderly. "It was better than *wonderful*, it was perfection, just like you." He kissed her again and tightly held on to her. He sighed and vacantly eyed the ceiling.

She noticed his detached mood, but she needed to finally get some things out in the open. Things she felt she should have told him long ago, but the timing just never seemed right. She hated keeping secrets from him, and she felt he needed to know all that she had concealed from him. *Would now the best time to tell him?* She took a deep breath and plunged in as she looked up at him from his chest.

"Nick, there's something I need to tell you; it's about me and my family. I didn't know when would be the best time to discuss this, but with their upcoming visit, you need to know the truth." She looked at his handsome but withdrawn face, but it was as if he hadn't heard her. Something had disturbed him, and she had to find out what it was.

"What's wrong Nick?" Gabrielle lifted a hand to his cheek and softly stroked with questions in her eyes. "You've been so distant. What's upset you? I can see something's bothering you."

He couldn't bring himself to look her way, he tried to avoid eye contact with her and looked straight ahead.

"I'm fine, we just need to talk," he kissed her hand and held her tighter to him. He loved having her in his arms she felt so good and he didn't want to let her go, "but, later okay?" He closed his eyes, swallowed hard and sighed. "I just want to lay here with you in my arms, you make me feel sane in my absurd world." He looked at her. "So, what were you saying about your family?"

"What I have to say can wait, because I won't sit still when I know that something is troubling you. Please tell me what it is, because, I want to know now, not later."

"Gabi, I-alright," he sighed audibly. "I didn't know how to tell you this, but I have to leave town for a bit."

"Leave town? Why? What for?"

"I have a business obligation that I have to fulfill." Nick

opened his eyes and vacantly stared straight ahead, realizing that the moment he had been dreading was upon him.

"When do you have to leave?" She quizzed.

"Tomorrow." His hand stopped smoothing her hair; frozen in place.

"You're leaving tomorrow? How long will you be gone?" *Tomorrow*? Suddenly she felt a constriction in her throat.

He removed his hand from her hair and reluctantly thought *I guess this is it, and now we have to do this dance*. He took a deep breath to prepare himself.

"I'll be gone for about three weeks."

"You have got to be joking!" She lifted up and faced him. "You're leaving town, tomorrow? For three weeks?"

"Yeah." He said pressing the base of his palms to his eyes.

"Why didn't you tell me this sooner?"

"I'm telling you now. I knew you wouldn't take it well, and I didn't want it to ruin our last night."

"You were right; I'm not taking it well." Her face displayed her confusion and displeasure. "Ruin our night? Forget about ruining our night. What about my family's visit? They will all be here in a matter of days, Nick."

He looked at her and saw the disappointment on her face; he turned away.

"You were supposed to meet them, I expected you to be here."

"I know that, and I'm sorry, Gabi. It can't be helped."

"You said a business obligation. Couldn't it be postponed

until after you meet my parents? Can't it wait until after Christmas? Or can't you at least come back for the holiday itself?" Shaken by the news, she struggled to try to make some sense of it all and fix it somehow.

"What's with the twenty questions, Gabi? Look, I've already told you. It's something that can't be helped, and no, it can't wait. I won't be here. At all!" He snapped, and immediately he regretted his tone with her.

"I don't mean to question you. I'm just so confused."

"I'm sorry, Gabi, I didn't mean to be cross with you," his voice softened. "I don't want to spoil our last night. We'll talk about it later, okay?" He averted her gaze, unable to look her way.

"Alright," she could see he was getting upset too. "If your business thing can't wait, I'll explain it as best as I can to my family and smooth things over with them. I'll make it all right. Don't worry about it, Nick." She said with uncertainty. *How am I going to tell my parents that he won't be here when they were coming specifically to meet him?*

With the knowledge that he'd be leaving tomorrow, she became panic-stricken; her hand went to her necklace and she nervously fidgeted with the pendant. Coming to the realization that she wouldn't see him for three weeks. She anxiously summoned the courage to speak. "Well, Nick, since you won't be back until after the New Year, there is something else we need to discuss."

Nick wasn't sure how to tell her what he needed to tell her:

the truth about why he was leaving. He looked at her with a mirthless smile. "I'm all ears."

She turned around and sat on her bare heels to face him directly, pulled the sheet up, and covered her breasts. She looked serious, and it was now his turn to look anxious.

"Ahem." She nervously cleared her throat. "Um, I need to let you know something that I just found out."

The hairs on the back of his neck bristled.

"Well, this sounds ominous." He stared at her intently. "Go on, tell me, Gabi." *She can't possibly know already, can she?*

"Nick, I just found out," she hesitated as she pushed her mussed hair behind her ears. She took a deep breath then blurted it out. "I just found out... I'm pregnant."

His face went ashen and the shock took over his whole face. "You...you're what?" He sat straight up. Stunned, he managed to ask, "How can that be? You're on the pill."

"I am or I...I was." She stammered. "I guess they don't always work. Dr. Bauer thinks that since I'd been so new to them, that it may have happened when I got sick with the flu a few weeks back. When I couldn't keep anything down?" She had a reminiscent smile.

"Remember how you came over and took care of me? You brought me chicken soup and crackers..." She reflectively lifted her eyes to see the shocked expression on his face, and she quickly continued. "He's really not sure how it happened either, but he is sure of one thing. I'm definitely going to have a baby."

Dazed, Nick ran his hand through his dark locks; images of the beaten Enrico, his mom, Gina, and Sal assaulted his mind. He moved to the edge of his side of the bed, swung his muscular legs around, and placed his bare feet on the floor. He looked defeated as he leaned forward and positioned his elbows on his knees; with closed eyes he rested his chin on his interlaced fingers silently letting her words sink in.

After what seemed like an eternity to her, he stood abruptly and announced succinctly: "Well, you'll just have to get rid of it."

"Get rid of it?" She gasped as she protectively clutched her flat belly.

"Yes." He said matter-of-factly.

"You know, Nick, I didn't expect you to jump for joy, but... you really want me to get rid of our baby?"

He reached down and began picking up his clothes; he grabbed his boxers and jeans from the floor and pulled them on. "It's the only reasonable thing to do." In one quick motion Nick zipped up his jeans, closed the button, and squeezed his belt closed.

Gabrielle quietly disentangled herself from the bed sheets and stood. She opened her closet door and lifted a long tangerine satin robe off the hook and slipped it on her naked trembling body. As she tied the sash around her thin waist, warm tears welled up in her eyes.

She turned to face him; his back to her as he pulled his turtleneck sweater over his head.

"I'm not sure I can do that." Her voice just above a whisper.

"I didn't catch that!" He snapped. "What did you say?"

"I said I can't do that, Nick!"

"Can't Gabi? Or is it that you won't?" He stated with building ire; "You're the one with all of the power here, and I guess that's just the way you like it, isn't it? You and all of your women's lib crap." He paused. "On top of everything else that's going on in my life, I don't need this right now."

She silently eyed the floor.

"Tell me, Gabrielle, what do you want to do?" His eyes, resembled frozen cubes as he coldly faced her.

She blankly stared at him; she couldn't believe what was happening. He lifted his eyes heavenward and interlaced his fingers and placed them at the base of his neck.

"I won't be trapped me this way, Gabi." He glared at her and placed his hands irritably on his hips.

"Trapped? That's what you think? That I'm trying to trap you into something?" The brimmed tears rolled down her cheeks.

"Well, isn't that what's going on here?" The bed separated them as he stood in front of her. His words were harsh, and he knew it, he felt they needed to be.

"I can't marry you." He tilted his head as he pressed his lips together. "I couldn't now, even if I wanted to. So you can get that thought right out of your head."

"I haven't said anything to you about marriage." Her mind reeling as she sniffled back.

"Gabrielle, I know you well enough to know that you're the girl who is looking for the happily ever after. The husband, the white picket fence and kids running around in the yard," he felt a lump forming in his throat, and he swallowed it down, "waiting for Daddy to come home from work."

Seeing her cry had been gut-wrenching for him, and he felt even worse knowing that he'd been the cause of her tears. But he had to do it, a necessary evil, like pulling a Band-Aid off a hairy arm. He continued, "I gotta tell you, that kind of life is just not for me. Not now." He paced back and forth in her dimly lit bedroom. "Gabi, how could you let this happen?"

"I didn't do this alone; you have some responsibility here too, Nick. You're the one who got *me* pregnant, remember?"

"You're the one who was supposed to be on the fucking pill, *remember*?"

She couldn't argue that point as she looked down at her hands and shuddered a sob. He could see how upset she'd become, but he went on.

"Look…if this kid is mine, then I should have a say, don't you think? I'll tell you right now. I don't want this mistake screwing up my life or my future."

"If? How can you say that? You know this is your baby."

"You know there's an old saying, Gabi. *Mama's baby, papa's maybe?*" He regretted saying it as soon as he heard the words come out of his mouth.

The wounded expression on her face was more than he could stand; he turned away from her, his back to her. He picked up his socks and quickly pulled them on.

Better she thinks of me as an ass, because in essence that's just what I am. After all I've done.

"Nick, you know you were my one and only."

He couldn't trust himself to look at her, because of the pain he caused her. "I may have been your first, Gabi, but how can I be certain that I've been the only one?"

Gabrielle was stunned, her usual feistiness had abandoned her. Pulling some tissues from the box on her nightstand, she blew her nose. She moved around the bed and stood directly behind him and spoke dispiritedly. "Because, in spite of everything else you've said, you are right. You do know me. The kind of girl I am. You know I wouldn't give myself to just anyone. I'd have to be in love with him. You are that man, the only man that I've ever loved." She sniffled back. "You are the man I chose to give myself to."

Her hand glided up the wide expanse of his back. "You have me, body, mind, and heart. I love only you." She reached her arms around his slim tapered waist and embraced him from behind.

"I know, I'm sorry for what I said. I know it's mine and I know you've been faithful."

They stood this way for few moments. He then took a hold of her hands and released her grip as he turned to face her. Nick cupped her face within his hands as he exhaled heavily and sorrowfully.

"I wish you didn't love me." His voice, remorseful. "God,

I wish you'd never even met me. I'm not good for you. I never have been, but when I met you I selfishly knew, I had to have you. You stirred something inside me, that I never knew existed." His own eyes glistened. "Gabi, you are so beautiful, so intelligent, brave and talented."

He moved a finger to the corner of his eye to thwart a tear of his own as he continued. "You didn't deserve for a man like me to come into your life and screw things up for you. I know I've hurt you and for that I'm truly sorry. Please believe me." He kissed each of her tear stained cheeks and tenderly kissed her lips as he squeezed his eyes shut.

"Gabrielle, I have always been a selfish man, a self-centered son of a bitch. I knew that about myself and I was okay with it. Meeting you changed me, I wanted to be a better man. I wanted to think of someone other than myself." He lowered his eyes. "And I did, but in doing so, I've made some irreparable choices. Now I have to live with those choices. You deserved a much better man than me to have given yourself to."

He took her in his arms, comforted her, he held her quaking body as she softly wept. He held her until she received the strength he willed into her within his embrace until she no longer trembled.

"I'm not perfect either," she spoke with a strained voice. "But I love you, Nick Caine, flaws and all. And even though you've never said it to me, I know in my heart that you love me too." She gently continued, "this baby is a part of both of us. I can't have him or her disposed of."

In a dreamlike acceptance she said. "Hmm…Listen to me, will you, calling it him or her. This is so surreal for me, too. To think, I have a little person growing inside of me, and not just any little person, our little person." Her voice became soft. "I believe that with love we can get through just about anything. I'm not talking about marriage." She shook her head to emphasize that point. "I'm not expecting you to marry me, that's not what I want. Especially given the way you feel about it. I would never want to *trap you* into anything." Her voice became stressed. "You asked me before what I want, I just want you to be there, be with me through all of this. I need you. I can't do this alone."

He pressed his lips onto her hair. "That's just it, Gabi, don't you see? You don't have to do it alone. After you get the abortion there won't be anything for you to do alone. Our lives continue on, uninterrupted by this one slip-up." *I can't believe what I'm asking her to do, but there's no other option, not now.*

"I can't do this, Gabrielle." He said plainly as he held her in his arms. "I have to be honest with you." His eyes went heavenward and shifted to the side with acceptance. He blew the air from his lungs. "You deserve to know the truth."

Her body became rigid under his embrace.

"I came here tonight…to break things off with you."

"Wha…What?" Gabrielle inhaled abruptly as she tried to free herself out of his grasp, but he held her tightly in place as he continued.

"I've met someone else." His voice held no emotion.

Gabrielle strained against his steadfast hold.

"No Gabi, you've got to listen to me." He tightly shut his eyes.

She struggled to free herself from his grip.

"She is someone who has means, someone who can be a true partner for me." His tone rose a little; it was a voice even he scarcely recognized.

She couldn't believe what she'd just heard as she hissed through clenched teeth. "Let go of me, Nick!"

He opened his arms and freed her. She backed away from him as she beheld him in disbelief.

"You've met someone else?" She wiped at her nose with the tissues. "You came to break up with me?" She placed her hands on her hips as the embers began to form in her eyes.

"So that's the real reason you've been so preoccupied tonight. And, of course, you couldn't tell me any of this before you took me to bed, now could you?"

"You turn me on, Gabi, and I wanted you. I *always* want you." He glumly looked away. "I have wanted you from the moment I laid my eyes on you."

"You *want* me?" Bewildered, she added scornfully. "If that were true then you wouldn't have turned to another woman." She paused for a moment. "What you're telling me, is I meant nothing to you?" She sniffled back. "I've just become another one of your many conquests of *lovely ladies*? Someone to screw when the urge struck you?" Her face contorted miserably, instantly she felt used. "Was I the only one with real feelings here, Nick?"

He had a pained expression as he turned to face her, but he said nothing.

"Just what was I to you?" She had to know, her eyes welled up with more tears and filled with hurt.

His eyes went downward, yet he remained silent.

"Tell me something, have you told *her* that you love her?"

"That's immaterial. With her, I'll have the kind of future I've only dreamt of." He crossed his arms in front of himself. "My life will be different; I'll want for nothing." He paused. "She's very affluent, lives in the right circles, and knows all the right people."

"Oh, now I see." She mirrored him as she crossed her arms over her chest. "What you're telling me is that it's not about love at all. From what you've said, she's your new benefactor." She paused. "What if I had money, Nick? Would you still be leaving me for her?"

"Number one, I know you don't have money, and number two, I wouldn't accept money even if you did, Gabi."

"You know, I thought we had something truly special here." The dazed stare in her eyes apparent, she shook her head unbelievingly as she spoke. "Now, I see. I was just another notch on your bedpost." She sniffed, with sad eyes she looked at him, "even tonight you just wanted to *'fuck me, but good'*, one last time before you ended things with me. I'm right, aren't I, Nick?" She gave him a rueful broken smile.

"What a fool I've been. To actually think I'd found love with a *good* man."

He turned away from her and headed out of the bedroom. "Look, this is getting us nowhere, Gabrielle."

"Enlighten me," with bare feet she followed after him. "Who is she?"

Silently, he walked over to the wall nook that housed her telephone; keeping his back to her he picked up the pen and scribbled something on the pad of paper near the phone.

"Aren't you going to answer me?" She persisted.

"I just don't see what the point would be." Nick sighed with his reply.

"You don't see the point?" She stared at the back of his head. "I need to know, that's the point. Don't I, at the very least, deserve that much from you, Nick?"

At the dinner table he picked up the wine bottle, poured wine into his glass and drank it down.

She stood in front of one of the other chairs, and looked closely at him.

"Alright." He looked away from her. "If you have to know and if you think it will make you feel any better, I'll tell you. You're going to find out soon enough anyway." He bolstered himself up. "It's Margaret Bradford." He replied flatly.

The words resonated through her; she became a little lightheaded and grabbed the back of the chair in front of her as if he'd slapped her. Gabrielle had been dumbfounded. *So this really is about his financial gain. Have I just dodged a bullet? If he knew the true scope of my wealth, would he stay and pretend to love me?* She couldn't stop herself; she let out a sardonic laugh.

"You want me to destroy my child so that you can start your new life with a clean slate?" She shook her head in disgust. "You make me sick, you clearly are not the man I thought you were. I'd say go to hell, but from what you've told me tonight, I have a feeling you'll be living there soon enough." Gabrielle refused to let him see her cry again as she steeled up her back and stared straight ahead without looking his way.

He walked over to the boot tray and put on his boots and coat. He took his wallet out of his inner coat pocket and fished some bills out of it. He placed them on the table near her hand. "I left a number on the pad of someone who will help you with this…situation in my absence."

"Convenient," she scoffed, "done this before, have you?"

He ignored her comment as he turned to walk toward the door. She looked down at the bills he placed on the table.

"You're forgetting something, Nick."

He turned to her; she picked up the bills from the table.

"Just so we're clear here. The last thing I need is your fucking money." Glaring, she threw the bills at him. "I don't want anything from you, not now. Not ever, believe me on that."

He let the bills fall to the floor in front of him. "I know you need the money, so don't be foolish, Gabi. Get the abortion for both of our sakes." His voice softened. "Why let this one mistake ruin the rest of our lives?"

"That's what this innocent baby is to you? A mistake that

would ruin our lives, yours in particular." Her voice filled with disgust. "The only real mistake made here, was me, falling for a selfish bastard like you. Just go, get the hell out of my apartment, you second-rate, son of a bitch." She turned away from him as she held her head high.

He reached the door and turned the knob. Nick pulled the door open but turned back towards her. "For what it's worth, Gabi, you weren't the only one with feelings. I really do..."

"For what it's worth," she cut him off and turned to face him. "I really don't give a damn how you feel about me anymore. Now slink your way out of here. Enjoy your life as a kept man." She paused. "And, on second thought, I do think you should go straight to hell. You and your rich bitch Margo."

He quietly stepped out into the hall and closed the door behind him.

She blew out the candles on the table and walked to the door and twisted the deadbolt shut and put the chain lock in place. She went to the oven, turned it off, picked up her wine glass and downed it. Empty glass in hand, she grabbed the wine bottle and reached for the hall light switch. She turned off the lights then headed for the living room.

On the radio Neil Diamond seemed to be mocking her with his aptly chosen words:

I've been misunderstood for all of my life
But what they're sayin', girl, just cuts like a knife
The boy's no good

Well, I finally found what I've been lookin' for
But if they get a chance they'll end it for sure
Sure they would
Baby I've done all I could
it's up to you

Girl, you'll be a woman soon
Please come take my hand
Girl, you'll be a woman soon
Soon, you'll need a man

"That's where you are wrong, Neil, I don't need him or any man." She fumbled for the knob on the stereo and shut it off.

She turned off the lights in the living room and threw another log in the fireplace and it slowly sprang to life in the dimly lit room. She lifted the bottle, poured more wine into her glass, and ambled over to the window. She watched Nick through the sliver of an opening of the living room curtains as he brushed the snow from his car, the city had been illumined by its fresh covering of white. She knew that he couldn't see her in the darkness of her apartment, but she could see him clearly as she unhurriedly sipped her wine in the darkened room.

After removing the snow from his car, Nick looked up toward her window longingly for a moment. His face appeared somber as he entered the car; he gradually drove away. A lone tear trailed down her cheek as sadly she realized she wouldn't ever see him again.

She poured the remainder of the wine into her glass, emptying the bottle as she drank it down. She stepped through the hall and glanced at the pad of paper where Nick had hastily written down a name and a phone number. His solution for what he deemed *'their mistake.'*

Entering her bedroom, she couldn't believe all that had transpired. Only a short while ago she'd been here with the man she loved, expressing that love to the fullest, now she was brokenhearted.

What should I do? Her mind, in a whirlwind. *Should I correct the mistake and 'get rid of it' as Nick told me to do?* That just felt so wrong to her, but the idea of carrying his child to term seemed just as displeasing. *Why had I fallen so fast and hard for him? He's gorgeous, an undeniable fact, from the moment I saw his eyes, I'd been hooked.* She had never met anyone who could make her feel the way he had.

When she met him nine months ago she would have never thought that she would find herself in the place she now found herself in. Pregnant, alone, and after she talked with Linda, without a job. *There is no way in hell I'd continue working at VonShelles for that bitch, Margaret Bradford, however as indirectly as it may be.*

Gabrielle's head throbbed as a headache loomed; there were so many questions running through her head. Questions she didn't have the answers to: *why did I continue seeing him after the Claudia Avery debacle,* and *how could he have chosen that awful Margaret Bradford over me?* That one, she could answer: *money.*

Grabbing the pillow; she lay on her bed, the pillow smelled of Nick's scent and oddly gave her comfort as she hugged it tightly to her trembling body. *How can I still love him after all he's said and done to me tonight? How could he even suggest that I may have been with someone else? And why did he tell me to always remember how much I meant to him? Maybe, I should have told him that I come from a wealthy family... No, I wouldn't want him if that would be the only way to have him.*

She was confused by the anger, hurt and the yearning for him still. Her body ached for his touch as she wished she could turn back time to feel his sweet kiss on her lips and his hands in her most intimate of places.

Knowing they were over and done had been too much for her to bear, and hot tears filled her eyes as she wept into *his* scented pillow. Sleep soon overtook her.

47
❦ Gabrielle ❦
New York City – Saturday morning - December 20th, 1969

Gabrielle awakened from a fitful sleep, her head still throbbed. The small lamp on her bedside table still on; she blinked and squinted her eyes to see the clock on her nightstand table. It was dark outside, and the clock read 3:10 a.m. She sat up, placed her fingertips at her temples, and pressed with circular motions.

The floor had been cold on her bare feet as she stumbled through the door and walked across the hall to the bathroom. She flipped the switch on, and the bright light above the sink lit up the room. Nausea got the better of her as she placed her hands on the toilet's tank lid and braced herself as she retched into the bowl.

Gabrielle moved to the sink, lifted her head and looked at her reflection in the mirror. The whites of her eyes were red and her lids swollen, even her lips were puffed.

The light caught the glint of the moonstone in her necklace. *'Never take it off'*, *he'd told me.* She found the clasp and removed it, and for the first time she noticed the inscription on the back.

'Per sempre nel mio cuore' engraved on one of the hearts and the words 'Forever in my heart' on the other. "I never was in his heart." She said, throwing the necklace into the medicine cabinet.

She vigorously brushed her teeth to eliminate the horrid taste from her mouth; Turning away from her mirrored image, she moved toward the tub and turned on the water for the shower.

She let the warm water pour down on her head, and she reached for the bottle of Breck shampoo, poured the thick golden liquid into the palm of her hand and lathered her wet hair. Her thoughts were still of him, remembering his touch on her skin. She wanted him even now, she hopelessly loved him, and she felt the tears sting her eyes again.

Why did I have to get pregnant? Why did I sleep with him in the first place? How could he have done this to me and then try to claim to have had feelings for me? "Remember this always" he'd said before he had me, he knew that this would be our last night together, how could he have used me in this way?

The questions remained, only she had no answers. Her emotions overwhelmed her as her whole body quaked within her sobs. Her strength waned, in her tear-filled sorrow, she sank to her knees in the tub and held on to the side of the tub.

Gabrielle continued to sob as the water rained over her crumpled body. She let the water pelt her tender skin, and she willed herself to stop thinking of him and the hurt she felt. Her tears subsided as she tried to calm herself yet again.

She pulled open the shower curtain and grabbed her towel off one of the nearby hooks and dried her body. The orangey colored Ten-O-Six lotion on a cotton ball, stung as she smoothed it over her face and neck. Plugging in her hair dryer, she began the chore of drying her long thick hair. She gathered her dried locks into ponytail with a hairband.

Feeling so much older than her twenty-four years, she came to the realization that Nick Caine had just taught her a painful lesson.

Her pounding headache, she surmised, may have been because she has not eaten much of anything since breakfast yesterday. However, the mere thought of food and eating made her feel more nauseous. Taking out the aspirin bottle from the medicine cabinet, she took two pills and tossed them into her mouth as she filled a Dixie cup with water and swallowed them down.

Lifting a soft white chenille robe from the hook on the back of the bathroom door, she snuggled into it as she tied the belt. She pulled some tissues from the box and put them into the pocket of her robe. She padded her way into the kitchen and saw the flaccid salad on the table. She dumped the contents of the bowl into the trash; she did the same with the lasagna from the oven. The kitchen's wall clock displayed the time as 3:42.

Gabrielle walked into the dimly lit living room. The room was cool as the fire had burned out long ago. She opted to turn up the thermostat instead of building a fire.

She sat on the comfortable sofa, and pulled her feet up and rested them underneath her; she placed the soft wool knitted throw on her lap. Her eyes settled on the cleared area where the Christmas tree stand awaited a tree; she and Nick were supposed to go pick one out together today.

Nick had been right about one thing, meeting him did screw up things in my life. Remembering the day when she met him in Central Park, she now asked herself. *Why hadn't I just gone straight home after work that Saturday?*

She wanted to talk to Linda about everything that had gone on; however, Linda was one of the few from VonShelles who went away for the weekend to escape the snow.

Maybe that's a good thing, I'm not sure that I could share everything about my dilemma or let her know just how dumb and irresponsible I've been. Getting knocked up while on the friggin pill like an idiot, then getting dumped by my so-called Mr. Perfect so that he could be with that wretched woman Margaret Bradford.

She rose and went to the hall phone, putting a shaky finger in the '0' she dialed.

"Operator." The woman's voice on the line had been brusque.

"Ahem," she cleared her throat, "hello, Operator, I'd like to place an international person to person call to Milan, Italy."

After a series of clicks the phone rang and the familiar voice came on the line.

"Pronto!"

Hearing Suzette's voice, the emotion got to her. Gabrielle

felt a lump in her throat as the tears welled in her eyes.

"Hi Suzette, it's me." She croaked out. "I didn't wake you, did I?"

"Gabrielle?" There was alarm in Suzette's voice.

"Yeah," she wiped at her tears, "it's me."

"No, you didn't wake me; it's just a little after nine in the morning here. I've been up for a couple of hours." She paused. "What's going on?"

"I'm wondering or hoping… do you think you could come to New York a little early? Before the rest of the family gets here."

"Come early? Why? What's wrong?"

"I…I'm in trouble," she sniffled back, "and I need you." She couldn't stop the tears as they slid down her cheeks.

"Gabi, I need you to tell me what's going on. What kind of trouble?" Suzette spoke evenly.

"It…it's Nick. Nick broke up with me last night." Gabrielle took a tissue out of her pocket and wiped her nose.

Suzette was perplexed, but she sighed with relief. Guy trouble she could deal with. She couldn't believe that her sister could be this worked up over some guy.

"Gabi, I know you really liked the guy, but don't let him breaking up with you get you so upset. It's his loss, remember that."

"Suzette, I don't just like him, I…lov…love him. I love him so…so much, even after everything…I'm still in love with him." Gabrielle wailed as she took in shallow breaths. "I just can't shut these feelings off, I wish I could, oh God, how I wish I could. I don't know what I'm going to do."

"Is it because he was your first?" Suzette paused, she didn't want to appear insensitive. "Well, Gabi, someone had to claim that title." She remarked, realizing that being sensitive just wasn't her style. "It's not that big of a deal, believe me. You're young, gorgeous, and living on your own in New York City. Trust me, you're going to have many lovers in your life, as you should. Gabi, you need to embrace the hurt you are feeling right now, learn the lesson, and move on. You will be better equipped for your next lover." She continued her thought. "You know it's like Maman has always said, *'men are like a bus; you miss one there's always another one coming.'* You're much better off without him, trust in that."

Gabrielle clutched the phone tightly in her hand as she placed her other hand on her belly. "Please Suzette," she sniffled. "I don't need to hear all of the usual clichés or your glib remarks."

"I'm sorry. I don't mean to dismiss what you're feeling. I just wanted you to know that any man who would break up with you right before Christmas, and before he was set to meet your family, is hardly worth your time or your precious tears."

"I know that, but…," Gabrielle tried to interject.

"Gabi, I think you have to agree with me when I say, it sounds like he's a pretty selfish guy and that he doesn't deserve the feelings you have for him. Maybe he's smarter than I thought, because just think if he had met Papa and then broke up with you…, well, let's just say I wouldn't want to be on the receiving end of Louis Laurendeau's anger. His ass would be grass and Papa would be the lawn mower." Suzette chuckled at her own joke as Gabrielle sighed.

"Suzette, please… be quiet and listen to me… I have to tell you something important. I'm pregnant."

There had been a momentary silence on the other end.

"Does he know?" Suzette asked.

"Yes, he knows."

"That son of a bitch. I'll be on the first flight out."

To be continued…

Follow Gabrielle and Nick's journey in the next book, *Awakened Devotions*.

About the Author

BeJae Ladd is a first-time author, a working wife and mother with two married adult sons, and a grandmother to six. She is from the Midwest near Waukesha, Wisconsin, and loves to travel and read. Her love of the written word prompted her to dust off the novel that has been in her head for over thirty years and tell the story of Gabrielle and Nick.